Oh My Stars

Stars

S-Jay Hart

MW01174893

Thanks

This book has honestly been such a labour of love for me. When I first started reading Lesfic around the start of lockdown here in the U.K, I was inspired by so many talented writers. On days when I struggled with our government's rules of not being able to leave the house other than for 45 mins of exercise per day, sapphic authors really kept me sane. When I decided I wanted to try my hand at writing, (something I only ever did for myself and only by hand, in notebooks that I have boxes of under my bed) I reached out to a few authors who I was fortunate to Beta read for, and the support that I have had in writing this has been immense. So I really do want to make sure I thank them all.

Firstly to Lily and Jacqueline, who saw Oh My Stars in its beginning stages. Two wonderful humans who saw the bare bones of a story and told me to run with it. Thank you both for your unwavering support. You are two of the most beautiful souls to walk the earth and I adore you both. Sorry it took me so long. X

To my writer friends Luc and Sabrina for letting me steal your time and pick your brains. For sending me messages on the front pages of books that I will remember forever. You're such fountains of knowledge, thank you for letting me wade in the kiddy pool of your expertise. I am humbled to know you both.

To Erica, who not only became a friend but became family. You were the first lesfic author I read and I know if I ever live to have half the talent you have, I'll be so lucky. Thank you for not only your eyes on this, but for letting me know I'm not alone when I felt like I was an imposter. For sending me pictures of the most innocent healing smile on days when I have barely been able to function. Thank you for sharing your life and your days with me. Thank you for your trust. Give the Lord the biggest squeeze from his fave British Auntie, oh and take one for yourself I suppose LOL x

To the beta squad. You guys are always there, be it Carlsbad, Cornwall, Verity or the crazy spirals of my mind. Let's pick a place and meet up, drinks are on me! Special mention to Conny, general badass with an accent, timeline queen and awesome person who reminds me to hydrate. Thankyou for taking the time to help me work through the days I wanted to give up. Thank you for sharing your heart and stories with me. I hope one day the world gets to see your beautiful words too.

To my family, who had put up with me being locked away in my room for hours on end and who have encouraged me every single day. You are the most wonderfully beautiful humans and I am so privileged to walk through life with you. I can't wait to see how you change the world.

To Alex, Ash and Lols… my holy trinity. I'd be lost without the three of you. Alex, your TikTok game is always on point. Ash you're the best little sister I could have ever asked for. Late night talks and dancing it out have saved me. Lols, I am sorry I wasn't a catfish, but I'll never be sorry I got a best friend. Always xx

To Ange who has supported me in ways unimaginable. Who has listened to me ramble when I've needed it and always made me believe it was possible.

Finally this is for YOU. You changed my life the day I met you. I know the waters are rough but I hold onto hope that one day we reach the other side. Never stop swimming.

Little star,
feels like you fell right on my head.
Gave you away to the wind
I hope it was worth it in the end.
You and my guitar,
I think you may be my only friend.
I gave it all to see you shine again
I hope it was worth it in the end.

- **Elliott's Song**

We will always have 6am
X

Chapter 1

Honey

Rosenberg's Deli was bustling, busier than usual for a Monday. It wasn't even lunch time yet, but the sounds of coffee being brewed and excited chatter filled the air. Honey smiled as she noted her almost empty cake cabinet. Across the room, a whirlwind of messy brown hair flitted from table to table, as her eldest sister, Sasha, moved around the open space, making polite conversation. Ever since Honey and Sasha were little and helped their grandparents after school, Sasha had loved nothing more than speaking with their customers. The 'gift of the gab' her grandfather had called it, a silver tongue, whatever it was, she had it. If asked, Honey would state with absolute certainty that her sister's infectious and constant good nature was what had enabled them to continue their family's success when they took over Rosenberg's Deli eight years ago.

Honey allowed herself a moment to pause and admire the way her sister danced around the white tiled floor, moving from table to table with the ease of a ballerina on opening night. It made sense. Running the deli was, in some ways, a well rehearsed dance, one they had been training for since they were young. Honey had always held a soft reverence for Sasha, who must have sensed Honey's stare and met it with a questioning look.

"Did we miss something? A town event or something?" Sasha whispered conspiratorially. Her eyes darted around the room, "Not that I'm complaining, but we haven't seen a rush like this since…"

"The Cookie Conundrum of 2016," Honey said, smirking as her sister leant across the countertop and grabbed her arm.

"Oh, I'd almost forgotten about that," Sasha sighed, "I was going to say since Gramps and Gran started selling fresh brewed coffee but yeah, the Cookie Conundrum."

"What is so important that we are talking rather than serving?" a voice asked accusingly, stepping into their little bubble. A taller, more intimidating brunette raised her brows and folded her arms across her heavily pregnant stomach.

"Nothing Ky, just reminiscing about old times," Sasha sighed at their other sister's intrusion.

Honey caught Sasha's quick eyeroll and stifled a laugh.

"Well maybe that could wait until we actually have some free time. I didn't expect it would be this busy today, and I need to be out of here at three. The twins have baseball practice and Ariella has her piano lesson, and I have to do all of this while lugging a very cranky three year old around with me. Don't let anyone tell you it's the twos that are terrible, three is absolute hell."

Honey sighed thinking about the sheer exhaustion of having every moment of her day planned, but that was just how Kyla ran her life, and that of her children's. Honey supposed that if she had to corral and entertain four children daily while making another, she too, would be a little less carefree.

"There are tables that need cleaning," Kyla said, scowling sharply. She glanced disapprovingly over at Honey, flicking one hand in the direction of the counter, " I don't know if you noticed but you have a line forming."

Honey looked at the end of her counter where the octogenarian, Mrs. Robbins, Verity's longtime librarian, stood clutching a woven basket, overflowing with her usual selection of baked goods.

Still warm roasted garlic and tomato focaccias were tucked in next to soft, maple bacon brioche buns and underneath Honey caught the vibrant stripes of the Rainbow bagels, which she had originally started making exclusively for Pride month but that had surprisingly become a hit with the locals and so became a staple.

"One person does not make a line, little sister," Sasha said, rolling her eyes in a mock annoyance that caused Honey to snort back a laugh.

Kyla Rosenberg was every inch the middle child. When she was younger, she was often so quiet that Honey and Sasha forgot she was there. But as an adult, Kyla had found her voice and ran the deli pretty much like she ran her very busy home: with a firm hand. The taller woman's steely gaze darted toward Honey, her obvious annoyance evident in the way her lips pursed, and her hands rested in balled up fists on her hips.

"I'll get right to it," Honey said with a forced smile, stepping away from her sisters and over to where Mrs. Robbins was now inspecting the almost empty cabinet with dismay. "Don't worry Mrs. Robbins, I saved an entire box of Blueberry Banana Bonanza, just for you."

"Oh! You're such a sweet girl, you know how I love them. I've been starting my days off with one of those tasty little treats for the last twenty two years," Mrs. Robbins jokingly patted her barely there stomach, "It wouldn't feel right to go without. Or worse yet, to have to go into Irregular Joes."

Irregular Joes was a chain coffee house that had opened two years ago, Rosenberg's Deli's only source of competition in Verity. For a while, it had seemed like Irregular Joes could have possibly taken away a good portion of their business. For weeks there had been lines down the street but it didn't take long for the luster to wear off. Soon, the small, close-knit town of Verity had filtered back through their double doors in search of locally sourced, fresh produce, and a personal touch Irregular Joes just couldn't provide.

That, and no one could bake quite like town sweetheart, Honey.

"We definitely couldn't have you doing that now, could we?" Honey smiled, grabbed a brown box tied with a purple ribbon, and slid it across the countertop.

"I'm one of the only people who can say they've never been that desperate to go in there. No, it's Rosenbergs or bust for me, sweetie. You and your family have always taken care of this town, we owe it to you to make sure this place is around forever."

"We thank you for your loyalty, Mrs Robbins."

"Please, it's Ida. You're not a child anymore, I've seen those books you ask me to order for you at the library. Besides, Mrs Robbins makes me feel old." She raised her eyebrows and Honey felt a blush warm her cheeks.

Ever since Andie had left, Honey had been devouring sapphic romances like her life depended on it and Mrs Robbins was her dealer.

"My apologies, Ida. Here," Honey bent down and retrieved a small paper bag from under the counter, "For Keats. They're blueberry and pumpkin flavored."

She watched as recognition filled the elderly woman's eyes. When she had the time, and now she was alone she always had time, Honey had started baking pet-friendly treats alongside her usual goodies. Mrs. Robbins' old tabby cat had been her willing test subject for the last few months.

"Ah. Thank you sweetheart, Keats will thank you too. He really enjoyed the last batch of catnip croutons. He couldn't get enough of them." She tucked the paper bag in her wool, woven tote, waved over her shoulder, and then shuffled out of the deli.

Honey glanced around and noted that most of the tables that separated the three sections of the deli, were occupied with patrons chattering and indulging in their breakfast pastries and cups of freshly brewed coffee. She stepped out from behind her counter and crossed over to where Sasha stacked plates and cups precariously before carrying them back to the small kitchen.

"Do you think you could watch the counter for me while I run out?" Honey said, hoping for a quick agreement rather than the lengthy interrogation she knew was a possibility.

While Sasha didn't entirely approve of Honey's strained relationship with Andie, of her two sisters, she was the one less likely to voice it.

"Sure. Business or pleasure?" Sasha winked and waggled her eyebrows at Honey, who stifled a laugh.

"Well, seeing as how my girlfriend is currently nine thousand miles away, it's definitely not pleasure. I have to go move some money around at the bank and…"

"No! Not this again," Sasha sighed, emptying the plates and stacking them in the dishwasher. "You can't keep doing this, Honey. You aren't her personal ATM."

Honey felt her stomach churn. She understood her sister's reservations. She knew she only wanted what was best for her, but Honey really did love Andie. She wanted to help her. It was the one thing within their relationship that she felt absolute certainty in. She took joy in knowing she was able to help those who she loved, and Andie loved her too.

Didn't she?

Honey grabbed Sasha by the hand leading her out of the kitchen and over towards her counter hoping to keep their conversation private.

"Please," Honey said, lowering her voice. She didn't want Kyla to weigh in on a situation that was already making her feel even sadder than she had been this morning. "It's hard enough to deal with missing her the way I do. I just want to help her. This is the only way I can from this side of the ocean… Please."

"She's out there having the time of her life, and you're here with your life on hold, just waiting!"

Too Late.

Honey winced as Kyla's rough voice spat her unwanted opinions from over her shoulder. She knew she shouldn't turn around and acknowledge Kyla's comments because no good would come from doing that. They'd never really seen eye-to-eye, especially on matters pertaining to Honey's choice of girlfriends. Kyla just couldn't help herself when the words forced their way out of her mouth.

Honey was unable to meet her sisters' hardened stare.

"Why don't you just say what we both know you're thinking, Ky. I'm pathetic, I know. I just, I love her. I'm supposed to help her."

"Is she coming back? Did she say when?" Kyla asked sneeringly "It's been a year and a half, Honey. I told you when she left that I doubted we'd see her again. I don't know why you're holding onto this. You know she's not coming back, right?"

Honey felt little comfort from the sympathetic smile Sasha offered her before moving to wipe down the table nearest to Honey's counter. She didn't have to look over at Kyla, Honey could hear the smugness in her words.

"I don't know if she's coming back," she admitted, her voice breaking. The overwhelming sadness she had lived alongside for the last year and a half was forcing itself out into the open. "But she's spent so long waiting for this and I support her. She's out there, living her dream and I'm happy for her, really I am. I just miss her. That's all."

Kyla scoffed, shook her head and walked away leaving Honey feeling smaller than she ever thought was possible. She had to believe that Andie would return, because the alternative meant possibly acknowledging a reality that Honey wasn't quite ready to face.

Sasha's hand landed on Honey's shoulder and she felt a reassuring squeeze. Pushing back the tears that threatened to fall and pushing down the sadness that flooded her, Honey met her eldest sister's gaze.

"What about your dreams, Buzzy? When do you get to live your dream?"

When did she?

Honey had never been uncertain of what she wanted. She wanted it all. Safety, stability, someone to come home to, someone who adored her as much as she did them, and children. Gosh, did she want children. For a little while when they first got together, Honey had rushed headfirst into planning all of the above with Andie. She allowed herself to naively indulge in dreams where tiny, bare feet, slapped on the hardwood flooring of the cottage as the open space filled with laughter and smiling faces.

That had all stopped when Andie had attended her first Rosenberg family gathering and excused herself within ten minutes to head home, claiming a migraine she couldn't shake. Honey followed an hour later, clutching some of her Nonna's special Pastina soup. But instead of finding Andie immobile on their bed with the throbbing migraine Honey thought she had, she found Andie dressed in her gym attire with a bag slung over her shoulders. Andie had confessed, without remorse, that she simply couldn't handle the noise at the gathering, and Honey had momentarily understood. She had even felt a little guilty for not easing her girlfriend in slowly, but then Andie shook her head, inched toward the door, and uttered words that Honey knew should have been a warning to her.

"All those screaming kids, yikes! I guess your family isn't big on birth control; I bet you're glad you're gay."

It had hit Honey square in the chest and left her speechless. She could only watch in silence as Andie headed off to the gym.

They hadn't broached the subject of children since, but Honey hoped that in time Andie's attitude towards having a family would change. She wondered often if Andie's time in Australia, away from those she loved, had softened her to the possibility of family life. If it was something they would ever get to talk about.

"If she comes home, I guess that will be a discussion."

Honey forced a smile, the weight of those words lay heavy on her heart. *If she comes home.*

Sasha tilted her head and swung a protective arm around Honey's shoulders, "Oh Buzzy, you really do miss her, don't you?"

"So, so much." She bit down on the inside of her lip to reroute the pain, as tears threatened to break the boundaries of her eyes.

"At least she called you to say happy birthday, right? Are you excited for the Buzzday celebrations at the Hive tonight?"

"Yeah," Honey lied.

The truth was, Andie hadn't even acknowledged that it was Honey's birthday. Sure it was possible she had forgotten, or maybe she intended on calling later, when she knew Honey would be finished with work. Honey's mind toyed momentarily with the romantic notion of arriving home and finding the porch filled with a thousand yellow daisies. Ever since she had watched Max's proposal to Lorelai in her favorite comfort show "Gilmore Girls," she had always secretly longed to come home to find something similar.

It was dangerous, Honey knew, allowing yourself to hope. Hope was often a gateway to disappointment and heartbreak.

Sasha's grip around Honey's shoulders tightened, offering her reassurance and she whispered softly, "Go. Do your thing. We got this."

Chapter 2

Liv

Liv Henderson was excited, nervous and tired…So. Damn. Tired.

For a little over a week now, while working long hours and battling a submission deadline, Liv had been waiting for her phone to ring with news of the arrival of the newest addition to their friend circle. As the day gave way to night a mere fourteen hours ago, Baby *'first name still unknown'* Hadley, had made his way into the world on the front doorstep of the family home—almost fourteen days overdue, leaving his parents and Liv absolutely breathless.

Liv loved children, longed for them, yearned for the soft touch of a tiny hand in her own, needed to hear the soothing sound of a soft breath in her ear as she rubbed circles over a back so small that her hand would cover its entire expanse. Liv had wanted children for as long as she could remember.

Then she had met Marcie.

Marcie Jacobs was allergic to children— or so she proclaimed any time a small human dared to glance in her direction. She would pull her scarf up over her stern mouth, her shades down over her dark gray eyes and narrow her gaze, so that they were guaranteed zero further interaction.

It was shocking, really, that Marcie disliked children so much when she was, in fact, the eldest of nine. The way she explained it to Liv, a year into their relationship, was that she had never really been able to be alone. She had done her time helping her mother raise her siblings after her father had passed away unexpectedly at the age of forty-three but that she never intended on raising another human, ever again. And so, Liv's dream had ended there. Too deep into a love she thought was her forever to walk away. Too smitten with the gentle curving of her lover's lips, too needy for the rough touches that straddled affection and desire.

Now it lingered only in her sleeping hours, *where she rocked back and forth in an oversized comfy chair, on the front decking of a house a far cry from their luxury apartment in the city. A beautiful head of blonde curls tickling her chin as she hummed softly, while the stars twinkled in the sky.* When she woke, she would be clutching her pillow in a motherly embrace, her back turned to the soundly sleeping form of her girlfriend whose dreams, she was certain, were a far cry from her own.

"Here, hold this," Liv directed cheerily, handing over a medium sized package dotted with blue and yellow crepe paper.

Watching her girlfriend's nose crinkle and eyes widen, she snorted softly, pulling open the door to the car and nodding for Marcie to get inside.

"You don't have to be so cautious, it won't explode," she said, rolling her eyes dramatically as she watched Marcie move into position slowly, panic written across her face.

"Is this a cake?" Marcie spat, her tone disapproving and almost bored. She cocked her head to the side and examined the package with scrutiny. Her eyes squinted to match her still wrinkled nose.

"Yes and no," Liv slid into the driver's seat and reached behind for the seatbelt. She giggled as she leaned over and gently stroked the soft colored fabric. "It's actually baby supplies wrapped up to look like a cake. These are little onesies, vests and some socks. You know how often babies need changing. It's cute, right?"

"I'd have preferred actual cake," Marcie lamented pushing the gift away from her so it rested against the dash. "Do we have to go?"

Liv sighed softly and gripped the steering wheel tightly. "Taylor is your work partner, they are our closest friends and they just had a baby. Don't you want to congratulate them?"

"I can congratulate them over the phone and avoid being spat on. This suit cost almost a month's pay. I'd rather not have it ruined by sticky jam hands and then have to send it out to the barely competent dry cleaners on the corner. You know what they did to my coat!" Marcie huffed, looking down at her outfit. In a gray fitted pantsuit, with a pristine white blouse tucked in at the waist, Marcie looked every inch the sharp businesswoman she was.

Liv sucked her bottom lip into her mouth, and bit down gently to stave off her growing agitation. Starting the engine, she concentrated on directing herself out of the underground parking of their apartment block.

"You don't have to worry about that. I think he's a little too young for jam hands, Mar," pulling out into the street, she could feel

rather than see Marcie's annoyance. It filled and then suddenly
sucked all the air out of the already tense space, "What if I promise
to do all the holding?"

"They're going to want me to touch it?"

Liv felt Marcie's body go rigid and watched her girlfriend
blanche, from the corner of her eyes, as she made her way out of the
city and headed for the suburbs. Part of her wished she had chosen to
take this trip alone but she knew she couldn't make up a lie about
Marcie being at work, Taylor would know. No, instead she knew she
would have to grin and bear it and play buffer for the rest of the
night.

She began to think up ways of ensuring that their friends didn't
get offended at Marcie's flagrant disregard for the tiny life they had
created, while not making a big deal out of how much she was going
to enjoy holding the little one herself. She didn't want to sit through
another night of having to brush off dreams that haunted her, while
pretending they didn't exist. She wanted to revel in her friends'
happiness.This hadn't been an easy process for them. It was the
culmination of four years of constant heartache and deserved to be
celebrated, not turned into a secret pity party for Liv's broken
dreams.

She could feel the familiar ache of longing sitting over her heart
as they pulled onto the gray paved drive that sat next to the perfectly
manicured lawn of a modest townhouse. Liv turned to face Marcie,
who was doing what she did best, disassociating into her online life.
God Damn Phone.

She watched for a second as Marcie's deft fingers slid over the
screen, her eyebrows knotted in concentration until she landed on
something that caused a smirk. A very sexy smirk. Liv tried to
remember the last time she had seen this response on her girlfriend's
face and she wondered, with a small hint of jealousy, what or who
had caused it.

Rather than asking outright, knowing it would only cause Marcie
to become even more defensive and distant, she blew out a breath
and exited the car.

Liv glanced at Marcie as she stumbled up the path, now clutching
the gift as though her life depended on it. Only Liv could see the
action for what it was. The offerings provided a perfect barrier

between Marcie and the small human that lay beyond the threshold. If she held the gift close to her, she wouldn't have to hold the baby.

Shaking her head, her long black curls dancing around her shoulders, Liv contemplated telling Marcie to at least fake her enthusiasm, but was stopped as the door opened and three faces appeared. Liv smiled, throwing her arms into the air and doing her best to contain her excitement at the tiny bundle of human swaddled in Jen's arms.

"Hey!" she whispered enthusiastically. She could feel how wide her own smile was by the aching in her cheeks. "Oh my gosh! How are you both?"

Liv followed their friends into the house and through to the sitting room. She watched as Taylor's hand rested softly on her wife's back, guiding her gently down onto the sofa, her eyes full of love, admiration and exhaustion.

"Tired, but happy," Jen admitted, her tone indicating that her precious bundle wasn't yet asleep, as she shuffled to get herself comfortable. She winced a little and yet still smiled in Liv's direction. "So happy. Do you want to hold him?"

Liv watched Marcie take a step away from the sofa, as she fought to keep the distance between herself and Jen. She felt embarrassment creep up her cheeks at her girlfriend's obvious reaction and felt the need to immediately turn the focus to herself.

"May I?" Liv said, turning her focus back to Jen and the baby.

"Here, say hello to Aunt Liv," Jen said and lifted her arms to offer him to her. A precious exchange.

The weight of him filled her arms and simultaneously, her heart.

"Welcome to the world little one," Liv said softly. She closed her eyes and inhaled, allowing the scent of his newness to wash over her. "Gosh, I could get addicted to that newborn baby smell. That's a thing right?"

"It's most definitely a thing. I can't help but want to have him in my arms constantly. I know I shouldn't. Taylor's convinced I'm already spoiling him, but I just can't help it. I'm in love." Jen sighed dreamily and Liv's smile widened.

"Entirely understandable," Liv said and watched Jen curl herself in a fetal position on the couch. Her friend's eyes began to close and Liv realized that possibly, in her excitement to see this new addition, she may have intruded on much needed recuperation time. She turned back to the doorway and attempted to pull Marcie's focus to the reason they were here. However, Marcie lingered, no longer looking scared but instead looking once more at her phone with that lascivious look in her eyes. Rather than become annoyed, Liv kept her gaze focused on her girlfriend, cleared her throat gently and spoke softly.

"Isn't he beautiful?"

Liv wasn't sure if it was the question she had asked, or being caught on the phone once again that caused Marcie's cheeks to flush, but neither made her move closer to the baby.

Instead, Marcie glanced over, as if getting too close would cause her to catch something. "He's something," Marcie muttered under her breath, and Liv felt a heat rise in her chest. Her eyes darted around the room, hoping neither of their friends had heard this statement. Not missing a beat, Marcie spun on her heels, plastered on what Liv knew was a fake smile, and turned to Taylor, whose gaze was fixed longingly on her almost sleeping wife.

"Did you hear about the Sanderson project?"

"Marcie, really? We aren't here to talk about work." Liv said.

She was now definitely annoyed and so ashamed that her girlfriend would instantly try and change the focus of why they were here in the first place, to work. One of the things that annoyed Liv the most was that they could be having the most intimate talks and Marcie's mind would still be at the office. Yes, she was focused, hardworking, and driven. She was incredibly competent in her job as a real estate agent and was known for being a shark when it came to sealing the deal. She could smell compliance like blood in surrounding waters. She was relentless in her pursuits and Liv had witnessed that firsthand when they had met.

"Actually, it would be nice to have a little normalcy, the last two days have been a little crazy," Taylor said, her gaze flitting between Jen and Liv apologetically before turning back to Marcie. "Could I interest you in a glass of wine?"

"I'd love a glass." Marcie smiled, already crossing the room and heading for the kitchen without so much as a glance at her girlfriend. Taylor followed close behind, turning as she reached the doorway.

"Elizabeth?"

Taylor's use of her full name caused Liv's shoulders to tense. Only her parents and Marcie insisted on calling her Elizabeth. She preferred the nickname her brother had dubbed her with when his toddler tongue couldn't wrap around that many consonants. Her parents had thought it cute for a while, but being the people they were and living the life that they did, with all its unspoken but very visual privileges, they soon refused to call her anything other than the nine letters they'd given her at birth. In fact a few select times during her teens she had been berated for breaking curfew and her parents had gone so far as to include her middle name -Beatrice- when dressing her down. She introduced herself as Liv to everyone she had ever met, including Marcie, but when her girlfriend first learned of her full name she had asked Liv why she intended on going by a name clearly meant for a child. Since then, she had only ever called Liv by her "adult" name and encouraged her friends to do the same.

Liv shook her head and held back a sigh. "Um, no thank you. I've got my hands full and I have no intention of putting him down just yet."

"He's perfect isn't he?" Jen voiced sleepily from her seat on the sofa.

Liv felt her heart swell at the solid weight resting in her arms. Her gaze traveled over his slightly mottled baby skin, cheeks covered in milk spots and downy hair sticking out at all angles.

"A literal dream," she sighed. "I'm sorry about Marcie. She's just really focused on this project. I feel like I haven't seen her in weeks and when I do she's just everywhere and nowhere. Sorry, here's me lamenting about my woes when you've just pushed a watermelon out of your lady parts."

A soft giggle filled the air and Jens eyebrows knitted together in mock indignation "Did you just call my child a watermelon?."

"He's the cutest watermelon... of course."

"Of course."

"How are you, really?" Liv sensed how exhausted Jen was, she could see the soft blue circles cowering beneath her bright green eyes. She had read that women often survived the first few months of parenthood on adrenaline and adoration alone. Looking once again at the beautiful bundle in her arms she understood why. He wasn't even hers and she felt so much love for him already. She resisted the urge to bring him closer to her and inhale his sweet baby scent again.

"Sore, tired, elated, absolutely shitting myself. Contrary to popular belief they don't come with a manual. There's no one who shows up at your doorstep with a *'How To'* book that tells you everything you need to do to make sure you get it right. It was easy when I was pregnant. I kept me safe, I kept him safe, you know? But here, now… it's like oh, he's real. He's here and I have to make sure this wonderful little human does good."

Nodding along at the full force rant that spilled from her friends' lips, Liv resisted the urge to smirk. Jen had always been so level-headed and here she was completely unraveling at the hands of this beautiful new addition, who was yet to know his purpose and power in the world. She chuckled internally and shifted his position, both hands cradling his head as his body rested in her closed knees. Face to face with him she felt her heart race with possibilities and her chest fill with want.

"With great cuteness comes great responsibility."

Her gentle response prompted another spiel from Jen who had tucked her legs further into herself, her head resting lazily on her crooked elbow for support.

"I had a panic attack last night," she whispered, her voice shaky and rough. "I was sitting in the nursery watching him while he slept and it just all of a sudden hit me. We aren't a two anymore. We aren't just T&J able to skip work for a long weekend and head to a cabin in the woods or sit watching the stars from the porch of a beach house. We can't just leave. Now we have to plan, and I'm a planner but my god, Liv! Did you know babies need so much stuff?"

"I did, actually," Liv giggled.

"And you didn't think about warning me before I got pregnant? What kind of friend are you?" Jen laughed too.

Cupping the baby's head steadily, Liv brushed his cheeks with her thumbs affectionately and watched in amazement as his natural instincts kicked in and he rooted with his open mouth for her thumbs.

Sadness washed over her at the thought of never having this for herself. She wanted it. She wanted it so much, all of it. The tiredness, the fear, the attachment, the unconditional love. Hell, she even wanted the stretch marks. Something indelible that reminded her each time she ran her hands over her stomach or glanced in the mirror that they had once been one.

Feeling Jen's gaze firmly on her, she cleared her throat and allowed her eyes to leave her lap.

"I'd like to think the end product outweighs the overwhelming scariness. You know, you can still do all the things you did before both with and without the little watermelon. I'd happily take him off your hands for a few hours, or days. When he's older and you're ready to part with him for longer than an hour, that is."

"You're the best. I don't think Marcie would share your enthusiasm though. You think being one of nine would have meant the maternal instinct was strong in her. Fear of failure is such a powerful thing. She did everything she could to avoid ending up like her mom. I don't think she ever looked back when she finally left home."

Liv knew all of this to be true. Marcie rarely talked about her experiences growing up, but everytime one of her siblings reached out, Liv could see the instant resentment that would shadow her girlfriends face. She heard the voice in her head reminding her that she knew what she had gotten herself into when she had decided to stay with Marcie, the one that yelled *'I told you so'* whenever Liv realized Marcie's desires wouldn't change. Feeling uncomfortable all of a sudden, she shifted in her seat and tried to change the subject.

"Do you want to nap? I read somewhere that it's best for you to rest when he does, so if you feel the need to just doze off while I'm here, go for it."

"You sure you wouldn't mind?"

"Of course not," Liv smiled. "I'm completely content to just sit here and marvel at the perfect little human you made. You did such a good job, mommy!"

"I did, didn't I? Don't steal him. I know the temptation is there, but I'll keep everything crossed that once Marcie finally makes an honest woman out of you, you'll waste no time changing her mind so you can make a perfect little playmate for Theo." Jen yawned, her voice trailing off as she closed her eyes and sighed.

"Oh! That's your name is it? Theo 'Heart Stealer' Hadley." Liv felt his tiny hand open and close around her index finger. Her heart swelled at the gentle touch and she marveled at how such a simple gesture brought to the forefront the yearning she had pushed down for so long.

Not sure how much longer she could do this, a wave of guilt washed over her as she thought about the fact she had potentially been lying to Marcie all these years. Then fear gripped her, and she wondered if they would survive the truth. She wasn't sure if her heart was ready to let go of Marcie's just yet. When you're with someone for so long your lives become so intertwined it's hard to know who you are without them. If Liv had to be honest, she wasn't sure who she was outside of work and her relationship, she had been lost for the longest time. How frightening to be lost in familiarity, in a place and with a person who was supposed to make you feel safe.

"It means 'divine gift'" Jen breathed, her tone indicating she was on the precipice of sleep she had been starved of for a while now. The corners of her mouth lifted and Liv nodded her head slowly, glancing back down at the welcome weight in her arms.

"He's exactly that."

***

The minute she had buckled her seatbelt, Liv felt Marcie breathe a sigh of relief that traveled on the chill of night and slipped through the open window. The warmth Liv had felt holding Theo, still filled her chest.

"I'm glad that's over with." Marcie said, looking at Liv as if her comment would be agreed with.

Liv pulled out of the driveway and rolled her eyes hoping her friends hadn't overheard Marcie's exclamation. She had already felt shame wash over her the longer Marcie had stayed in the kitchen and when she had refused another chance to hold Theo it had been hard not to catch the sympathetic look Jen gave her. It could have been worse, Liv supposed. Sympathy was better than being offended. She knew that Jen understood, but damn it, couldn't Marcie have made an effort? Let down her walls just this once and just have held Theo?

Liv smiled to herself at how natural it had felt to sway him softly into a slumber she envied. She thought about his soft features, button nose upturned slightly, pursed full lips that screamed Jen and soft downy hair that threatened to burn amber.

He was breathtaking, Liv was still a little enamored as they drove away. Her eyes never left the road for fear of them betraying her and showing Marcie glimpses of the truth. Liv knew it was all written there in cerulean blue. While Marcie reveled in the relief of never having her life become even a smidgen of what their friends' now was; Liv was awash with sadness. Heartbroken at the resolve that the weight she longed to feel in her arms would always reside in her heart.

"I didn't know how much longer I could stand there listening to all the baby talk," Marcie spoke and Liv straightened her spine, sucking in a breath.

"They're new parents Marcie and they're smitten. They have every right to be, he's beautiful."

"He's loud," Marcie deadpanned, leaning her head against the window and once again glancing at her phone.

Liv shook her head, trying to remember when their relationship had slipped into this. She tried to pinpoint when she had first started to tolerate Marcie, rather than simmer under her once lustful gaze.

"He's a baby, they cry to communicate," Liv said, biting down on her bottom lip to stop herself from losing her cool altogether.

"I'm just glad we decided to never go down that road. I like how our life is. I like knowing I can go home and relax...and sleep. Those circles under Jen's eyes," Marcie scoffed and this time Liv felt her brow noticeably furrow. "Ugh, no thank you. The only thing I want keeping me awake is you, and that sexy red number I got you for Christmas."

Liv glanced over at Marcie as they came upon a red light, she shook her head and pursed her lips. "You didn't get me anything red for Christmas."

"Sure I did."

An awkward silence filled the car. Marcie's fingers stopped swiping over the screen of her phone. Liv watched as those eyes she once dreamily drowned in, turned into stormy, dark depths that hid secrets. Her lips parted and a breath dared to pass the threshold of her mouth but no noise filled the air. The traffic light switched back to green and Liv found herself focused straight ahead once more.

"Nope, you definitely didn't buy me any lingerie for Christmas, Marcie. Maybe you have me confused with your other girlfriend."

Chapter 3

Honey

After throwing off the work day in a trail that led to the bathroom, Honey turned the dial on her shower to a pleasant seven and waited for the beep to let her know the temperature was optimum. She caught a glimpse of herself in the full length mirror, trailing her hands over the softness of her hips and the rounded curves of her fuller breasts, she sighed softly. She had always been a little curvier than her sisters. She often joked with their parents that by the time they chose to have her, any hopes of being tall and slim had been squandered. She didn't mind so much now she was older, but as a teen, however, she had hated being the smallest of her friends, standing at a small but respectable, five foot two. Her height combined with a heart shaped face, wide eyes and perfectly upturned button nose meant she was always confused as being younger than she actually was. Add into the mix the kindness and gentility she emanated and it was no wonder that the more outspoken of children at school nicknamed her "The Disney Princess."

The shower beeped, pulling her away from her reflection and she glided through the fog of steam to stand under the faux rainfall that often soothed her when the real thing wasn't available. Honey was a pluviophile. She found joy in the rain, in the way the world seemed during and after. It was almost as if the world had participated in a factory reset. Rain had the power to take even the messiest of pathways, objects and even hearts and make them clean.

When the first rain fell after Andie had left, Honey had run outside immediately. She had watched for weeks, waiting for the slight change in the air. The misting on the windows that turned to promising droplets, had carried comfort and solace as they made their way from the skies. She had stood outside in that storm for over an hour, until her clothes were weighed down with a heaviness she shed from her soul. She had held her arms upwards to the gray skies in thanks, her heart a little lighter than it had been in months.

"Alexa, play Paramore - When It Rains" her voice echoed through the room, finding the circular machine sitting on her cabinet and with its blue blinking light it obeyed her request.

"When It Rains by Paramore, on Amazon Music."

Honey smiled and closed her eyes as the opening notes to her favorite song danced around the room, bouncing off the walls. She inhaled deeply and began to sing along, imagining she was headlining her own stage at Warped Tour, as she always did.

"Just a quick set today," she giggled. It had to be, the birthday celebrations at her parents house would be starting in just two hours. Their moderately sized home would be filled to bursting with her ever expanding family. All there to help welcome her to thirty.

As she lathered her dirty blonde hair with shampoo she smiled and tried to remember that despite not having the one person she wanted the most there with her, she wasn't alone. She hadn't truly been alone in her whole life. In a few hours time, she would be the center of attention, as her nieces and nephews clutched at her hands and legs begging her to play games with them. There would be the usual friendly argument over who got to sit next to her at the dinner table, even though they'd sorted out a rota years ago when Honey had sealed her position as the favorite aunt to all her sister's children. She felt a wash of gratefulness following the rivulets of water that cascaded down her olive skin and as she sang along to her favorite band, she rushed through the rest of her bathroom routine.

***

"Happy Birthday Buzzy!" came a shout from the wrap around porch of the old house on the top of the hill. Honey had decided, as she was oft to do, to check in on Marvin, her neighbor and the man who had kindly let her rent the little cottage she lived in. Towering over her at six foot but with a gentle smile that broke past the wrinkles of time on his weather worn face, he was one of Honey's favorite people in the world.

"Marvin, you remembered!"

She knew he wouldn't have forgotten. He was getting old but that was one thing that had remained intact, his memory. He prided himself on it and it showed when every Thursday he would beat her -with ease- at Chess.

"I may be old but I still got all my faculties. Well, most of them." He winked, settling down in the old wooden rocking chair he had made himself many moons ago, "You got time to indulge me in a quick game?"

Honey found herself slipping into the chair opposite before he had even finished speaking, holding up the cardboard carrier she had lugged across the field with her.

"As if I could resist. Cider?" She pulled a bottle out. Leaning the lip of the metal seal against the edge of the table, she brought her hand down precisely and was rewarded with a pop.

"As if *I* could resist. You know me too well," Marvin smirked, reaching out his shaking hands and nodding his thanks, "So, your girl's coming home soon, right? I'm going to miss our little game nights."

Honey lifted another bottle from the carrier she had placed beside her feet and angled it against the table, biting down on her bottom lip. She brought her hand down a little harder this time. The lid was not the only thing breaking free from its seal. Sadness swam in her stomach, her feelings for Andie drowning against waves she could no longer control.

"Actually... you could have my company for a while longer. If you're okay with that?" She said, moving her king pawn forward two spaces and Marvin mirrored that move back.

"She's not coming back?"

"I... I don't think so." Honey's gaze darted to the floor, her thumbs scratched nervously at the label of the bottle cradled firmly in her palms.

"Well, her dedication is admirable but I'm not sure I could stay away from my girl that long. At least, not willingly." His watery gaze moved past the open screen door to the picture hanging in the hallway. There in sepia tone, lived an incredibly handsome young man radiating love through his gaze at the stunningly beautiful woman in his arms.

She had known Marvin and Bea all her life and had admired them like they were her own grandparents. After all, they were best friends. She had been at Marvin's side when Bea passed ten years ago. She had been the one to hold his hand the first night he came home to a house that no longer smelled of whatever fantastic pie or baked good she had thrown together. Honey had watched with an aching heart, as a man she once was convinced was so tall he could touch the clouds, shrunk before her. It had broken her to see him walk aimlessly around the space that had been perfect for two, but now seemed far too big for one.

"I know what you mean. I miss Bea too. She made the best peach cobbler." Honey's mouth watered as she thought about the lightly golden crumbs, dusted with brown sugar that hid the soft sweetness of peaches underneath. Gosh, if she could have one gift for her birthday it would be to taste that cobbler again.

"Yup. Couldn't boil pasta worth a damn, but she made a mean pie. You kids were always around here as quick as a flash when you were younger."

"The smell would carry six blocks over. Of course we all knew where it came from. Legend had it that the first to the door would always get the biggest helping. I remember wishing for so long that I could be a little taller, so I could beat everyone to get here. When I accepted that I wasn't going to grow overnight, I started to practise running every chance I got." Honey laughed into the cool air and noticed the night start to approach on the horizon.

"Oh, she knew. She watched you kids out of the window. Helped her with missing our own grandchildren. She would watch you running up and down that road, noon and night, in all weathers. Do you remember that winter when the snow reached a few feet? You must have been about seven. All the other kids were out filling the walkway with snowmen but not you. Oh no! You were out there clutching a shovel, clearing a path from your grandparents place to ours. To anyone else it was a sweet gesture. It looked like you didn't want us falling over. I'd like to think part of that was true, but she knew you were stacking up the odds in your favor of getting here first. After that she started making sure yours was the biggest helping regardless of how fast you ran. She had a soft spot for you, it was hard not to with those big eyes, blonde pigtails and the sweetest gap-toothed smile. *You* were always her favorite. In fact let me just…" he pushed himself up slowly from his seat. Shuffling his way towards the door, he went inside.

Honey stayed seated on the porch, her eyebrows knitted together in curiosity and a smile of remembrance on her face. As he re-emerged, Honey noticed his limp appear visible, a symptom of his tiredness and triggered by the cold. She stood quickly from her seat and crossed the floor to offer him some assistance.

"Careful," she whispered, helping to lower him gently back into his seat. In his hands he clutched a rather worn booklet, bound with a deep purple cover and containing loose sheets of yellowing paper that stuck out at odd angles.

"Here," Marvin smiled, holding the book between them and nodding his head encouragingly.

Honey tilted her head as realization of what he held in his aging hands hit her.

Bea's recipe book had been the talk of the town in the months after she passed. Actually, long before that. The town rumor mill claimed that she had once been offered a substantial amount of money for the cobbler recipe that lingered between those covers. It was said the offer had come from a company looking to market it to the masses and would have secured her enough capital that she wouldn't have had to worry about money ever again. They could have moved East, closer to their only son and his children. They could have watched their own grandchildren grow up, instead of the children in town. However, Bea had turned it down, and rather foolishly -or so the town said- remained in Verity Vale, in the house on top of the hill.

"Oh, Marvin, is this her recipe book? I can't take this."

"Nonsense. You can and you will. She would have wanted you to have this. I'm only sorry it took me so long to pass it on."

Honey shook her head as he pressed the welcome weight into her hands. A warmth of affection filled her chest, spilling out of her eyes as she closed her hands protectively around the bound pages. Glancing up at him she saw nothing but sincerity and affection. She hoped that he saw all of that and more reflected in her own gaze. This wasn't simply a bunch of recipes, it was love. Memories in black and blue ink that spanned years before Honey was even a notion conjured in her parents wildest dreams. This was the most thoughtful birthday gift she knew she would receive, undoubtedly.

"Wouldn't you rather keep this in your family? Perhaps give it to one of your grandchildren?" she asked sincerely.

"Oh, I haven't seen them in the longest while. Don't assume I ever will again in my lifetime. They stopped calling when Bea died. I think they forgot this place exists." Honey watched him lower his head. He lifted one hand and gently caressed the oak chess pieces he hand carved himself. The unspoken words resounded in her ears.

They forgot I exist.

Honey's mind drifted to thoughts of how people could do that. Forget about someone they loved, so easily. Forget that someone loved them so much and longed for them even when it hurt. Honey thought about Andie sunning herself on golden sands and wondered if she ever thought of her. If there were moments where the smell of freshly baked blueberry muffins would transport her back to Verity, to Honey and the life they had, or if she simply pushed all that aside now in favor of surf, sea and somebody else.

A hand on hers pulled her from her reverie and Honey blinked away those thoughts. Willing them deep down in her stomach where her fear of abandonment wrapped around them and kept them for when she was alone. She really wished she could let them go.

"Buzzy, are you okay?" Marvin asked, reaching out a hand and making contact with her.

"Sorry, I was somewhere else for a second," she apologized and mustered up a fake smile she knew he could see through. "Are you sure about this?"

"Positive. I think this is exactly where she would have wanted her recipes to go." He smiled and the corners of his mouth pushed away his wrinkles. If Honey looked hard enough she could see remnants of the handsome man on the wall. Someone he used to be, but still was underneath the layers of time and loss.

Her smartwatch began to vibrate, telling her she had an incoming call from Sasha. She shook her wrist and gave Marvin's hand a gentle squeeze.

"Are you sure I can't convince you to join me at the Hive?" she asked, smiling as the affectionate name for her family home rolled off her tongue. She knew that's why Sasha was calling. Honey was officially late for her own birthday party and she could bet that Kyla was already pitching a fit.

Marvin laughed. "Oh no, I've got a glass of scotch and Tolstoy waiting for me. You go and enjoy what's left of your special day. Thank you for wasting a little of your precious time with an old fool like me."

"Marvin," Honey smiled, bending at the knees and making sure she made direct eye contact with him. She wanted him to understand that she meant every word that fell from her lips, knowing he was convinced that she only came over out of some form of obligation. Sure, she lived in the cottage at the bottom of the hill, on land and in property he owned, but their friendship meant the world to her. She wanted him to know that.

"Marvin, time with you is never wasted. You're the best friend I could ever have asked for."

"What a sad existence if I'm the best you've got." He chuckled, but Honey could hear the scratch of sadness in his voice. She reached for his hand and gave it a squeeze.

"I happen to think I'm extremely lucky to have you for my best friend. The luckiest in fact. You're positive about not coming?" she glanced across the fields and down the hill to where her bright yellow Jeep sat waiting for her. A sunflower amongst a Van Gogh sky.

"I'm sure. Go be with your family." Marvin sighed and Honey straightened up, leaning forward and placing a kiss on his cheek as she went.

"You are my family Marvin."

Her wrist began to vibrate again and she took a step back watching as Marvin moved to stand. He picked up his almost finished bottle of cider and lifted it into the air in a silent toast she knew was for her. Honey began to gather her things. She placed the untouched but open bottle back inside the cardboard carrier, she would finish drinking it once she arrived at the Hive. Her parents always insisted she stay over the night of her birthday and though she dared not admit it to them, she secretly loved spending the night in the twin sized bed, surrounded by band posters that indicated the soundtrack of her youth.

"Oh Buzzy, before you go." Marvin said, his voice indicating a tone Honey knew all too well. He hit a lower register that emanated warmth whenever he was about to dish out sage advice and Honey had received her fair share over the last two years.

"Ooh, Birthday advice?"

"Let's call this everyday advice. Life advice. Don't go settling just because you haven't got what others have. I know it's tiring when you feel like you're constantly running against people faster than you are. Remember, you're running the same race but it doesn't matter where you place. You'll get the reward you deserve in the end regardless."

"You really believe that, don't you?" He gave a nod and a smile.

Walking towards the stairs she glanced back over her shoulder at where he stood in the hallway of his home, tall and stoic, but with a softness you could see in his eyes.

"Sleep well. I'll see you in the morning. We'll have birthday cake for breakfast."

Marvin's laugh echoed through the hallway of the big house, he clapped his hands together before resting them on the doorframe. "You always did make your own rules. Happy Birthday Buzzy!"

***

The drive across town to her parents' home always made Honey feel great. It wasn't a long drive and she could have walked it, but walking in the dark was something she tried not to make a habit of. Verity Vale was a relatively safe place and everyone literally knew everyone. Still, Honey, by nature, was careful and cautious.

The familiar stores passed by in a blur of striped awnings and fairy lights, as Honey drove through the center of town. Her chest swelled at the sight of the enormous window front of her grandparents' store, well, her store now, sitting pride of place in-between Alex's Hardware store and McCormicks Book Nook. Two businesses that were relatively new to Verity, but their owners were absolutely wonderful people. This part of Verity got really quiet at night, unless there was some form of pre-organised event or gathering. Honey loved how everything slowed right down when the street lights came on.

She turned onto the back road that took her away from the center of town, passing the one bar they boasted and continuing into the oncoming night. Honey didn't really mind that the street lights faded from her view. She had been driving this route for as long as she could remember and knew the bends and straights like she had paved them herself. That was true of the whole town though, so much so that she could probably drive to her parents, or anywhere in Verity for that matter, with her eyes closed. She would never attempt it though, nor would she vocalize that thought to her family. Kyla already thought she was flaky, she didn't need to further fuel that fire.

Honey arrived at her parents home in less than ten minutes. As she pulled onto their gravel driveway she took in the sight before her.

Streamers, balloons in every color and an enormous banner that read, HAPPY BUZZDAY! in alternating yellow and black lettering, were illuminated by string lights that hung from the awning.

She could tell from the inconsistent sizing and form of the letters that it had been a creative process undertaken by her many nieces and nephews. The thought of them all huddled around her mother's dining table to make it, warmed her heart. Honey unclipped her seatbelt and moved to grab her phone from the passenger seat, hoping her mother didn't choose that moment to come flying out of the door and catch her in the act.

She had promised her mother years ago when she first started driving that she would always put her phone in the glove box or in a bag away from her, whilst the car was in motion. As Honey gripped her phone it lit up with Andies' name. Excitement merged with hope in a dangerous mix. She swiped her thumb across the screen and brought it to her ear. The smile she had been wearing fell away instantly.

"Like this. Is that good?"

Muffled voices breathed heavily down the line and for a moment Honey considered it was a wrong number, but it had flashed with the picture she had taken of Andie three weeks after they had met. The day Andie had taken her to a park, pushed her on the swing and pulled her back into a kiss before asking her to be her girlfriend. This wasn't her voice. Maybe her housemate had accidentally dialed Honey's number and this was all some mistake. Surely this wasn't what it sounded like. It couldn't be.

Her stomach bottomed out as she heard the unmistakable raspy tone of her girlfriend, moaning a name that wasn't hers.

"Tessa! Yes! Right there. Fuck, Tessa! I'm so close."

Before she could comprehend what she was doing the phone flew from her hand, across the passenger seat and fell to the floor. Honey felt sick. Her hands shook and she felt her throat closing over, trapping the screams she so desperately needed to let out. For months she had suspected something was happening but had so desperately wanted to be wrong about it. Now she knew. The reason Andie hadn't been in touch was because she had not only moved away, but moved on. Tears burned at her eyes, rolling down her cheeks in warm rivulets of regrets and denial she had held onto for far too long. She sucked in a staggered breath, trying to ground herself.

She couldn't do this, couldn't face going into her parent's home right now. All those eyes on her, all those hugs and smiles, it was too soft, and right now Honey felt hard, she needed hard. Gripping the wheel tightly with one hand and shifting the gear into reverse with the other, she backed out of the driveway before anyone could see her. Her autopilot well and truly activated, she made her way mindlessly back down the darkened roads towards her home. Her heart was racing as fast as her mind. She tried to talk herself out of an over-reaction but felt her breathing become labored and the brain fog that usually signaled the start of a panic attack, set in.

Pulling up outside her cottage, Honey turned off the ignition, feeling the old car juddering to a halt. As she attempted to catch a breath she caught sight of flashing lights up the hill. Before she knew what she was doing, Honey threw open the driver door and ran towards the lights, her legs trembling with each step she took.

The ambulance had left tracks in the grass as the gravel walkway wasn't wide enough for a vehicle that size to stay on. The fight to stay upright when her entire body screamed at her to fall, was hard. Her heart pumped blast beats to a song she didn't want to hear as she watched strangers wheeling out a gurney. Marvin lay there, a glassy look in his crystal blue eyes.

This couldn't be happening. Not today. Not now.

"What's happening?" she asked, or at least she thought she did. She wasn't entirely sure the words were making it out into the open, half convinced they too were drowning in her tears.

"I'm sorry Ma'am, you are?" a larger woman asked as her gloved hands squeezed repeatedly on a soft, blue sphere covering Marvin's mouth and nose. Honey rushed to his side and reached for hands that were warm earlier and now held an unfamiliar coldness.

"I'm his neighbor. Is he okay? What happened? Marvin!"

"He's had a heart attack. He managed to call in an emergency but by the time we got here he was unconscious. Do you know if he has any family close by?"

Honey shook her head, sobbing as she rubbed his hand gently, willing some of her warmth back into him. Helpless, Honey reluctantly let go of his hand as the paramedics counted to three before lifting together and smoothly transitioning him into the back of the ambulance.

"I… I'm all he has. I'm his family, he's my…he's… Marvin! It's me, It's Buzzy!"

"We're taking him to Verity West if you'd like to follow us."

"Yes. I'll follow." Honey said. She pushed her hands against her cheeks and swiped at the tears that were now flowing freely. Not knowing what else to do, she took a step back and watched as the doors to the ambulance closed, blocking the woman and Marvin from view.

Darkness had spilled itself across the sky. An indigo expanse dotted with stars Honey would usually wish upon. A cold chill accompanied the night, holding hands as they wrapped themselves over everything reachable and threatened that which they couldn't.

She wasn't sure how long she had stood there, rooted to the spot. But by the time Honey managed to make her body move again her cheeks were stained, sore and chapped from where cold had met warm and her tears were now dry.

She walked up the wooden steps of the porch and closed the door. His spare key resided next to her own on the small green lanyard she kept in her pocket and she would give it to him when he came home. He was going to come home, wasn't he?

As she headed back down the hill to her car, the reality of everything finally hit her and she doubled over, one hand resting on the hood. This couldn't be happening. Surely if the universe was playing some cruel joke it could have picked a better day.

Her whole body lurched suddenly and she emptied the contents of her stomach onto the gravel. It wasn't much. She had been saving herself for what was always too big a dinner cooked by her mother.

As her shoulders wracked with sobs, Honey made a silent plea with the birthday goddesses that if they let Marvin be okay she wouldn't ask for anything else ever again. To anyone else she knew it would sound silly. Asking for a life, in exchange for wishes that rarely came true. Honey hadn't had the best of luck with birthday wishes but she was a huge advocate for believing in something bigger than herself. Something that guided rather than controlled how people's lives unfolded. Something that provided gentle nudges rather than pushed you off cliff edges. Honey always thought the universe was smart and had a reason for everything, but she couldn't fathom the reason for today's events. If asked to be honest, she wasn't entirely sure she really wanted to.

***

The sounds of doctors and nurses being called over the address system filled the hallways of Verity West. Alarms signaled codes in colors Honey wished to never hear again. It had been two hours since she had walked through the doors and asked to see Marvin Henderson. Fighting against the claims of 'no visitors unless they're family' and explaining that in each other's eyes they were exactly that, Honey had been shown to the waiting area by an orderly who gave her a sympathetic smile she wished would fall off his smug looking face. Her ears rang with a cacophony of sound and so it was no surprise when she almost missed her wrist vibrating and her phone ringing in the pocket of her jeans.

"Buzzy where are you? Everyone's waiting. Buzzy, is everything okay?" Sasha said.

Hearing her sister's voice made Honey want to collapse into her arms. She choked back a sob and the words scratched her throat as she spoke her next words. "I'm at the hospital."

"Are you okay?" Sasha's concern was evident and Honey all of sudden felt like she couldn't breathe. She shifted herself further up the wall and rested her head on her free hand. Pulling her knees into her chest, she tried to make herself as small as possible, so as to not be in the way of the ever increasing foot traffic.

"I…I'm fine. It's M…Marvin, he…" she couldn't finish her thought. She didn't know what was going on. She had been sitting for so long in the hallway and no one had come to see her. No one had given her any information. The last time she had asked, the woman behind the desk had rolled her eyes and made it seem like asking was an inconvenience.

"Do you want us to come be with you?"

It was at that moment Honey was absolutely certain that her adoration for her sister knew no bounds. It didn't matter what she was going through or where she was at, she knew Sasha would drop everything in an instant to be with her. That's what family was, unconditional and unwavering support. It had always been there, a backbone in her life.

A foundation stone of hand holding on her first day at school when Honey was so scared of the large building and even larger number of children heading into it. It had been there at sixteen when her first love Clarissa Stevens had broken her heart and Sasha had slipped between the sheets of Honey's twin sized bed and cried alongside her. It had been there when, three days after Andie had left and Honey had all but forgotten how to function, Sasha came over to the cottage, letting herself in and turning on the shower before practically picking up her littlest sister and holding her under the spray herself. Honey knew that if she so much as breathed the word her entire family would rally around, because that's what they did but she didn't know that she could handle all of that right now.

Her whole body was vibrating at such a high frequency that she could feel everything, from the light hairs on her arms standing on end, to the pressure from the laces on her Doc Martens pressing into her feet. It was painful. Everything was painful.

"No, stay there. Tell everyone I'm sorry and I'll see them all soon, okay."

"Give Marvin our love Buzzy."

Honey looked over as double doors opened and closed in a never ending stream of doctors and nurses whose eyes avoided hers. She tilted her head backwards and closed her eyes, feeling completely helpless and frustrated at the lack of news.

"I will...Sasha, I'm scared. What if he, what am I supposed to do?"

"I'm sure he will be fine Buzzy, he's old but strong. Don't get yourself too caught up in the what ifs. Wait until you know for sure and call me if you need me, okay? I love you." Sashas voice soothed her slightly.

"I love you too."

Honey lowered the phone from her ear and swiped her fingers across the screen. Accessing her contact list, she hovered over Andie's picture. Her subconscious was screaming at her to reach out for a source of familiarity, but then she recalled the breathy moans that had reverberated in her ears a few hours earlier. She dropped the phone into her lap and glanced over at the double doors, willing someone to walk through them and let her know that everything was going to be okay.

How odd that the only person who could provide comfort was a stranger who knew nothing of Marvin but his vital statistics. They didn't know that he once taught English Literature and could recite Robert Frost, Shakespeare and Chaucer in his sleep. Or that he placed importance on the lyrics of Mos Def, Common and considered What They Do by The Roots to be poetry in itself. The hands that now touched him didn't know how it felt to really hold him. The eyes that gazed over him, didn't look at him with the reverence Honey did. They didn't know that it wasn't just *his* heart they had in their hands. It was hers too.

The double doors swung open once more and a sympathetic gaze fixed on hers. She willed it away. She didn't need that comfort, she didn't want to hear the words that her heart already knew.

Footsteps filled her ears as the rest of the sounds deadened and dampened around her. It felt like someone was holding her underwater the way her lungs were crying out for air. The room began to spin on an axis she wasn't prepared for and she shook her head slowly, willing him away. Her blonde hair fell around her shoulders, framing her tired face.

No. This wasn't real, this wasn't happening. It couldn't be.

The doctor was looking at the wrong person, he had to be. Marvin wouldn't just give up. He was too strong, he was too real. He wouldn't just leave her.

When the footsteps paused in front of her, toes almost touching her own in an attempt to draw her attention, Honey felt a desperate gasp escape her. She wanted to scream at them to go away and that they were making a mistake. Didn't doctors make mistakes all the time? They had gotten it wrong. He wasn't gone. He couldn't be. He had to stay.

Didn't he?

A gentle apology reached her ears and Honey pushed herself to her unsteady feet. She couldn't understand any of what was happening right now. How someone who had been so very much full of life was no longer here. Anger swam inside of her stomach as people continued to walk the halls, phones continued to ring and the stupid doctor with his stupid apologies kept talking at her. She couldn't lift her gaze from its fixed position on the floor, her heart and head felt too heavy and so, giving in to the strong flight response she wasn't aware existed within her, she ran. Her feet moved with full autonomy until she had reached her Jeep. She took the keys from her pocket, opened the door and slid into the driver's seat. Slamming the door shut, her head fell against the steering wheel and she broke.

Colors flashed before her eyes. The rainbow balloons filled with air Marvin no longer breathed. The purple cover of a book filled with writing from a woman he had missed for so long. Deep blue eyes swimming with sorrow and apologies Honey didn't want to hear, and then… black.

Chapter 4

Liv

The view from the seventh floor was spectacular. Liv loved to stand at the full length windows of their apartment and watch as the sunrise chased away the midnight blues and breathed life into the city in a welcome warmth of orange.

Her hands wrapped around her favorite mug. The warming scent of cardamom and clove filled her lungs as she inhaled the Chai she always started her mornings with. They had lived here for almost seven years, Liv and her girlfriend. It was convenient for Marcie in her job as one of Fenton and Smith's top real estate agents, to live so close to the center of the city. It didn't bother Liv that she had to commute to work every day. She used the hour and half to do productive things like listen to her favorite British podcast, Something Rhymes with Purple.

Liv loved words and their meanings. She had fallen in love with the English language whilst listening from her mothers lap, as she read bedtime stories in a polished accent meant for classic literature. As a child, Liv would fold herself into her mother's soft curves and tangle her hands in her own black curls, ones she grew into with age, safe in the comfort of her mothers' arms.

It was no surprise to her parents when Liv informed them of her decision to study to become an English professor. It also didn't surprise them that in order to do this she packed up her life at eighteen and headed for England, Oxford specifically. After spending four years gaining her Masters in English, Liv was loath to return home. She had made some wonderful connections both in and out of the lecture halls. It didn't take long, having credentials that reflected her impeccable effort, for her to secure a position as the youngest member of the English faculty, at a small Liberal Arts college just outside the city boundaries. The campus was devoid of the gothic buildings and spires Liv had come to adore during her time in England. But she loved the view that the window in her office afforded her, of the clocktower in the main building.

Liv prided herself on being able to adapt, no matter where she went and what she did. With each place she visited, Liv found herself falling in love with life a little more along the way.

She had been back for almost two years, when a chance meeting at a coffee shop had ended up with her wearing Marcie's drink. Liv had turned down the offer of having her once white blouse professionally cleaned and had left the coffee shop with little more than a glare of annoyance at the beautiful woman before her. When she had returned the next day, her order had been paid for and a note had been left containing a heartfelt apology and a phone number. Liv had swooned a little at the persistence. Tall, lean and with eyes that sparkled with mischief and unspoken promises, Marcie lit a fire in Liv and she fell in love quickly, or at least what she thought was love. Her heart had raced with excitement and the breathlessness that comes with being noticed. She didn't realize the latter would be so short-lived.

Liv sighed at the memories, and brought her still steaming cup to her lips to take a sip. The sound of her phone vibrating against the granite countertop in the kitchen pulled her from the breathtaking view and her daydream of what once was.

She hurried, barefoot, across the white tiled floor barefoot in order to retrieve the noisy offender before it woke Marcie from her slumber. Noticing the name across the screen Liv swiped quickly and brought the phone to her ear, "Hey Mom, to what do I owe the pleasure?"

Liv tried her best to keep the sarcasm from punctuating her tone. Her communication with her family was very limited and only ever out of obligation these days.

"Dear," her mother's ever exasperated voice sounded down the line. Liv mentally prepared a list of excuses to get out of what she was sure was another invite to a dinner at her parents' place. "We have some news that I'm not sure how to break to you, so I will just come right out with it. Your Grandfather has passed away."

"Oh. Wow. Is um, is dad alright?" Liv reached out and placed her cup on the countertop. She splayed her fingers on the cold clean surface to steady herself, as she listened to her mother's voice. She had never really been close with her father's parents. She couldn't actually remember the last time she had seen her grandfather, but part of her was sure it had to have been when her grandmother passed ten years ago. Liv felt so detached from that part of her life, thanks to her father's estrangement, that she couldn't really recall the exact details.

"He's surprisingly doing much better than I expected. He's got his assistant helping plan the funeral and he wants you to know that you aren't obligated to go. His words specifically being that he is *"going under duress"* and doesn't want you or Daniel to feel you have to."

Liv nodded her silent understanding. She knew her father would detach himself from this situation. He wasn't the most affectionate of humans and his emotional range straddled disinterest and anger in equal measure. Liv knew something had happened a long time ago, a disagreement of some sorts which had meant that during her teen years her summers were spent skiing the slopes in Europe, rather than spending them in the quaint town she had visited only a handful of times as a small child.

"I mean, I could take some time off work I suppose and see if Marcie can too."

"Oh no Elizabeth, don't do anything drastic." Her mother's flippant tone was no surprise. Genevieve Henderson was materialism personified. A societal magpie, she filled her life with all things bright and shiny. She wore designer clothes and was no stranger to paying over the odds for her morning cup of coffee. It was surprising, given her upbringing in high society, that she had fallen for Liv's father. He was, despite his social standing now, still a veritable country boy who grew up knowing exactly where his milk came from. Although he had worked incredibly hard to make something of himself, Liv wondered what he had given up in exchange. What part of his life had been pushed aside and forgotten for monetary comforts.

The answer was his life before college, his parents, his childhood home and a huge part of himself. She wondered if that was why she found it so difficult to get to know him, because he didn't know who he was himself.

"How did it happen?"

"He had a heart attack. Although he was approaching ninety so I guess it was only a matter of time really. Your father is surprised he lasted this long, honestly. It's a shame they didn't spend more time together over the years, but you know your father."

Liv did as much as she didn't. She knew he was stubborn and angry and if he didn't approve of something he didn't waste his time on it. To the rest of the world time was precious, to Liv's father, time was money. That was why her mother was calling her with this news and not him, it wasn't important enough a topic, or Liv wasn't important enough a person to command his time. Something inside of Liv shifted at that thought. A wave of sadness washed over her at the thought of her grandfather's passing. Shame entered the mix too as she wrestled with the truth that he was practically a stranger and she wasn't sure she was entitled to feel that loss. Her mothers loud sigh sounded down the line.

"Anyway, I will let you get back to your life. We just thought you should know."

"Of course. Thanks Mom. Give my love to Dad, okay?"

"I will Dear. Send our love to Marcie. We will see you sometime during the summer. Bye now!"

Their conversation was over as quickly as it began. Liv placed her phone back on the countertop and glanced at the clock on the wall indicating that she had an hour to ready herself before work. She wasn't sure how to process what her mother had just told her. The news that her last remaining grandparent had passed away was numbing in a way she never expected. When Liv had lost her grandmother ten years ago, she had only been twenty-three and so it hadn't really shaken her; fresh out of college and focused on her new job, she had been too self absorbed back then.

Standing in the early morning silence of her kitchen, Liv felt a finality settle around her. A gentle breeze slipped under the front door carrying a whisper of a voice telling her exactly how much she had taken for granted in her life. It wasn't that she had always just assumed her grandfather would be there, but growing up they had been two people who had existed only sometimes. She wondered if over the years they had thought of her, despite their distance. An act of love that Liv wasn't entirely sure she understood, or deserved.

When Liv thought about love in all its variations –and being a hopeless romantic she thought about it often– she considered that maybe love was more than giving a voice to it. Maybe real love was something that exists even in the absence of physical connection.

She wasn't sure she had ever felt love like that and sadness blossomed in her chest like a heavy weight threatening to anchor her heart to the depths of her stomach.

Silence still lingered in the air as Liv tiptoed along the hallway towards the bedroom. A sudden laughter slipped through the crack in the open door to her room, telling her that her girlfriend was now awake. She paused and watched, through the gap, as Marcie, phone held to her ear, whispered in reverent tones down the line. The words were unintelligible, but there was that salacious grin sitting knowingly on her well rested face.

Placing her hand on the door, Liv pushed it open, causing her girlfriend to drop the phone into her lap, losing it amongst the pristine white sheets that were pooling around her bare waist.

"Gosh Elizabeth! Do you have to sneak around like that? You could give someone a heart attack!"

Marcie's words shouldn't have cut like they did, but given the call she had received just moments ago Liv couldn't help it when her shoulders began to shake and tears rolled down her cheeks. Before she could explain herself, Marcie had crossed the room and placed a hand on her arm. Blinking away pools that flooded her aqua eyes, Liv sniffed and recounted the phone call with her mother. She shook her head apologetically as she swiped at her cheeks, her chest staggering as she grasped at air and willed it back into her struggling body.

"I didn't even know you had a grandfather, Elizabeth. You haven't spoken about him in the eight years I've known you. Not once. How is it you are this upset?"

Liv wasn't sure if she should be amazed at Marcie's obvious lack of tact or ashamed at herself for the home truths that fell from her girlfriend's mouth. Had she really never told Marcie about her grandparents? This was a woman who supposedly knew almost everything about her, a woman she had been building a life with for the last eight years and yet she didn't know anything about her family. The reality hit Liv that she didn't know anything about her family either, and now she would never get the chance.

"I don't know why I'm this upset. You're right of course. Gosh, I feel like such a fraud. I guess I haven't ever spoken about them because I don't really know what I'd say. My grandmother passed away ten years ago but it was her who put in all the effort. She would call weekly when we were younger and ask about us, to speak to us. Sometimes my father would pick up the phone. More often than not he would ignore her calls. Daniel and I weren't ever really encouraged to forge a relationship with them."

"Did your father have a bad childhood?" Marcie asked, dropping her hand from Liv's arm and moving back towards the bed. Liv felt the loss of comfort like cold water washing over her, freezing her in place. She watched as Marcie searched amongst the sheets for the lifeline she had lost moments earlier.

"Far from it…" Liv croaked, trying to regain her voice as well as her footing as she moved slowly across the floor, "Dad was an only child and from what I gathered, he was doted on. But they didn't have much. Sure, they had some land and owned their own home, but it had been passed down from his fathers' father. *Inheriting* doesn't equal *"worked hard for"* and we both know how my dad feels about working for things."

"Well, his outlook clearly works because look at his children. You and Daniel both own your own homes, work at the top of your respective fields and want for nothing. I only wish my own parents had half the drive your parents do." Marcie's voice radiated annoyance and Liv wasn't sure if it was the irritation of not finding her phone yet or because she was simply talking to Liv, which was a very real possibility.

Liv began to slip into the clothes she had left out for herself earlier, pulling on her slacks and buttoning up her favorite light blue blouse.

Marcie cheered as she finally found the phone and held it in the air triumphantly. Her eyes moved back to the device and once again Liv lost her to whoever was on the other side of the screen. Her girlfriend's thumbs tapped out the speediest response to whatever had been asked of her, causing a smile to creep up on her previously strained features. She couldn't stay quiet anymore, no longer willing to overlook Marcie's inexcusable ignorance. Liv felt her stomach bottom out as her mouth spat words she had been harboring for longer than she cared to admit.

"Who is she?" she asked, stepping closer to Marcie and dropping her hands to her sides. Anger met heartache inside of Liv and agreed to share space for a while. Marcie lifted her head rapidly and her eyes widened. It was then Liv's suspicions were confirmed. She waited for Marcie to deny it, to say something at all but her silence was deafening.

She began again, "How long?"

Marcie swallowed and Liv watched her clutch the phone closer to her chest, holding it close to her heart. A place Liv realized she hadn't lived for a long while. She expected to feel broken. After all, when people find out their lives are falling apart, aren't they supposed to fall apart too? Instead her resolve was unwavering, her heart not pounding in her chest but beating a steady rhythm as if encouraging her with each beat. Letting her know that she had this under control.

"Wh…what are you talking about?" Marcie stammered, looking around the room at anywhere but Liv. For a split second, Liv could have sworn she saw panic creep across Marcie's face, hand in hand with shame, but then her gray eyes steeled and she furrowed her brow. Marcie hated being challenged.

"The woman you've been texting. Who is she?"

"Elizabeth, You're being silly. It's no one."

"Does she know that she's no one?" Liv countered. She lifted her eyebrows at Marcie's flippant disregard for both her and the person on the other end of the texts. She could see Marcie's tongue moving, attempting to wrap around lies as she opened her mouth, poised to speak untruths her mind had conjured up quicker than a rabbit from a magician's hat, "Don't you dare lie to me Marcie!"

The change in the woman before her rippled through the air, Liv watched her harden as she glanced down at her lap and then sat up ramrod straight and closed her eyes. On a blown out breath came the admission Liv expected.

"It's Cora."

"Cora from the office, Cora?" Liv balked. A vision of the bleached blonde, twenty something, who had been Marcie's assistant for the last three years, filled her mind. "Your assistant?!"

"She's not my assistant anymore. She got her license last year. She's a fully-fledged agent now."

"She's a child, Marcie!" Liv cried, throwing her hands into the air in exasperation.

"She's twenty-four!"

The same age Liv had been when they had met. She scoffed at Marcie's response and shook her head.

"How long have you been fucking her? Please tell me it's a recent development and that you haven't been sleeping with the both of us." Liv sighed.

Guilt screamed silently into the space between them as Marcie breathed in deeply before answering, "Almost twelve months."

Liv felt it hit her square in the chest. Marcie had been sleeping with her barely adult assistant for a whole year. A whole year and she hadn't noticed, or had she?

Liv's mind played back memories like an old movie. Waking to an empty bed, glancing at the clock and seeing 3:00am. Sitting at a table in a crowded restaurant, eyes fixed on the door waiting for someone who never came. The unexpected charges on their joint account for restaurants she never went to, for places she'd never been…for gifts she never received. So many of these things that she had noticed but had rationalized as work obligations had simply enabled Marcie to do what she had. No, this wasn't Liv's fault. She hadn't cheated, she wasn't in the wrong and this wasn't her weight to carry.

While everything in her was screaming at her to react, she knew no good would come from it. Tears burned at the corners of her eyes, but they didn't fall and that's when she knew. She knew it was over between them. It had been over for a long time, she just hadn't realized, too blinded by love, or something that had masqueraded as such for a while.

She angled her head to the side and took a step back, assessing the scene in front of her. Marcie remained on the bed, the phone she clutched playing a gaudy tune as it vibrated in hands that once knew every inch of Liv's skin. Her stomach churned at the thought of how those hands knew another person now and while it felt weird, it didn't hurt her as much as she thought it would and it was that notion that triggered a release within her.

"You should answer that." she said.

The phone continued ringing and with each bar of repeated notes that went unanswered, Liv watched Marcie become increasingly more on edge. Marcie moved to stand from her place on the bed but before her feet could touch the ground Liv held up a hand in front of her.

"I'll go. I have to get to work." she said, blowing out a breath and turning on her heels.

"Elizabeth!"

Marcie's voice was shaky and laced with an uncertainty that was alien to hear but it didn't stop Liv from her mission, which was to leave the apartment as quickly as possible. She had reached the front door when she heard the ringtone silence, hushed tones filtering in her ears as she imagined Marcie revealing to Cora that they had been outed.

She reached for the keys she kept in a small, white, wooden box on an end table near the door and chanced a glance behind her. She wasn't sure why she half expected Marcie to have followed her out and begged her to come back and listen. To fight for whatever it was they had. To cling to the remnants of what once was. To throw around platitudes and apologies alongside reassurances that it wouldn't ever happen again and assure her that she would end it with Cora so they could get back to the life they had conjured up in dreams during the beginning of their relationship. But she didn't and Liv felt...relieved.

Stepping out of the apartment and into the hallway, Liv wondered if this was really happening. Her body felt a little fuzzy, almost as if she was standing on the periphery of herself watching everything unfold and feeling a little numb. When the door to their apartment slammed shut, a gust of air followed her down the hallway and on it, whispered promises of new beginnings. She didn't hug her arms around herself in an act of comfort or protection against the sudden cold. Instead she allowed the cold air to wash over her. Sometimes in holding on to something, you can accidentally drown when all you have to do to survive is let go. So Liv began to loosen her hold on a life she wasn't entirely sure she wanted anymore, and with each step she took she welcomed the possibilities of something new.

Chapter 5

Honey

A week had passed and with Marvin no longer there to brush away the soil displaced by winds that howled through the surrounding foliage; a thin layer of dust gathered on the wooden decking of the wrap-around porch. Honey found herself unable to do anything other than simply sit and stare. Grief still held her in a tight embrace. The chess pieces from their unfinished game sat unmoved, an eternal checkmate she wished would come. She hadn't been able to leave the porch in the first few days after Marvin's passing.

Returning from the hospital in a daze of disbelief, Honey had all but ran up the hill towards the house shouting his name. He never answered. Instead little markers lingered, small reminders that he *had* actually been there, he *had* existed. The thick woolen blanket that he often spread across his lap when cold nights set in and his tired legs were in desperate need of cushioning from the elements, was still draped across the back of the chair he had sat in only hours before. His voice still lingered in the night sky, speaking birthday wishes and wisdom Honey longed to hear one more time. She thought back to earlier and their interaction, trying to remember what their last words to each other had been. Had she remembered to kiss him goodbye? Had she told him that she loved him? Did he know how much she admired him, how much she adored him… how much she needed him?

She had sat in her chair, across from where his memories remained and tried to bargain with the universe. She begged whichever sky deity was listening, to fix this. To send him back. To have her wake up from the obvious nightmare that had been this day. When bargaining didn't work and the skies began to lighten, dawn filtering through the clouds and trees bringing a new day, a new life without him, she crossed the wooden flooring, to the porch swing he had built with his own two hands. Seeking support for her shaky legs, she lay down and curled into herself, closing her eyes she addressed him directly.

"You weren't supposed to leave me too. I don't know what I'm supposed to do without you. Who will offer me life advice? Who am I supposed to beat at cards or have thrash me at chess? Who will eat my pasta, watch old movies and tease me for the grunge I listen to? You were supposed to stay with me longer than this. Wasn't I worth staying for? Everyone I love seems to leave and I loved you so much. I never got to really thank you for everything these last few years, not properly." She pulled her sleeves up over her hands and swiped at her free-flowing tears, "I know you needed to be with her. I know you have waited so long and your heart's at ease now. I wish you could have stayed and I know I'm being selfish in wanting that but I just wasn't ready to lose you. I want to thank you for filling my heart with so much love these last ten years. I'll always feel like the luckiest person ever, because I had the best friend in the world. Bea if you're listening, wrap your arms around him extra tight. He's been missing you for so long."

It had been Sasha who found her lying still on that slowly swinging seat, warm from the morning sun but shivering from the blanket of loss that she had been draped in since she heard the words that he had gone. Honey had been grateful for the support of her oldest sister in the following days as she helped get her back down the hill.

There had been uncertainty as to what would happen regarding Marvin's funeral arrangements. Honey knew he had a son and grandchildren out there in the world.

Somewhere.

She wondered if they too had fallen to their knees upon his passing, if they too had felt empty ever since. Grief manifests itself in many different ways. Some people wear grief like a cloak, hanging heavy over their shoulders, hiding them from the outer gaze of those unaffected. Some people carry it around with them like an anchor, weighing them down as they struggle to swim against the tides of everyday life. Some remain silent and stoic and that is a danger in itself. To stay quiet and not give grief room to breathe, is like trying to extinguish a fire with a teacup of water. The emotion burns at you until it's all encompassing and you are destroyed from the inside out. Honey carried her grief like Atlas carried the world.

The day of the funeral arrived and left with the changing winds. People Honey had never met before came to say goodbye to a man they had barely known. Unfamiliar faces filled Marvin's large home for hours after the service, swapping stories and talking about the lives they lived away from him. Honey had watched as a man who resembled Marvin stood at the screen door and glanced at his phone screen, while muttering under his breath something Honey couldnt entirely hear. She swore she had made out the words "a terrible inconvenience."

She had left before she spoke out of turn, running back down the hill and into her cottage. Upon closing the door she slumped to the floor and let her head fall into her hands. Tiredness took her before anger could fill her completely.

The house at the top of the hill looked different now. The chess game they never managed to finish had been packed up, the porch cleaned and the blanket that hung over the back of Marvin's chair was no longer visible. Any sign he had once been there had been tucked away, hidden from view as if removing visual reminders could ever wipe away the memories that lingered. As the days passed Honey couldn't bring herself to cross the field and go sit in the seat she once thought of as her own. Instead, with each day that passed she sat outside, on the little blue bench in her own garden and replayed those memories in her head. It was her way of feeling close to him, of staying connected but today the loss weighed too heavy on her heart.

Today she crossed the gravel driveway, hopped into her bright yellow Jeep and headed for the solace of the Deli.

***

"I wonder what will happen to the land now?" Sasha mused, her eyes softening as she took in Honey who was fastening her apron around her waist.

"I think you need to look at contacting Brewer's Estates and seeing if they have anywhere local on the market. I think the house on the corner of Maple went up for sale a few weeks back. I guess old Jones finally shuffled off this mortal coil."

"Wow Kyla, really?" Honey shot a wide eyed gaze at her older sister. "…Marvin died a week ago."

"Hey! I loved Marvin, we all did. But you really need to think about what could potentially happen now, Honey. It's not like his son is going to come back and take over the land. I see For Sale signs on the horizon and I bet you the new owner will not be willing to keep renting to you at the same price of, you know…free. You have to start being an adult about these things. One of us has to be practical about this. If you don't want to leave then maybe you could get in early and state your interest to buy the big house. It could use tearing down and rebuilding."

Honey didn't know whether to scream or cry but she could feel each emotion holding hands in her chest and marching towards her tongue in a united front of disdain. She narrowed her eyes and took her bottom lip between her teeth tightly, her full pink lips displacing their color as she bit down everything she really wanted to say to her sister. A hand on her shoulder squeezed away a little of the rage that simmered beneath the surface and Honey was extremely grateful for Sasha in that moment. She didn't want to argue with Kyla, especially not at work. She knew that her sister was being practical and honest but the truth hurt to hear and sparked an anxiety in her she had tried to push down the last few days.

Of course someone would be coming to sort out the house and they'd either sell or rent it out, or maybe even move in themselves. Honey knew that they'd be informed that they also owned the little wooden Cottage at the end of the hill. The place she had called home for the last ten years. She knew there was a distinct possibility that she would have to pack up and leave no matter how much it hurt her heart to think about it. It made her feel so incredibly sad to think that someone else would spend summer months on their hands and knees in the vegetable patch she started. Someone else would watch from the bright blue bench she upcycled, as the blossom left the trees, dancing on the gentlest of breezes and promising their eventual return.

"I know you're sad, Buzzy. I know you and Marvin were close these last ten years, since Bea passed. I know it hurts you that he's gone and that it's going to break your heart to watch that place get sold but, Kyla despite her lack of tact, is right. We really do need to make sure you have a place to live." Sasha's hand rubbed soothing circles on Honey's back.

"It's just hard to think of having to leave that place and I'm not sure I'm ready mentally or financially to buy something so big. I'm just me and that place has energy far too big for me to claim. I saw how lonely it made him feel after Bea's death. I don't know that I could live there without thinking of him all the time. I don't want to live in constant loneliness, I don't want to buy that place because it's the only way of keeping him close to me. I know we shared more than the nights we spent on that porch. Marvin was more than my neighbor. He was…"

"A friend, I know. It's okay to think about him, Honey. Remembering means never forgetting. He deserves to be remembered."

Honey cast a downward glance, leaning into her sister's reassuring touch, "You know, I walked across the field last night with a couple of ciders, ready for our weekly game of chess and I had been sitting on the porch for fifteen minutes before I remembered he wasn't there anymore." She admitted, her voice small and laced with sadness, she dropped her head into her hands.

Sasha sighed, rubbing her hand over Honey's back in a soothing motion indicative of how their mother comforted them as children. "Oh Hon. Maybe you should take a few more days. I'm sure Lissy won't mind running your counter. She's always telling anyone who will listen about how she needs more cash for her trip to Europe this summer."

Honey knew her eldest niece Lissy would happily work extra hours. Eighteen and with the ambition and drive to rival any adult, she was absolutely worthy of Honey's admiration.

While Sasha and Kyla had been closer in age, their three year age gap was barely noticeable but Honey had been a surprise, ten years after Kyla. While she always considered herself close with her sisters, sometimes that age gap was incredibly noticeable. She had been almost a teenager when Lissy was born and so they practically grew up together. When Honey had come out to her family shortly after she turned sixteen, Lissy had toddled into the living room wearing a "Love Is Love" t-shirt. When she had subsequently had her heart broken for the first time and Sasha had cried alongside her, Lissy had crawled into her arms and distracted Honey with demands to watch Tangled over and over again. It figured that Lissy' favorite "princess" was an adventurer who saw the good in everybody because that's exactly who she had grown up to be. Honey and Lissy had forged a close bond in those formative years and now that they were both adults -well almost, in Lissy's case - they still remained really close.

"I can call her." Sasha offered and Honey shook her head, reaching for a cloth and wiping down her countertop.

"No, it's okay. I'm fine. I just… I miss him."

"Well missing him isn't going to keep you warm when you're sleeping on the streets." Kyla shouted from across the floor, clearly not on the same page as Honey about arguing at work. She bit back a retort and instead chose to narrow her eyes at Kyla's response. She wondered exactly when it was that her sister had become so unfeeling, so detached. Kyla was tired, Honey could see it in her eyes and how she carried herself around the shop, but that wasn't an excuse for being rude. Kyla turned her back on Honey and Sasha and waddled towards the kitchen. That waddling walk had been an almost permanent fixture in the last few years that she had started having children.

The Henderson clan was as big as it was loving. Gray had followed three years after Lissy, completing the two children limit that Sasha had always said she wanted. Kyla, on the other hand, had filled her home. The eight year old twins, Liam and Josh, were into absolutely everything. Ariella who was almost five could be found walking around with her cute button nose buried in a book and three year old Savannah was absolutely keeping the entire family on their toes. Throw into the mix that she was six months pregnant with another set of multiples and Honey knew Kyla was struggling to keep everything together. Still, that was no excuse for how harsh she had become.

Honey moved around to the other side of her counter and busied herself by shuffling around the small trays containing the freshly baked cookies and muffins, in an attempt to staunch the tears threatening to spill. Even as she tried to distract herself she could still hear Kyla playing ignorant as the conversation between her sisters continued from across the room.

"You could have given it a day or two, Kyla. You know how much this hurts her. She just lost someone she loved like family." Sasha said.

"She'd had more than a week, Sasha. It's not my fault she gets so attached to people. She loves too easily, a little dose of harsh reality will do her good. Come on, you know I'm right. She lets Andie walk all over her and we both know she's still sending her money. I know you both think you're being discreet, but you suck at keeping secrets…you always have. She practically looked after that entire place and Marvin by herself for the last few years but she could still be made homeless in all of this. I know you said she considered him family, but I heard from Alice Walker that he left the entire place to his granddaughter. His *actual* granddaughter… not Honey. Did you even know he had a granddaughter because I sure as hell didn't?"

"I think I remember one visiting when we were younger, maybe. Look, all I'm saying is give her a break. Be a little less, well… Kyla."

"No can do. If I stop being me this place stops being functional and if I'm not mistaken there are currently six mouths… other than ours who are dependent on this place running smoothly."

Honey lifted her gaze and watched Kyla waddle away into the back, but not before she had thrown back her signature disapproving glare. The one where annoyance mixed with frustration in a look specifically reserved for Honey.

Marvin had willed the house to his granddaughter. She played those words over in her brain. Of course she knew it was the right thing to do, to keep the house in his family, but Honey still felt a little strange. Nausea crept up on her, she could taste a bitterness on her tongue. Inhaling deeply through her nose, she closed her eyes and tried to steady herself.

"I'm sorry about her Hon." Sasha said with a sympathetic tilt of her head.

"You have to stop doing that. She's forty years old and can apologize for her own big mouth. She obviously doesn't have the best of opinions about me and I'd be more upset if she ever had. We both know she thinks I'm just the flaky little sister who is always looking for attention, doesn't know anything of the world and can't hold onto a relationship. I'm surprised every day I wake up and still have my counter space."

Honey picked up a blue striped cloth and started wiping down her already clean countertop. She pushed harder at a stain on the surface that was refusing to budge, the frustration of her situation still not enough force to remove the blemish. Suddenly her motions were stopped by a hand on her arm, looking up into Sasha's deep blue eyes she found a softness that had always managed to cushion the hard edges of Kylas disapproval.

"Hey! Stop that!" Sasha demanded. "You work hard here…harder than all of us. You source, grow and bake your own produce. You stay late most nights to do the books even though we can absolutely afford to hire someone. You make sure we always have our shifts covered when the kids get sick or need picking up from school. You're the best sister anyone could ever ask for and one day you'll find someone who sees how awesome you are and they're not going to ever want to let you go."

Honey lifted the corner of her mouth, unconvinced by her sister's words but not wanting to seem ungrateful. She sighed, "I don't know about that. I scared Andie off all the way to Australia. I mean she literally ran to a place where everything is trying to kill you, rather than commit to a life with me. What does that actually say about me?"

"The fact that she chose to leave someone who has the biggest heart I've ever known says more about her than it does about you, Honey. It says that she wasn't who you were supposed to be with. I know your someone is out there, somewhere."

"How can you be so sure?" Honey asked, defeat in her eyes. She clenched her fingers around the towel, needing to rid her body of the negativity she felt coursing through her.

"Because I see how much love you have to give. You're the worker bees favorite aunt and I'm not even mad. That's six kids who are completely and utterly enamored by you and I know you don't believe me but you've got two sisters who adore you too. Even if one is too lost in her own narrative to tell you. You deserve *your* love story too."

Sasha's reassurance was enough to cause a small smile to find its way back onto Honey's heart shaped face. "Thanks Sash. I love that you still believe that."

"One of us has to." Sasha smiled. Giving Honey's arm a gentle squeeze, Sasha moved away from the counter as the light twinkling of the bell above the doors signaled their first customer of the day. Honey inhaled deeply, closing her eyes and giving her body a small shake to loosen up.

Sasha was right, someone had to hold onto hope, Honey just wished it could be her.

Chapter 6

Liv

"Did I hear correctly? You're taking time off?"

Hannahs' voice filled the confines of Livs' office. Although small in stature, no one could ever accuse this woman of lacking presence. She thrust a reusable cup out in front of her and Liv reached for the warmth. The waft of cinnamon confirmed that it was a cup of Chai and Liv sighed happily. After the night she had, there was nothing she needed more than this. Bringing the cup towards her face she inhaled deeply and smiled, remembering the first time she had encountered her powerhouse of a best friend standing before her. Hannah had been Liv's friend ever since her first day when - panicked about the thought of leaving the safety of this exact room-Liv had committed to having her lunch alone.

She had been curled up in the soft seating of the oversized chair she had intended to use for reading between classes and was unwrapping the brown paper bag she had haphazardly thrown her peanut butter sandwich in that morning. It was only when she took a bite and panicked as her tongue almost became glued to the roof of her mouth that she realized she had forgotten to bring a drink, or refill her water bottle after downing the contents earlier that morning. She had momentarily debated putting down her sandwich and heading for the crowded cafeteria but since her mild anxiety was already in full swing at simply being new on campus she knew taking this risk would push her further over the edge. Her tongue had unglued itself from the roof of her mouth with a pop and she was making a mental note to reassess her jelly to peanut butter ratio next time she rushed together a packed lunch, when she heard a knock at her door. Without waiting for a reply this tiny whirlwind of a human barrelled through the doorway, wearing a warm smile and clutching two steaming hot cups of what smelled like Chai. Her savior had been dressed in pale blue dungarees and a tie dye shirt.

The same outfit she wore right now.

"You've never taken time off, Liv. In all the years you've worked here, not a single day, not even for an illness. I was beginning to think you were superhuman. Please tell me that you're healthy and the reason for your time off is that you and that gorgeous girlfriend of yours have finally decided to run away to a tropical island and tie the knot?"

Liv watched as Hannah moved towards the oversized chair opposite the desk and made herself comfortable. Placing the cup down on her desk, Liv began stacking together pieces of paper containing the notes for this afternoon's class on "British Literature", one of her favorites to teach. Liv shook her head.

"Actually, no," she began, scrunching her nose slightly as she spoke her next words. "Sadly this trip is not going to be pleasurable. My grandfather died two weeks ago and I have some loose ends to tie up."

"I'm so sorry, you never said anything."

Waving a hand nonchalantly Liv tried to push away all notions of sympathy her small friend was poised to afford her. After all, she didn't feel right about accepting any form of it when she was still struggling to justify the feelings of loss that sat deep in her stomach.

"We weren't really close. I didn't visit much growing up, maybe once or twice. They lived in a small village miles from here, miles from anywhere actually…Verity Vale."

"I've never heard of it." Hannah pushed off her Vans and lifted her socked feet up on the seat, her knees touching her chest she nodded towards Liv, the universal sign to continue speaking.

"Not surprising. My grandparents owned a piece of land and some property and they left it to Daniel and I. Typical Daniel, he doesn't want to deal with any of it so naturally it's fallen to me to go tie up the loose ends."

Liv didn't know why she felt the need to elaborate further, or even why she was allowing this situation to occupy her thoughts as much as it was. When her mother had called her two weeks ago she assumed she would feel a little something for sure, but with each passing day she found new feelings introducing themselves. When she went to bed every night she struggled to find solace in her sleep. Instead she would wake feeling drained, her whole body aching as though she had walked the almost 400 mile distance to Verity Vale, in her sleep.

"Is Marcie excited for this trip to Valency…"

"Verity Vale," she corrected, putting the papers down onto her desk and considering the best way around answering Hannah's question. Hannah had somewhat of a crush on Marcie and as much as Liv knew her friend would support her, she still felt extremely vulnerable about sharing the fact that she had effectively been traded in for a younger model and that her relationship had failed.

She shuffled to get comfortable in her chair and reached her arms out on her desk, thrumming her fingertips lightly against the deep oak wood. "Marcie won't be joining me on this trip, or any trip ever again, for that matter. Her and I have been, we are… we are not."

Liv struggled for the right words to explain what had happened without causing what she knew would be a major overreaction from her friend because honestly she didn't need it right now.

Since the argument with Marcie and the revelation of her having cheated, Liv had been avoiding all contact with her. She had returned that night, after work, to an empty apartment and rather than stay in a place filled with the ghosts of what once had been, she had packed a few essentials into a bag and left.

She was surprised that Hannah hadn't commented -being as fashion conscious as she was- on the fact that Liv had been wearing the same four outfits on a repeat cycle for the last ten working days. She was also grateful her friend hadn't caught on because as much as Liv felt certain this was for the best, there were moments of doubt that crept up on her like a thief in the night.

"I will be taking this and all future trips entirely alone."

Saying those words out loud didn't hurt the way Liv thought they would. The idea of having to do all of this alone didn't upset her, in fact, she had begun thinking that with the very obvious distance between them once she left the city, Marcie might cease the constant barrage of phone calls and attempts to find out where she was staying. It was only after Liv had answered a call from Jen two nights ago, where she informed her she was doing okay and just needed some space, that the calls dropped from every hour to three or four times a day. Still it was too much.

"Did something happen with you two?" Hannah asked in confusion, leaning forward and resting her elbows on her thighs as she clutched her cup between her hands.

Oh no, she just cheated on me. Liv's smartass mouth wanted to scoff, knowing that if this were the movies, her best friend would instantly start ranting and raving about how she never liked her or had always gotten a weird feeling from her. But this wasn't the movies, this wasn't make believe, this was Liv's life and it was very, very real.

Not one to talk badly about people, she preferred to go through life with the philosophy of *'what's for you won't go past you'*. She believed that not everything or everyone is meant to stay.

Sometimes people aren't permanent fixtures in your book, they're chapters, footnotes, side characters even. She had read somewhere that you have to experience every chapter, get to know every character, no matter what. You can't skip over things. Not if you want to truly understand the story that is life. Liv knew this was true, but how did you tell someone that a chapter was over before it began? How did you explain that you didn't need to dissect or over analyze what had happened because this was a book you didn't finish and you were okay with that?

"Marcie and I broke up." Liv admitted, trying to maintain a neutrality in her voice so as to not encourage further conversation on the topic, although she knew this was futile.

"How long do you think you'll be gone?" Hannah's quick question broke Livs' reverie and surprised her in equal measure. There was no awkwardness lingering between them, her friend had just done something Liv should have suspected she would all along. Afterall, Hannah was as wonderful as she was small. The corners of Liv's mouth lifted a little at her friend's compassionate understanding and she breathed out a sigh.

"I'm taking the next six weeks off but I have no intention to spend all that time there. I'll go and see what condition the place is in and then work on getting it sold. That'll take maybe a week or two, I guess. The rest of the time I have, I fully intend on trying to get this book finished. I have a month until I have to have it in my editor's inbox. If I can get that done quick enough, who knows maybe I'll start my next one. Maybe there'll be some inspiration waiting for me in Verity."

A bird flew past Liv's office window, pulling her gaze out onto the courtyard. Scores of students transitioned their way across campus. Two girls caught her eye, huddled together with their sides touching, both were smiling wistfully. She couldn't decide if they were friends or more. If they were standing so close together because they were so in love that not touching one another was impossible or if they were simply two friends reliant on the other for moral support as they meandered their way through the crowds. Liv wished she had someone to lean on as she meandered her way through this situation her grandfather and Marcie had put her in.

For a split second, after she had looked up the property on Google street view, Liv had allowed herself to fantasize how it would feel waking up in that massive old house. She had visions of glancing out of the bay windows and seeing nothing but green as far as the eye can see. She had thought about how instead of the rushing sounds of the city coming to life she would hear birdsong and the rustling of the branches from the surrounding foliage.

"How are you dealing with everything? A house is a huge responsibility to deal with alone.Especially when you're grieving."

Hannah was so right. It seemed a mammoth task to take on and Liv was dealing with grief, or at least she assumed that's what the constant ache in her stomach and chest was.

"I don't even know why my grandfather left it to us. My dad and his parents never really saw eye to eye. My dad hated Verity and couldn't wait to leave and once he scored a place at Haverton he never went back. I mean, we spent a few days there during summer as small children, but nothing substantial enough to forge the feeling of loss I'm feeling right now. I didn't even know them. I don't really remember what they looked like. Does that make me a bad person because I feel like it does? Are you close with your grandparents?"

Hannah tilted her head to the side and some of her wild brown curls spiraled out of the bandana barely holding them in place. "Yeah, I mean, there's only my grandma left but I visit her a few times a week. We go out for lunch sometimes."

"I don't even really remember their names. That feels bad."

"Do you wish you'd known them better?"

That question caused an uneasy feeling in Liv. If she admitted the truth, that she had never really thought about her grandparents, how would that make her look? Surely that alone was reason enough to not be entitled to the feelings of grief, longing and loss that encompassed her now. She wondered how it was possible to miss something, someone that you never really knew. Of course life was never really that black and white, especially when emotions came into play.

Liv knew more than anyone that once emotions took over you were no longer in control. You just sat back and strapped in while holding on to whatever you could, as you braced yourself for the inevitable crash. That's what it had felt like falling in love with Marcie. Like strapping herself in for the most deliciously dangerous ride of her life, each mile they took filled with memories she played back like a home movie in her mind when she needed some kind of comfort. But she had known, for a while, that they were rounding the last few miles of their journey. Liv had felt it, and she had been constantly bracing herself for the impact so when it had happened she suffered minimal damage.

Liv had spent nights in the hotel room she now called home, surrounded by room service meals she barely touched, berating herself for not having confronted Marcie sooner. For not demanding to know who it was on the other side of the screen she held in her hands, the first time she suspected her smile was for someone else. Liv chastised herself for not asking Marcie who was really on her mind when she went to bed. Who was staring in her dreams. But she hadn't been ready for the answers. She knew that now. Finding out that you're nothing to someone who was your everything was soul destroying and Liv hadn't been sure how she would keep moving forward after that.

"Hey, are you sure you're okay?"

Hands grasped at her own, anchoring her in the moment and warmth filled Liv as she glanced up at her friend and saw nothing but genuine concern. In that moment Liv loved Hannah for being exactly who she was, perfectly imperfect and unwavering in her friendship.

So maybe the person who would provide her comfort wasn't meant to be the 6ft Amazonian in a power suit that she had shared a home and her life with. Maybe it was the 5ft, pocket rocket of a human who always appeared unbidden, when Liv needed her most.

Pulling herself back into the now, Liv sucked her bottom lip into her mouth, pushing her fingertips into the desk and her heels into the floor, as she attempted to ground herself. She was moving forward in the only way she knew how. Taking each day as it came.

"I don't know if I'd say I'm okay right now, at this very moment. But I know I will be… eventually," she admitted as she sucked in a breath and allowed it to calm her. "I feel a little lost, I guess. There's always this innate feeling of needing to know where you come from. To know your past. They were my family and I didn't know them. What music they liked, what they sounded like when they spoke, when they laughed. How it felt to have them smile at you, I bet they both had great smiles. All I know is that my grandmother baked and at one point in time there were a few companies interested in marketing her pies. My father wasn't too happy when she refused. He always said that could have been their ticket out of Verity. I guess the problem was, they never wanted to leave. They were happy exactly where they were. They weren't living restlessly, constantly trying to find the next thing to do. They had each other, and in each other they had found someone worth being still for. I wish I knew what that felt like."

Hannah offered her a sympathetic smile, "Then take these next few weeks and maybe try to get to know them. I know you won't be able to hear them talk or ask them questions but there's bound to be clues all around you. All you have to do is look. Besides, you're well overdue for a break. Go find your own happy Liv, you deserve it."

***

Liv pulled another sweater off the hanger and holding it up against her chest ran through the realities of if she needed another one packing. She loved this sweater, with its multicolored stripes and chunky knit texture; it provided a level of comfort she relished. Of course Marcie hated it, hence its relegation to the back of the closet.

Glancing over her shoulder at where her suitcase lay open on the bed, clothes thrown inside haphazardly ready to be folded and allocated their place, Liv smirked. Now she could also justify bringing those ripped boyfriend jeans she had stashed at the bottom of her pants drawer. She crossed the room and tossed the sweater on top of the burgeoning pile of clothes then headed for the dresser and the soft worn denim she knew lingered there.

She had returned to the apartment at a time she knew Marcie would be at work, with the intention of packing enough clothes to last her while she was away. The rest of her stuff she would ask

Marcie to pack for her and have shipped to her parents house and she would collect them upon her return. A solid plan, or at least she thought so.

Stepping back into the apartment for the first time in days felt strange, everything seemed so foreign to her and for the first time ever she noticed how clinical the place was. She had removed her shoes at the door and almost ran for the bedroom in socked feet that slid, almost dramatically, along the polished floors. A hurried motion that set the pace for what she was about to do. She had spoken to herself the entire drive over here, reminding herself of her task.

Get packed, get out.

How sad it was that after all those years together, it was that simple.

She had half expected some of her things to have already made their way into boxes. However, Marcie was not really one to think of anyone but herself and so it was no surprise that she had walked into the home and everything was still as she left it. Broken but intact.

Liv hummed to herself as she folded her clothes neatly into her suitcase. She didn't hear the front door opening and closing and wasn't aware of Marcie's presence until she heard shouting into the air of the apartment, instructing Alexa to lower the volume on the soft jazz that was now playing through the speaker system that ran through the entire apartment.

Her heart began to beat fast in her chest. She had avoided all possible confrontation that could have arisen these last two weeks by staying away. Liv hated arguments, hated raised voices. Confronting Marcie had taken all she had and she still felt the heaviness of that each and every day. In Liv's opinion, if you were fighting with your significant other in order to win, then you'd already lost.

This was not a notion Marcie shared. Marcie had this fire inside her, this passion that was the driving force behind why she had been incessantly calling her, and leaving voicemails begging for a chance to explain. Liv didn't need an explanation. What she needed was to get her clothes and get out of here.

She wondered how long it would be before Marcie realized she wasn't home alone, having undoubtedly missed Liv's shoes at the door because Marcie's first stop upon arriving home was always the wine cabinet. The possibility that Marcie hadn't come home alone shot through Liv, tossing her stomach in somersaults she knew wouldn't land gracefully. When she heard glass hitting the kitchen tiles and the padding of bare feet on the floor heading in her direction, Liv steeled herself for the inevitable.

"You're home," Marcie breathed, a hopeful smile on her face as she stepped towards Liv. Exhaling through her nose, Liv turned back to the task at hand. She swung back towards the dresser and crouched at the knees, all the while avoiding making eye contact with her ex-girlfriend.

"I'm not home. I'm not back. I'm here to get some of my clothes and then I'm leaving... for good this time."

Marcie stepped towards her but Liv held up a hand, her splayed fingers a firm indicator for Marcie to stop moving, and she did.

"Elizabeth, please. Can't we talk about this? You've avoided my calls for two weeks now."

The desperation in Marcie's voice would have normally had such an impact on Liv that she would push away her own intuitive feelings and put Marcie's first but now she really didn't have to. She shook her head and carried on scooping up items of clothing in order to find what she was looking for.

"That right there should be an indicator of exactly how much we *don't* need to talk about this Marcie." She breathed in frustration. Hands grasping at an almost long forgotten comfort, Liv pulled the jeans out of the dresser and smiled. *Gotcha.*

Marcie remained rooted to her spot and Liv moved across the room, her bare feet sinking into the plush carpet as she made her way to finish organizing the mess that spilled from her suitcase. Looking over her shoulder, Liv wondered —not for the first time— if the distance between them had always been this evident.

At the beginning of their relationship, during a disagreement, passion would have taken hold of the situation. Liv would have been thrown onto the bed and the suitcase would have been haphazardly shoved to the floor. She would have been tangled up with Marcie's body, writhing beneath her while panting her name. Now she was only thinking about how annoyed she would be if her clothes were knocked to the floor, and her skin crawled at the idea of Marcie's hands touching her. As such, she was grateful when Marcie made no attempts to move from where she stood.

"Can we talk about this, please? I miss you."

Liv shook her head at that confession. There was absolutely no way she was falling into this trap. Marcie was adept at getting what she wanted. She had wanted Liv once upon a time and she had gotten her. She wanted to make partner at her job and was well on her way. She had so very obviously wanted Cora and oh, had she gotten her. It was that thought alone that made Liv's resolve a little stronger.

"You didn't have to miss me, Marcie. You had me, you made a choice to have someone else, so now you don't get to have me and that's something you just have to deal with."

"Please Elizabeth, you're being unreasonable. Don't you know how hard these last two weeks have been for me? We have to talk, Elizabeth. We have to fix this."

Liv couldn't believe the words that Marcie was saying, the audacity she had to ask her those questions. Of course Marcie would make herself the most important person in all of this. Of course her girlfriend's or rather ex-girlfriend's familial loss registered as a mere blip on the Marcella Jacobs checklist of importance. Selfishness was a suit Marcie wore well, although Liv swore it hadn't always lived in their shared closet. Unlike Liv's comfortable soft jeans that had sat in exile under her slacks and pencil skirts, Marcie's selfishness was her go to outfit and Liv had to bite her tongue and refrain from pointing her ex-girlfriend to the mirror.

To her own astonishment she realized that her usual desire for Marcie to be better was waning. Her earlier contemplations sat on the tip of her tongue begging for freedom. She continued folded her clothes away into their neat little places in her suitcase and she focused on breathing.

In, through the nose. Out, through the mouth.

It was the only thing Liv felt like she could control right now.

"That's the problem Marcie. I don't think there's anything here to fix. You did what you did for a reason. This hasn't been working for the longest time and rather than admit it we both pretended that we were fine. That this," she waved her hand back and forth between them, "...was fine. We aren't meant for one another Marcie. If we were, you wouldn't have wanted someone else and we wouldn't be standing here right now."

"I don't want her, Elizabeth. I want you."

"You don't want me, Marcie! You need me! There's a difference.You need to be validated, more specifically you need me to validate you. Because it's what I've always done." Liv said, throwing her hands into the air in exasperation.

"What am I supposed to do without you, Elizabeth? I can't do any of this without you. What about the house and the bills and the…"

"That's not your love for me speaking Marcie. That's your codependency talking and honestly, it's something you need to talk about with someone a lot more qualified than I am."

"So what, you're going to just pretend we never happened? Continue to ignore my calls while you run off to Villey Valley and leave me?"

"It's Verity Vale." She muttered under her breath, scrunching her nose a little as she cursed herself for not biting her tongue long enough for Marcie to leave.

Marcie, still clinging to the doorframe tilted her head to the side, a surprised look on her face at what Liv assumed was her utterance.

"Excuse me?"

Breathing deeply, Liv closed the suitcase and pulled the zipper around its track, sealing the contents safely before daring to meet Marcie's gaze. A part of her was afraid of what she would see when she spoke her next words.

"I wish I could."

Marcie took a step back, her eyes wide and mouth hanging open as if she had been deeply offended.

Liv had expected this reaction from her once it was revealed that they couldn't be fixed. By staying at the hotel and ignoring Marcie's attempts at talking, she had avoided having this conversation. Compassionately, she had reasoned with herself that her heart was still too raw from all the unexpected hurt she had accumulated. That her mind was still clouded with uncertainty about what would come next and so it was okay to take some time to work through this alone. This had felt inevitable though, coming at them like a ship on the horizon, and while in the days after Liv had left, the notion of being away from Marcie scared her, now it felt like a finality she welcomed with open arms. She now felt a blossoming in her stomach where for days she had felt a nauseating turbulence.

Nodding her head in the direction of the doorway where Marcie remained, she allowed her acceptance of their situation to manifest into the air surrounding them, "I'm not running off, anywhere Marcie. I'm leaving because we are over. We are done."

"You can't just leave like this, Elizabeth! Please, don't leave me! Can't you see how this is breaking me?"

For the first time in days Liv felt her heart soften at the desperation in Marcie's voice. The sadness that clouded her eyes almost drew Liv back in and for a split second she considered crossing the room and taking Marcie into her arms. Feeling the familiar weight that was strange to her now, as she comforted her and told her everything would be okay. But it wasn't okay, none of this was and Liv was brought back into reality with the stomach churning tones of Marcie's phone ringing. A twinkle of notes she would never be able to forget or forgive.

"You broke me first," she whispered.

Pulling the suitcase off the bed and adjusting the handle to her desired length, Liv exhaled. She shook her head, her long black hair falling around her shoulders in a veil of mourning she had worn for days now. Heading for the door of the room and pulling her essentials behind her felt freeing. Each step she took was like a running stitch on her heart, pulling her back together in the very place she had fallen apart.

Liv could have swore she imagined it, but the corners of Marcie's mouth dropped in a sadness she recognized all too well. Remaining in the middle of the room, Marcie stood, shoulders shaking, as the reality of their situation filled the spaces between them. Liv made her way down the hallway not stopping until she reached the front door where she slipped her feet back into her shoes. Hooking her finger into the back of her shoe and forcing it up and over her heel, Liv allowed herself a moment to take in her surroundings. The couch where she had curled up to read all those late nights she had waited for Marcie to come home. The comfy chair next to the bookshelf in the far corner of the room, where all her first editions lived. The large glass windows from where she loved to watch the world come alive. It all felt so strange to her now, not like when you came back from a vacation kind of strange either. No, Liv felt detached, like this wasn't her home anymore. She wasn't sure it ever had been.

Standing alone in a place that no longer felt anything like home, with most of her belongings in a suitcase her heart beat a fast paced thrum of anticipation. One thing was for sure, Liv thought as she considered Hannah's words from earlier. Maybe there was something waiting for her in Verity. Whatever it was, she sure hoped it was better than this. It had to be, right?

Chapter 7

Honey

She couldn't do it.

Honey shook her head as her fingers stroked the soft front covering of the book in her hands. Such a small thing, that had such a heavy weight attached to it. Of course she wanted to see what was inside. Curiosity was battling with a sadness inside of her, a sadness that told her if she opened it and read Bea's words then everything would end. There wouldn't be anything left. Growing up Honey had adored Bea, her grandmother's best friend had been a force to be reckoned with both in and out of the kitchen. She had a laugh that filled rooms and a heart that filled lives. When she had passed away, that feeling of being full had shifted slightly. An emptiness filled Honey and her heart and it was emphasized every time she saw it reflected in Marvin's eyes.

Marvin. With his equally abundant impact on the lives of those around him. He was another loss that caused a chasm within Honey to open up and she had been fighting ever since the day he left her, to avoid falling in.

Nausea crept up on her and caused a panic that Honey knew would escalate if she continued to sit still. Her hands had already started to shake and her heart thrummed warningly inside of her. She placed the book down on the small wooden table that sat underneath her window, stood up and began to pace the room, while she paced she whispered under her breath.

As an anxious teen, Honey had discovered that quoting her favorite passages from books was an effective way to combat her attacks. She found comfort in words the same way she did from baking and the rain. It was something that had bonded her and Marvin over the years. Sometimes they would even play a game of seeing how long they could carry on a conversation using only quotes. Marvin always won of course, he was a walking collective of everything ever written. He devoured books quicker than anyone Honey had ever met.

At least, he used to.

"And when I shall die, take him and cut him out in little stars, and he will make the face of heaven so fine that all the world will be in love with night." Honey said to herself, finding comfort in each word. It felt fitting that her mind had chosen to conjure this quote as it absolutely encompassed everything she felt when she thought about Marvin. It had been three weeks since his passing but she still missed him terribly. She had watched the stars in the sky every night since losing him, looking for the once familiar twinkle in his eyes, to break through the darkness.

The sound of tires on gravel attracted her attention and as she glanced out of the window she saw the familiar soft blue of the Chevy Spark her sister had bought Lissy for her seventeenth birthday, as it crawled up her driveway.

Honey crossed the room, opened the door and headed outside to greet her niece. Lissy had a key and would let herself in but Honey didn't feel like being met in her grief bubble just yet. A space she wasn't yet ready to share despite knowing Lissy would absolutely provide comfort and support. Honey wanted to try and keep a brave face, especially in front of her niece, who had always looked at her like she was the sun.

"Hi you!" Honey said, stepping into the daylight.

The sun felt warm against her skin, comforting in a way that made her wonder when it was she had stopped recognizing it and had started taking it for granted.

"Hey Aunt Buzzy!" Lissy returned, as she opened the passenger door of her car and pulled out two paper bags filled with food, Honey's stomach growled. "Mom said you probably hadn't left the house today and so I figured I'd come over. I mean, why wouldn't you want to spend your day off with your favorite niece! I brought us both a nutritious, well-balanced, mess of a meal!"

Lissy smiled wide and Honey felt her heartbeat slow instantly. Something about the gentle tone of Lissy's voice made Honey's shoulder drop and she started to relax.

"It's a lovely day today. What do you say we eat these how they're meant to be eaten?" Lissy asked, stepping into Honey's space and dropping to the floor right there in the garden.

She crossed her legs in front of her knowing that resistance was futile, Honey followed suit. Lissy settled the bag on the floor and reached inside. Honey was relieved to see Lissy pull out a striped reusable wrap, that the deli sold in their attempts to reduce waste and as reached for it she uttered her thanks.

Lissy was a whizz in the kitchen. Honestly, Lissy was a whizz at everything she turned her hand to. She was reliable and studious and followed rules to the letter, but Honey had always encouraged a little *outside the box* thinking.

When Lissy was small, she loved staying over at Honey's parents home and they would sneak down into the kitchen at midnight and rustle up some pretty questionable food items. They would dare one another to take a bite and roll around the kitchen floor, laughing at the grimace on the other's face whilst trying not to wake up Honey's parents.

Inside the paper bags were a concoction they had dreamed up during one of their many kitchen creation moments. A Midnight Madness with extra crunch. A double, peanut butter and jelly sandwich, with a layer of Froot Loops and Salt and Vinegar potato chips in between. There was something about the sugary little hoops and the tang of vinegar that just added to the greatness of PB&J and caused both Honey and Lissy a great deal of delight.

"Mmmm…" Honey murmured, nodding her head in appreciation as she took her first bite. Lissy mirrored her action and shimmied a little, causing Honey to giggle. She loved that Lissy did a happy dance when she enjoyed her food. The fact that she was unable to hide her emotions was one of the reasons Honey liked to use her as a guinea pig for any new recipes she tried. The truth would always be written on her niece's sweet, but now, very grown up looking face.

"Good right?" Lissy said, taking another ridiculously large bite and leaning into Honey.

The weight against her side was comforting and Honey realized her body had been craving the closeness of familiarity. They sat on the floor for a while, taking small bites out of their sandwiches, not really talking but content in the company of one another. When pins and needles threatened their way down Honey's leg she couldn't sit any longer.

"Thank you," Honey said, putting her sandwich on her lap and folding the reusable wrap back around it. "I know I haven't been the most functional human recently."

"Functional, schmunctional," Lissy said as got to her feet and brushed the crumbs off her ripped jeans and band t-shirt. "You lost someone important to you, Aunt Buzzy. So it's okay to take your time getting back to the rest of the world. Besides, having everything together is overrated. What is it you always tell me… find perfection in the imperfect. Focus on getting through the next hour, not the next year. Fall apart when you need to, because you're wonderful, in all your forms and anyone who thinks you're beautiful when you're complete, should love you still, when parts are missing."

"I really said all of that?" Honey asked, moving further into her garden and taking a seat on the little blue bench that sat under her window.

Lissy sat next to her, one corner of her mouth lifting into a smile, "Aunt Buzzy, you always give the best advice. Mom is great, but she has to say nice things to me. She's my mom. But you…you don't have to always be there for me, but you are. You always have been. Even when you could have seen me as an annoying little inconvenience, you never did. You treated me like I was the most important person in the room, always."

"That's because you are, Lissy. You should always remember that. When you leave here, wherever you go, remember that you are the most important person in the room. Surround yourself with people who see your worth."

"You need to surround yourself with those people too, Aunt Buzzy. I know we haven't talked about it much but, has she called?"

Honey felt shame rush her being and the need to defend Andie, who was out there putting good into the world, came on strong.

"No. She hasn't. I think maybe they have her too busy to talk right now." She said, looking up and off into the distance to try and stop Lissy from seeing the lies swimming in her threatening tears. The sun warmed her skin and she closed her eyes, taking a deep breath before some semblance of the truth fell out of her. "I don't think I'm going to see her again, Lissy. We both know she wasn't happy here, she couldn't wait to leave. I think maybe keeping me around, even in the background, was out of convenience for her, in the end."

She hadn't called again, hadn't even sent a text wishing Honey a Happy Birthday and she hadn't replied to the message Honey had sent in the wake of losing Marvin. She wondered if Andie had even realized she had accidentally called her, that Honey knew what she was doing and who she was doing it with. It was a situation that Honey was having trouble erasing from her mind. Even though recalling it caused a nausea to swell in Honey's stomach, she couldn't force herself to be angry; It wasn't who she was. Instead, sad acceptance won out.

"I hope she is happy out there, I hope she found whatever it was she was looking for."

A hand in hers gave a gentle squeeze and Honey swallowed her sadness, it tasted sour and she felt it all the way down in her stomach. Honey knew what Lissy was saying even before she continued to speak. Lissy was telling her, silently, that she agreed about Andie not returning to Verity, and while her heart twinged a little, it didn't ache entirely anymore and that –she supposed– was progress.

"It's sad how empty it feels around here now," Lissy folded the corners of her wrap absentmindedly. "I guess you never know the size of the hole people leave when they go, until you're confronted with it."

"I know what you mean, it's like, out there the world continued to turn and people continued to live their lives… but here, the birds stopped singing,"

"The flowers stopped growing." Lissy added, shuffling so close that Honey thought she might try crawling into her lap, like she did as a baby.

"… and the stars stopped shining." Honey said.

A cool breeze attempted to pass by, but wrapped itself around them as they sat there, huddled together on the little wooden bench. Honey felt the weight of Lissy's head on her shoulder and she welcomed it. Leaning into her niece she allowed the moment to unfold. They sat in silence for a short while, not a word was spoken and yet everything was said. Honey wasn't sure how her niece had known exactly what she needed but she had.

" Don't worry, Aunt Buzzy. I'm pretty certain you'll see them again."

***

Lissy had opted to stay at Honey's place for a little while longer and so as the breeze picked up outside, they had moved inside. They had talked around the sadness, filling up the silence with excited chatter about the trip to Europe that Lissy was taking with a friend, before she headed off to college. Honey had listened eagerly as her niece listed each hopeful stop on her travel agenda and for a moment she envied the excitement and freedom of youth.

"I can't wait to see it all, you know. Just be a part of the world." Lissy had rambled, throwing her hands around animatedly, from where she sat on Honey's sofa.

Crossing the room and placing a tall glass filled with sweet tea, on the table. Honey smirked at her niece's enthusiasm, as she sat down beside her. "You are a part of the world, Lissy. A very important part."

"You know what I mean Aunt Buzzy. Didn't you ever want to get away from here?"

It wasn't that the opportunity hadn't been there for Honey when she was younger. She too could have taken a summer to travel and see the world, but she wrestled internally with feelings she considered too heavy a tide to swim against. Verity Vale was all she knew and it fit her like her favorite cardigan. She felt like trying on new cities, hearing new accents and meeting new people would potentially cause her to expand and want more. While she knew there was nothing wrong with growing, she had worried that she would alter and change shape so drastically that eventually she would no longer fit comfortably in the place she knew she wanted to grow old. She didn't have a restless need to wander, she was happy being still. Although she never left her hometown, her dreams did. She missed them occasionally.

"I used to think it would be exciting to go to England, visit all those castles and walk along those cobblestone streets. You know, go see all those fancy men in top hats and jackets and drink tea with the Queen."

"No one actually gets to drink tea with the Queen, Aunt Buzzy," Lissy laughed and Honey felt lighter at the sound.

"I know that, but a girl can dream." Honey reached for her glass and took a sip. "Has your mom started lecturing you on making sure you don't pack your bag at the last minute and making sure all your documents are in order before you fly?"

"I'm pretty sure she handed me a packing essentials list the day I mentioned the trip. I've been inundated with talks about cultural differences for weeks now. Believe it or not, apparently we aren't very popular with the Europeans."

"All the more reason to stay here, with me!" Honey teased and the desired response of a giggle fell from Lissy's mouth as she bumped her shoulder into Honey playfully.

"Awww, you make it sound like you're going to miss me."

"I am. Of course I am. When you get back you're heading off across the country for college and I thought I'd at least have my best friend to myself for a few more months. You know, convince you that I'm cool before you find new friends and don't wanna hang out with your lonely, old aunt anymore."

Lissy's face softened and Honey saw glimpses of Sasha reflected there in its comforting warmth. "I'll always think you're cool, Aunt Buzzy. Even if you do spend an inordinate amount of time sighing whenever Hayley Williams from Paramore is mentioned."

"Hey, that woman is a literal goddess. It's not my fault you're stuck on the factory settings." Honey loved teasing Lissy about the countless guys who pleaded with her for dates. There had been a few brave little toasters who had come into the deli while she was working and plucked up the courage to ask her in front of Honey, Sasha and Kyla.

For a moment Honey thought she saw something pass over Lissy's face at that comment. An uncertainty mixed with something unspoken. She considered pressing it further and asking what that look was about but she didn't want to make her niece uncomfortable. Teenagers were like hedgehogs, if you exposed them to too much human interaction they'd curl up in a ball the moment they felt threatened.

"Are you going to stay for dinner?"

"Actually I sorta have somewhere to be a little later," Lissy said, pulling her phone out of her pocket, "I told a friend I'd drop by and help them with something. But I can stay a little while longer."

Honey thought she heard a lilt in her niece's voice at the mention of a friend. The kind of gentle excitement that came with a crush maybe. She felt oddly aware of Lissy's age now and how grown up she was. How mature. Here she was keeping her broken hearted aunt company instead of giggling with her friends about the cute boy who bagged groceries at the minimart.

"You don't have to babysit me, Lissy. If you want to go see your friends, then you should go. I appreciate you coming, and the Midnight Madness with Extra Crunch but go... have fun!"

"You know, I wish you and I were closer in age. You could come hang with us without it being weird, all of my friends love you."

"They just love the free cookies and muffins. Speaking of which," Honey teased, lifting herself from her sofa. She moved into the kitchen and pulled a clear container out of the pantry. Heading back over to Lissy, she handed it to her. "A fresh batch of Sprinkle Supremes. Remember–"

"Each one is a mouthful of positivity!" Lissy finished and Honey shook her head whilst laughing.

"I was going to say, don't eat them all. I'm not responsible for the sugar high you will inevitably get from those, should you choose not to share."

"Thanks Aunty Buzzy! Are you sure you don't need me to stay longer?"

"Oh Lissy, I need you to stay forever. But you have a life to live, so get to it little bumble bee... buzz off! Queen's orders!"

Lissy laughed and stood from the couch, stepping closer to Honey and pulling her into a hug. Honey's body stiffened at the full contact, it had been a while since she had felt that kind of comfort. It didn't take long before she relaxed in her niece's arms and when she did she noticed how tall Lissy had gotten all of a sudden. Honey was a respectable five foot six and she saw now that they were almost eye to eye.

As the embrace continued, Honey felt Lissy's hold on her tighten. She had to fight against her instinct to ask if there was something Lissy needed to talk about. But she didn't push it. She had always prided herself on being the person her niece came to for advice. She didn't want to jeopardize being that safe space for her. When Lissy was ready, Honey mused, she would be there.

Lissy's soft breath warmed Honey's neck as she whispered so low Honey almost missed the fact she had begun to talk.

"You know, I'd stay forever if I could, Aunt Buzzy. But this part of the world is starting to feel a little too small for me."

"I understand, Lissy. Really I do. You're meant for more than this."

"I wish you'd consider coming along. It's never too late to start living your dreams, regardless of where you left them. They can come true." Lissy said. She pulled back from their embrace a little and tilted her head.

Her long, waist-length brown curls fell over her shoulders. Honey reached out to scoop them back and away from her niece's beautiful face. She cupped Lissy's heart-shaped face and pressed their noses together, a display of affection they'd adopted when they were younger.

"I love you Lissy. More than you'll ever know, but I won't impose on your trip, that's your time with your friends. Besides, this little part of the world still seems pretty big to me. I love it here."

Honey walked her niece to the door, watching as her niece headed down the path, hopped into her little car and threw a wave out of the open window before she drove away. She remembered when she got her first car and the freedom that came with it, how she had felt so grown up. But shortly after she passed her test she realized all the places she wanted to go, she could get to on foot. She meant what she had said to Lissy. Verity still felt really big to her and she knew deep down there wouldn't ever be a reason to leave. Honey had a business she loved, a family she adored and a home she felt safe in. At least, she had the latter for now.

Chapter 8

Liv

The drive to Verity Vale was long and arduous but it was absolutely nothing her roadtrip pop/punk playlist couldn't soothe. Liv's sadness dissipated with every lyric she sang and she sang them extra loud.

She had left the apartment and Marcie, but honestly she knew this was more than that. Liv could see the end very clearly now. She would give it a few days and then send Marcie one final text asking her to pack up the rest of her belongings and have them sent to her parents house. Then she would block and delete Marcie from her phone, knowing that retaining any kind of contact would almost be an act of self-harm. If she was honest with herself, she had expected it to hurt more than this, expected to feel a little lost but, like the directions to Verity Vale she had programmed into her navigation system showed, even a wrong turn could be righted.

Bonnie Fraser's voice was quieted by the abrupt ringing of Liv's phone through the speaker system and she brushed her thumb over the button on the wheel to answer the call.

"Elizabeth, it's your father."

Liv rolled her eyes. Always with the formalities. For once she would have liked him to have greeted her like she imagined most fathers would their youngest child, *"Hello sweetheart"* or some other term of endearment so the call would feel even a fraction familial. Instead his introduction managed to make this seem like a business interaction and so she responded with equal absurdity.

"Hello father. What can I do for you?"

"Your mother called and told me you are going to Verity to attend to the situation regarding the house and land. I wanted to ask you for something while you are there."

Her father was asking her for a favor? Now there was something that definitely didn't happen, well, ever. Hand outs, leg ups and favors were definitely not a part of his rhetoric. She had been well aware of this ever since she dared to ask at the age of sixteen for help buying her first car and had been told to go get a job.

"There is a book that belonged to my mother," he continued, "It is... of some value to me. It contains her handwritten recipes. I looked for it during my short stay but I'm afraid I was unable to find it. If while packing away all of their things, you happen to come across it, I would appreciate you giving it to me."

Liv furrowed her brows. She had never in her thirty-two years heard her father get sentimental over anything and yet here he was asking for something that belonged to his mother. That thought alone softened Liv's notions of him and almost endeared him to her. She allowed her heart to acknowledge that maybe there was a warmth in him after all.

"Of course I'll look for it. Is there anything else you'd like me to keep for you. Pictures, clothing, anything of yours that they may have kept hold of?"

"No. Just the book. You can throw out the rest. Goodbye, Elizabeth."

And there he was. There was the man Liv barely knew.

In one simple sentence he had managed to dampen any hopes Liv's inner child had of finally having a father she could relate to, one who would show her affection. He was as unfeeling as he had ever been. She wondered what it was about this book that could affect him in ways his own children couldn't.

The music returning to full volume, Liv shook her head at her father's flippant attitude. How a person could be so detached and removed she would never understand, especially as she felt everything so deeply.

The built up concrete pillars of the city eventually gave way to a landscape of green and blue. The hustle and bustle of the busy streets filtered away and were replaced by the lilting hum of birdsong amongst the rustling trees and rolling hills. With each mile she put behind her, Liv felt her shoulders slacken, her back melding into the leather seats as she tapped out the beat of the music on the steering wheel. Night was lingering far behind the slowly waning sun and before long she saw a large sign welcoming her to Verity Vale. Confusion swept over her and she was convinced that her mind was putting her through some sort of Mandela effect. She was certain that the last time she saw this sign it had been hand painted and dotted with flowers.

"Why do I feel like I know this place?" she wondered out loud, taking the next left and lowering the volume on the built in navigation system of her little red, Mitsubishi Mirage.

Slowing down and glancing out of the window she noted the vast difference between her home and this quaint little town. Streetlights added to the ambience rather than provided essential reassurance for those walking home under the cover of darkness, although they weren't lit just yet. Liv was willing to bet that here, people took walks in the dark readily.

The main street boasted many stores, most of which Liv assumed were small family owned companies, judging by the hand-painted signs stating their last names. Lantham's clothing store, Jefferson's convenience store and Brewer's barbershop complete with its little stripy rotating poles. A cute little deli with an olive green awning was nestled snugly between a rustic looking bookstore and a hardware store. Outside of it, a small blonde woman twisted the key in the lock and headed away from the store with her arms wrapped around herself. Liv's eyes were drawn to the woman and how small she seemed. Her stature aside it was almost as if this woman didn't want to be seen. This behavior was familiar to Liv, she had spent a long time making herself small too. It was different seeing it reflected back at her, back then it had felt normal and now it only sought to make her feel sad and a little ashamed. Growing up she had always been a confident person. She wasn't sure exactly when she had dimmed her own sparkle but she internalized that possibly, it had been as a result of the eclipse that occurred when she met Marcie.

Her focus pulled back to the blonde woman who was now climbing inside a bright yellow Jeep. Liv chuckled inwardly thinking about how, the car aside, with her baggy dungarees, Doc Martens and hair pulled into the cutest space buns, this woman was *anything* but unnoticeable. She drew focus. She drew Liv's enough that she almost forgot she was driving, albeit at a snail's pace. Liv thanked the goddess for the small town's lack of traffic.

Passing the store, Liv's stomach began to growl. Keeping her focus ahead Liv made a mental note to remember the location of the deli and pay it a visit tomorrow. She had neglected to grab lunch earlier when she had pulled into a gas station halfway through her drive. She hadn't found the wilting green leaves sat in plastic containers at all appetizing. Hungry was never a great state to be in for Liv, she was a carb fiend and had been known to become quite unreasonable if her appetite wasn't satiated. She scanned the passing stores looking for a remedy to quieten her stomach.

A coffee shop called Irregular Joes was the only place on the street still bursting with life. Its black and chrome fixtures instantly signaling its intent to be this town's version of a big chain coffee house. However, its aesthetic felt entirely out of place with what she had already seen of Verity. She wondered if she herself would stand out like this coffee shop; if tomorrow when she took a stroll down this street, gazes would flit to her and people would think about how she didn't fit in.

Flipping the signal on, she pulled into an empty space and reached for her purse that was nestled comfortably on the passenger's seat. Hooking it over her shoulder she opened her door and stepped out of the car. A familiar but long forgotten scent mingled with the fresh pre-dusk air and Liv tilted her head, sucking her bottom lip into her mouth as she tried to place exactly what it was she was smelling. Her stomach growled again, she really had to get something to eat, or at least drink. Walking towards the coffee house she smiled at people who passed her by, feeling warm with each smile that was returned. A woman clutching the hand of a small child around four or five even accompanied her smile with a shy hello and Liv welcomed the brief interaction after her lonely drive.

An obnoxious beeping announced her arrival in the coffee house. Liv winced a little and tucked a stray black curl behind her ear as she approached the counter, squinting as she took in the illuminated backboard flashing images of drinks with names more gaudy than appealing.

"Hey! Welcome to Irregular Joes, my name is Lara. What can I get you today?" A petite redhead with freckles that visibly dotted her cheeks and nose, held a pen poised for Liv's reply.

"Oh, um I'll take a Chai Latte with Oat Milk, please. To go." Liv reeled off her usual order, smiling softly at the girl who she guessed couldn't have been any older than twenty. Her stomach continued its protest loudly. She hoped the cute server hadn't heard it.

"Sure. Can I take a name for your order?"

"Oh, yes Liv, my name is Liv."

Lara smiled so widely Liv wondered if it hurt her cheeks to be that happy all the time.

"Nice to meet you Liv, Welcome to Verity!"

"It's that obvious I'm new here?" Liv asked, and when Lara's eyes scanned the outfit she was wearing and winced, Liv had her answer. Still stuck in her mindset of weekdays are workdays, Liv had pulled on a pair of black slacks and a white blouse, she was halfway to Verity before she realized what she had done.

"Just a little, I don't suppose I could interest you in any of our muffins or cookies?" Lara asked playfully, trying to inject cheer into the conversation and doing so perfectly, while rocking back and forth on her heels. She scrunched her face and leant in, before adding in a conspiratorial whisper, "They're not as good as the ones they have over as Rosenberg's Deli but they're closed now and I'm gonna guess you've missed lunch?"

"That's obvious too, huh?" Liv teased and Lara nodded, stepping back and sliding open the door on the glass cabinet containing the sweet snacks. "I'll take a Blueberry Muffin, thanks."

The young girl reached for the biggest muffin in the display case, bagged it up and slid the bag along the countertop to where a steaming cup of liquid happiness sat with Liv's name literally written on it. Handing over a twenty, Liv nodded at the almost empty tip jar that sat beside the cash register.

"Keep the rest."

"Are you sure? That's almost an hour's pay."

"I'm positive. You've provided me with sugary goods and nectar of the gods and a super cute smile. I can't thank you enough for being my first real friendly interaction here in Verity." Liv smiled at the blush that crept up on the young girls face. She played nervously with the apron strings tied around her tiny front and Liv noticed a heart shaped pin on her lapel in alternating pinks and purples. "You're welcome. I hope I get to see you again. Although I fear once you've tried Honey's Peach Passion Promise you'll never settle for a Blueberry muffin fresh from the freezer, ever again." Lara's soft, flirtatious laugh prompted Liv's own to appear.

"I'll be sure to drop by again soon, I'm sure. It was lovely to meet you Lara."

Taking her drink in one hand, Liv lifted the hand grasping the muffin bag and waved goodbye.

***

The street lights disappeared the closer Liv got to her destination, but the sun had yet to set so her view of the quaint little town was not diminished. As she drove through the center of town and towards the outskirts, the smooth, paved road gave way to a dirt track that flicked small stones up, dinging the underside of her car. A few miles up the road she spotted a small cottage with its lights, its gable roof and flowering trellis covering the frontside of the house gave it an air of idyllicism that Liv expected from a small town like this. She considered the possibility that this was her grandparents' property but then her eyes were drawn to the bright yellow truck that sat on the driveway. Could it be her luck that the small blonde from earlier was her neighbor?

The navigation system instructed her to take a left at a small opening that once could have been a main road. Liv wondered how long it had been since anyone had driven the path; it was so covered in overgrowth and dirt. It had to have been her father when he was here for the funeral, although Liv knew he had refused to stay at the home, opting instead for a hotel in the next town over.

She took the obscured path cautiously, the uneven ground crunched beneath her tyres. She held her breath as she crawled up the incline towards what she assumed was her grandparents home. What she wasn't expecting was how big it was. A large colonial style house with a wrap-around porch came into view. She knew her father was an only child, but this was definitely meant to be a family home. Liv pressed on the brake and the car rolled to a stop and she was gifted a vision of a younger version of herself running barefoot up the wooden steps and throwing herself onto the porch swing, laughing voraciously.

"I remember that." Liv admitted to the universe softly, a small pain filled her chest at this memory she had so obviously pushed aside. She wondered what other memories she would unlock simply by being here. What long forgotten stories would slip back into her everyday narrative.

She climbed out of her car, wanting to take a look around and make sure it was livable before she committed to staying. Upon reaching the steps she winced at the paint peeling from the woodwork, curling where it clung for dear life after weather that threatened to remove it entirely. It wasn't just the crumbling steps that required work, the entire porch, or what she could see of it, was weather worn and in need of some serious attention. This was a mammoth job, but an essential one if she was going to have any hopes of selling this place for its utmost potential. Liv made a mental note to assess exactly how much of the home had been damaged, in the morning, when the view would be much clearer and her eyes less tired.

For now, she reasoned, she would get herself situated and give herself a brief tour and if all was well she would settle down in bed with one of the romance books she had packed, and her blueberry muffin.

She contemplated calling her parents to let them know she arrived safely, but it was Thursday night and her parents would no doubt be at some function of sorts. Loath to distract them or even waste a call and miss them entirely, Liv decided to give it a few days. Or at least wait until they contacted her.

She had, during a rest stop on the way, almost reached out and let Marcie know she was safe, but had reminded herself promptly that she no longer had to do that. She only had herself to answer to now, and yet she couldn't help but flick back to the day before, a smidgen of guilt enveloping her as she played back Marcie's pleas. That had evaporated like a puddle on a hot day upon checking her social media and discovering a picture of Marcie and Cora, dressed for a night on the town and clutching champagne glasses.

Liv reached out tentatively, guiding herself up the creaking steps and bending at the knee once she reached the top to search for the key her mother had told her days earlier was left underneath a porcelain frog. Freddie —as the writing on his chest proclaimed him— was sitting exactly where he was supposed to. Liv reached for him and tilted his ample weight back. Fingers connecting with the cold metal, she pulled her arm back and stood upright. She approached the door and slid the key into the lock. When she stepped over the threshold, her breath caught in her throat as she witnessed herself growing up in various stages from pictures in frames that hung in the hallway. Although she hadn't known her grandparents, they had so obviously wanted to know her. She hadn't even known some of these pictures existed, but she looked happy in them. Stepping further into the house, Liv felt a familiarity wash over her. The house felt warm and for the first time in weeks Liv felt safe.

***

A shuffling sound from outside caused Liv to panic. A thud accompanied the sound of her heart pounding as her book dropped to the floor. She pushed aside the fleece blanket she had wrapped around herself for warmth after being unsuccessful in lighting the log fire, and stood frozen, waiting for the noise to sound again.

The shuffling came again, louder this time and Liv mentally noted that another thing she wasn't prepared for was the possibility of having to fight off a carnivorous, wild animal. Back in the city her biggest predators were trash pandas and the guys that catcalled and shouted for her number from the open window of their cars. She wasn't entirely sure what creatures lurked this far north. Cautiously, she slid her socked feet towards the sound, scanning the hallway for something, anything, that could be used to protect herself should this intruder decide it wanted to eat her. She wanted to call out. Liv knew that doing so would either be the most sensible thing to do… or the stupidest. She knew her fears would ease if an answer came from outside, but if that answer was a growl, Liv knew she would run back into the safety of this big empty house and wait for morning to come. Her mind flicked through things she had picked up from watching those survival shows. The ones Marcie had forced her into watching, where celebrities spent the entire time trying to keep up with some barely attractive British survivalist.

"Make a noise or was it don't make a noise? Stand your ground! Make yourself big! They need to recognize you as a human." Liv muttered under her breath. A snort escaped her as she thought about if most days she wasn't sure she recognized herself as a human, how would a bear be able to do so, or anything else for that matter. "Stop overthinking this Liv. Just have a quick look and then you can panic."

When she reached the front door what she saw wasn't the silhouette of a bear snuffling around looking for food, but instead a small, shadowed figure staring blankly at the ground. Slowly opening the door, she flicked on the porch light. The shadow startled and the sound of bottles clinking together filled the air.

"I'm sorry, I didn't mean to startle you!" Liv said, before she realized what she was doing. It struck her momentarily that it should have been the young woman she saw before her, who should have apologized. After all, it was Liv's home she had intruded upon, at least it was for now.

"No, it's fine. *I'm* sorry it's just…" the woman said, holding up her hands and the offerings –a cardboard carrier containing four bottles of what Liv could see was cider– in front of her in surrender.

"What were you doing?"

"It's Thursday," the woman admitted somewhat sadly. She tilted her head as if the declaration was an appropriate answer.

Liv narrowed her eyebrows and the straight lengths of jet black hair she had scooped haphazardly into a messy bun, escaped their confines and fell in front of her face. She hoped the quizzical look that claimed her face was letting her intruder know that the explanation she offered wasn't sufficient.

"Oh, um Marvin and I, we play chess every Thursday. At least we used to. I keep forgetting he's not here anymore. I'm sorry."

Liv saw genuine sadness etched on the face of the blonde she now recognized from outside the deli earlier. She took in the woman's small stature, biting her bottom lip as her eyes roamed over the swell of her breasts down to the soft curves of hips beneath paint-stained dungarees. Breathtaking, that was the word Liv's tongue swirled around her mouth as she subconsciously took a step closer.

This woman couldn't have been more than twenty five, Liv thought, as she took in the nose ring and multiple piercings in her left ear. All indicators of youth bound up in her dress sense and impish features. But she also saw a dullness in what she bet was far from her usual sparkle, because by the outward aesthetic projection alone, Liv sensed light in this woman. Light that had obviously been dimmed by a powerful loss. Up close Liv could see that her eyes glistened with tears that threatened to spill and she felt the urge to take this woman's pain away. To wrap her up in the safety of her arms and tell her everything was alright. Which was a strange thing to feel about someone you had just met, right?

Liv wasn't even sure what was happening to her right now. Being here in this place full of memories she had no recollection of, but that hung on the walls like a story told in a language she didn't know anymore, was causing her to forget who she was. That was why she was here though, to find herself, and she toyed with the idea that maybe this woman could help her, if not by filling the blanks but providing a distraction she could bury herself in while she was here.

She considered the possibility of allowing herself a moment of weakness, something not typical of her and blaming it on her loss. Shame crept up on her, at that. *"Stop it Liv! Those eyes aren't for you. Those lips aren't for you either! She is not for you!"*

Unlike Marcie, cheating wasn't something Liv had ever considered, and although she knew it was no longer cheating, as their relationship had ended, a modicum of guilt blanketed her thoughts. Liv could accept now that she too had played a part in the destruction of their relationship but rather than look elsewhere for release, she had internalized everything. Keeping quiet was just as destructive and deadly to a relationship as cheating but Liv knew why she hadn't called time on them sooner. If she was honest, back in the city with the trappings of their shared life fully evident around them, the idea of not being with Marcie had frightened her a little. Marcie was a stability that Liv had longed for but their foundations had been crumbling and both ignored the obvious. Something so broken couldn't be fixed, could it?

Liv had read a while ago about the art of Kintsugi. A practice where Japanese craftsmen would pour gold into the cracks of broken things to repair them. In making them strong again they also made them beautiful. She loved the notion of finding beauty in something or someone's imperfections. Liv wasn't sure her and Marcie could ever have the potential to be something beautiful again. The acceptance of this was a weight Liv carried daily, and yet with every mile she distanced herself from the city, from Marcie and what once was her home, the lighter her load felt. With each passing mile marker on her journey to Verity, Liv had felt more afraid of having to return to familiarity than she had been of approaching the unknown.

"You knew my Grandfather?" Liv asked, shaking the intrusive thoughts from her head.

"You're Marvin's granddaughter? I'm so sorry...I'm just going to go. I am so sorry for interrupting you," the blonde said and something about her wavering words caused Liv to feel the need to apologize again. Here she was, this stranger who knew her family in a way she didn't. Someone who absolutely had a right to feel authentically the emotions Liv herself had been remotely feeling. Liv moved to stop her from leaving, stepping out onto the decking, she reached out a hand before pulling it back abruptly.

"Stay. Don't run away because of me. I was just having a nap after admitting defeat to a burner oven and wondering if all I was going to eat tonight was a subpar Blueberry muffin."

That did it. The woman stopped in her tracks and smiled softly. "I take it you don't cook on gas much?"

"Honestly you could have left it as "don't cook much" and it would still ring true. Sadly, one place I am absolutely useless is in the kitchen."

"I have a lasagne cooking back at my place. Normally Marvin and I head back after a few games and indulge in some with a bottle or two of cider," the petite woman gestured with her thumb over her shoulder and Liv noticed a blush pink up her pallid cheeks.

"I love pasta. In fact I'd say it's one of my four main food groups, alongside cheese, wine and desserts. I really appreciate the offer. It was an offer right?" Liv asked, dipping her head and watching that soft smile spread and lift the corners of her intruder's very kissable mouth.

Liv couldn't help the thoughts that raced through her mind, of how kissable the sad woman looked. Of losing herself for a moment in the sweet taste of her plump, pink lips. Thoughts of the secrets their tongues would whisper when they came together. Their kiss, a cure she could offer, one that Liv found herself longing for. A zap of something attacked her core, causing her to squeeze her inner muscles.

Liv took a step backward, placing a distance between them in order to avoid possibly losing herself entirely in those thoughts and this woman.

"Yeah, it was an offer. Well, I'm just over the field there. Do you want to change into something else?"

Liv looked down at the outfit she had changed into - oversized black joggers and a band tee that had evolved from day wear to bed attire over the years- and wrinkled her nose. Checking out the blondes mud covered Docs she bit down on her bottom lip. She hadn't brought shoes she was willing to get *that* dirty. Her own shoes had cost two months wages and Marcie would die if she knew she had crossed a small puddle in them let alone an entire muddy field. Marcie who no longer got to have a say on anything Liv chose to do. Hell, she could go swimming in a newt infested lake with her shoes on now and it wouldn't be any of Marcie's business. Liv smiled at that thought. Looking behind her she spotted an oversized pair of gumboots next to the old wooden coat stand. She slid her feet into them and nodded at the woman who watched her intently.

"I think I'll be okay. I'm Liv by the way. Liv Henderson."

"I'd kinda figured. Honey."

Liv narrowed her eyes at the term of endearment used by this sweet but rather bold woman who stood before her. Had she read her wrong, was she not this shy, unassuming, breathtakingly beautiful woman standing before her raw and real? The thought that everyone was masquerading as something other than what they were, felt a little jarring. A hand reached out, the softest touch grazing Liv's arm and causing the hairs on it to stand on end as laughter permeated the night silence. That was a sound Liv wanted to hear again and again.

"No! That's my name, sorry…. I'm not hitting on you, not that you're not worth hitting on because you totally are…" she pinched the bridge of her nose, closed her eyes and breathed a sigh of exasperation. "I'm Honey. Honey Rosenberg."

Liv's whole body lit up, her heart racing as she allowed herself to feel the gentle touch. Everything in her urged Liv to lean into this woman. To take a step forward and allow herself a moment of comfort. To allow Honey Rosenberg to take some of the weight from her heart and soul and in doing so potentially relieve Honey of her own heaviness.

A long forgotten feeling coursed through her body, she almost didn't recognize. The small, curvy, sweet blonde in front of her radiated the warmth of home and Liv was pretty sure it was absolutely genuine. She also knew it was not normal to be feeling this way about and for, someone she had only just met.

"Nice to meet you Honey Rosenberg. Let me go get my keys," Liv said, as she turned to reached behind her.

"You won't need them. No one walks this way at night and no one would chance walking up that driveway in the dark. It's a one way ticket to Verity West. Besides, Freddie is on guard." Honey pointed at the porcelain frog still sitting sentry at the door.

"Let me just pull it over then, you know to keep out any wild animals and such," Liv said, pulling the door closed. Honey laughed and Liv's whole body tingled at the seductive sound.

Walking down the steps in silence, following the footsteps of a stranger, felt more familiar than anything Liv had ever known and soon they had made their way down the hill. They crossed the large muddy field filled with crops thankful for the rain that had graced them this last week and Liv smirked at the squelching noise of each step she took. She scrunched her toes and tried to keep purchase on the oversized gumboots, careful not to lose one with each upward motion of her legs. The last thing she wanted to feel was wet socks, a massive pet peeve of hers.

Rabbit holes, squinted eyes and uneven ground caused Liv to stumble a few times but she managed to remain upright, as they walked in silence, guided by moonlight, towards the small cottage. Denim strained against Honey's ass as she straddled the wooden stile at the bottom of the field, and Liv couldn't tear her eyes away. Once Honey was over, Liv stepped up onto the wooden plank and threw one of her legs over, following Honey's lead. She was unsure if it was the shoes or the fact she couldn't shake the image from moments ago, but something caused her balance to falter, but before she could cry out for help she felt strong arms wrap around her waist. Daring to look into the eyes of the beautiful woman who saved her from a muddy fate, Liv saw something akin to attraction reflected back at her in those warm brown eyes. Could it be possible that Honey felt this too, this unmistakable, undeniable... whatever it was between them? No, Liv assured herself silently, Honey was just doing what any decent person would have done when they saw someone about to hurt themselves.

"Falling for me already, eh?" Honey joked and Liv giggled easily at the teasing implication.

A lightness filled the air surrounding them as she righted herself, Honey's hands lingering still on her lower back. Attraction licked at the flame inside of her, causing the heat to burn steadily in Liv's chest and core.

Honey Rosenberg was unexpected, a welcome distraction from the uncertainty Liv's life was drowning in. Possibility was a dangerous contender in a life already planned and Liv's had been planned and in action for the last eight years. Despite recent events, Liv wasn't sure if she could truly pull herself away from something she had entered into all those years back, long enough to look at this situation objectively. She didn't know if it was even possible to fall for someone when you had supposedly given your heart away long ago. All she knew for certain was that it wasn't fair to anyone involved to have this be at the forefront of her mind right now. But as she stood under the crescent moon -in shoes and a life she didn't fit into- there was one thing she couldn't deny and that was that she really enjoyed the way Honey Rosenberg looked at her.

Chapter 9

Honey

Not again.

That was the first thought that entered Honey's mind as she stood on Marvin's porch, ciders in hand and sadness in her heart. She hadn't realized what she was doing when she had crossed the field earlier. Her autopilot was still engaged most days and it wasn't like it was the first time she had gone over to the big house. Normally it was the result of a long day of work, where normality snuck up on her before she could remember her normal had changed. Today had been an incredibly busy day.

The deli had been bursting with life from the moment Kyla flipped the hand drawn sign that hung on the double doors to "OPEN" and watched their regulars filter in. Honey had been grateful for the help of Lissy, when the cabinets she had filled with freshly baked goods at six am, had depleted by ten.

Lissy was a pro at running the counter, she had her mother's ability to converse with anyone and Honey's sweet nature. It meant that when Honey excused herself into the kitchen out back to rustle up a few more sweet treats, she could focus entirely on baking how she always tried to, with her whole heart. She tightened the strings on her green apron and pulled her blonde curls back into a high ponytail, rolling the sleeves on her black and white raglan tee, up to her elbows. Honey loved to lose herself in the measurements and repetitive motions. Her muffins and cakes were the talk of the town, prompting comparisons to Bea that caused her heart to swell.

Honey still hadn't managed to pull herself together enough to delve into the loose pages of the purple bound book, a parting gift from Marvin she hadn't expected to be the last thing he gave her. Everytime she glanced at it from where it now sat on the small bedside table, she felt a tug on her heart. It was almost as if she was doing a disservice to the memory of two people she had adored by not opening the pages and having their legacy live on. But their legacy wasn't the ink on the loose pages of a book, no matter how treasured it had been.

No.

Their legacy had just demolished, impressively she might add, two plates of homemade lasagne and was currently standing in Honey's modest living room, staring at the walls adorned with ukuleles and guitars.

There was no doubt about it, Liv Henderson was beautiful. Honey found herself stealing a glimpse of the perfectly polished and poised woman from across the room as she washed the dinner dishes in the sink. Ocean blue eyes and long, slightly wavy hair that dipped to her lower back, Liv was a perfect vision in clothes that spoke of soft hugs and comfort. Despite her current outfit, everything else about Liv Henderson screamed big city living. From her perfectly manicured nails down to the way her sleek black hair was pulled back into a high ponytail, accentuating the magnificent portrait that was her face. Honey had found herself a little more than distracted a few times during dinner. At one point, a small coating of sauce had lingered on Liv's bottom lip and as she poked her tongue out to swipe at it deftly, Honey had almost excused herself to go recuperate in the bathroom.

During their meal the conversation had stayed relatively formal. Compliments and thanks were passed back and forth across the small wooden table. Each lift of a glass bottle had sought to soothe the lingering nervousness that inevitably accompanied first dates. Honey had scolded herself internally for that thought, this was most definitely not a date. Liv was here because she had lost her grandpa and was hungry. She most definitely wasn't here looking for love.

"Do you play these?" Liv asked, her fingers skimming a pineapple uke that had been fourteen year old Honey's first purchase with earnings from her weekends washing dishes at the deli. Honey felt her throat go dry as she watched Liv's long fingers stroke the length of the rounded instrument. So soft and considerate, as if she knew this was something precious to be revered.

"Yeah, some of them, sometimes. That one I haven't played in a long time though."

"They're beautiful. I wish I had learned to play an instrument. My parents wanted me to play the piano but I have no shame in admitting I'm tone deaf."

Honey snorted a little at this revelation. She loved how open Liv was being, it was refreshing to be around someone who didn't seem to take themselves so seriously.

"You have a lovely home," Liv said, moving to caress another mounted uke.

Honey watched Liv take in her surroundings, she knew it wasn't much. Most of the furniture in the house had already been here when she moved in. The wooden table in the kitchen and most of the wooden fixtures were the products of long hours in Marvin's workshop. Honey loved how each piece had a story to it, each piece had been built with love. It's always said you should fill your home with love and luckily for her, Honey had walked into one that radiated it.

"I guess technically, *you* have a lovely home. This place belongs to you now. Mar... your grandfather let me rent it from him. I mean, he refused to let me actually pay him in anything but chess matches, warm meals and the occasional bottle of cider." Honey admitted, the taste of loss still lingered on her tongue, bitter and coarse. She glanced down at her feet, fingers nervously picking at the label on her bottle of cider.

"You're worried I'm going to ask you to leave."

Not looking up, Honey nodded. She was absolutely terrified of that possibility but she hadn't even really vocalized it in her own presence yet, so to have a stranger say it, took the wind out of her. She inhaled deeply and nodded. "I'm worried about a lot of things, but yeah I love living here. It's all I have left of him."

She moved into the living room and sat herself down on the sofa, her legs suddenly too jelly-like to keep her upright. A tightness gripped her chest at the reality of possibly losing her last connection to Marvin. She didn't register the motion of the cushion sinking as Liv lowered herself into the space next to her, but she felt the warmth of a hand on hers and turned her head to meet those incredible blue eyes. Liv's voice was a whisper, but the words held a comfort Honey hadn't expected.

"I don't know for sure what my plans are, with the house I mean. But I promise that I'll keep you informed every step of the way. I didn't know that this was part of the property. My father never mentioned it."

A flurry of questions filled her. Honey wondered why a man so insistent upon cutting all ties with this place would forget to mention the ownership of the little cottage. She thought about the funeral, how Liv's father had moved about the big house as if it was alien to him, and she supposed in some ways it was. He had grown up in those four walls, but it was clear to see how he had grown too big for them. Watching him as he stood shaking hands with the people coming and going after the service was like watching a shark in an enclosure ten times too small. He was stiff and agitated, such a contrast to soft and pliable Marvin, who was the largest personality Honey knew and yet always seemed like he was comfortable in his surroundings.

"Why did you never visit him?" Honey dared to ask, feeling Liv's hand squeeze her own as if jolted by the spark that was her question.

"Honestly. I don't know all the details. When you're young you don't really ask, I guess I felt like it wasn't my place to question but to simply do as I was told. The relationship between him and my father was strained, Although thinking about it I can almost guarantee it was my father's issue. He's not the warmest of people. Sometimes I wonder if coldness towards people is catching because my mother used to be so loving."

Liv's admission made Honey feel sad. She knew how lucky she was and couldn't imagine ever not having warmth from her parents, even if sometimes they were a little overbearing and a *lot* over-protective. She sensed that even Kyla's lukewarm temperament was more loving than what Liv was experiencing. She squeezed Liv's hand reassuringly and offered her a small smile.

"Gosh, I shouldn't really complain about them. They're a perfectly normal family and we live perfectly mundane lives." Liv said, lifting her gaze to Honey's and letting her shoulders drop as she sighed heavily.

Honey had the urge to close the space between them and comfort the woman in front of her, she knew the heaviness that accompanied people's expectations. Maybe she could take a little of it on her own shoulders, ease Liv's burden, but it wasn't her place. Instead, she chewed on her bottom lip and nodded.

"That sounds like a lot of perfect. Don't you ever get tired of it all…don't you ever just wanna lose yourself in the imperfect?"

"I haven't ever really had the chance to. Being anything less than
perfect in the Henderson household was always a no-no. It's
probably why I am the way I am."

"Which is?"

Liv snorted and moved her hands in a downward gesture "Well
contrary to what my attire this evening says about me, I'm a little bit
of a perfectionist. I don't tend to find myself in many messy
situations."

Honey could definitely see that. She thought back to earlier and
how Liv had sat at the small, wooden dining table looking almost
uncomfortable, her back ramrod straight and her hands resting in her
lap when she wasn't eating. She had attributed some of this to being
a guest in a stranger's home but when Liv had started eating, Honey
noticed she held her knife and fork with delicate hands and ensured
she covered her mouth when she dared to take too big a mouthful.
Honey considered that Liv probably never did anything without
decorum. Then that notion was quashed with the image of her almost
nose diving in the field and falling into Honey. A welcome weight to
arms that had been empty for too long.

"You almost found yourself in a messy situation earlier. Those
gum boots are far too big for you. You would have gotten mud all
over your clothes and if you can't light a log fire or cook on a burner
stove, I'm gonna guess you definitely wouldn't have been able to
work Marvin's washer. It's older than he is…was," a breath caught
in Honey's throat as her sentence trailed off.

Their hands still touching, Honey allowed Liv's weight in her
palm to soothe her worries. Her heart beat faster at the touch.

"Liv, I'm so sorry for your loss," she said, her voice strained with
sadness.

Silence filtered through the space they shared and in that moment
they weren't two strangers having just shared a meal. They were two
people who had lost the same someone, but who had each lost
something so incredibly different. Liv had lost a link to her past, a
part of her family. She had lost the ability to mend what had been
broken many years before she even existed. Losing all chances to
feel and reciprocate love in its most precious form. Honey's loss was
that of a friend, of someone she loved with her entire heart. Someone
who had guided her through the difficult situations she had found
herself in, by providing laughter, company and advice she would

always do her best to adhere to. Honey had lost her North Star, the focus point she always looked for when she needed help finding her way home.

A tear rolled down her cheek. She felt its warm kiss stroke the side of her face and cling to the arc of her chin. She sniffled a little and then felt the gentle touch of Liv's thumb tentatively brushing at the path her sorrow had traveled. It was uncontrollable then when she leaned into the touch and let it soothe her. Brown met Blue and it was like the heaviness she had carried with her since Marvin had passed, was lifted, as Liv's voice whispered her reply.

"I'm so sorry for *yours*."

***

After having walked Liv back over to the house and showed her how to get a fire going, Honey had returned back home and found herself unable to sleep. Her mind raced with the changes she felt in the air at the arrival of this beautiful woman. Small electrical currents coursed through her, waking parts of Honey that had laid dormant for almost two years. Her skin still tingled from the soft touch of Liv's hand on her face and the chemistry she had felt immediately.

While it hadn't been a surprise that someone from Marvin's family would be coming to attend to the house; she hadn't expected that someone to have the same magnetic pull Marvin himself boasted. She couldn't ever have dreamed that Liv, with her comforting smile and gentle ease, would have walked, or rather have fallen, into her life.

The way Liv spoke told Honey that she was educated, the words she spoke told her that Liv was as kind-hearted as her grandfather. It was funny, Honey thought, that you could be so like a person you never really knew. How genetics passed on qualities, like hidden secrets that you unlock without truly knowing their origin. Honey saw pieces of Marvin in his granddaughter and she blamed those for the instant connection she felt to her.

She rolled over in her queen sized bed and pulled the comforter up around her shoulders for warmth as she glanced out of her window. Across the way, Honey could just about make out the lights in the front room of the Henderson house. She pictured Liv curled up on the sofa, the fire turning to embers that would warm her through the night. A book in her hand and the patchwork blanket that drooped over the back of the sofa, tickling the floor as Liv drifted off into a safe slumber. Honey's own eyelids began to feel heavy and as the light across the field flickered and dimmed, she welcomed sleep like an old friend. As she straddled the line between dreams and reality, she wondered if in tonight's dream that beautiful, no longer stranger, up the hill would come find her.

Chapter 10

Liv

Birdsong. That's what woke Liv from the deep slumber she had fallen into last night. Blinking away the remnants of last night's sleep from her eyes she slowly took in her surroundings and realized she had fallen asleep on the sofa. That explained the pain radiating from the base of her neck, down her spine and making sure she felt every single one of the thirty-two years she was.

"Ugh!" Liv groaned, sitting upright and raising her arms to the sky in a sun salutation or the closest she was going to get today. Her entire body was begging for more rest, she couldn't blame it yesterday had been a lot. She tilted her head from side to side until the pressure was released with a small series of pops and cracks; a yawn escaped her mouth. Liv caught a taste of something unpleasant and realized it was her own breath.

"Yuck!"

Her toothbrush and toothpaste were still sitting in the confines of the suitcase she hadn't unpacked but simply abandoned at the bottom of the staircase yesterday.

Liv pushed herself to her feet and crossed the wooden floor of the living area in an almost "*Risky Business*-worthy slide." Retrieving the much needed essentials from the case, Liv moved towards the stairs and headed for the bathroom.

She still wasn't familiar with the layout of the large house. The ground floor boasted a main living area, dining room, utilities room and a kitchen twice the size of the one in her apartment. A door in the kitchen led to even more land out back which was largely overgrown but she could almost make out the boundaries of what was undoubtedly once a beautifully attended garden. The first floor consisted of four bedrooms each with their own bathrooms. In the middle of the two largest rooms sat a linen closet filled with bedding and towels folded neatly into piles.

Liv hadn't known what to expect when she walked through the door yesterday and had kept her initial tour brief, simply checking that there were no animals or any major damage to the house that would require immediate care.

Moving up the creaking steps two at a time, Liv reached the top and made a beeline for what she had remembered to be the largest of the rooms. The bed was still made with corners that looked like they'd been folded and tucked meticulously. She made a note to ask her father if her grandfather had been in the military.

Standing in front of the mirror she unscrewed the cap of the toothpaste and squeezed a generous amount onto her brush. While brushing, she pondered for a second on how many of her questions Honey would have the answers to. A blush warming her cheeks as her mind flitted back to their dinner last night. Liv didn't know what she expected when she thought about her first night here in her fathers past, but she knew couldn't have conjured up Honey Rosenberg even in her wildest dreams.

A cute, compact, blonde-haired, free spirit with a voice that matched her name. And gosh could she cook. Liv had suppressed a groan more than once during dinner last night. If she wasn't absolutely certain that the blonde hadn't been watching her, she would have definitely made eyes at the plate of food she had been served. Liv was unsure how long it had been since anyone had cooked for her, let alone cooked that well.

Finishing her task and heading back down the stairs to try and figure out the plan for a cup of tea, Liv's mind remained firmly stuck on her super cute neighbor.

"Definitely taken," she mumbled under her breath although she knew no one could hear her.

There was absolutely no way that Honey Rosenberg wasn't already someone's everything. Last night, walking around the modest living space of the small cottage, she had seen a picture on a shelf of a woman who looked like the cat who got the cream, her arms wrapped posessively around Liv's doe-eyed neighbor.

A few moments of frustration later, after admitting defeat to the overly complicated burner oven, Liv resigned to try and approach Honey and ask for a complete run through of each of the appliances in the house. For now she would have to head back into town and grab a cup of tea from the coffee shop. As she slipped into her faded blue jeans paired with a fitted gray henley and a pair of blue and white checkered Vans she usually wore for Sunday morning walks around her local park, she headed out the door. Across the field she noted the bright yellow truck was missing. Musing that Honey must have been awake earlier than the birds this morning, Liv was grateful for the hospitality she had shown her last night. Especially walking her home after dinner and the subsequent time she had spent lighting the fire that had burned through the night, keeping Liv at a comfortable warmth that ensured a peaceful first night.

The pinging of her phone alerted her to a text and seeing it was from Hannah she made to reply. She had sent her a quick text yesterday to let her know she had arrived safely, had met her new neighbor and would tell her more in the morning. Hannah clearly had been waiting anxiously, her text filled with exclamations that Liv could practically hear punctuating the text she read.

"Come on!! The sun is up Liv, so spill!! You drove 400 miles and this person was what…waiting on your doorstep?! Come on, I'm dying to know the details!! Let me live vicariously through you!"

Shaking her head as she laughed, Liv typed out a reply.

"The sun is barely up. Have you been eating Sour Patch Kids again? I told you they're an after lunch snack, not a breakfast food."

"Okay, Mom! Tell me about this cute neighbor… better yet!"

Liv's phone began to ring and she swiped to answer the call.

"So is she cute? She's cute isn't she?" Hannah's volume was almost too much for Liv to take and she winced at her overly excited friend.

"Hello to you too!" Liv said, rolling her eyes as a scoff of derision sounded down the line.

"Spill!! Now!!

"Okay, okay. I was having trouble getting the fire lit, or rather anything working in this place. It's like the land that time forgot."

"Did she sweep in a light a fire in you?" Hannah gushed and Liv rolled her eyes at her friend's ridiculous play on words. Choosing not to react she continued with her story.

"Just when I had given up on the idea of ever eating again, she showed up on my doorstep."

"And asked you to eat her?"

"Hannah!" Her friend was a handful and Liv missed her already.

"Get to the good stuff. I'm already five minutes late and I swear Dean Stevenson just walked past and saw me leaning the seat back in my car to have this conversation."

"It could have waited until you were on your lunch break."

"You could have waited maybe, but you've met me. I don't have patience. Please give me something to hold onto to help get me through this miserable day." Hannah whined and Liv could imagine her reclining in her seat hiding in the staff parking on campus.

"She showed up on my doorstep clutching ciders meant for someone else, apparently she used to spend time with my grandfather. But um, yeah, she invited me over to her place and we had dinner and talked a little. She's really sweet."

"Okay but is she cute? Is she potential girlfriend material?"

"Hannah I am so not there right now. Besides, I don't even know that she's gay and even if she is, she's absolutely not single. There's no way. Although she did sort of flirt with me last night."

"She did?"

"I might have had a Liv moment, fell off the fence and she caught me." A blush warmed Liv's cheeks as she remembered the way Honey had held her as she fell. How certain she was with her touch and how confident she was when she spoke.

"Is the word fence being used metaphorically or literally here?"

"The latter. Anyways, she asked me if I was falling for her already and I just sort of didn't know what to say."

"Liv, you need to get it together. If her being on your doorstep and catching you when you fell isn't enough of a sign for a romance reader like you, then I don't know what is. That's a meet-cute for the ages."

"Maybe."

"I know I told you to find your happy, but maybe your happy found you. Some girls get all the luck, go figure," Hannah sighed dramatically. "Look, I really have to go, but we *will* talk about this again soon, don't worry. I'm glad you got there safely. I love you."

Liv didn't even have the chance to respond. She slipped into her car and drove slowly down the remnants of the once clear pathway, mulling over her friend's words as she took in fully, the place she was to call home for the foreseeable future. The vast expanse of wheat fields that danced in the gentle morning breeze, a sea of gold that stretched to the property boundaries where tall trees stood, racing to touch the bright blue skies. The cottage Honey occupied was so small, Liv wondered if it had been intended to be lived in at all. It was big enough only for one, definitely not a family home.

Compact and cute, she mused. Just like her neighbor.

The streets leading into town were still quiet leading Liv to suspect that this was more to do with the actual population of Verity Vale, rather than the time of day. Up ahead, a young boy of about twelve walked a rather rambunctious Dalmatian. The boy spoke animatedly to the dog who jump-stepped as it stared back at him, pure joy in both their eyes. Liv had always wanted a dog, or maybe a cat but Marcie hated pets equally as much as she hated children and so that was another want that Liv had resigned to never having.

She had just reached the center of the town with all its green striped awnings and aesthetic storefronts when she noticed a familiar yellow that caused a flutter in her stomach, unnerving her as much as it excited her. Honey's Jeep was parked outside of the deli. Seeing an open space just behind the truck, Liv pulled in and began to gather her things.

"Hey you!" a voice sounded and Liv looked over her shoulder to see Honey looking -if possible- even more beautiful than she had yesterday. Her blonde hair was expertly pulled back in Dutch braids and the white crop tee she wore with baggy denim jeans perfectly exposed her bare midriff. Liv's eyes flickered to Honey's soft curves. Her cheeks warmed and she heard Honey cough a little ducking her head to try lift Liv's eyes to meet her own.

"You okay there?"

"Yeah, sorry. Still trying to get myself together. I haven't had a cup of tea yet and I'm absolutely non-functional without my morning cup."

There was no way Liv was going to admit to having been wide awake since Hannah called, nor was she going to admit out loud that her body had felt like it had electricity running through it ever since they had hung up.

"You still couldn't figure out the stove?"

"Absolutely not. I was sort of hoping I would bump into you," Liv admitted and she could have sworn she saw a blushing on Honey's cheeks, that mirrored her own.

"Oh yeah?"

"Yeah. I was going to ask what it would take to bribe you into giving me a *For Dummies* run down of how to work the fireplace, burner oven and well… I guess everything else in that house."

"I don't deal in bribes," Honey deadpanned and Liv found that response a little jarring from the woman who had only been anything but sweet to her since they met. She took a moment to consider that maybe she had read Honey wrong. Maybe all these years of trying to figure out Marcie's mood swings and motives had meant that her ability to read people had gotten a little rusty. Sometimes in adjusting yourself to fit other people's narratives, you can lose a part of yourself unknowingly. "I mean, unless they're of the sugar variety. I happen to have a bit of a sweet tooth."

Giggling at Honey's confession, Liv felt reassured in her earlier assessments. Honey was definitely a sweet person and she was absolutely someone Liv wanted to know more.

"Would you like me to make you a cup of tea? We aren't open yet but I think I could speak with the boss and sneak you in?" Honey gestured over her shoulder with her thumb.

Liv leaned to the right and looked over at the deli whose sign still read closed. She didn't want to get Honey in any trouble but she also *really, really* needed a cup of tea.

"You're sure won't get in trouble?"

"Absolutely positive. The boss is a bit of a pushover, come on."

They walked towards the deli and Honey grabbed at the door and pulled it open. Gesturing for Liv to step inside, Liv complied, albeit worriedly.

She glanced around the large open space, round white tables with cute, matching wooden chairs dotted the floor. On the right was a glass counter and behind it stood a tall woman with a protruding stomach, filling the display with a variety of cold cuts. Liv wondered if this woman was the boss, but when she didn't even look over at her and Honey, Liv concluded that maybe she was just another employee. At the back of the room were shelves containing wicker baskets brimming with fresh produce, vegetables and fruits in vibrant colors that made the room come to life. A cute brunette clutching a basket of apples to her chest threw them a warm smile as she placed the basket on the floor and then headed for what Liv assumed was the storage area at the back. She felt a warmth cover her lower back, heating her skin through the tee she had pulled on earlier and looked worriedly at Honey.

"Take a seat and I'll be right back with your tea. Any preference?" Honey asked.

"A Chai would be amazing if you have it, that is." Liv considered that she could have declined Honey's very sweet offer, crossed the street and got exactly what she wanted from Irregular Joes, but as she looked at the way this woman smiled at her, a feeling blossomed inside her like the first flowers in spring. Liv felt like if asked, she would never deny Honey anything and to feel like that so quickly meant that this -whatever it was between them- had the potential to shake her foundations.

Honey had crossed the floor and slipped behind the counter on the left, grabbing at items in a coordinated shuffle. The spicy scent of cloves and cinnamon filled the air, mingling with the smell of freshly baked pastries and cakes, Liv closed her eyes and allowed the delicious smell to fill her lungs.

"Here you go, one Chai, I wasn't sure if you wanted cream or sugar so," Honey placed the cup down on the table in front of Liv, along with a small metal jug containing creamer and a handful of assorted sugar and sweetener packets. Liv thanked her softly and watched as she slipped back behind the counter and emerged once more carrying a plate with her.

"You're sure I won't get you in trouble?"

"Oh, yeah. Don't worry. Like I said, the boss is a bit of a pushover."

This reassurance eased Liv's fears a little and as she wrapped her hands around the warm porcelain mug she felt them almost evaporate entirely. Liv could feel Honey's warm, brown eyes still fixed on her as she took a sip from her mug and felt her shoulders drop.

"You're gonna want to eat that while it's warm. Trust me," Honey winked and Liv glanced at the muffin that Honey had gifted her. Light brown and dotted with fleshy pieces of what looked like peaches, Liv hoped it tasted as wonderful as it looked and smelled. She glanced up to thank Honey but she had already made her way back around the other side of the counter. A figure filled the seat next to her and Liv jumped a little, the brunette from the produce section smiled at her.

"So you're the granddaughter huh? Nice to meet you, I'm Sasha," she said, extending her hand in greeting. Liv accepted graciously and smiled back at her.

"Nice to meet you too. Sorry to impose on your morning, Honey said it would be okay."

"Oh it's perfectly fine. Any friend of Honey's is a friend of mine." Sasha waved away Liv's apologies and she wondered if everyone in Verity Vale was as nice as the people she had encountered over the last 24 hours.

"Are you the boss?"

Liv wasn't sure what she had said to make Sasha laugh, but the sound was more comforting than teasing and the woman slapped her hand down lightly on the table.

"Me? No, you sorta met the boss already."

Sasha's gaze flitted across the room directing Liv's eyes to where Honey now stood, hips swaying softly to the music that hummed from her phone.

A green apron hung from around her delicate neck and Liv licked her lips at the sight of Honey's bare, lower back where a bow had been tied with nimble fingers.

She imagined her own hands pulling on the release of the bow, the apron strings dropping to the blonde's sides and her fingers tingling as she ran the flat of her palms around the exposed flesh of Honey's waist. She felt the hairs on her arms stand to attention as she got lost in a daydream of what it would feel like to hold the smaller woman close to her, resting her hands in that delicious hollow of Honey's lower back. She inhaled deeply, as a wave of desire crashed over her. Honey was so far from Liv's usual type, she seemed quiet and reserved, but so unwaveringly sweet and Liv wondered if these very noticeable differences were what made Honey so much more desirable.

Maybe here, in a new town living an almost new life, Liv could choose something different. What she had tried before definitely hadn't been working for her.

Honey spun on her heels and their eyes connected briefly before Honey's stare dropped to Liv's lips and back up again. There was absolutely no question if something existed between them, it was practically screaming at Liv, she could see it in the way the blonde sucked her bottom lip between her teeth and fluttered her eyelashes. Whatever it was, Liv swore Honey felt it too.

"Don't let the braids confuse you," Sasha's voice filled Liv's ear and for a moment she forgot that she wasn't sitting alone,

"Underneath that sweet exterior my little sister is an evil genius... well not evil, but a genius nevertheless. Honey *is* the boss. Well, her own boss. We all are, we own this place together. You should eat that while it's warm and watch out for the center. It gets a little messy."

The plate pushed towards her, Liv's hand rose automatically and tore delicately at the wrapper around the soft, still warm muffin. Bringing it to her lips she bit down, the sweet peach pieces the perfect contrast to the gentle hints of cinnamon in the batter. She groaned inwardly a little at how decadent yet delicate the flavors were as they danced amongst her taste buds and made her stomach flutter with satisfaction. It was the second bite that really outed Liv, she squeaked in delight and embarrassment, as a sharp taste coated her tongue unexpectedly and her brain struggled for a moment to place exactly what it was. Then it hit her.

Passionfruit.

The middle of the muffin oozed with a perfectly textured passionfruit curd. The words from the young girl Liv had encountered at Irregular Joes last night, filled her mind. She had just had her first taste of Honey's Peach Passion Promise. Lara was right, she would never be able to settle for anything less than this, ever again.

Chapter 11

Honey

"So, she's cuuuuute." Sasha sang as she rounded the table closest to Honey's counter, picking up the empty cups as she went along. Honey had expected this. To be honest, she had wondered after inviting Liv in for a cup of tea, exactly just how long it would take for her sisters to say something. She expected it to be Kyla rather than Sasha though and she also expected it to be something blunt.

"I'm sorry, who's cute?" Honey feigned ignorance, instead she concentrated on switching the empty display trays for freshly filled new ones. The lunch rush would be descending on them shortly and she had to be prepared.

"The granddaughter."

"She has a name, Sash." Honey sighed, rolling her eyes and sliding the door to the glass cabinet closed.

"And I bet you wanna scream that name don't you? Ugh, if I were ten years younger," Sasha sighed.

."..and not straight…and not married," Honey finished, smirking.

As far as she knew Sasha had never even entertained a girl crush before. She had met her husband Greyson at eighteen and had been smitten ever since. They were sickeningly in love and Honey envied them. Sometimes when she sat alone at night, curled up in her chair reading, she thought about what she wouldn't give for someone to look at her the way Greyson looked at her sister. It felt quite a sad realization that she wasn't entirely sure that Andie had ever looked at her like that. Not even in the beginning.

"She's hot. Like, serious but not so uptight she wouldn't be fun. I like her."

"You don't even know her!" Honey giggled, shaking her head.

Sometimes Sasha's world view in which everything was black and white and easy, was tempting to be sucked into. She was absolutely a sucker for romance and was also the biggest believer in Honey's ability to have a happy ever after.

"I know I like her better than Andie, that didn't take me long to figure out. Please tell me you're going to ask her out!"

Honey balked at the idea, her stomach flipped around the waves of nervousness at the thought of asking Liv out. Sure she was beautiful -breathtaking even- and Honey had absolutely found herself attracted to Liv, the instant she saw her. But asking her out, especially at this time was a hard no.

"Sasha, she's here because her grandpa died. I don't think dating is top of her list of priorities at the moment. She's probably not even interested."

"Oh, she's interested. For sure," Honey scoffed in disbelief and Sasha tilted her head, her eyes wide "What? I saw how she looked at you." Sasha's perfectly sculpted eyebrows narrowed and waggled a little at the insinuation.

"And how was that exactly?"

"Like she wanted to eat you like that muffin you gave her."

"She did not look at me like that." Honey denied, grabbing a dishcloth and wiping it back and forth over the already pristine countertop. Her sister's notions were bordering on insane and Honey knew she meant well but inside she felt something a little like hope making itself known. It took hold of her breath and kept it for itself, whispering in her ears that maybe Sasha *had* seen something on Liv's beautiful face.

But Honey knew that hope was like a helium balloon in a child's hands, one strong gust of wind partnered with a loose grip and it could all blow away. She would have loved to have held onto the possibility of something, but after everything she had been through the last two years, she wasn't sure if her need to be loved was clouding her ability to see things clearly. Honey was sure of some things though, the way her heart sped up when Liv was near her, the way her body shivered with anticipation each time they stepped close enough to one another to touch. The way she had warmed as Liv had thanked her for the cup of tea, with a hug that made Honey's nerve-endings tingle.

All signs pointed to Liv.

The door sounded, letting them know a customer had arrived and Sasha moved back to her side of the deli, but not before glancing over her shoulder and throwing Honey the most mischievous smirk she had ever seen.

"I've always told you, one of these days those muffins are gonna land you a wife."

***

After work Honey went home and hopped into the shower intending to wash the day off. She did her best thinking under the rainfall spray, like when she decided to cut her waist length hair into a shorter more manageable style, and then dye it bright pink. Like when she had decided, after looking at her reflection in the glass screens of the deli all day, that she would definitely get her nose pierced. Like when she decided to ask her sisters to partner up and keep the deli open after her grandparents passed.

As the spray washed over her, she allowed her mind to flit to something she had been wrestling with internally for the last few days, Andie. She hadn't contacted Honey at all since that phone call. Andie had moved on, found someone else to give her what she wanted. It was as clear as day that she had been nothing but Andie's personal ATM. While Honey had been handing out affection and love alongside the monthly cash injections, Andie had only been interested in the latter.

Honey needed closure, it didn't feel fair to continue to sit in a state of unknowing and uncertainty. She knew what she had to do, although she doubted it would make any difference to Andie.

Stepping out of the spray and wrapping herself up in a towel, Honey headed for the bedroom where she had left her phone. Sometimes the hardest thing to do was make the first move but Honey knew from her countless nights playing chess with Marvin that whatever move you make, difficult consequences can arise. She had gone over and over in her mind exactly what she would say when she made this call. How she knew they should have said their goodbyes long ago, but her heart hadn't been ready to let go, despite never truly having a hold on Andie's.

She would make sure she remained stoic, no tears would be shed; Honey wasn't sure she had any left all these years later. She wanted to make sure that she thanked Andie for opening her to the possibility of love. This however was something Honey knew her sisters would call her crazy for, if they knew exactly what had prompted this conversation in the first place and she didn't need another lecture from Kyla, punctuated with looks of pity and disdain. She didn't know that she would be strong enough to listen to well meaning platitudes from Sasha as she would undoubtedly throw her arms around Honey in a comfort that would prompt tears. So, Honey had buried the truth alongside shame and embarrassment, carrying them in the lockbox that was her bruised heart the last few months.

Sliding her thumb across the screen and clicking the contact widget she scrolled for Andie's name. Tapping on the screen, she crossed the room and sat herself down on the edge of her bed. Shaking legs were not a good foundation for someone who had been crumbling on the inside for so long. She inhaled deeply, as down the line the ringing pattern began, a metronome beat her heart raced past.

"Hello?" Andie's voice was terse and clipped. Honey thought she would hear even the slightest bit of shame considering what had occurred, but it didn't make itself known.

"We need to talk." Honey said. Surprising herself with the control she had over her voice, despite the rest of her body not complying.

"Well can it wait, I'm at work. I can't just drop everything to talk to you." Andie's annoyance laced her words and Honey found herself no longer surprised. It was like for the first time she could truly see what her sisters were talking about when they complained about how Andie spoke to her.

"No Andie, it can't wait. At least, not anymore. Actually that's what I was calling to tell you. I need to tell you that I'm not waiting around for you anymore."

"What? H, this really isn't the right time."

That was enough for Honey, who shot up off the bed and began pacing back and forth across her carpeted floor, in an attempt to tamper down the flourishing anger she felt inside her chest.

"When will be the right time? When you finish work and forget to call me? When you decide that you need me to start sending you money again? When you're ready to admit you're with someone else or when I pick up the phone to hear you having sex with someone else? The right time for us to have had this conversation would have been before you left. Before I spent months holding onto hope that you would come back but you knew before you left we wouldn't see one another again, didn't you?"

"Honey, I ..." something akin to shame laced those words. Honey could hear the way it turned her soon to be ex-girlfriend's once confident voice to an almost whisper.

Shame is a powerful emotion that lingers long after events have happened, or words have been spoken. It outstays its welcome and takes up space that is meant for other things.

Honey felt ashamed of herself for allowing Andie to take up as much space in her life as she had. She blamed herself for giving this to her willingly, for convincing herself that what they were to each other was something meant to last. Honey knew now that Andie was a crack in her foundations, a weakness that if not dealt with could bring her down entirely.

"Honestly Andie, I had convinced myself that I needed to hear exactly what you had to say. I told myself to give you a chance to explain but I don't need you to explain. I don't need to hear your lies and excuses, not anymore."

"Honey, please."

There it was. The pleading Honey had known would occur as Andie's mind caught up to the reality of what was happening and made a last ditch attempt at fighting for whatever this was...or used to be.

She stopped pacing the room, and stood in front of the window. Outside the sun slowly said goodbye to the sky and greeted the horizon. Across the field, at the big house, the porch swing moved back and forth. A small figure was draped in a blanket, curled up reading a book. She smiled and clutched at her towel as a welcome shiver made its way down her spine and found her center.

Liv Henderson was relaxing on the porch swing, looking more at home with each passing second. Honey closed her eyes and allowed her mind to momentarily wander to what would happen if she crossed the field. She imagined smiling softly at her new neighbor, who would shuffle along the wooden swing, lift the blanket and invite Honey to join her with a soft smile that said more than words ever could. She could almost feel the warmth Liv would radiate, the unquestionable softness of her touch and how the sweet smell of her perfume would enveloping her. She shook her head softly, her drying curls dancing around her shoulders.

"Honey. Please can this wait?"

"No, Andie. I need you to listen. We are done. I'm… done. I spent so long waiting for you to come home, when really, this was never your home. *I* was not your home. I was just a layover on the way to your destination and I hope that whoever it is you're sleeping with now, knows that she's just a layover too. You'll never be satisfied Andie, no matter how much I give you, and I gave you everything… all of me and what I got in return was a broken heart and a bunch of wasted hope. So don't call me anymore, please! Don't try and justify what happened or put up some silly attempt at a fight for something that you don't truly want. Because I'm not sure you ever really wanted me, not how I wanted you. I used to think you were the sun, you were all I could see. I stared too long and became blinded by you. No matter what happened, I would *always* choose you but I need to put myself first now. I have to choose myself. This is me, choosing… me."

"Honey, I'm sorry."

"No, Andie. You're not. I don't think you're capable of sorry, not yet. But maybe, when you look back on this in a few years time and realize exactly what it was you gave up on, you will be. I hope you find whatever or whoever it is you are looking for."

Honey's chest filled with pride as she allowed what was happening to register. She had taken the first step in acknowledging the end and not only that, but she had embraced it. Honey had done something Kyla had been pressing her to do for the longest time, only she had done it for herself. She had been ready to see this for what it was. Ready to accept it and move on and that was such a powerful feeling.

"You too." Andie's voice was soft now, cushioned by defeat, the wind knocked out of her once magnificently blowing sails.

Honey didn't need to say goodbye, it was something she had said every time they called over the last two years. In reality their goodbye had been said long before that, the last time Andie had said goodbye and meant it had been the night she came home from the gym announcing her imminent departure. Honey just hadn't been able to hear it, or hadn't wanted to see it then. Andie's words reverberated in her ear as she lowered the phone and pressed the end call button.

Her eyes darted back across the field to where possibility sat, on a swing whose story Honey desperately wanted to tell her, draped in memories she didn't yet have. Honey watched Liv sway back and forth in the swing and her chest fluttered. It was possible that what she was looking for, had come looking for her too.

***

"Care for some company?" Honey chanced, climbing the steps to where Liv sat, swinging back and forth on the creaking porch swing. She held a four pack up in front of her and shook the cardboard carrier a little, hoping her offerings would be accepted. She wasn't disappointed.

"Honestly, I'd love some." Liv said, pulling back the blanket that she had draped over her. "I've sort of felt a little disconnected today. Don't get me wrong, being here has absolutely helped me focus on getting my work done, but it can also fuel the desire to become a hermit and never speak to another human again."

"Who needs social interactions when you have a view like this, right?" Honey teased, moving over to join her neighbor on the swing.

"It's a stunning view." Liv admitted as their eyes met and Honey felt her heart speed up a little at the inference. Surely Liv wasn't talking about her. There was no way her cute, new neighbor was making eyes *and* a pass at her. She cleared her throat and pulled her bottom lip into her mouth hoping the lack of light meant her blushing cheeks wouldn't be noticable.

"I didn't know there were this many stars in the sky. They're really out there, huh!" Liv said, leaning her head back to get a good look at the sky. Her long black hair fell from the messy bun she had wound it into, resting now over her shoulders. Honey wanted to run her hands through Liv's hair, feel how soft it was as she wound it around her fingers and pulled her into the softest of kisses. One that would elicit a moan that Liv wouldn't be able to stifle.

Suddenly aware of the silence that fell between them and that she was moments away from being caught staring, Honey blew out a breath and moved to mirror Liv's position. "I imagine light pollution is a very real thing in the city."

"Oh yeah, light pollution, noise pollution… ugh I can't believe people actively choose to live there when places like this exist. Everyone should move here."

Honey smirked, of course someone new here would instantly see its merits. The dry dirt hadn't had a chance to cling to her clothing yet, let alone embed itself in. But she guessed it wouldn't take long for the luster to wear off. No, it wouldn't be long before Liv, the chic city girl, would shuck off her gumboots and head back to capitalist central. Honey couldn't imagine what that would be like, to wake up everyday to a place where the noise was constant. A place where silence really was golden. One thing she absolutely loved about living here in Verity was that the day began and ended calmly, with the soft chirping of birdsong and the gentle twinkling of the stars.

"A glowing recommendation, but not one we really want to become public opinion," she breathed, rocking the swing back and forth with her heels. "If everyone came to live here, so would the light pollution and the noise pollution too. Where would we escape to then?"

Liv took a moment to respond, her legs dropped from their position on the swing and Honey felt resistance against her pushing and the swing came to halt.

"We could escape to the stars themselves!" She stood from her position and moved towards the edge of the porch, pointing a finger towards the sky. "I can imagine that one there to be particularly hospitable. I mean, imagine the view from up there."

"Stars aren't inhabitable, Liv." Honey said, shaking her head.

"Neither are half of the rentals in the city, but people still live in them." Liv teased, glancing over her shoulder. The way the moonlight kissed her face made Honey jealous.

"You know you're not selling me on the notion of ever leaving here for the big city."

"Why would you want to leave?" Liv turned back to the sky, "Everything anyone could ever want is here."

"Apparently not everything."

That admission had fallen from Honey's mouth before she could stop it. Liv spun on her heels this time, offering Honey her attention. Honey wished it was her absolute attention, she could feel the sexual tension burning between them or at least, what she thought was sexual tension. But she wouldn't make a move and so nothing would come of it. A girl could dream, couldn't she?

"Are you okay? Do you want to talk about it."

"I made a difficult call today, one that shouldn't have taken me this long to make. My girlfriend... ex-girlfriend now I guess, well, she's been in Australia for the better part of two years and today I told her that I wasn't waiting around for her anymore."

"Wow, that's..."

"I should have done it sooner. I don't know why I didn't. Actually that's a lie, I know exactly why I didn't do it. I was scared of being alone, but I'm already alone. I've been alone before and I've been alone since she left. We didn't really talk anymore, not unless she needed something from me. Money. Attention. Validation."

"That doesn't sound like fun."

"I know it sounds stupid but I think I held on so long because I'm not great at saying goodbye."

"That doesn't sound stupid at all. In fact that sounds pretty normal. I don't think anyone who starts something is ever prepared for the end. I think as humans we absolutely think in terms of forever. Who wants to go into a relationship thinking about the breakup? That's hardly healthy. You should give yourself some credit for realizing that you couldn't keep putting yourself through all of that. Self-care is important."

"Maybe you're onto something with the whole living on a star thing."

She glanced off to the side and blinked back the tears burning at her eyes. Liv was speaking nothing but truths and Honey had waited so long for someone to validate what she had been too scared to voice herself. The words caressed Honey's heart in a way she hadn't expected. She didn't know why but it was different hearing these words from Liv rather than her sisters. She supposed it was because they had an obligation to soothe her soul, Liv didn't. Honey felt those comforting words reach inside of her, illuminating her darkest places.

"Wanna build a rocket ship and fly lightyears away from our problems?"

"Don't tempt me. Sadly, I have too many responsibilities to attend to here that are much more pressing than my lack of love life."

"Then humor me, at least for tonight. Let's just pretend that nothing exists outside of this, outside of us and the stars and night sky."

"How do you propose we do that?"

"Come with me." Liv held out her hand and Honey instantly reacted. As her hand slipped into Liv's, a jolt of possibility made its way through her body. She shivered slightly and although she tried to blame the cool night air for the goosebumps that traveled the expanse of her skin, lighting up each part of her like the fourth of July; she knew the real reason for this was blue eyes and a smile she was ready to fall into without question. This instant trust she felt between herself and Liv was staggering and yet Honey wasn't scared.

They made their way out towards the back of the property, where the grass wasn't as tall but was still not as perfect as it had been when Marvin was around. Honey thought about asking Liv if she knew how to work the ride-on mower that Marvin kept in the shed out back. But considering she didn't know how to light a fire, Honey guessed Liv would have no clue about operating a machine like that.

Coming to a stop in the middle of the field, Liv released her hand and shook out the blanket she had grabbed from the porch. Laying it down on the grass, Liv sat down on it and lay back entirely, looking at Honey with wide eyes.

"Well... are you going to keep standing there and miss the show, or are you going to join me?" she asked.

Honey considered her options. If she continued to stand here, Liv would probably get up and they would head back to the porch. It would be awkward because she would have put herself out there and Honey would have rejected her. But if she lay down next to her, she would be inches away from Liv's body. The same body that she had cuddled up to in her dreams every night this week.

Honey lowered herself to the ground, being careful not to touch Liv as she got herself comfortable on the blanket. She wasn't graceful and in her shuffling around on the lumpy floor, threw out a hand that inadvertently touched Liv's hip. She pulled it back quickly, an almost apology on her tongue before she noticed Liv was smiling at her. Honey took a few deep inhalations to steady herself, her body was wound so tight right now. She had to get herself together.

They sat in silence and watched as the stars dotted the sky, welcoming night as it slid around them, illuminating them further. Honey had grown up under these night skies and had surprisingly, in all her years, never done anything like this before. Lying here now she couldn't help but feel guilty in having taken for granted the view she was offered.

"I know this is probably not so new to you, but this very well may be the most amazing thing I've seen in a while." Liv said.

Honey continued to stare straight up at the sky. The words she wanted to say stuck in her throat a little. She wanted to tell Liv that all of this was new to her, being with someone like this, watching the stars, just being still. It was all new to her. She ached to tell Liv that the most amazing thing she had seen in a while wasn't the collective of stars tethered together by invisible strings humans had used to create pictures in order to make them memorable. No, the most amazing thing Honey had seen in a while was the blue in Liv's eyes and that was something she would never forget.

They had flirted back and forth a little, there had been glances and exchanges of smiles that fanned the flames of desire in Honey, but she knew it was too soon to say something so openly forward and so she didn't.

"It's been a while since I saw them. The stars that is. They sort of went into hiding a little after Marvin died."

"What's changed, do you think?"

"You," she wanted to say. *"You have changed everything and I've only just met you."* Honey knew that Liv's question was probably wanting more of a scientific explanation rather than the emotional one she felt compelled to give and so she shook off her feelings and shrugged.

"I guess I'm ready to see them again, now."

Liv's hand found hers on the blanket and gave it a gentle, reassuring squeeze. Honey's heart thudded against her chest as she glanced down, willing Liv's hand to stay where it was. She silently willed Liv to entwine their fingers together and anchor her to the ground because right now Honey felt like she was floating. She chanced a look at the woman lying next to her, her long hair was spread on the blanket and she had her nose scrunched up as if she was trying to work something out.

"I know you said earlier that you're not great with goodbyes," Liv's voice was a whisper, and turned to meet Honey's gaze. When their eyes locked, something passed between them that Honey wanted more of. " But I want you to know, I think you're wonderful at hellos."

Chapter 12

Liv

A few weeks had passed since Liv had arrived in Verity and the house once unfamiliar to her, now whispered secrets out loud, as if welcoming her home. She knew that the third step creaked loudly on the staircase and so each morning she would omit the last few steps, landing with a flourish as her socked feet hit the hardwood floor. She knew that the log burner she had seen as a hazard a short while back, was actually a more efficient way of heating a home; especially now she knew how to stack her logs. She had her neighbor to thank for that. Her beautifully breathtaking neighbor.

Honey Rosenberg was a fountain of useful knowledge. It also didn't hurt that she was adorably cute with her wide, chocolate brown eyes and curly blonde hair. Liv had found herself -when in her neighbors presence- unable to control the way her eyes moved over Honey's soft curves.

Since their night watching the stars, they had spent nearly every night in each other's company, sitting out on the porch and talking about anything and everything. As such, Liv had become accustomed to the way Honey's laughter sounded, and how it made her heart skip a beat. Although their touches had been brief, small accidental brushes of their bodies as they walked past one another, hand holding the night they watched the stars, they were addictive. Liv knew she should be careful, but there had been moments when she had found herself purposely seeking Honey's gentle touch.

Honey had spent hours showing Liv around her grandparents' home over the last few days, talking her through everything from how to light the fire to ensure maximum warmth, to which cleaning products to use on a stove that looked like it was in pristine condition, despite its age.

Not only had Honey come over most nights but sometimes during the day, she would drive home during lunch hour and knock on Liv's door bearing gifts. Liv had started to feel a tightness in the waistband of her jeans, a clear indication of overindulgence. But with cakes as delicious as Honey made, it was a price Liv was absolutely willing to pay. To combat this she had ordered some new clothes online, things more suitable to the environment she now called home, after having come to the conclusion that half of her packed items were definitely not suitable for life in Verity.

Liv however, was finding herself *entirely* suitable for life here. She had adapted her once rigid morning routine to her surroundings. Instead of watching from the seventh floor as the city came to life, she stood on the porch, warm mug in hand and watched the sun bring everything to life. She had been doing exactly that, when her father had called again this morning.

"Elizabeth," no greeting, just straight to business. Liv could hear in his voice that this was not a call to ask her how she was doing, and she was right, "Have you found the book yet?"

"I'm sorry. The book?"

"Yes, Elizabeth. Please tell me you aren't wasting your time down there doing anything other than packing up the rest of that place and getting it ready for sale." His voice was firm and Liv could imagine his forehead creasing with the annoyance that clearly laced his voice.

"Good Morning to you too, father," she muttered under her breath.

The truth was, Liv had only gotten so far as to pack away her grandparents' clothing, and that had only been due to the need to unpack her own. The boxes that had accumulated as a result of this, sat in the second largest room. It had been too much for Liv, too heavy, putting things that belonged to someone else away. Like ending a story she had no right closing the pages on.

Liv had discovered that her grandfather hadn't donated any of her grandmother's clothing after she had passed and so the wardrobe had remained a reminder for him the last ten years. She had imagined him opening the door to retrieve his own shirt and seeing her clothes hanging there, the faint scent of her clinging to the dresses, brushing off onto his own clothes. His weathered hands caressing the fabric as gently as he did her grandmother. She knew he was a kind and gentle man from small things Honey had said, and the sepia-toned evidence that still hung on the walls of the house. It had pained her heart and in some ways restored her faith in love a little, to know someone could still be so in love with another person that they kept hold of pieces of them long after they'd had gone. Liv wanted that kind of love in her life, something so strong that not even distance could dampen it.

Her father's voice filtered into her daydream, popping the bubble with his harsh tones.

"Elizabeth, are you listening to me? This is important. I asked you for one thing while you were there. Now find the book, stop playing house and come home and fix whatever it is that's gone on with you and Marcie. She spoke with your mother yesterday and told her you were refusing to answer her calls."

Unbelievable.

The truth was, yes, she *had* been dodging Marcie's attempts at interaction. For a good reason. But Liv hadn't wanted to get into this with her parents, knowing the exact route it would take. Her father adored Marcie. He hadn't been super supportive when Liv came out as a teenager, but had completely accepted Marcie and even spoke to her as an equal, which was often more than what Liv herself got. She knew his reaction would be loud, messy and absolutely nothing Liv wanted to hear, but she couldn't keep it from them any longer. She had to tell them what had happened, the whole truth. But speaking things into existence makes them real and Liv hadn't openly said those words to anyone yet. Not even to her own reflection on nights she stood in front of the mirror and tried to find the woman she had lost.

They were absolutely, unequivocally, over. They'd become two very different people who had tried walking the same path but now it had become too narrow to stand side by side. Liv had felt like she was constantly walking behind Marcie, and what she really wanted was someone to walk beside. She wanted to walk a new path, maybe a path unpaved.

She sucked in a breath of exasperation and opened her mouth to defend her situation but her father cut her off instantly, "I don't need the details. You're a grown woman but I expect better from you than running away from your problems."

"You mean like you did–" she uttered out loud before she could stop herself. She heard very clearly, her father's indignation and annoyance, in the breath he blew down the line.

"Find the book, sell the house and come home Elizabeth! Do it quick before that place sucks you in and drowns you like it almost did with me!"

***

Four hours later Liv found herself standing in the largest bedroom staring at the messy end result of sorting through more of her grandparents' belongings. She had searched everywhere for the book her father wanted so desperately and she was starting to think that maybe it was something he had conjured up.

Unlikely.

Her father was a man who only dealt in facts, in reality, and she had to wonder what it was about this book that he was so desperate to have it. She no longer believed it was his wish to hold onto the memory of his mother, to marvel in her handwriting on the pages of the book or to learn any secrets that may have lived between the pages. Liv suspected he did not intend on replicating any of the dishes she had written down. Her father's idea of putting together a meal was sitting in a fancy overpriced restaurant and ordering the most expensive dish while dousing his taste buds in scotch. She wasn't entirely sure why he wanted it, but she felt the pressure of finding it, like a thousand pound weight on her shoulders.

A knocking sounded through the house. Disheveled and a little exasperated Liv shuffled out of the bedroom and headed down the stairs. Opening the door she noticed Honey looking rather sheepish and wearing a pale blue sundress dotted with daisies. Her hair was hanging around her shoulders in loose curls that Liv found herself wanting to fist, as she pulled the smaller woman in for a kiss guaranteed to take her breath away. Her building attraction to this woman was becoming increasingly evident, so much so that Liv had started to have daydreams and even sleep filled dreams of Honey. Ones that left her feeling very frustrated and occasionally very wet.

"Hi," Honey smiled, rocking back and forth on her heels nervously.

"Wow, you look...wow! I'm sorry, did we have plans?" Liv asked, wondering if she had forgotten a discussion they'd had the night before while drinking ciders on the porch.

Her father's earlier call had sent her on a wild goose chase she didn't really want to be a part of and the last thing she wanted was to have her relationship with Honey be collateral damage.

"No. I um, just thought I'd swing by and see if you were busy. You are, aren't you? I should just go," Honey clicked her Doc Martens together at the heels and turned to leave. Liv couldn't allow that, she stepped over the threshold of the door and reached for the small blonde.

"I'm not busy. I was just looking for something."

That was a loaded statement and Liv smirked at her own words. Everybody was looking for something or someone, but not everyone found what they were looking for. If you did, you were lucky.

Liv's fingertips grazed the warm skin of Honey's forearm and she was surprised when rather than pull away from the touch, Honey stepped further into it. The air thickened between them and she heard Honey gasp. Rather than shaking off thier connection, Honey glanced at her arm and scanned her eyes over Liv's body, until they were staring deeply into one another's eyes.

"I was wondering if you would like to take a break and come have some fun. You've been stuck in this house for days and I think you could use a change of scenery."

"What did you have in mind?" Liv's voice was hoarse, she coughed a little, trying to clear the desire from her throat and hoping it wasn't as noticeable as it felt.

"Well, it's my niece's birthday today. She's turning six and we are having a party over at my parents' house. There will be a lot of children there, and they're loud but they're sweet and there will also be a lot of adults too. My mom always makes too much food and so—" Honey blushed as she rambled and Liv found her heart fluttering as she heard the obvious adoration in her voice as she talked about her family.

She made a mental note to call Jen and Taylor over the next few days so she could see Theo, who had no doubt grown immensely since she last held him. Obviously she would have to talk to them about what had happened because there was no way Marcie would have revealed her cheating ways to their friends. That part she wasn't looking forward to. She knew Marcie didn't have many friends, she was tonic not everyone could handle. The last thing Liv wanted to do was turn anyone against her ex, or steal Marcie's support system from under her. She would wait and see if they broached the subject and lean into it with as much grace as she could muster. The negativity Liv had carried with her when she arrived had started to dissipate over the last week and she had no desire to slip back into that way of thinking.

"You want me to come with you...to your niece's sixth birthday party?" Liv asked, a smile tugging on the corners of her lips.

She knew she would say yes just to be able to spend time with Honey but anxiety swam in the pit of her stomach at the idea of being surrounded by strangers. She had no problem standing in front of new students year after year. It didn't really matter if they liked her, they just had to be able to learn from her. This was different though. Liv wasn't sure why, but she wanted Honey's family to like her. She suspected it had something to do with the way her stomach was flipping right now just being in Honey's presence.

"You don't have to say yes, I just thought maybe you would want to meet some new people. Have some company other than me for a change." The cutest thing about Honey, Liv mused, was that when she was nervous she rambled. "It would be a shame to waste weather as beautiful as this...oh and there's a bounce house!"

Honey's eyes widened at the mention of the inflatable house and Liv could practically feel her neighbor's excitement at the prospect of having a go. She tried to think back to when she had last jumped on a bounce house. She must have been about five years old, back when her life was carefree and she had been oblivious to the world's expectations.

"Oh well, if there's a bounce house then count me in. Why didn't you start with that?" Liv teased, and when Honey rolled her eyes and smiled that butterfly inducing smile of hers, Liv ached to make it stay there. "I'd love to come with you. Are you sure your family won't mind?"

"Absolutely not. My mom has been bugging me non-stop since you got here about bringing you over for dinner."

"Ah, so this was all your mom's idea." Liv said, her fingers moving slowly down Honey's arm towards her hand. She couldn't help it, she had to make some sort of physical connection, her body was drawn to Honey's like a magnet. "That's a shame, I was hoping you were gonna ask me out on a date sooner or later."

Honey's mouth dropped open and Liv smirked at being able to cause this reaction in her cute neighbor. She expected Honey to pull away from her but was surprised to find that she instead turned her palm upwards. Liv's fingers smoothed over Honey's own as their fingers entwined.

Silence lingered between them, zipping between the invisible bubbles of tension in the air. The way Honey was looking at her, her wide eyes filled with evident desire, had the hairs on Liv's arms standing on end. Her breathing became labored and Liv knew she had to step back and take a moment. If she wasn't careful she would move in for a kiss and that would lead to her undoubtedly losing herself in the beautiful blonde in front of her. If she kissed Honey, she wouldn't ever want to stop.

She looked back over her shoulder, "I'll just slip into something a little less, well, grungy. Come on in. Take a seat, make yourself at home."

Not wanting to break their connection though, Liv's fingers remained tangled with Honey's as she guided her inside, out of the midday sun. The way their hands fit together made Liv even more reluctant to let go and as they reached the foot of the stairs, she hated that she had to. She nodded for Honey to head into the living area. Honey turned on her heels and the bottom of the sundress billowed out, offering Liv a glimpse of her toned thighs. Her tongue darted out to wet her suddenly dry lips and even though her entire being screamed at her to follow the beautiful blonde, she resisted. Liv took the stairs two at a time as she made her way to her bedroom, not wanting to leave her neighbor alone long enough to reconsider the invitation.

She couldn't wait to spend more time with Honey. During the last week she had grown quite fond of her and looked forward to their lunchtime chats and nights sitting outside watching the stars, while drinking fruit ciders that tasted like summer. Their friendship had come easy, instantaneously and the connection between them was unparalleled. Liv couldn't ever remember being this comfortable with someone so soon. This invitation felt different though, this was spending time with her around other people, people Honey loved. The two of them, as a combined entity. This felt like it meant something, like their friendship was evolving into something unexpected.

She sifted through her clothes trying to conjure up an outfit that was suitable for a six years olds party, but at the same time complemented the outfit of the beautiful woman standing in her living room. She wanted to give Honey something to fuel the desire simmering between them, Liv's desire had been bubbling away since she opened the door.

Honey's dress was snug in all the right places, showing off her ample cleavage and curves that made Liv want to map them with her hands. She had been sneakily mapping them with her eyes over the last week and once or twice, had woken from dreams with her hands shaking and her center pulsing. She wondered how it would feel to really hold Honey in her arms. If she would be soft and pliable, allowing Liv to take the lead. Would she feel firm, stiff, like Marcie's body had felt pressed against Liv's during the rare moments when affection had been scheduled between them over the last few years. She wondered if Honey ached to touch her too. She didn't strike Liv as a person who scheduled affection, she radiated it. From the lingering gazes she gifted her with, to the gentle but intoxicating laughter that threatened to give Liv an entire zoo alongside the butterflies she already felt when she was around her.

Honey Rosenberg was wondrous.

But there was something else that lingered in the corner of Honey's mouth, a disappointment, a fear Liv found herself wanting to kiss away. Since she had discovered, a few nights ago, that Honey was not taken, but had been in a situationship with someone who didn't appreciate her, Liv had started harboring hope. Hope that this spark between them could be explored, chartered and potentially manifest into something neither of them expected. Liv knew she had to be careful with Honey. That the hurt she carried alongside insecurity was because of someone who had moved thousands of miles away and never looked back. It was heartbreaking hearing exactly what had happened. How Honey, who was this wonderfully real and honest person, had given herself to someone who had taken her for granted. Liv didn't know how anyone could leave Honey behind, she imagined it would be like committing to perpetual winter.

Deciding on a pair of black skinny jeans and an oversized white blouse with the top two buttons undone, Liv dressed as quickly as she could. She pulled her jet black hair out of the messy bun she had donned the last two days. Her hair falling in natural waves now over her shoulders and down her back. Taking a glimpse in the mirror she pondered if she needed to wear any makeup. Normally she would spread a little concealer under her tired eyes, but she had been so well rested recently that it wasn't needed, so she applied a little mascara, eyeliner and lip gloss before heading back downstairs. But not before giving herself a pep talk in the mirror.

"Be cool, Henderson. She's sweet, maybe a little too sweet for you. Yes, she trusted you enough to share her story with you. Yes, you think her ex is an absolute asshat of a human for hurting her the way she did. But rushing into anything right now could be a bad idea. It's okay to admire her from afar, or even a little up close… but that's it. Admire her. Be her friend."

Liv took in her reflection, noticing the subtle changes in her body since arriving here. Her skin had taken on a little tan from the hours she spent outside on the porch swing reading or working. The dark circles that usually sat under her eyes had almost all but disappeared and she attributed that to the amazing sleep she was having as a result of the fresh air. But what she noticed the most was the smile painted on her face, a gift from the beautiful blonde waiting for her downstairs, the one with the electric touch and deep brown eyes that felt like home.

She had spent so long telling herself that there was absolutely no way in any universe anything could happen between her and Honey. They were friends who drank cider on the attention starved deck of her grandfather's patio and watched the stars in silence. They were friends who ate lasagne and then lay on the floor of Honey's living room in a carb coma, listening to slowed down piano covers of Paramore songs. It didn't matter that there was a certain spark of attraction between them. It didn't matter that the silence between them was never awkward but instead comforting in a way Liv had never known before. Honey was off limits. She was a wonderfully kind person who had offered Liv instantaneous friendship and asked for nothing in return. Liv had reasoned with herself countless times, that she should stop this almost infatuation before it got her into trouble, but her libido was putting up quite the resistance. She willed those thoughts away as she headed for the stairs.

"Do I look okay?" Liv asked, as she reached the bottom of the stairs with a bounce. Figuring them to be the best choice of footwear for a garden party, she slipped her feet into her blue checkered Vans.

"You look good. I mean, you look okay. I mean–"

Honey tripping over her own words was amusing, and Liv had to admit she really enjoyed how the younger woman floundered, before blowing out a breath of embarrassed exasperation. She could either let Honey continue with her adorable outburst and enjoy how the blonde's cheeks would warm and her breath stagger, or she could mirror a little of that back. Liv thought it was so brave to stand in front of someone you had a crush on and be so transparent. Not only brave but it was both bold and sexy and Honey was the epitome of sexy, standing there in a dress that had Liv longing to slide her hands underneath it.

"Just okay? Wow, never had a woman compliment me like that before," she said and the panic that rushed Honey's face had Liv reaching out to calm her down. "Relax Honey, I didn't mean to make you uncomfortable, I was just teasing you."

"Oh!"

As she watched Honey steady herself, pushing her hands down her dress, smoothing out invisible creases, she wondered what she would see if their eyes met. Would her eyes reflect the tone of her voice? Would Honey's resolve melt like ice cream on a warm day? Honey continued to straighten her dress, tugging it down around her thighs and Liv wanted to tell her to stop trying to hide, that there was no need to hide because she saw her and what she saw, she really, really liked.

"Shall we go?" she asked instead, clearing her throat and waving a hand toward the entrance.

Honey nodded and they shuffled awkwardly towards the hallway. Liv pulled back a step, giving herself a moment to admire the gentle sway of her neighbors' hips and the way her dress moved with each step she took. A smirk formed on Liv's face as she watched the blonde curls bouncing around her neighbors freckled shoulders. Everything about this woman was vibrant, warm and so welcoming. She longed to sink into Honey, even with the uncertainty of what would happen as a result of doing so.

As they reached the end of the hallway, Liv swiped the key from a glass bowl situated on a small table next to a wooden coat stand. Clasping the cold metal in her warm palm she moved towards the front door and her body connected with something solid. Her hands shot up in front of her, reaching out to steady herself and then she realized exactly what she had bumped into. Honey's back was pressed against her front and her hands were resting on Honey's hips. Her warm, soft, perfectly curved hips.

An internal war waged in Liv and while her thumbs itched to rub soothing circles over the thin fabric of Honey's sundress, her head was yelling at her to take a step back, apologize and remember that this woman was her neighbor. That this invitation meant nothing other than Honey just being friendly. That she had overstepped a boundary and there was no way that anything could happen between them.

Honey was still transitioning through feelings that had occured as the result of a woman who never truly appreciated her, and she would be remiss to ignore that. Liv also was still dealing with feelings from ending her own situation and so she knew she should be rational. She told herself to take a step back and stop all the thoughts running through her mind, but rationality has no place in lovers' laments. Honey was a book Liv wanted to curl up with, a story she wanted to get lost in. She reasoned with herself that if she felt Honey flinch at her touch she would remove her hands from their resting place and apologize but when Honey glanced back over her shoulder at Liv and actually smirked, then leaned once more into Liv's touch, she found herself breathless.

"Just so we're clear, you look more than okay. You're beautiful," Honey said as she opened the door, stepped out into the sunlight and left Liv standing in the doorway, completely and utterly breathless.

***

The first thing Liv noticed about Honey's parents home was its size. The house was situated deep into Verity Vale, but not far enough they'd been in the car long. A few minutes on a winding road had given way to a gravel drive that sounded their arrival with the crunching of tires. The home was much bigger than her grandparents' and was absolutely, no question about it, made with a large family in mind.

As they stepped out of the truck and into the midday sun, it was evident to Liv that the Rosenbergs' had absolutely lived up to the purpose of such a grand home. She could hear a generator buzzing, no doubt providing air to the giant inflatable bounce house that currently echoed the squeals of delight from so many small children that Liv couldn't guess exactly how many there were. The smell of charcoal, fresh cut grass and cotton candy permeated the air, wrapping around her like a warm welcome in a place she knew she was a stranger.

Liv readied herself as Honey reached into the back of the car, pulling out a small pile of wrapped gifts. Panic washed over her as she realized she had turned up at the Rosenberg home without not only a gift for the birthday girl, but without a bottle of wine for Liv's parents. Her mother's voice echoed in her ears, scolding her for her rudeness.

'A Henderson never shows up to a function empty handed, there are appearances to keep up, impressions to be made and reputations to uphold'.

Liv wasn't sure what to do, sure it wasn't a large distance to go, if they were to head back to one of the stores that sat in the heart of Verity. But it would be unfair to expect Honey to drive her back and potentially risk missing part of her niece's day. She cursed at herself for being so distracted by her libido and the way Honey's sundress clung to her hips, that she had forgotten her manners.

"Are you okay?" Honey's warm voice washed over Liv, pausing her self-deprecation and causing her to look over the hood of the car.

"I didn't bring a gift." Liv stated apologetically, looking around nervously.

"It's okay. She's not going to notice the lack of gift Liv, she's six. She's going to be more interested in the prospect of making a new friend," Honey assured her, kicking the car door closed and rounding the vehicle. "If it's really bothering you. Here."

Honey nodded at Liv to hold out her hands and when she complied, tilted the top most gift into her waiting palms.

"I can't take credit for one of your gifts Honey."

"Of course you can. It's a set of books she's been hinting at for a while." Honey began to walk towards the house and Liv followed suit. The gentle kindness Honey continued to show her was a constant surprise for Liv, who was absolutely certain that in all her time living in her apartment in the city, she hadn't so much as said hello to her neighbors.

"So the birthday girl belongs to Kyla?" Liv asked, trying to remember the brief family rundown Honey had given her one night during their hangouts on the porch.

"Yes. Ariella is number three in what will soon be six," Honey smiled as she spoke and Liv panicked momentarily.

She repeated the little girl's name in her head over and over until she was sure it was cemented. The last thing she wanted was to make a bad impression on Honey's family. She wasn't sure why this moment felt so important, but it did. "Don't worry I won't expect you to remember all the names. We are a pretty big family and there will be cousins and aunts and uncles… and I'm scaring you a little right?"

With each step they took Liv found herself even more enamored by Honey. The way she smiled through her awkward ramblings made Liv want to reach out and hold her hand. Steady her and remind her to breathe, or better yet, pull her close and kiss away the nerves that flew from her lips and into the already noisy air. But friends didn't kiss, at least not newly minted friends as they were.

She shook her head reassuringly.

"No. Not at all. I'm looking forward to it. You're sure I'm dressed okay?"

She felt Honey's eyes scan her body, the warmth of her stare blanketed Liv protectively and made her feel wonderful. She cast her mind back to the conversation they had engaged in the other night, about how Honey's ex left without looking back and Liv found herself baffled, because having known Honey and having been in her presence, she couldn't imagine looking anywhere else but directly at her. Honey was beauty personified. The cute upturn in her button nose that begged to be kissed, the freckles that dotted her cheeks, daytime constellations Liv longed to study and her lips, well Liv hadn't been able to stop thinking about what it would be like to taste them, no matter how hard she tried.

"It's a six year old's party, you're going to spend the entire time in the garden fending off hands covered in icing and slushie kisses."

Kisses. There went her imagination again.

What Liv wouldn't give to just lean in and press herself softly to Honey. To whisper against her lips and tell her all her secrets from between sheets and eyelids. Honey was deep water Liv wanted to dive headfirst into and she honestly didn't care if she was strong enough to swim. She was certain that if she made a move, took a step towards Honey and reached for her, that they'd find themselves undoubtedly coming together. There was a danger in that though.

Liv knew of the instability of uncertainty and yet she longed to be a little selfish. It was obvious that Honey was a little attracted to her, she could see it in the way Honey's freckles dotted the pink blush of attraction whenever Liv caught her looking. But neither of them were ready to act upon it yet, their earlier interaction at the house clear evidence of that.

"You think they'll like me?" Liv asked, climbing the wooden steps to the front door and pausing briefly.

"Yeah," Honey said, certainty lacing her voice before giving way to nerves that forced the rest of her declaration out in a shy whisper, "I mean, I like you. I might be biased though."

Honey removed a hand from under the gift pile she had carried out of the car and wrapped her hands around the door handle, pushing it open and motioning for Liv to follow her inside.

The staircase was wrapped with a flower garland, soft pinks and yellows accentuated the shabby chic decor of the interior. The hallway was full of shoes in various sizes, some placed neatly on a shoe rack, others in piles, the first sign of disarray in what looked like a pristine home. Liv glanced around the walls and saw the familiar faces of Honey's sisters' staring back at her from various stages in their formative years. She also noted some faces she didn't know, but who were unmistakably Honey's nieces and nephews, as every one of them shared her nose.

They moved further into the large house, following the sound of laughter and music, until they reached the kitchen. Standing at the island in the middle of the open space was a girl of around seventeen, her long brown hair pulled back into two french braids that ended at her waist. She was crouched over, a book in her hand, her face laced with concentration. Honey slid the gifts she was carrying onto the island and the young girl looked up, a smile breaking the seriousness that Liv knew all too well came as a result of being an older sibling.

"Hi Aunty Buzzy." When she spoke, her voice was soft and sweet just like her aunts. Liv wondered if that was a result of trying to avoid being seen and heard or if it was simply how girls here were. Sweet, unassuming and entirely all too entrancing. The teen's green eyes flickered over at her and when she smiled, Liv returned a smile of her own.

"Hey Lissy," Honey began, stepping around the counter and throwing her arms around the younger girl.

Liv watched Lissy lean in for a hug that made her a little jealous. She knew it was silly to feel this way but she wished she could feel, even for a split second what it was like to be in Honey's embrace. Honey pulled back and glanced back at Liv, pulling her back into the interaction.

"This is Liv… Liv, this is Sasha's daughter, Lissy."

Liv lifted her hand to wave and offered a smile to the teen who returned it instantly. Honey glanced around the room, searching for something.

"Where are the guys?"

"They're out back playing with the archery set up, naturally."

Glancing over at the double french doors Liv could see now the decking was overflowing. People stood in small groups, clinking glasses and clutching beers as the conversation filtered through the room. Small children weaved between the scattered adults, some waving foam swords, others simply squealing with delight and excitement. Even though the house itself was smaller than Liv's parents, the Rosenbergs' garden was much bigger. Back home they had a tennis court that doubled as a basketball court but it wasn't spacious enough for something as cool as an archery set up.

"You're not out there showing them how it's done?"

Liv noted that when Honey asked this question, pride lacing her voice, Lissy shook her head and glanced off to the side sadly. She wasn't sure what that was about but there was definitely something that Lissy wasn't telling her aunt. Liv wagered the teen hadn't told anyone, because she looked like she was carrying the weight of the world on her shoulders.

"Maybe later. Let them have their fun."

Honey seemed satisfied with that answer and so turned to catch Liv's attention, making sure to keep her involved in the conversation.

"Lissy has Olympic hopes in archery."

This statement caused another almost painful look to appear on the teen's face, lingering behind the fake smile she was wearing. It was a microexpression well hidden to people who hadn't known this feeling. Lissy was doing a fantastic job of hiding the discomfort she felt at this conversation but Liv had spent so many years wearing her own discomfort daily and so she recognized it instantly.

"Doesn't seem fair to use my skills at a child's birthday party," Lissy mumbled, bending the top of her page, ear-marking her place before closing the book in her hands. "Besides, there's a *Paint Your Own* table with a butterfly shaped mug I've had my eyes on since I got here."

"Oh, I love to paint!"

Liv's declaration caused Honey to glance over at her in surprise, "You do?"

She had been relatively quiet since walking through the door, taking in the home Honey had grown up in. Seeing the sadness in the teen's eyes, compelled Liv to try and befriend Lissy. Teenagers were ridiculously hard to connect with at the best of times, regardless of how nice they were underneath all that angst. The truth was, although she hadn't lied and she did enjoy it, Liv hadn't painted in the longest time. At home any free time she had was spent either reading material to include in her lectures, working on her books or, something she considered an ongoing lifetime project, making her way through the fiction section of the New York Times bestsellers list. Something she was absolutely way behind in since her arrival in Verity, but something she also didn't mind when the reason was as cute as Honey.

"Surprised?" She arched an eyebrow at Honey, and threw her a cheeky smile. Honey returned the gesture, her smile reaching her warm eyes.

"You're a constant surprise, Liv."

"In a good way?"

"In the best possible way."

This response warmed something in Liv, the ebbs and flows of attraction began a rising tide in her stomach. Honey's welcome stare moved over her slowly before becoming distracted.

"Ah, here comes the birthday girl!"

A small blonde-haired child squealed her way across the room. She was dressed in a sundress that mimicked Honey's own and Liv's heart sped up at the sight. How much Honey loved children was very much evident in the way she bent at the waist and threw her arms open for the small version of herself to fall into. Liv felt her heart anchor into her stomach, sitting like a ship called *Possibility* on the waves already crashing inside her, willing to brave turbulence in hopes of new land. As Honey scooped up the little girl and nuzzled her nose, Liv felt herself falling.

"Aunt Buzzy, you're here!"

Small hands cupped Honey's heart shaped face, delicate touches that Liv longed to feel for herself. It was clear to see the adoration pass between them both and while she felt a little like she was intruding on such a sweet moment, she allowed herself a second to take it all in.

"Hey there sweet girl, you've grown again."

As she moved a hand back and forth from Honey's forehead to her own, the small girl giggled, "Birthday inches…"

"More like birthday miles. I think you're taller than me and you know what that means."

"When I'm bigger than you I owe you a Jetpack. On account of all the ones you've given me."

"Precisely!" Honey nodded and Liv giggled at the thought of the tiny girl carrying her aunt on her back. Honey lowered her niece back to the floor and Liv felt her own insides warm when deep blue eyes glanced over at her, a gap toothed smile proffered instantly.

"Hey, you brought a friend!"

"I did, I hope that's okay? Ari, this is my friend Liv."

Liv smiled as the tiny blonde stepped towards her and took her in with silent reverence. She knew that children were known to reserve judgment on adults or situations they were unfamiliar with. Sometimes they would hide behind their parents legs, watch cautiously from a safe distance until they were certain they were safe to interact. Honey's niece was clearly an exception to the rule. Instead of tentative steps and glances from behind the safety of her aunt, Ariella continued to close the distance between them and then smiled widely.

"You're pretty," she said, wrinkling her nose in a way that had Liv convinced that all of the Rosenberg girls had cornered the market on adorable mannerisms.

Before she could thank the smaller girl, a stampede of tiny feet pounded the floor followed by a cacophony of high pitched declarations of excitement. A blur of blonde and mousy brown hair rushed past Liv, surrounding Honey's legs, hands grabbing at her until she dissolved into a tangled mass on the floor. The look on

Honey's face as she descended was a mixture of embarrassment and a sultry shyness that made Liv's heart flutter against her ribcage.

"Excuse me while I make a further fool out of myself," Honey apologized, from her position on the ground. She disappeared under the mass of children until the only sign of her being there was her unmistakable giggle that Liv felt in her core.

This is what she wanted. This was what she longed for. This feeling of family. Obvious displays of affection that filled a room with so much love and joy you couldn't help but succumb to it. Liv needed it more than she needed air.

When she thought about her future and all she had put on hold, it was becoming so much more apparent that she had been wrong to settle. The life she had been living wasn't ever going to be enough. She had given too much of herself away trying to make love stay. Loving someone so much that you change who you are to fit into their narrative means you become a story untold. Liv didn't like the idea of that. It sat heavy within her, weighing her pages down like a paperweight of expectations. She was a page unturned, a book held open and destined to never be finished. More than anything she wanted to control her own ending, but when you've been with someone for so long it's easy to allow their life to become yours. You become a shadow. Standing here in this house, with all of this vibrancy and life around her, Liv's internal pen was poised and ready to write a new chapter.

Her chest filled with adoration as Honey emerged from beneath the hands that tickled her, humming a low buzzing noise. Instantly all the children began to find their footing and scream loudly as they ran away. Honey got to her feet, smoothed down her sundress and then, holding her arms out in front of her began to take large steps towards them, grabbing wildly at the air. When she caught the smallest little girl, who wriggled in a half-hearted attempt at getting free, Honey made a munching noise and pretended to eat her.

Liv's own laugh crept up on her like the first wave in open waters, her body vibrating with excitement and nervousness. She adored this glimpse into her neighbors personality and adored how unabashed she was when it came to showing love and affection for her niblings. If Liv hadn't already known she felt something for Honey, this would have definitely tipped the scale. Still clutching the giggling girl to her chest, Honey made her way outside to where the rest of the children lingered, eyes cautiously fixed on their aunt.

"Buzzy is going to be a while," a voice chimed and Liv smiled as Sasha approached them, wrapping an arm around her daughter's shoulders and pulling her close. "Can I get you a drink?"

Liv flipped her gaze away from Honey to Sasha and thought she saw a smirk of knowing on her face. Nodding her head in thanks, she followed Sasha and Lissy through the kitchen and double doors into the open air of the backyard where Sasha led them over to a large table filled with bottles of every liquor imaginable.

Before she could even decide what to drink she could hear Marcie's disgust at the fact that the drinks were being poured into red plastic cups. She would have complained that they were not in college and adults should never drink from a plastic vessel after the age of twenty two. Liv didn't know what had happened to make Marcie as full of high expectations as she was, she wished she would lower her bar a little and just enjoy life more. Like Honey, whose blonde hair was swaying over her face, sticking to the sheer gloss she had coated her luscious lips in. Honey who didn't care about the fact that she was now pretending to be some sort of child eating monster in front of her neighbor and potential crush. Honey, who was now running barefoot on the grass, her sundress inching up her thighs in the most delicious way, causing Liv's gaze once more to falter.

She cleared her throat and flicked her gaze back to the table.

"You'll explain to me the whole, 'Buzzy' thing?" she asked, her mind trying to focus on Sasha, who popped some lime wedges into a shaker and then reached for a spoon of brown sugar.

"Oh, that! It's silly, really. Buzzy Bees... Bees make honey." Lissy replied, shrugging her shoulders and glancing off to where Honey had her arms full once again, with small, adoring humans.

"That makes sense."

It was fitting that someone as adorable as Honey Rosenberg had a cute nickname, to go with her soft laugh, entrancing wide-eyed gaze and unapologetic authenticity. Watching her throw herself around the floor with her niblings, Liv loved that Honey wasn't obsessed with how she appeared to anyone else. She lived life in a way that was real and raw. She was an open book with all her pages visible and filled with life and Liv wanted to be a chapter in that book.

Heck, if she was honest, she wanted to take up a little space on every page that came after this. Embed herself in this beautiful woman's narrative.

Loud laughter drew Liv's focus and she wondered if Honey's laugh would become part of her forever soundtrack. If Honey's smile would become a permanent feature on the cover of Liv's story. She wondered if Honey's words would weave into the dialogue of her life. Words yet to be written but waiting, unbidden for the right time.

She wanted that, she wanted it all. Putting it simply, she wanted Honey.

As Sasha shook the metal canister vigorously, Liv chased thoughts of forever from her mind, hoping it hadn't been apparent on her face. She felt a little like her life, her entire existence almost, was being shaken up at the hands of a Rosenberg.

Sasha poured the contents of the shaker into a cup containing what Liv had seen was vodka, fresh passionfruit and ice and handed it to her. Thanking her she brought it to her lips and took a sip. Her tongue slid along her lower lip capturing the sweet remnants of pulp that lingered there. The drink was deliciously sweet without being too overpowering. It danced over her taste buds, awakening them instantly. She brought the cup to her lips and took another sip while her gaze flitted across the backyard filled with noise, searching for Honey.

She had come to Verity Vale to find herself, to find links to a past that she hoped would explain the ever growing emptiness she had harbored for so long, but all it had taken was time, and a soft smile, to make Liv feel more complete than she had ever known.

Chapter 13

Honey

"The worker bees have finally allowed the Queen to leave the hive," Honey mock complained around ten minutes later as she made her way across the yard to where Liv was sitting at the crafts table with Lissy and Sasha. Liv was currently painting a porcelain figure that on inspection looked a lot like an elephant, only this elephant wasn't your standard grayscale. Liv had re-imagined this one in a gaudy mix of fuschia and violet.

"Are you having fun there with your pink elephant?" Honey teased.

Liv leaned her head back, took in the figurine before her and laughed, "I hadn't even thought of that."

Honey moved around the table and sat herself down in the space next to Liv, hoping it had been left unoccupied intentionally. Lissy, who sat opposite Liv, was entirely focused on the butterfly mug she had expressed wanting earlier. Her tongue peeked out of the corner of her mouth as she steadily guided her brush over the wing shaped handles.

"Are you going to join us?" Liv asked, nodding towards a foldable wooden table an arms reach from them, which housed the plain porcelain figures for painting.

"Maybe. I could use a drink first though, the Queen needs some sugar."

"Here, have some of this. It's really sweet."

Liv pushed her cup across the table, towards Honey and she wasted no time reaching out her hand for the refreshment. After running around like a madwoman for what she knew was minutes but had felt like hours, she was in desperate need of refueling. It was like that during family get-togethers though. Honey would walk into any environment and instantly be inundated with hugs, kisses and find herself the center of so much attention.

She brought the cup to her lips, the smell of lime instantly filtered through and she wrinkled her nose in recognition. Caipiroska, her sisters go to drink and the scent of one too many drunken nights in the company of her family. Honey guessed by the gentle blush that had settled on Liv's cheeks that she had ingested at least two of these sweet but silently lethal cocktails. Sasha never went easy on the vodka, even when they were younger.

Honey recalled the night of her twenty-first birthday when rather than go out with her friends she had opted for a night in the backyard, fire pit burning and curled up in the lawn chairs with her sisters. She had intended to keep the night low key and take it easy, of course it wasn't the first time she had drank alcohol. Her high school best friend, Kelly Morris had goaded her into taking a sip of whiskey once during a sleepover, but it had burned Honey's chest and she wasn't sure she enjoyed it. In fact she wasn't sure if she would ever enjoy any alcoholic drink after that, which she had decided would be perfectly fine with her. Sasha had explained to her, after hearing this, that maybe she just hadn't found the right drink and so, sitting in her pajamas in the backyard of their parents home, they had a cocktail night. The first Caipiroska Honey consumed went down smoothly, it was so sweet and light she barely knew it was alcoholic. But by her fourth she was definitely aware and so was the lawn chair she had stood on as she belted out the lyrics to Misery Business by Paramore at the top of her lungs.

She leant closer to Liv and handed back the cup without taking a sip.

"You know, those things are lethal. Don't let her ply you full of them unless you want to forget everything. I swear she uses at least triple the amount of vodka required." Honey teased and Liv's eyes widened at the contents of the cup before shifting over to where Sasha sat smirking with the same drink-infused blush on her face.

"I do no such thing. It's definitely no more than a double. I can't say for sure though, I free-pour these days," Sasha snorted and raised her cup in the air towards Liv who mirrored the gesture. Honey shook her head.

She was glad to see that while she had been heavily occupied by her nieces and nephews, someone had taken care of her guest. She had felt bad for almost instantly abandoning Liv, but she couldn't say no to all those cute faces. It's how she secured her favorite aunt status and she wasn't ever going to relinquish that title not for anyone. No matter how beautiful they were and ugh, Liv was so damn beautiful.

Liv looked so comfortable, Honey thought, so at ease sitting in the busy backyard surrounded by the entire Rosenberg clan and their extended family. She definitely didn't seem out of place.

When Honey had asked Liv to come along she hadn't expected her to agree. Years of getting a solid no from Andie, when she asked her to family events, had left Honey with a residual amount of anxiety. She had felt it balling her chest that morning as she had crossed the field to get to the big house, but the idea of spending time with Liv was exciting and so she had pushed through her anxiety and put a little trust in hope.

She knew her family could be a little too much, they were loud and large, they laughed and sang, but they were her everything, her foundation. They were a large part of the reason she had never even contemplated leaving Verity. The safety and support she felt would always exist, but it wouldn't ever feel as strong from a distance. Sure things weren't always great with Kyla but, Honey knew deep down that her sister's love for her was currently clouded by her own stress.

"Aunty Buzzy, come play hide and seek with us!" came a voice from over by the table filled with snacks in every color of the rainbow, sugar central, as it had become affectionately known.

Glancing over she could see the twins Liam and Josh hanging off the arms of their older cousin Gray, having obviously roped him into playing, albeit reluctantly. Gray was a good sport with the little ones, he always had been despite the age gap. He was a very quiet and stoic teenager, with long brown hair that tickled his now very defined jaw. He had grown up before Honey's eyes and each time she saw him she wished time would slow down.

Clad in jeans and a hoodie emblazoned with a band Honey had never heard of, he was every inch the emo teenager that Sasha had been back in her day. It always made Honey smile at how much like her sister, Gray was.

Surprisingly, for all her sweetness now, Sasha hadn't always been the rational level-headed sister. She had been the one to rebel against all their parents' rules growing up, loud music, staying out after dark and there was even a guy on a motorbike with a mohawk at one point. During their disagreements back then, their mom always told Sasha one day she would meet her match, and Gray was as close as it seemed she was going to get. Honey felt a little like Sasha had gotten off lightly though, because Gray adored his little cousins and despite his lacking conversational skills these days, he was actually really sweet.

Honey laughed, as Gray removed his headphones and wrapped them around his phone. He shrugged his shoulders and threw a look her way, one that said *'if i'm playing, you are'*. She turned to Liv who was clutching her paintbrush in one hand and her half filled cup in the other, not wanting to leave her again.

"What do you say? Are you up for finding a quiet space for a few minutes?" Honey asked, and her stomach turned a somersault as Liv's eyebrows rose a little.

A salacious grin spread across Liv's face as she quickly dropped the paintbrush to the table. Luckily there was a wipeable sheet over the table, typical of Kyla to think of damage control.

She stood up from the table and looked down at Liv, allowing herself a moment to appreciate the woman in front of her, who was in turn –or so it seemed– appreciating Honey too.

"I have to warn you, I haven't played hide and seek in a long time, not officially." Liv confessed, standing up and brushing her hands over her clothes. Something flashed behind her eyes that made Honey pause. Maybe later tonight, if she could convince Liv to extend their time together, they would sit outside again and have drinks while watching the stars and she would ask what that look was all about.

Liv had started opening up a little to Honey, two nights ago. Honey now knew that Liv was a professor of Literature at a small liberal arts college, just outside of the city where she lived. This wasn't at all a surprise to her, knowing that Marvin too had been a lover of literature. Honey had told her as such and it had caused tears to well up in Liv's eyes. She had apologized for upsetting her, not realizing how little Liv knew of her grandparents until she revealed that this trip was her attempt at finding parts of them, and in the process a part of herself. It saddened Honey that Liv hadn't known her grandparents, because from what she had already seen Liv was proving to be just as wonderful as they were. It pained her to know that Liv felt like, in not knowing them, she didn't know herself either and so she decided to do all she could to help Liv on her journey. She promised to tell her everything she knew about Marvin and Bea, retell every story from her past that they starred in, it was the least she could do.

Honey had this urge to fix everything for the woman in front of her and do all she could to make her smile, because when Liv smiled, well Honey wasn't sure all the stars in the sky could ever compete with that view.

Impatient cries of 'hurry up' rang from across the yard as children scattered everywhere, while one of the twins stood with his hands over his eyes counting down loudly from thirty.

Honey began scanning the distance, eyes wide as she noted the places on the property where the rest of her nieces and nephews had gone into hiding. Liam had begun climbing the treehouse situated in the large oak at the back of the yard, so that was out. Gray had hold of three year old Savannah's hand and was running, as best as he could with her stubborn resistance, towards the bounce house. Not the most solid place to hide, but definitely the most fun. She caught a glimpse of a bare leg slipping under the cloth draped over the large table where the food had been spread out. Ariella had always been a little smarter than the rest and while she was really adept at finding the best hiding spaces, she definitely wasn't as good as Honey. She had grown up here and spent most of her childhood hiding outside from her sisters and their friends.

She had no desire to leave her guest alone again this afternoon and so she already knew where they would go. Somewhere the children wouldn't dare to look, at least not until they were desperate. A place guaranteed to buy Honey and Liv a moment's reprieve.

"Do you trust me?" Honey asked, holding out her hand, her eyes wide as she swallowed a 'please' that threatened to give away her need for the other woman.

Liv nodded and placed her hand in Honey's, an act of certainty that caused them both to inhale sharply. Shy smiles appeared on their faces as their fingers effortlessly entwined. A modicum of fear that Liv would retreat and let go of her hand crept in and so Honey began to cross the yard in the opposite direction to the children. She headed for the overgrowth at the side of the yard, where her dad obviously hadn't gotten to yet, in his normally meticulous gardening plan.

Pulling Liv carefully through and behind the shrubbery, they came to a stop and Honey gave Liv's hand a gentle tug, wordlessly instructing her to crouch down. They watched and listened carefully as Josh counted out the last remaining numbers before spinning on his heels, scanning the entire yard and heading right for the treehouse. *Poor Liam*, Honey thought, *sometimes that twin telepathy thing really sucked.*

Her heart pounded against her chest as adrenaline raced through her. She would have loved to have passed it off as simple excitement from the game, or overexertion due to being the Queen in a hive of very excited worker bees. But Honey knew it had nothing to do with any of that. Honey knew the cause for her racing heart was the blue eyed owner of the hand that still lingered in her own.

She looked down at where they were joined, hands clasped between bent knees. Holding onto Liv felt exactly like she imagined it would, like being anchored safely to the ground, when her body was determined to float. Honey swallowed the lump that had formed in her throat at noticing the proximity of their bodies and wondered if Liv could hear her heart pounding from where she crouched. It felt like the baseline of a song she wanted to slow down, but she didn't know how to; her world was turning almost too fast.

A staggered breath stumbled from her mouth and she poked out her tongue, wetting her lips. This woman had stolen not only Honey's attention but all moisture from her body. Well, not all of it, not entirely, because Honey could feel a warmth pooling at her center. Her thighs pressed together in an attempt to stop her very obvious arousal from coating them any further.

"So," Honey ushered her words free from their prison in her throat, being careful to remain quiet, lest they get caught "you having fun?"

She glanced over in the direction of the children, glad they had chosen to hide in the entirely opposite direction. The last thing she wanted right now was anyone interrupting whatever this feeling was filling the space between them.

Liv smiled directly at her and a stray strand of jet black hair slip forward to cover her face. Honey instinctively reached out to tuck it back behind Liv's ear, but quickly stopped herself.

"I'm having the best time. Thank you for inviting me."

Liv's words were genuine and Honey marveled at how absolutely different their interactions were, compared to those she had with Andie. Part of her reasoned it was because Liv was just a friend and as a result, had zero obligations to do anything out of a need to appease her. But the fact that Liv actively chose to accompany her today spoke volumes about who she was as a person. She was absolutely the type of person Honey wanted in her life and each time she looked at Liv it was becoming harder to deny the fluttering in her stomach.

"Even being stuck in this bush, waiting for the worker bees to find us?" she asked, continuing to look between the broken branches of the shrubbery to where Josh had just discovered Gray and a squealing Savannah.

She tried to avoid making eye contact with Liv when she asked this, and acknowledged it was because she wasn't sure if she wanted to see it when Liv's eyes told a truth her mouth refused to speak. Honey knew what it felt like to hear the words you wanted to, but to see something entirely different reflected in someone's gaze. She wasn't sure she could handle that again.

Something about the lingering silence between them tugged at her though, her brain yelling at her to look and so she did. Pulling her warm brown eyes over to Liv's, what she saw there caused her to gasp. Liv was staring at her with heavy lids, a dreamy look on her face and she was smiling so earnestly that Honey wanted nothing else but kiss her.

A sudden gust of wind shook the foliage hiding them. Liv rocked gently on her feet and leaned further into Honey's side, squeezing her hand as she tried to maintain her footing. The effects of the Caipiroska undoubtedly kicking in. Liv giggled a little at her own lack of balance and a heat traveled the expanse of Honey's body at the sound.

"Especially this part. I haven't had this much fun in… I don't know how long. Seriously, thank you for this."

"I'd say you're welcome but you're going to get us caught if you keep giggling like that."

Liv's voice dropped to a whisper, the smile replaced by a more serious look as her eyebrows raised and sent another jolt of attraction right to Honey's center.

"Maybe you should help me stay quiet then," she suggested, tilting her head and smirking a little.

"Yeah?" Honey asked, breathlessly.

She was almost certain she understood exactly what it was Liv was asking of her, nevertheless, Honey loved to have things confirmed. After all, consent and communication was sexy, right?

When Liv nodded her head slowly but certainly, leaning further into Honey's space, she didn't waste any time closing the gap between them. Their lips came together softly, a whisper of a kiss that threatened to cause the light simmering attraction Honey felt, to boil over. Still holding Liv's hand, she brought her other hand to the side of Liv's face and cupped her cheek, eliciting a breathy moan that she felt against her mouth. She parted her lips a little and felt Liv's tongue swipe at her bottom lip. As she slid her hand around and up the nape of Liv's neck, fisting her hair, Liv moaned again. She was reactive and Honey loved that she wasn't afraid to let it show, but she most definitely didn't want to be interrupted right now.

"Shhh they'll find us," Honey whispered against Liv's mouth, pulling back a touch and noticing her eyes were closed and her well kissed lips were swollen, "I don't know about you but I *really* don't want to get caught right now."

Liv shook her head, not bothering to open her eyes. Instead she leant back towards Honey, her tongue deftly sweeping at her lips, no doubt tasting the remnants of their kiss.

Glad they were on the same page, Honey pulled Liv in for another kiss. This time the gentle movements of first kisses gave way to an insatiable hunger. Honey hadn't been kissed in so long, in fact, if asked, she would ashamedly admit to being a little touch starved. So much so, that when Liv dropped her knees to the ground for more solid purchase, letting go of her hand and wrapping both her arms around Honey's hips, she felt her entire being melt into Liv's touch without caution. Her rational mind was silenced by the absolute need to lose herself in this woman. She lowered her own knees to the ground, steadying herself, not bothered about the dirt she knew would muddy her skin. Straightening herself, she moved further into Liv's embrace. When she felt Liv's thumbs rubbing at her hips she rolled herself into the touch, pleading silently for more. She loved how it felt to finally be kissing the woman she had been dreaming of since her arrival a few weeks ago. She loved how right it felt as their lips pressed against one anothers. Honey loved the taste of passionfruit and lime that lingered on Liv's tongue as it danced with her own, encouraging Honey to continue sucking on her tongue and below her waist her body was screaming for relief.

As if sensing this, Liv's hands began to slide around the curve of Honey's hips and down towards her ass, pulling her firmly against her. Every nerve in Honey's body stood to attention as goosebumps brailled her bare skin. She stroked her dexterous fingers up Liv's spine, over her clothes and felt the taller woman press into her, moaning once more into her mouth.

Yeah, she absolutely didn't want to get caught just yet.

Chapter 14

Liv

They hadn't been found. The children had, eventually, given up looking for Honey and Liv, distracted from their game by the large blue birthday cake covered in sparklers rather than candles. Liv wasn't going to complain, not only did they win the game, but she felt like she had gotten a wonderful prize. Gosh, did Honey know how to kiss. After what must have been at least a half hour they had managed to come apart long enough to decide how they were going to head back to the party, without arousing too much suspicion about their whereabouts and actions.

Liv rocked back on her heels and brushed the dirt from the knees of her jeans, praising herself a little for choosing black ones that morning. Honey however wasn't so lucky, Liv chuckled at the dark marks on Honey's bare knees. She ran her fingers gently over the marred skin as Honey stood upright and Liv felt her still at the touch of her hand. She thumbed at the dirt, her fingers fluttering lightly against the backs of Honey's knees, just below the hem of her sundress.

"Oh!" a breathy whimper fell from Honey's mouth at the contact.

When Liv looked up from her position, the sight she saw before her took her breath away. This was an angle she definitely wouldn't mind viewing Honey from, over and over again. Her blonde curls cascaded over her shoulders that were rising and falling with each staggered intake of breath, her nostrils flaring slightly, a sure sign of how much she was affected by this.

Before she could stop herself Liv leaned forward and placed a gentle kiss on each knee, the weight of Honey's hands rested on her shoulders in an attempt to steady herself. Liv couldn't help but think about how right this all felt. How nothing about the woman above her felt unfamiliar. Honey Rosenberg was a book Liv had read before, although she couldn't remember when exactly. She was a story Liv knew with every fiber of her being, and with each touch, Liv felt the long forgotten words being revealed.

"We should go sing…eat cake," Honey breathed and Liv nodded, standing up straight and brushing herself off once more.

As they began to emerge from their hiding space, Liv scanned the partygoers cautiously. She knew that all it would take would be one comment from an adult about something happening between her Honey and her face would give everything away. She was very expressive, or so she had always been told growing up. Her mother once told her it was a shame she never quite got into acting, despite taking musical theater classes as a child, because her expressions would have won her an Oscar. The problem was that despite Liv's ability to run the gamut of emotions, she lacked the ability to disguise them. Once she felt them, they painted her face instantly and that often meant people knew exactly what she was thinking, good or bad. Like now, she mused, as Honey turned around to face her and reached out a hand for hers.

"You don't have to be so afraid. We are two consenting adults and I for one definitely don't regret it. Do you?"

Liv shook her head, her eyes wide enough that she hoped Honey could see the absolute certainty in her reaction, because she was *so* certain. She didn't regret a moment of their first kiss or the many that had followed after. Everything about that kiss and having Honey in her arms felt… right.

It had felt so good to finally touch her, and to have Honey's hands on her, too. As her fingers had traveled the length of Honey's spine, down to her hips she had the urge to slip underneath the light fabric of Honey's dress and caress the soft skin where Honey's thighs met her ass cheeks. Not sure if that was too much for a first kiss, she had refrained, she absolutely didn't want to get this wrong. This, what was happening with them, meant something. She wasn't entirely sure what just yet, but it felt… important.

Her brain had screamed at her to pick Honey up, her body longed to feel Honey's legs wrapped around her waist and as if she had read her mind, Honey had lifted one leg and anchored it on Liv's hip. Those thighs were absolutely becoming one of Liv's most favorite things about the blonde, second only to her freckles. She had been drawn to them the moment they crouched down. Sure she had spent time with Honey a lot recently, but they had never been close enough that Liv could see the supernovas of amber that burst in her eyes and count the smattering of brown flecks that danced over her soft skin. She had been thinking about kissing the constellations on Honey's skin, when she had been caught staring earlier.

They crossed the grass and headed towards the table where Honey's entire family stood, readying themselves to sing the Happy Birthday song. Liv followed an entire step behind Honey, running her eyes over her outfit, checking for signs of disturbance. She lifted a hand to her loose black locks and ran her fingers through her hair. It felt like her entire body was vibrating at such a high frequency, like a bottle of soda that had been shaken, her emotions threatened to spill out of her at first release. Even though she was happy at being here, and everyone had been so welcoming, she longed for more of the quiet stillness that came with Honey's lips on hers.

Lost in her reverie, Liv came to an abrupt stop when her front collided with Honey's back and her hand once again felt full.

"Is this okay?" Honey whispered over her shoulder, her eyes darting down to where their hands swung between them.

Something flickered in Honey's brown eyes, something akin to uncertainty, not the nervous kind that Liv could have attributed to this small act of affection in a public forum. She knew Honey's parents most definitely knew she was gay. No, this uncertainty was most definitely something Honey was carrying with her from her last relationship, maybe even the one before.

They had talked a few times about Honey's ex and how long they'd been together in the little cottage at the end of the hill, before it became too small to contain Andie's wanderlust. She had listened as Honey explained how Andie had crossed an ocean and never really looked back. She had the same look on her face right now and it almost broke Liv seeing this so early in whatever they were going to be. She needed Honey to know that she most definitely wanted to see what they could be.

"This is perfect," Liv confirmed with a smile, giving Honey's hand a gentle squeeze of reassurance. It didn't feel like enough of a connection and so she stepped to Honey and slipped an arm around her waist, holding her close.

Their moment was punctuated by a countdown led by Sasha, who then managed to coax the most enthusiastic Happy Birthday song from the family surrounding them. Liv smiled as she picked out Honey's soft melody amongst the others, even the way she sang was soothing. Liv joined in, for the first time in a long time not having to worry that her singing would embarrass anyone. It felt freeing.

Looking around at all the smiling, welcoming faces of the Rosenberg crowd, Liv allowed herself to entertain a notion of coming to Ariella's birthday party next year, and the year after that. As Honey leaned further into her, she knew she could happily stay in this moment forever. The joy that radiated was as warm as the sun that shone down on them, a family, a real family who liked each other. It was a novel notion, but one Liv yearned for.

Then out of the depths of her subconsciousness, a thought crept up on her and blossomed in her chest. A thought that Honey, who obviously liked children, could possibly have the same dreams that Liv did. That they could potentially share a vision of the future.

When Ariella leaned over the table to blow out the candles, her messy blonde hair held back by Kyla, Liv watched her glance up at where she stood with Honey and smile.

"I know my wish," she said, eyes still focused on Liv and her aunt. Liv felt Honey's head fall to her shoulder and without thinking she leaned in and kissed her hair softly. As everyone broke out into cheers and a few of the adults fired off small confetti canisters, Liv took a moment to make her own wish.

What was the harm, after all?

***

The drive back home was very different from the drive to the party. Liv no longer sat in her seat trying to focus on anything but the cute blonde driving and singing along to the playlist streaming from her phone. Instead she was sitting as close as she could without becoming a potential hazard, her hand on top of Honey's, resting over the gear stick.

"I had a really nice time," Liv admitted, meeting Honey's gaze as she flicked her eyes to the side quickly. "I think the birthday girl enjoyed her presents. You know her really well."

She recalled watching with a wide grin as Ariella had unwrapped the gifts Honey had brought along, beaming at her aunt from across the table before leaping from her seat and throwing herself once more into her arms. It had warmed Liv from the inside watching this exchange, the love between the two of them never more evident than when they both leaned into the other, their identical button noses pressing into each other as they laughed.

"She's easy to buy for. I just think about what I would have wanted as a child and get it for her. Ky always says I could pretend she's mine and no one would ever question it."

Liv's heart fluttered at that image. She knew she shouldn't have said the words that danced on her tongue, but they hit the air before she could stop them.

"Do you want that... kids, I mean?"

Heat rushed to her cheeks and she averted her gaze, suddenly finding the view from her window very interesting. They crawled the main street at a pace that allowed Liv to read the signs above the shops, in an effort to stall the race her mind was gearing up for. It was pointless, her mind ran the gamut anyway. Her insides churned with the countless possible responses she could imagine coming from Honey's mouth.

She was unsure why Honey's response felt important, but she could feel the weight of it surrounding her. It sat on her chest, holding her in place like the restraints on a rollercoaster she had opted to ride without thinking. She knew why she wanted to *ask*, because despite the small amount of time that had passed since she had arrived here in Verity, she had become somewhat attached to the beautiful blonde who she shared space and smiles with. Something burned deep inside her whenever brown met blue and it didn't matter the distance from which they passed one another.

During the early hours of the morning, she would watch the sunrise from the porch, while Honey danced the gravel path –almost silently– and slipped into her jeep, ready to head to the deli. During the night she would steal small glimpses of her neighbor under the expansive night sky, sipping beer with lips Liv had before now, longed to taste. Lip she now knew were encouraging, insistent, and were everything she had imagined them to be.

This spurred her on and gave Liv courage to speak again. She breathed out the question once more but this time with a little less vigor, "Do you want them?"

"I have a huge family. I love my nieces and nephews very, very much and I see how much joy they bring to my sisters," Liv could hear a waver in Honey's quiet tone, a sadness of sorts, almost hidden among the words, but flowering nevertheless. Liv wanted to know exactly what or who had planted that there because while she was never one for confrontation, she decided she could absolutely send them a very strongly worded email. She squeezed the hand that still held contact with Honey, an invisible string binding them together in that moment, trying to reassure her. Honey must have felt it, because she continued.

"I absolutely want that for myself. All of it, even the heartache that I know comes along with it. My parents never had it easy with us. Sasha was a bit of a wild child believe it or not. Kyla always had an argument for everything and I… well, I was a surprise. Their plans were scuppered a little when I arrived ten years after they had agreed they were done. My grandmother always called me "inaspettata", it means 'unexpected'."

Liv felt that.

Honey Rosenberg was definitely unexpected, in the most amazing of ways.

From the moment Liv had heard that her grandfather had died and had left her the house on the hill, she knew she would have to take this trip alone. In some ways, Liv had been alone for a while before she arrived in Verity, even though her life was full of people. She hadn't realized it until that first night as she curled up on the sofa in silence, hungry, cold and tired with no one she felt like she could call. She had known how difficult this would be, but had readied herself to spend some time alone. What she hadn't expected was Honey to come in and change all of that, to change her.

That first night, as Liv had tapped out a message on her phone telling Marcie to pack the rest of her things and have them dropped off at her parents home, she had accepted the end. She couldn't keep holding onto something that no longer existed, simply because she was afraid of what her life would look like without Marcie in it.

Honey had appeared on her porch that night and had slipped beneath her skin with the first contact they had made. With her laughter, smiles and her sweet generous nature, she warmed Liv more than any log fire could. Honey had been a literal wake up call, and Liv couldn't have conjured up what was happening with them, not even in her wildest dreams.

A hand squeezed her thigh and sure she had missed something, Liv looked up to see Honey smiling at her, from across the seat. The car was stationary, having pulled up, Liv now noticed, outside the quaint little cottage Honey called home.

"Do you want children?" Honey asked, putting the stick into neutral and lifting the handbrake. She turned in her seat and Liv felt the way Honey's gaze traveled the expanse of her body. "I feel like we have spoken so much about my life already. I practically monopolize our night time talks and so I feel like I haven't gotten around to truly getting to know you."

"I think you got to know me pretty well back at the party."

Liv couldn't help the flirtatious tone that wrapped itself around her words and when she watched Honey's chest stutter and a giggle pierce the air, she knew it had been well received. She leaned in a little closer, angling herself in the seat so they faced one another and she could really take in the woman across the Jeep from her.

It was true, their nights had mostly been spent talking about Honey's life here in Verity. Honestly, Liv had been thankful for Honey taking the lead in talking as it had removed some of the pressure she had felt the last few weeks since her grandfather had passed. In the beginning she wasn't sure she had the capacity to put into words everything she had been feeling, or even explain who she was when she wasn't here. Liv in the city was a far cry from Liv here, and if she was being completely honest with herself, she was still figuring out which she preferred.

Now, knowing her neighbor the way she did, she was certain that if she explained her situation to Honey she would be met with nothing but understanding. Honey would probably tell her that she was sorry, and offer her a soft smile and sympathy, which would wrap around Liv like a warm blanket. But she hadn't been quick to share that side of herself, the side of her. The side of her that had known for months there had been someone else in her girlfriend's life, and yet she had chosen to walk blindly through a relationship that wasn't working. She was afraid of having Honey, who looked at her with adoration and desire, see her as someone weak, someone pathetic. Someone who had failed at love.

Now however, sat looking into Honey's deep brown eyes, Liv felt the urge to tell her everything. To tell her about the secret phone calls and charges on a joint account that had been explained away plausibly in the beginning, or so Liv thought.To tell her how the distance between her and Marcie had felt like living, no... existing, around a Grand Canyon sized hole in what used to be a place they called home. She also wanted to tell Honey that since she had been here she had never felt so secure…so steady. But she also didn't want to scare her.

She was sure there was something occuring between them both, a candle ignited and burning low and slow. That kiss earlier had said more than their words ever had, and had Liv longing to watch the flame of their relationship flicker, as it gathered air and grew. But she also knew that the heaviness of what she had left behind could snuff it all out in an instant.

"I'd like to get to know you better." Honey admitted sheepishly, her voice soft and reverent.

Liv's heart fluttered at the confession, at the way the whispered words fell between them. Her hands itched with the need to reach out and touch Honey again and ground herself with the warmth radiating from the woman opposite. She ached to kiss her slowly, once more, and hope that everything she needed to say would pass between them, where their bodies touched. She wanted Honey so much and something inside her told her that Honey needed her too.

"Is that so?"

"Definitely. Did you want to stay and talk for a little while?"

"Just talk?" Liv teased.

Honey's eyes flickered up and fixed on her and Liv knew she was in trouble. She couldn't stop herself from flirting with Honey, and it was so unlike her. She wasn't this forward, ever. In actuality she was more the reserved one in her relationships.

Honey sucked her bottom lip into her mouth and trapped it between her perfectly straight teeth before sighing dreamily, "I think we can definitely do more than just talk."

***

"When you said we could do more than talk, this wasn't what I had in mind at all" Liv admitted, handing over a spatula to a very busy Honey.

The minute they had crossed the threshold of the small cottage, Honey had switched into business mode. She had scooped her hair up off her neck and wound an elastic around it that Liv hadn't noticed it on her wrist earlier, but made a mental note to see if that was a regular occurence. She admired a woman who was always prepared.

Honey had offered her a drink, and after pouring them both a glass of wine, had slipped an apron over her head before reaching into the drawer next to the sink and throwing another apron across the room, at Liv.

"I have a few things I like to make at home, for the deli."

Honey moved with precision around the cozy kitchen, plugging in her stand mixer and popping into it the butter and sugar she had pulled from the cupboard moments earlier. She stopped in her tracks and Liv watched as she spun on the spot, her eyes wide and a look of abject horror on her face.

"I'm so sorry. I know this isn't what you had in mind. I just thought if I got this out of the way now we could, I don't know, watch a movie or something. Talk."

Liv saw conflict and fear attack the beautiful smile Honey had worn moments earlier, pulling the corners of her extremely kissable lips into a frown that she longed to make disappear. So she did.

She stepped forward into Honey's space and slipped an arm around her waist. As she dipped her head and brushed their lips together softly, she could feel Honey's smile start to return. Her fingers played with the fabric tied into a bow at the dip of Honey's lower back, weaving into them in an attempt to hold her more solidly. She flicked her tongue against Honey's top lip, and Honey opened her mouth, deepening their kiss. She tasted like sunshine. Like summer days and warm blueberry muffins.

"It's okay," Liv breathed, pulling back a little but still holding onto the apron strings, "I was just teasing."

"Feel free to continue teasing if that's the way you apologize," Honey smirked, leaning forward and placing another kiss on Liv's lips before turning back to the stand mixer and flipping the switch.

Liv stepped off to the side and waited for further instructions. She had never seen someone command a space the way Honey did her kitchen. She moved with ease, not really measuring the ingredients but simply adding what *'felt right'*. The notion of putting trust in something just *'feeling right'* scared Liv a little. She hadn't truly been spontaneous in any aspect of her life since she left for England all those years ago, well that and this trip. She smiled as Honey spoke to Alexa and a soft piano melody echoed through the living area and made it's way into the kitchen.

Moving around the other side of the kitchen island, Liv pulled out a stool and slid onto it, waiting patiently for her instructions.

"Have you always enjoyed baking? Your mom seems like the 'baking mom' kind."

"Yeah. My mom loves to cook and she always made too much food growing up. She still does. But baking was not her forte. Actually, don't tell her I said this but, it still isn't."

Liv laughed at this admittance. True to the warning there had, in fact, been far too much food at the party. Even with Honey's rather large family in attendance. Honey's mom had almost had her leaving with countless trays of leftover potato salad. Honey had interjected and saved her by telling her mom, without thinking, that Liv had actually been sharing most of the meals Honey cooked for herself. This had caused eyebrows to raise, not just from Honey's mom but from her siblings too. Sasha had smiled at the admission, but the way Kyla looked at Liv sent shivers down her spine. She got the feeling that there wasn't much she could do to change that reaction and so she averted her gaze and thanked Mrs Rosenberg for her too kind offer.

"Your family seems great."

"They're wonderful." Honey tipped a small vial of brown liquid into the mixer and began sifting in some flour. "Tell me about your family. I mean I know about your grandparents, but what about your parents? Do you have any siblings?"

"There's not much to tell. I have one sibling, a brother. We don't really talk much. He has his life, a wife and a child. My mom is, well, different now. She used to be really soft spoken and kind. You know, the type of mom you could go to with all your problems and you knew she would fold you in her arms and let you cry it out. Now she's more interested in appearances than reality. She hasn't been herself in years. I think the last good memory I have of her was before I left for England, when I was eighteen"

"Wow! Did you go there for school?"

"Yeah, at first. I wanted to stay longer but an American teaching English Literature and Linguistics to Brits is a little ironic, don't you think?"

Honey giggled as she put the dishes into the sink and washed them over with the warm water she had filled the bowl with earlier. Liv stood and crossed the room, slipping beside her and dipping her own hands into the water. She hip checked Honey and took the sieve from her hands under the water.

"I got this, you carry on baking. Let me help."

"I didn't invite you in to do my dishes, Liv."

"I know, I want to help. Besides, if we are going to keep talking about my family I need the distraction. Trust me."

She felt Honey's warm breath on her neck as she planted a kiss just behind her ear. Her knees almost buckled and she pushed her hands against the bottom of the sink to discreetly steady herself. This woman had the power to bring her to her knees, and Liv resisted every urge screaming at her to do exactly that. She cleared her throat and swished her hands in the water as Honey stepped back over to the slowly churning mixer.

"I don't want to make you uncomfortable. We don't have to talk about this."

"It's okay. It's just my dad. He's got a lot of expectations that I don't quite live up to and one of those was that he expected me to be home by now."

"You live with your parents?"

"Oh no, just… not too far from them. Not that we see much of each other, if I can help it. He's not too fond of my career and life choices. Throw into the mix that I didn't just do as he said and get out of here and it makes for morning phone calls that I keep trying to avoid."

"I'm sorry, Liv. Is that what caused the sad look on your face earlier this morning?"

"He's pressuring me to find something of his mom's. At first I thought he wanted it for nostalgic reasons, but I don't think that man has a sentimental bone in his entire body. He just wants what he wants, because he wants it. I'm not packing up quick enough for him. My indecisiveness about the house is frustrating for him. He keeps telling me to find what he wants, put the house up for sale and come home. But honestly, I don't know where home is. I haven't felt at home in years."

Honey slid the muffin tin she had been filling, into the pre-heated oven and closed the door. Walking over to the sink she handed a cloth to Liv and urged her to dry her hands.

"Here, let's leave them to soak. Come sit. That's an awful lot for anyone to take on their shoulders."

Glancing down Liv realized she was shaking a little. Her chest rising and falling rapidly as something akin to frustration radiated through her body. A gentle touch on her forearm guided her out of the kitchen and over to the living room, she followed on autopilot.

"I'm sorry. I don't know why I let him get to me so much." Liv said, lowering herself onto the sofa. Honey slipped into the space next to her.

"You don't have to Atlas everything, Liv."

She raised her eyebrows at Honey's reference.

Cute, an amazing baker and smart, this woman was absolutely the whole package. Liv couldn't help but wonder, once more, what had caused her ex to leave. Maybe there was something lurking beneath the surface, but if there was, she was struggling to see it.

"Maybe we could find what you're looking for, together. If you'd like, I could help you pack up some of their things. "

A sadness tinged Honey's offer and Liv felt a little ashamed. Here she was lamenting about her family troubles to a person whose family were practically the Brady Bunch. She wrinkled her nose and shook her head, lifting a hand to her forehead and running her palm firmly over it in a soothing motion.

"It's okay. I couldn't ask you to do that. You already spend far too much of your time with me."

"Oh."

Liv felt in her gut, the disappointment lacing Honey's tone and she quickly dropped her hand and closed the small space between them on the sofa. She reached out and grabbed onto Honey's knee, bridging the distance between them. Her body was shaking with a desperation to make herself understood. She heard it the minute it left her mouth, she hadn't intended it to sound like she didn't want to be around Honey, because she did…more than anything. Even before the kiss they had shared earlier, Liv had this undeniable need to spend time with her neighbor that was as unexpected as it was strong and she wanted her to know that.

"I didn't mean it like that. I... I want to spend time with you. I'd really appreciate the help too. I just don't want you to feel obligated to help me, that's all."

"Why would I feel obligated to help you?" Honey asked, tilting her head and staring at Liv with eyes that held Liv with a reverence she had never known before.

"You know, because we um... because we..."

"Because we like one another?"

Liv blew out a breath. "Yeah, that."

"I never took you for the shy type, Liv Henderson. In fact, you've been very forward with regards to all of this. It's nice though, knowing I can make you flounder too." Honey's eyelashes fluttered and she glanced between them, inhaling deeply. Liv took this as a sign to move closer and so she did. She lifted her hand to cup Honey's chin, tilted her face until their lips lightly brushed one anothers and sighed.

"Yeah. You definitely do that."

Chapter 15

Honey

The sun slipped under the partially lifted, blackout blinds Honey had forgotten to lower last night, crawling its way slowly up her comforter and warming her bare skin in an attempt to coax her out of bed. She flipped herself onto her back and with her eyes still pressed together, smiled at the memories of yesterday.

Liv had kissed her or had she kissed Liv? Resolving that they had kissed one another countless times and each one had been more perfect than the last, Honey sighed dreamily.

The first kiss had been a precursor to some pretty amazing kisses through the night. After the muffins were finished, they had remained on the sofa. Liv's arms had wrapped protectively around Honey as they lay down, their bodies pressed close together on the small surface. After a while, Honey had found herself heavy lidded, breathing deeply as all of her worries and insecurities were kissed away by lips that it seemed, couldn't get enough of her. Liv was a wonderful kisser, from the way she tentatively flicked her tongue at Honey's top lip, to initiate the start; to the way she sucked her tongue when the kiss became passionate. Honey was absolutely sure that in all her life, she had never been kissed quite like that.

She sighed loudly, exhaling her satisfaction at the memory as she rubbed her hands over her still tired eyes. They hadn't said goodbye until 3am and if Honey was honest, she had to engage all of her willpower to not ask Liv to stay. Her head had wrestled with her body, with rationality kicking her libido's ass, in a move that saw them whispering their goodnights into the stars before Liv had crossed the field and headed home.

Home.

The fact that her brain was thinking of the big house as being Liv's home, made Honey sigh once more, only this time in frustration. She absolutely knew that this would have a timeframe, the limit most definitely did exist. Sure enough, as soon as Liv had the house packed up and the sale was in place, she would be heading back to the city. She would leave and Honey had just agreed to help her leave faster. Of course, Honey knew she could ask her to stay, but in her experience she was aware that she wasn't the type of girl people stayed for.

Anxiety bubbled in her stomach at the thought of losing another person she had allowed herself to get close to.

No, this wouldn't do. Getting attached so quickly, so soon had to be a bad idea, right?

She thought about the look Kyla had given her yesterday at the party as Liv's arms had wound around her middle, her lips ghosting Honey's ear as they sang Happy Birthday. It had been easy to read, Kyla never had been one to hide her emotions. She had stared at them and shook her head before throwing a look over to Sasha that said, *'This will not end well.'*

Honey didn't want it to end. It hadn't really even begun. She had to be realistic and sometimes being realistic really sucked. She hadn't ever really done casual before. Each of her girlfriends had been something significant and although they had all ended, she knew they were a *'blessin' or a lesson'*, as her mom would say. She wondered which Liv would be, with her beautiful dark hair and ocean blue eyes that longed for warmth. Honey knew Kyla would say that she still wasn't over the lesson that was Andie, and maybe to a degree she was right. But this, whatever it was, even in this beginning stage was proving to be something more than Honey had ever expected. She was certain that if this continued, if she kept sharing those butterfly inducing kisses with her rather sexy neighbor, eventually she would share so much more of herself that when the time came for them to really say goodbye, it would be hard. Who was she kidding, it was already going to be hard. She was in deep.

Pulling the duvet up and over her head, Honey attempted to block out the promising sunny day encroaching on her dark thoughts. She made a decision there and then, to allow herself a brief pity party. and then get on with her day.

For now, the sun could wait.

***

"Just say hello or good morning. It doesn't have to be a big deal," Honey muttered under her breath as she lifted the tray of muffins she was carrying into the air, holding them steady as she maneuvered her way over the stile.

Although there was a footpath leading between the houses, it meant going down to the bottom of the gravel path and around and so Honey had found it much quicker and easier to cross between the homes via the large shared field. Marvin hadn't minded, he had told Honey that '*a walk in nature, walks the soul back home*'. She had thought of that quote every time she had crossed the field and today was no exception.

Battling against her own thoughts and her nerves, she finished crossing the space between the two homes and shuffled her muddy Docs up the creaking, wooden stairs.

"Just because you shared a few kisses doesn't mean she's going to want more. Just say hello, give her the muffins and then get to work. It doesn't have to be a production."

"What doesn't have to be a production?" came a voice from over on the porch.

The swing to Honey's right squeaked as Liv stood up and crossed the decking to stand in front of her. Honey could smell gentle hints of Jasmine and something else she couldn't quite place, clinging to the gentle morning breeze. She was wearing a pair of baggy joggers and an oversized sweater, her long hair pulled haphazardly into a messy bun. Honey thought no woman had ever looked sexier than Liv did in that moment.

"Uh, hello morning," she stuttered, closing her eyes and screwing up her face as she realized her word fumble. "I'm sorry, I didn't see you there. I was going to say hello, or good morning but my brain couldn't decide which one to go with and clearly it decided to say a mix of both."

Honey's shoulders dropped as a heat rushed to her cheeks. So much for not making it a whole production. She held out the tray of muffins they had worked on together last night and smiled.

"Hello morning to you too," Liv laughed. "Are those for me?"

"I figured you deserved to taste the fruits of your labor." Honey handed over the tray and brushed her now empty hands over her denim dungarees, while rocking back and forth on her heels. Liv glanced at the tray and her tongue darted out of her mouth, swiping at her bottom lip as she took in the muffins. Honey gulped at the sight.

"I didn't really do much. I washed a few dishes and handed you a few items. I definitely don't deserve all of this."

"I can take them back." Honey teased, holding out her empty hands but knowing they would remain that way. When Liv pulled the tray closer to her chest and looked at Honey with mock disgust, she giggled.

"Don't you dare. I just poured myself a cup of tea, can I get you one?"

"Actually, I was just passing these over and now I have to head into work." She didn't want to say no. Everything in her was screaming at her to stay. To continue this delicious back and forth they were engaging in, only from the comfort of the porch swing, while clasping steaming mugs of Chai, which she knew was Liv's favorite type of tea.

"Oh, okay."

"I'm only going to be there a few hours today as Lissy is manning my counter. Europe is beckoning, and school is over for the summer, so I'm letting her pick up a few hours on the slower days."

"That's really nice of you." Liv smiled, and Honey felt the cool air brush over her bare arms. She wrapped her arms around herself in a hug, trying to retain a little warmth and felt a small flicker when Liv's eyes took her in.

"I was thinking that when I get back I could come over and give you some of that help I offered last night, maybe...if you want," her voice trailed off at the end. She didn't know if bringing up what happened last night was a good idea considering the way her brain had lectured her this morning about leading with her heart.

Liv stepped closer, the oversized sweater shifting to expose her collarbone and shoulder.

"That was a genuine offer? It wasn't just because you enjoyed the kissing?"

"No! I mean, I very much enjoyed the kissing..."

Honey couldn't take her gaze off Liv and her exposed skin. As she moved closer she felt Liv's nose bump against her own and before Honey could stop herself, her lips found Liv's. She tasted like cinnamon and cardamom. Kissing her felt like walking into a warm room after months in the cold. Like sinking into freshly made sheets after a warm shower.

Being with Liv felt like falling.

"Good," Liv whispered against Honey's mouth before deepening their kiss.

Honey lifted her hands, her fingers dancing lightly over Liv's shoulder along her collarbone and around the nape of her neck before sliding into the wisps of hair that always managed to avoid being tied up. Her other hand fisted the loose fabric of the sweater, holding Liv in place while she kissed her senseless. Liv moaned and Honey felt her legs buckle slightly. She slipped her tongue into Liv's mouth and felt Liv's own flicker against it.

They kept getting distracted by kisses, not that Honey was complaining but she knew if this continued she wouldn't leave, and she really had to head to work to hand over the rest of the baked goods from last night. She pulled back reluctantly, unfurling her hands from Liv's hair and clothing and pouting a little so Liv would know it pained her to stop, too.

Liv chuckled and Honey tipped her head to the side before taking a small step back.

"Your lips are a distraction and as much as I would love to stay here and continue this… conversation, I have to get the rest of those to the deli before Kyla pitches a fit about how late I am. Knowing my luck she's already put two and two together."

"She doesn't approve of you being gay?"

"Honestly, i'm not entirely sure if it's the being gay she doesn't approve of or just me. She's never really been my biggest supporter. I used to think it was because I usurped her title as youngest but now I'm just convinced that she just dislikes me as a person. No matter what I do she just doesn't seem to approve."

"I'm sorry. I won't keep you any longer, even if I do wish I could."

"I'll be back in a few hours. Then you can keep me for as long as you want."

Thoughts of forever announced themselves in Honey's mind and began hiking the trail to her heart before rationality could catch up with them.

"I'll look forward to it." Liv said and Honey couldn't stop herself from stepping and pushing up on her toes to steal one more kiss.

She turned away and walked down the wooden steps, glancing back over her shoulder, only when she was a far enough distance away that she wouldn't be tempted to run back into Liv's arms.

Liv was still stood on the porch, one hand clutching at the tray and the other held to her face, her fingers ghosting over her lips. She looked positively radiant in the morning sunlight and for a split second Honey allowed herself the delicious thought of how Liv would look as she just woke up. Next to her. Wearing nothing but that beautiful smile and the soft cotton sheets they'd share. Raising her own hand into the air she waved goodbye before heading back across the field. The quicker she got to the deli and did what she had to, the quicker she could get back to the woman waiting at the top of the stairs.

***

She had been baking for three hours and had stupidly convinced herself that she was home free, when Kyla had burst through the doors.

"So you're dating her?" Kyla, as ever, was abrupt and to the point.

Honey pulled out the empty trays from the display cabinet and headed back towards the kitchen. Kyla didn't ease up, she followed her through the double doors wearing a scowl and muttering something under her breath, Honey picked up the words *irresponsible* and *thought you had learned your lesson.* As much as she tried to ignore her obviously irate sister, she knew it was only a matter of time before Kyla got so loud the customers would hear her.

She put the empty trays into the large stainless steel sink and pulled down the hose to spray them off.

"No Kyla, I'm not dating Liv. I'm not dating anyone. Not it's any of your business."

She added a liberal amount of dish soap to the trays and rubbed it around with a cloth before reaching for the hose once more.

"Well what the hell was that at the party yesterday. You sure looked like you were dating. She had her arms wrapped around–"

"I know where her arms were, Kyla." Honey interjected, slipping the trays onto the drying rack and reaching for a nearby hand towel.

Wiping her hands clean, she took a moment to think about what was going on with her and Liv. She wasn't entirely sure of anything other than it felt good. Honey hadn't felt this good in a long time and she didn't want her sister ruining it by asking questions that she really didn't feel the need to have answers for just yet.

"I'm just saying, you don't need to be rushing into anything. Look what happened with Andie. I think it would be irresponsible of you to just throw yourself at a woman who doesn't even live here. You get that right? That she doesn't even live here?"

The way her sister stressed that last point made Honey tense up. It felt like a kick to the stomach, a low blow that she should have expected from Kyla given their history, but Honey always tried to see the best in people. She spun on her heels and threw her hands into the air.

"I know she doesn't live here, Kyla! I'm aware that she's just visiting. I don't know what we are to each other, yet. I don't know if I *need* to know yet. All I do know is that whatever it is, I like it and so does she. We are both consenting adults and we are having fun, which is something I haven't had in a long, long time. So stop pressing me."

"You're hoping she's going to stay, aren't you?"

Kyla's words came at Honey like a freight train, taking the wind from her without warning. Her chest tightened and her words dissipated on breaths she struggled to let out. Because the truth was, she did think about Liv staying. Every day she woke up she thought about the woman across the field and what life would be like if she stayed. Each night they had sat out watching the stars and drinking cider from the bottle, it had felt a little like having Marvin back. She didn't want to lose that, to lose Liv.

"She's not going to stay Honey. She's going to pack up all the stuff, serve you an eviction notice, list the *entire* property and drive off back to the city with a pocket full of cash. She's going to leave and she won't look back. You can't trust her."

"You don't even know her!" Honey shouted, not liking how her voice cracked as tears burned at her eyes. She blinked slowly and allowed them to roll freely down her face. Damn, she hated getting emotional. Her sister had always mistaken her anger for weakness and the uncontrollable tears Honey always shed didn't do anything to help change that.

"I don't need to know her. I know you! You always do this. You always make bad decisions when it comes to women, you throw yourself at them and expect them to fall as quick and hard as you do!"

That hurt. Of course Honey knew she was quick to fall in love. She knew she gave all of herself to the person she was with and that she wanted a love like the ones on the pages of her books. She didn't know how to be any different, how to love someone any less and she didn't want to.

"Wow! Just because the decisions I make aren't the ones you'd choose, doesn't mean they're bad. We can't be right all of the time Kyla, how else are we supposed to learn from our mistakes?"

"You've made enough mistakes that you think you'd have learned by now!" Kylas words were cutting, sure she was known for having no filter and lacking tact but this was a step too far.

"What did I ever do to you to make you dislike me this much?" Honey croaked, swiping at the tears pooling at her chin.

She shook her head in defeat. It was no use asking, she would never get an answer from Kyla when it came to this. Her sister was never going to change her mind about her, and Honey didn't know why she kept hoping she would.

The double doors swung open and a gust of fresh air followed Sasha through to the kitchen. She glared at them, eyes wide and hands on her hips in a look very reminiscent of their mother.

"Hey, what's going on here?"

Honey couldn't take it. That look of disapproval was fine coming from Kyla, but it stung far worse coming from the one person she always knew she could count on. She didn't have to stay here, she couldn't.

Deftly untying the knot at the small of her back, she lifted her apron over her head and threw it haphazardly on the steel countertop, before patting her dungaree pockets to make sure she had her car keys.

"Nothing is going on other than me leaving. I've made all of the cakes and pastries for today, the last batch is in the oven now. Can you ask Lissy to take them out in ten minutes, please. I have to go. I have plans," she said calmly, but unable to control the waver in her voice.

"Honey!"

She heard Sasha's voice trail off as she quickly covered the distance of the deli and headed for the exit. A part of her felt terrible that she hadn't stopped to say goodbye to Lissy, but she had to get out of there. Everything in her was screaming at her to run, to skip getting into her car and run all the way home instead. Before she could realize what she was doing she could hear the pounding of her feet on the sidewalk, the squeaking of her Docs as they protested her every step. Her heart thrummed rapidly against her chest and she felt the wind drying the tears still slipping down her cheeks.

Trees became blurs of green and children's laughter cycled through her brain on a never ending carousel, as she picked up her pace. She weaved between people, moving too fast to acknowledge those who greeted her and the few who enquired as to what was wrong. She didn't want to stop and make small talk, she wasn't capable of that right now. She had somewhere to be and that somewhere was anywhere but here.

The pinching of the faux leather against her feet caused her to wince as time passed and she cursed herself for not wearing practical shoes today. She hadn't known she would be going for a mini marathon when she assembled her outfit this morning. The sweat traveled down her neck, rolling in rivulets down her spine as the sun rose higher in the sky, preparing itself for the midday show.

When she finally came to a stop, and before she could take in her surroundings, a voice filled her ears. A soft, calming voice that soothed the pounding in her chest and caused her breathing to slow.

"Honey, is everything okay?"

Her go to response was to say she was fine, but Honey found herself shaking her head. Blinking against the sunlight and allowing her brain to focus now on where she was, she realized she *had* ran all the way home. Well, not home exactly... but to Liv. Her brain had subconsciously sought out comfort and this was where her flight response had taken her.

Honey wasn't sure if she should feel ashamed that she was already allowing herself to get attached, Kyla's word's from moments before surfing the waves of anger in her stomach, or if she should consider exactly what all of this meant. As her brain started to war with itself, she felt Livs arms around her and she melted into her touch.

"Come inside."

A warm mug of tea was placed into her hands, the steam finding her face and filling her chest with the scent of chamomile. She clutched the porcelain and smiled softly at Liv who stood in front of her, holding her own cup.

"You don't have to talk about it if you don't want to. We can just…sit. Drink tea."

Honey couldn't find the energy to reply. Instead she lowered her head once more. She hated that she had let her sister get to her like this.

She had known this morning, after glancing at the digital clock on her car screen that informed her she was two minutes late, that Kyla would come at her immediately. She had braced herself when she walked through the doors but thankfully, her sister hadn't been around and so she had allowed herself a moment of reprieve before slipping into the back to get a start on the day. As the hours passed, she had allowed herself to become complacent and so when Kyla did come in ranting and raving, Honey had her guard down. A rookie mistake where Kyla was involved.

A weight settled next to her on the sofa, Liv draped a blanket over Honey's shoulder and rested against her side. Turning her head she watched as Liv let the fabric fall around her own shoulder before snuggling into Honey's side, still clutching her mug. True to her word, she didn't push Honey to talk and yet the silence that enveloped them didn't add to the heaviness she was feeling.

"None of this feels wrong." Honey whispered, squeezing her eyes shut and breathing deeply through her nose, "I don't know what is happening with us but nothing about you feels like a mistake. I know that this is new and we both have hurt we are still carrying but… it's not a mistake is it?"

She glanced up at Liv and saw the softest smile there had ever been.

"I don't think being with you could ever be considered a mistake, Honey."

Honey felt her body still at this admission. The soft reverence with which it fell from Liv's mouth was all encompassing, the words something Honey had longed to hear for so long now. But ones she still found herself struggling to believe.

If being with her wasn't wrong why did everyone leave? Why did Andie run across the world? Why did Marvin die? What would happen to her heart if Liv left? As much as Honey wanted to hide beneath the weighted safety of those words, she knew that eventually, Liv *would* leave. There would come a day where she watched as another piece of her heart drove down that gravel road and never came back. Her heart beat overtime at that thought, a thrumming distraction from the somersaults her stomach was turning. She felt the question on the tip of her tongue.

"Do you ever think about staying?"

It tasted like hope and inevitable sadness but rather than waiting for an answer she closed her eyes, concentrated on her rapid breathing and cuddled further into the body next to her.

Chapter 16

Liv

Liv thought about staying all the time. She had thought about it every morning as she shuffled down the wooden stairs into a kitchen filled with memories that had started flooding back to her. She thought about it as she poured herself a tea, headed onto the front porch to sit in the swing and watched the morning greet her like an old friend. She thought about it as she typed into the darkness, the pages of her newest book. An unexpected romance, in which a woman who has been lost for so long finds herself, in the place she least expected to. She thought about staying each and every time her mind flickered to images of Honey's smile and her heartwarming laugh. Liv thought about staying here, constantly.

But she also thought about leaving.

She knew what it must have taken for Honey to ask this of her. To sit here in her very obvious heartache and be vulnerable without being needy. She had to be honest, Honey deserved that. Liv wanted to reassure her that she wasn't leaving, but the most she knew she could offer was consolation in the form of her not leaving...yet.

"I do... think of staying here." Liv admitted and she felt Honey's breathing slow down. "I think about what my life would look like here and how different it would be to what I have back in the city. I think about what I'd be leaving behind if I stay. I think about what I'd gain. I think about you... I think about you more than I probably should. I know we have only just met and are practically strangers, but Honey, something in me recognizes something in you and so, yeah. I think about staying here with you... all the time."

Those last words swam around Liv, rising into her chest and causing her heart to skip a beat. A swishing of uncertainty in her stomach made itself known and she held onto the breath she was desperate to exhale.

Anxiously waiting for Honey's response, her mind swam with thoughts of having said too much. Honesty was hard at the best of times, but being honest at such an early stage in their relationship could only bode well. Liv wanted that. If she and Honey were intending on continuing down this path, then honesty had to be present from the get go. Honey was always upfront with her and vulnerable, the least she could do was return it, no matter how hard it was and even if she could only do so in a minimal way, at first.

Silence filled the large room, dancing through the air and tickling the dying flames of the fire Liv had lit when the morning had greeted her coldly. Then the silence was broken by a soft murmur and as Liv turned to take in the woman in her arms, she realized Honey had fallen asleep.

She regarded Honey, her beautiful face with the soft sloping of a nose that begged to be kissed. The smattering of freckles that dotted her face, as if the goddess who created her had shaken her paintbrush haphazardly and created a masterpiece. Her soft lips, the top a cupid's bow that had shot an arrow right into Liv's heart the moment she tasted Honey. She longed for that taste again, but more than that, she longed for this. For the simplicity that came with a new beginning. For this stillness. Making sure that the blanket was wrapped around Honey securely, she settled her own body into hers and closed her eyes.

***

A rustling sound conjured her from her sleep, her eyes heavy with the dreams she hadn't expected to follow her all the way from the city. Blinking the dreams away, Liv realized she was lying horizontally on the sofa. Honey was no longer next to her. She stood up and stretched her arms towards the sky, a yawn escaped her and she glanced around the empty room. For a split second she worried Honey had left, that she had been freaked out by waking up with Liv wrapped around her and she had ran. But then the doorway to the living area was filled with a sight Liv knew she would never tire of seeing.

Honey's hair stuck up at odd angles, she wore an innocent smile and one of Liv's sweaters she had left thrown over the back of the rocking chair in the corner of the room. A place Liv curled up, almost daily, while she took in a few chapters of her most recent read on her Kindle. Honey looked radiant in her just woken state. An invitation of comfort and safety all wrapped up in Liv's sweater. Liv's heart thudded in her chest, reminding her she was still alive and should therefore say or do something other than stare at her neighbor.

"Hey you!"

"Hey sleepyhead!" came back Honey's loving response. The way her words swam with affection comforted more than any blanket ever could.

"You're wearing my sweater," Liv nodded at the oversized garment that almost caressed Honey's curves, "It looks great on you."

"I hope that's okay? I was a little cold when I woke up. I'm sorry I fell asleep on you. I think the stress of the last two years just caught up with me and decided that if I didn't stop of my own accord it was going to take me down."

"Do you want to talk about what triggered it today?" Liv asked, not wanting to push Honey, but wanting to assure her that she was there should she need to vent.

Honey exhaled sharply and stepped across the room, reaching for Liv's hand. She knotted their fingers together and fixed her gaze between them.

"Do you think we could talk about something other than how much of a mess I am? Maybe you could distract me."

Honey stepped closer and Liv reached out for her. She smoothed her palms over the curves of Honey's hips. She reacted instantly, her head rolling back and her eyes closing as Liv's fingers danced the length of her spine before tangling in the blonde curls at the nape of her neck and pulling her closer. Liv bent at the neck and kissed a path from the sensitive spot behind Honey's ear, along her jaw and back. Honey moaned softly and wrapped her arms around Liv's neck. Guessing she needed support, Liv held Honey's waist tighter. They stood like that for a little while, allowing themselves to find a much needed comfort in one another. Liv loved how Honey fit perfectly next to her, how her forehead begged to be kissed and she did just that before deciding it wasn't enough. She cupped Honey's chin and tilted her face up, guiding their lips towards one another she slid her tongue along Honey's lower lip before flicking it against her top one. A wordless instruction she knew would be obeyed.

Kissing Honey felt like freefalling. Like standing on the top of a mountain after a four hour hike and marveling in wonder at how the clouds kissed the sky. Like simultaneously coming up for air and having it stolen from you in a way that made you uncertain of if you'd survive.

When Honey amped up the pressure and lifted a leg to hook around Liv's waist, Liv concluded that if passion was a person then Honey embodied it. They stood in the open space of a home once flooded with love; strangers who had just met, but whose undeniable chemistry spoke of a familiarity they both wanted to explore.

"That was... wow! You're really good at that." Liv breathed, pulling her head back a little but still clinging to Honey like a lifeline she very much needed.

Rubbing her thumb over the denim that covered Honey's thigh, where she still gripped the leg hooked over her hip, Liv pushed her own hips gently into Honey's center. Honey gasped sharply, untangling her fingers from Liv's long locks and ghosted them over her thoroughly kissed and gently swollen lips.

"I'd like to think it's more that *we* are good at that. I know *I* haven't been kissed like that in a long time," she replied, tilting her head innocently and something about the way she moved made Liv want to discover everything that made Honey move this way.

Sure, it frightened her a little how easy this all was. How quickly she had effectively moved on and how all encompassing Honey was, in that ever since Liv met her, she hadn't been able to see life outside of her. But Liv simultaneously felt like she could sail even Honey's roughest waters, and on days when land wasn't visible, she had the sneaking suspicion that she wouldn't panic because this woman was safety in abundance.

"The fact that you haven't ever been kissed like that is both a shame, and something I'm thankful for. I don't like the idea of someone else kissing you.Which is probably a discussion we should have because I'm not entirely sure what it is we are doing here. I just know that I like it, really like it," Liv admitted, and Honey blushed. "You deserve answers though, to all of your questions. I want you to know that your feelings, wants and opinions are all valid and I want to make sure I address them as best as I can."

At that comment, Honey dropped her hands to her side, her leg lowering to the ground. Every instinct in Liv told her she had offended her neighbor. She wondered if she should take it all back, her nervous system telling her to reboot, to apologize for coming on too strong and moving too fast, especially when she saw a flash of confusion furrow Honey's brows.

She prepared herself internally for the words she would hear next, knowing there was a very real possibility that this had ended before it began. This was the part where Honey would tell her she couldn't do this. That she was still healing from everything that happened with the ex that didn't appreciate what she had. That she couldn't move on as quickly as that. How could anyone move on *that* fast?

Liv felt ashamed as she pondered on the fact that she too had participated in something that had her ready to give herself entirely, so soon and so what did that say about her relationship with Marcie? More to the point, what did it say about her? She didn't want Honey to potentially think that she was fickle, that her feelings even in this burgeoning stage weren't to be taken seriously.

Steeling herself and tightening her jaw, waiting for the fallout, she was surprised by a soft hand on her own cheek tethering her to the moment.

"I really appreciate that... and you're right, we should talk. I know I asked a loaded question before I fell asleep and I do sort of want to hear the answer, even though a part of me is scared to know it. But, right now... can you just kiss me again?" Honey said softly, lifting herself onto her tiptoes and nuzzling Liv's nose with her own.

Liv felt her stomach flip at the action and returning the gesture she closed her eyes in satisfaction, expelling all her worries in a single word.

"Gladly."

***

"Do you have any idea what all of this is?" Honey asked, and Liv lifted her head from underneath the bed. She saw glanced over at the small closet and saw Honey on her tiptoes, pulling at a battered cardboard box, that was overflowing with photographs. Greytone and sepia memories of people she wished she knew, slipped from the box and fluttered to the floor. Shrugging her shoulders and scrunching her face in confusion, she elicited a chuckle from Honey. They both went back to their tasks, Liv dipping back under the bed as Honey continued to dislodge the box from its shelf.

Minutes later she heard a muffled sound and a crash that caused her to jolt upright, being careful not to hit her head, and cross the room at lightning speed. What she saw was most definitely not what she had expected to see. Instead of seeing Honey buried deep in boxes, she saw the cute blonde standing frozen to the spot, her arms held up in front of her like she had tried so hard to stop the inevitable. All over her body and the floor, were envelopes, some opened, some still sealed, with cursive script adoring the covers.

"Are you okay?" she giggled as Honey, wide-eyed with shock, started shaking the papers from her body to the ground. The box fell at their feet and Honey bent to start scooping the letters back into it, shaking her loose curls.

"Talk about letters from nowhere. I thought I had a grip on the box but I clearly didn't. Remind me again why I, the smaller of us, got the high shelves and you got to look under the bed?" she joked.

Her heart healing laughter reverberated in Liv's ears.

"Um, you said something about wanting to know what it was like being back in the closet, I believe." Liv teased and Honey glanced up at her from the floor, scrunching her nose in the most adorable way. That action made Liv want to pepper her face with kisses.

"Well, like I knew it would, it sucks! I think we should swap," she pouted and Liv imagined all the ways in which she would turn that pout into a smile. All the touches and words she would conjure up out of thin air.

She liked this playful back and forth between them, their chemistry and compatibility was undeniable. They complemented one another in a way she had never really felt with Marcie. Their back and forths had been dangerous in that it would provide the basis for arguments; with Honey their exchanges felt like a dance she was learning the steps to, but that she was picking up effortlessly

"Oh you do, do you? I see how it is, you make a mess and expect me to clean it up."

"Actually, I think I'm the one on her knees doing all the hard work. I'm helping *you, remember. You're* the one looking for lost things."

Crouching down and helping to scoop the letters into the box, Liv scanned the papers. Each page was filled with a cursive script and she got the feeling that someone had really put thought into writing them. The letters were tinted yellow with age. She lifted one closer to her face and her eyes were drawn to the name at the top of the page.

"My Dearest Bea,"

A ghost of a voice resounded in her ear. A memory long forgotten, resurfaced as she scanned the rest of the page. She began picking up letter after letter, reading the same greeting.

"They're all letters my grandfather wrote to my grandmother. Love letters, I think…" she trailed off, sadness tinting her words.

Honey, who held a collection of letters in her own hands, smiled softly at her but Liv could see a measure of sadness sitting in the corner of her mouth.

"He would have called them life letters. Love and life meant very much the same thing, to him." Honey said.

"There are so many of them," Liv stated, sitting back on her heels and picking up more envelopes with the tops torn, glancing at the writing inside. "What do I do with them? Do I read them? Is that an invasion of privacy? I already feel like I'm imposing on a life that isn't mine just by being here in this house. With every piece of clothing I folded to put away or each piece of furniture I considered moving, I felt like I was messing with a picture that was perfect without me."

"His life was never perfect without you," Honey whispered, running her fingers over the forever memories she held in her hands. "He loved you very much. He was sad that he didn't get to see you, Liv. After he lost Bea, he thought he had lost you too. But he never stopped loving you, ever. Just because people leave or even choose to no longer be in our lives, doesn't mean how we feel for them has to change. Loving someone from a distance is just as meaningful as loving someone in person. Sometimes even more so. It shows that your love has no bounds, it's unconditional. His love for you was unconditional."

Liv felt the sadness in Honey's voice and watched the way she curled up on herself, as if willing herself to be smaller. She noted the tears filling Honey's eyes, a hurt she didn't know how to feel, still raw enough to find the surface.

"I wish I had known him the way you did." Liv admitted, shuffling closer to Honey and running a hand up her arm, a comforting gesture that afforded her a sweet, soft smile. "I'm sorry I can't take away the pain and sadness *you* feel at losing him. If I'm honest I feel a little ashamed of that. He was *my* grandfather after all."

"Don't feel ashamed, Liv. If I could give you all my memories, well… I wouldn't, but I'd be happy to share them with you."

"Were they really good people, Honey?"

"Honestly, they were wonderful. I see a lot of them in you. You're pretty wonderful yourself."

"You really believe that don't you?"

"All I know for sure is that I've only had you in my life for the briefest time and yet you make everything better. You make me feel… better."

"I know exactly what you mean. I never expected any of this when I came here. I never expected to feel this much. I thought maybe there would be something here, some piece of me that I left here all those years ago. Something that would fill this hole inside of me, that would tell me who I am. When I got here I thought to myself, how am I supposed to know if I find what I'm looking for, if I don't really *know* what I'm looking for?" she admitted rather than asked. When Honey glanced up at her, Liv knew she couldn't keep hiding the way she felt from her.

The words that had been following her around the last few days, the voice that told Liv that she had found more than she could have ever imagined here, in Verity… in Honey, pressed against her tongue. This was so much to feel, so soon. But it was undoubtedly real.

***

The afternoon came and went without any further envelope showers. Liv hadn't even noticed how late it was until she heard her stomach rumble and realized she had forgotten to have lunch.

Running the roll of packing tape over the top of the cardboard box marked 'donations', she breathed a sigh of relief. Three boxes, all from this one room. It seemed surreal to Liv, that a person's life could be condensed into such a small space in death, when they very clearly filled so many other spaces in life.

Her stomach growled again and a wave of nausea washed over her. She needed carbs and she needed them promptly. She bent at the knees and wrapped her arms around the box, lifting it into the air and crossing the room. As she headed out into the hallway she placed it on top of a box containing old vinyls, indicated by Honey's looping scrawl. Even her writing was effortless, feminine and delicate, swooping curls at the tail of the letter 'Y', and a flourish on the letter 'S'. Honey's writing was indicative of her character and Liv allowed her mind to conjure up an image of a letter in her hands, written in that script, that read.

"My Dearest, Liv."

Shaking herself from her daydream before she could find herself falling in love like stepping into quicksand, Liv listened for any indication as to where the beautiful blonde could be. They had decided after the envelope shower and heartfelt confession, that Honey would tackle the room at the end of the hallway, which had once been her grandfather's home office. This gave them both, Liv hoped, a moment to ruminate on the emotions that had filled the room earlier.

She padded across the hallway in search of Honey and paused in the doorway of the room. A smile crept onto Liv's face as she watched her walking back and forth, humming softly with each item she picked up and put in the appropriately marked boxes. Honey paused when she came to a thick cable knit cardigan and Liv watched how, as she ran her delicate hands over the weave, her face softened. Importance and sadness came together on Honey's beautiful face and Liv felt herself soften at witnessing an obviously emotional moment. Honey brought the cardigan to her face, closed her eyes and breathed deeply.

"It still smells like him…" the words were meant for no one in particular but they filled the entire room, a whisper of a memory that would remain long after they left.

Liv thought about what would happen to all of the memories this house held, if she sold the property. If they would leave, floating out of open windows into the fresh air of summer days. If they would remain, tucked into the furthest corners of the rooms, becoming part of the narrative the walls would speak about if they could talk. She wished they could talk, maybe then they could tell her the parts of her story she knew she was missing; parts long forgotten.

A resentment had been building up inside of her since she arrived. A steady distaste for her father and his estrangement, his distance from this place that so far had not made her feel even remotely 'trapped' as he had told her countless times it had made him. It was typical of her father and how he operated, that everything always had to be done his way, how and when he wanted it. Liv hated that he had a way of making everything about himself. It was a controlling aspect Liv hoped she hadn't inherited.

Feeling herself slipping deep into the heaviness that often accompanied her interactions with her parents, she tried to center herself by focusing her attention on what was happening in front of her. Honey had wrapped the cardigan around herself, her small hands pulling the sides together until they overlapped around her curvy frame. She then closed her eyes, breathed deeply, and Liv watched as she centered herself in the moment. She felt a little torn between, feeling a little like she should announce herself but not wanting to ruin such a private moment and yet she didn't have to make a choice. The minute Honey opened her eyes, they found Liv's.

"It's like a hug," Honey smiled softly, and Liv crossed the room determined to provide a real one. She felt Honey's arms wrap around her as they sank into one another with ease.

"You can keep that, if you'd like."

"I can?" Honey asked, and Liv pulled back a little to take her in, but still kept her close.

"Of course you can," she said, closing the space between them, wrapping her arms around Honey and placing a comforting kiss on her forehead. "You can take anything you want, Honey. Anything that reminds you of him, that holds a memory you both share. If you want it, it's yours."

"Is there anything you're going to keep? Any memories you have of you both?"

"Honestly, I don't know if the memories I have are even real. There are ghosts of them that linger in my mind and the longer I'm here, the more they make themselves known. Nothing fully formed, just small inklings of things." Liv shook her head and chewed the inside of her cheek, "I think he might have tried to teach me to play chess. I can remember painting these small wooden figures and getting black paint all over my white dress. I remember my father getting angry and loud. I think maybe I baked here, in the kitchen. I keep seeing mixing bowls and a blue apron. It has to be here because we were never allowed to go near the kitchen at home. The cook was the only one allowed behind the big doors, even as I got older, if I needed a drink I had to ask for it. It's probably why I'm useless at cooking now. I know this probably sounds really silly but, I swear sometimes I can be sitting on the porch and I can smell cinnamon and peaches."

"That doesn't sound silly at all. I know I've not told you much about them, I just…wasn't really sure how much you wanted to know. If I'm honest, I thought you'd come here, clean up, fix up and then sell up, but you've been here for a few weeks now, and I'm sort of hoping you're going to stay a little while longer. You seem happy here, Liv."

"I am happy here. I can't remember ever being this happy and I'm not even sure how it happened but I know that I want to try and make this feeling stay. I like who I am here." It was the truth, and a welcome one at that.

"You don't like who you are when you're away from here?" Honey asked against her chest, Liv nuzzled in closer.

"Honestly, I don't know. I feel like I've been a ghost of myself for so long that I lost track of who I am, what I wanted. Away from here it's easy to get lost and to remain lost. I'm trying to find myself."

"It seems like you're searching for a lot and that's a heavy weight to carry alone. I hope you find everything you're looking for, Liv."

Liv tightened her arms around Honey, holding her as close as she could. Her heart thudded in her chest and she wondered if Honey could feel it. She wondered if Honey knew that each beat was a product of the life she was breathing back into Liv. An overwhelming urge to tell her everything, filled Liv. To open herself up to this woman and hide nothing.

She wondered how Honey would react to knowing her life story to this point, from running away to England as a teen under the pretenses of studying, to arriving here carrying so much sadness and insecurity alongside obligation, in her suitcase. She wondered how Honey would react when she told her she had never really felt she belonged anywhere, until she felt her lips against her own. How she had thought she knew what love was, but then she had met her and something inside her told her that she had never really known love, not the way she wanted to. Not the way she deserved to.

Liv wasn't certain that she could do all of this without scaring Honey away though. Here before her was this beautifully accepting woman who didn't pressure her, who didn't demand answers to questions Liv wasn't sure she even knew how to answer. Honey was so sweet and pure, Liv worried that she could potentially hurt her and that was the last thing she wanted to do. She didn't deserve to be a stepping stone on Liv's path to finding herself. Honey deserved so much more than that.

Everything Liv thought she knew was changing. Her entire outlook on life was blurring and transforming with laughs, smiles and moments filled with everything Honey offered, everything Liv never knew she needed. Honey's words ran through her mind, and left her wondering if she really could find everything she was looking for in this small town, or if she had already found it.

Chapter 17

Honey

The sun filtered through the gap between the blackout blind and the windowsill. Honey rolled over as the noise of a text alert roused her from another night of restless sleep. She was positive it would be Sasha checking in, or at least trying to. It had been almost a week since the argument with Kyla and Honey had, for the first time ever, taken time off work. Not wanting to get into a discussion that could turn into an argument, she had sent Sasha a text letting her know that right now she was taking a break. That she needed to give herself some time to work through some things but that she would be back, eventually. The truth was, she wasn't entirely sure what she was going to do, or how to resolve this. She had never been in an argument before and never one that had kept her from the deli.

Turning over in bed she reached out and slapped her hand through the air, in a blind fumble for her phone. She had left on her bedside table last night and normally she knew better than to leave it so close. It was too easy to become sucked in by social media and baking videos on TikTok and so she normally put her phone on her desk on the other side of the room, while she slept. The last few nights however, had been filled with long conversations and midnight flirting with the woman across the field. Last night specifically, it had taken a turn for the sexy.

Honey wasn't sure what had gotten into her, but between her anxiety over everything happening with her sisters and being unable to bake the last few days, she was suffering some sort of frustration. Flirting with Liv seemed to ease that a little.

Who was she kidding? Flirting with Liv eased it a lot.

Although Honey wasn't entirely sure that she could call what had happened last night mere flirting. Somewhere between the hours of dusk and dawn their conversation had become hot and heavy. So hot in fact, that Honey could still feel the familiar ache between her thighs.

"Ungh!" she groaned, her voice slightly hoarse from a mixture of the morning and the moaning she was absolutely unabashed about vocalizing last night.

She gripped her phone and brought it to her face, pausing momentarily to consider her next move. She could swipe to view the text from Sasha, one that she knew would undoubtedly leave her feeling guilt-ridden and sad, or she could listen to the thudding in her chest and pulsing between her thighs and fire off a text to Liv that would guarantee a delicious start to the morning.

"Definitely the latter," she spoke into the quiet of the morning, smirking as she tilted her head, tapped her fingers on the screen and composed a single word message that she sent without second guessing herself.

"Satisfied?"

The reply was instantaneous.

"Barely. You?"

Honey smirked and turned herself over onto her stomach, legs bending at the knees and coming up behind her, bringing the comforter with them. She giggled as she typed, feeling an excitement bubbling from her core. These delicious back and forths had her feeling like she was young again.

"Well, can I do something to help with that?"

"I'm thinking you absolutely can. I mean, after last night we know you're perfectly capable…"

Honey heard the teasing tone laced between those words, a string of promise ready to pull her to safety if she held on tight enough. Recalling the noises Liv had made last night over the phone, and how worked up they had gotten her, she knew it wouldn't take much to provoke a repeat performance. Honey pressed her thighs together and sucked her bottom lip between her teeth, biting down lightly as she composed her next text.

"Perfectly capable? Oh that sounds like there's room for improvement. How about you come over here and let me try and change that."

She wrestled with herself over if she should press send, having never been this brave before but her thumb decided for her. Almost instantly her phone showed the moving ellipsis that signaled Liv's impending response. A moment of panic stilled her breath in her chest, as she considered what Liv was taking so long to type, and then the ellipsis disappeared. Honey stared hard at the screen, her heart pounding in her chest, her stomach now swirling as excitement threatened to turn to fear.

She twisted herself around and sat up in bed, her eyes still fixed on the screen, willing the reply to come. It didn't.

The possibility that she had possibly pushed things too far introduced itself and she dropped her phone with a flourish, watching it disappear into the sheets. That's what Honey wanted to do right now, disappear into the sheets. She internally chastised herself for her brazen forwardness. Never in her life had she been as openly willing as she had been these last few weeks. This side of her was so far from how she knew she was normally; her entire life she had held back to make sure she did what was expected of her. What was right. When she was with Liv, she felt like she had no restraints, she didn't have to hold back because each time she had stepped forward Liv had met her where she was. Each touch had prompted a touch, each kiss had been met with a kiss and each admission of desire had been met with another admission.

Then, last night she had given in to something selfish. She had allowed herself to enjoy a tantalizing back and forth that had resulted in whimpered breaths as her fingers conducted a symphony between her legs. Honey had teased, tempted and taken what had been offered willingly, at least she hoped it had been given willingly. She worried momentarily, spurred by the disappearing text, if Liv had felt obligated to reply last night. If she hadn't been as open to it as she had seemed. Had she missed something in their communication, too focused on her own delicious wants and needs, to see an uncertainty that could have been hiding behind the texted responses?

"Shit!" she exclaimed, tilting her head back in disbelief. "Shit! Shit! Shit!"

Her phone alert sounded once more. A series of assigned bleeps signaled Sasha's attempt to make contact, but Honey was not in the mood to answer her sister's messages right now. Not when she could have potentially messed everything up with Liv.

She gripped the sheets and pulled them over her head, as she sank into her shame, determined to remain there until it disappeared, or she did.

A pattern of taps sounded through the quiet and a light tremor shook the door in its frame as it continued. Sitting upright, Honey furrowed her brow and listened with baited breath for the sound to come again. She wasn't disappointed.

Throwing back the comforter, she swung her legs out of bed and padded her bare feet along the landing, towards the intrusive sounds still coming from the front door. The taps sped up, becoming almost hurried, insistent, and Honey found herself becoming agitated as she stomped her way down each stair.

"I swear to god, Sasha, if this is you beating my door down to get me to come back to work, you better have an apology signed in blood and sealed with a gold stamp, because that's what it's going to take to fix this!" frustration evident in her voice, she approached the door and continued, "It's been a week, Lissy knows how to bake and I know you know how to use a stand mixer too!"

When she pulled the door open, Honey expected to have to continue with her diatribe, but the words paused on the tip of her tongue as she took in the sight before her. Standing there, hair slightly disheveled in loose waves that hung around her shoulders, and wearing nothing but a t-shirt, boyshorts, gumboots and a look that spoke more than words ever could, was Liv.

"It's you!"

"You asked me to come over, didn't you? If you were joking or expecting someone else, I can leave."

Honey watched her brow furrow, as Liv's beautiful stormy eyes looked anywhere but directly at her. Before she could assure her that she was not in fact expecting another person, Liv took a step back.

Honey reached out a hand, tangling her fingers in the fabric that hung from Liv's lithe body, and pulled her across the threshold. Clumsily, their bodies came into contact with one another from their hips to their noses, which brushed against the others, nuzzling together. Honey blinked, her eyelashes fluttering, heavy with a tiredness synonymous with late night exertion. She could see clearly, the same sleepiness reflected in Liv's gaze. Moving slowly, she leaned into Liv's touch, closed the distance between them and kissed her softly. Her tongue ran a path over Liv's full bottom lip, flicking upwards at the divot where her cupid's bow dipped and Liv groaned at the contact. Honey pulled away and dropped her hands from Liv's waist to her hands, her fingers seeking solace in the spaces between Liv's own. The next words she spoke fell in whispers, but each word was clearly punctuated, to make sure there was no way Liv could assume she had made a mistake.

"I was serious. So. Very. Serious."

Liv's smile was all it took for Honey to take action. She pushed the door closed, and watched with anticipation, as the woman in front of her kicked off the oversized gumboots that had landed her in Honey's arms weeks ago. Liv was lithe and lean, a tower of odd angles that provided a contrast to the gentle parabola of Honey's own frame. She reached out a hand, desperate for contact and let it sit on the bare skin of Liv's lower back that had revealed itself, as she bent over to push the stubborn left gumboot from her bare foot.

When Liv finally shook her foot free, Honey took a fistful of her t-shirt and pulled her in for another kiss.

"Upstairs?" she breathed and when Liv nodded, they moved together towards the stairs.

They reached the doorway to Honey's bedroom and the rational side of her brain caught up to her actions. She spun on the balls of her feet and turned to face Liv, whose eyes, she noted, were focused firmly on her. It was things like that, Liv's unwavering attention and unfaltering eye contact, that made Honey feel like whenever they were together, she was the only person in the world.

"Is everything okay?" Liv asked, her hand squeezing Honey's where they remained connected.

Honey glanced briefly down at the floor hoping to find answers, but also partly to avoid the intense stare that warmed her entirely. The minute she dared to look up, goosebumps traveled up her arms and sent a tingle down her spine.

Liv was breathtaking. Not just in the way she stood before her, with her disheveled hair and sleepy gaze. Not just in the plain white t-shirt, with blue lace boyshorts peeking from under the hem. No, every aspect of Liv had Honey holding onto hope. Every gentle touch and softly spoken reverence had her clinging to the possibility that this could be something, well, permanent.

"We absolutely don't have to do this, if you're starting to have second thoughts."

Liv's words were a reassurance Honey realized she didn't need, but she was so grateful to hear. Walking over to her bed, Honey sat down on the end and patted the space next to her. Liv, still holding Honey's hand, sat down and turned to face her.

"When I'm with you I don't have second thoughts. My first and *only* thoughts are of you," Honey admitted, her hands trembling. She felt a light pressure as Liv squeezed them reassuringly.

"I know exactly what you mean. It's so easy to get lost here. In Verity…in you. I haven't thought of anything else in weeks. This place and you, have become such a part of me, that I forget what I came here to do."

"I never meant to become a distraction."

"No, Honey," Liv's hand slipped around the back of Honey's neck, applying a light pressure and then their eyes met. "Make me forget…please."

There was a pain in Liv's voice that Honey wanted to soothe. She knew she should ask what was going on. She suspected another call from Liv's father could be behind all of this, but she wasn't sure if Liv was ready to share that part of her life just yet. She hadn't given up much about her life and Honey knew it was absolutely something they should discuss but not one to rush someone, she would wait and hope that when the time was right Liv would speak to her. Right now, all she wanted to do, was wrap Liv in her arms and hold onto her tight. Be her anchor in stormy seas, a lighthouse in stormy weather. She leaned forward and placed a kiss at the corner of Liv's mouth.

"How about I give you something to remember instead."

Honey shifted herself to her feet, nodding her instructions for Liv to move further back. As she did, Honey bent to crawl the length of her bed. When Liv's back rested against the headboard, Honey moved to straddle her. Liv's hands rose instantly, steadying Honey as she lowered herself into Liv's lap and kissed her deeply. She felt her entire body slow, and her breathing become heavier, as she instinctively ground her hips into Liv's. It felt delicious. She moved her hands down Liv's chest and gripped at the fabric of her t-shirt.

"May I?"

Liv nodded and wasted no time rocking side to side to untuck the t-shirt from underneath her. Honey slid her hands lower and lifted the material over Liv's head. The lengthy waves that Liv hadn't bothered to tame that morning, became bundled up in the fabric and then fell over her bare shoulders. Honey tossed the t-shirt to the floor and with a deep inhale, she allowed herself a moment to take Liv in. Really take her in.

Liv's bare skin was flawless, glistening with a light sheen of perspiration that Honey wanted to taste and so she did. She leaned into Liv and placed a kiss on her shoulder, dipping her tongue out and licking along the ridge of her clavicle until she felt Liv shiver beneath her. Her hands began to trail a path over Liv's bare skin, from her hips up to her small breasts, that were now pebbled from the rush of cold air that crept through Honey's open window. Liv's nipples were hard and tall, as Honey brushed them with her thumbs she felt the urge to take them into her mouth and soften them with the warmth of her tongue. She swallowed back that desire, not wanting to rush this, knowing deep down that the tension that had built between them, was just as delicious as her impending release. Her eyes continued to travel down Liv's stomach to the blue boy shorts that hugged her hips. She swallowed back a moan as she noticed a damp patch at the apex of Liv's thighs. Liv made no attempt to move, her chest was heaving with anticipation of Honey's next move and when she lightly traced her fingers back down Liv's body, a small moan escaped them both.

Honey loved seeing her this way, raw, real and so breathtakingly stunning. Liv was so soft, Honey wanted to fold herself into her.

"You're so beautiful," she said, trailing her fingertips across Liv's lower abdomen.

When Liv's thigh rose and connected with Honey's center, a slight panic took over her as the wetness between her own thighs increased. There was absolutely no denying how incredibly turned on she was, how much she wanted, no, needed Liv. Honey felt her own body signal the need for more friction and yet she didn't want this to be over before it began and that was becoming a very real possibility. She tried to lift herself up on her knees, to create a distance between them and allow her body a moment of reprieve. Liv however, had other plans and Honey felt the grip on her hips tighten, as Liv held her in place. Liv lifted her thigh again, connecting with Honey's center and she moaned into the air. Her head rolled back on her shoulders as she hooked her limp arms around Liv's shoulders to steady herself.

"If... if you keep doing that I'm not sure how long I'm going to last," she admitted, closing her eyes and scrunching up her nose in slight embarrassment.

Liv knew just what to do to get her worked up and it came as no surprise that the first touch of their skin had ignited such a powerful response. Honey bent her head to Liv's shoulder and began to kiss a trail up her neck and along her jaw.

"I don't see a problem with that," Liv breathed.

Honey could feel her wetness now, soaking through the fabric of her underwear, coating Liv's thigh as she continued to rock back and forth. The friction was pulling her deliciously towards release and she could feel the beginning flutters in her stomach. Without hesitation she reached for Liv's hand and moved it between them, guiding her to the place she needed her most. When she felt Liv's hand push the fabric of her underwear aside, her fingers fluttering over her core, Honey bit down hard on her bottom lip.

"Fuck, Honey. You're so wet,"

Honey nodded away any embarrassment she may have felt. The way Liv spoke was with such reverence that it was impossible to feel anything but aroused, and she pushed herself further into Liv's touch. She didn't want this to stop. The way she felt right now, like every part of her was on fire, ignited in that delicious way that always signalled amazing sex, was long overdue. She moved her hands up Liv's body, cupping her breasts and pinching lightly at Liv's incredibly taut nipples. She wanted to make her feel even an iota of how good she was feeling right now. As good as Liv had made her feel all night, as they texted back and forth the things they wanted to do to one another.

Emboldened, Honey gave a gentle but firm tug at Liv's nipples, and like she suspected would happen, Liv arched her back in ecstasy.

"Yes! That feels amazing," Liv whimpered encouragingly and Honey repeated the motion once more. When Honey felt Liv's fingers swipe through her folds she paused in her ministrations momentarily and proceeded to remove her own t-shirt. She had to feel all of Liv, needed to feel her body against hers, without barriers. She wanted to close the space between them until their hearts beat in sync, passing declarations of desire between them with each thud.

Tossing her t-shirt to the floor, Honey felt her spine curve into Liv's touch, as the hand not between her legs, moved up to tangle in the hair at the nape of her neck. When Liv tugged, Honey moaned unabashedly. She loved having her hair firmly fisted and pulled, it was absolutely one of her biggest turn ons.

"Tell me what *you* want," Liv whispered raggedly in Honey's ear, and she wasn't sure she could organize her thoughts to answer that, with the way Liv was making her feel right now. Although she was normally shy when it came to asking for what she wanted and she wasn't sure she would have mentioned this particular desire to Liv, Honey was not surprised that Liv knew exactly what to do, where to touch her, how to touch her to have her body shaking the way it was right now.

None of this felt out of the ordinary, Honey felt like she had known Liv's body before, from the way she moved to the way she tasted, she felt familiar, inevitable. She wondered if Liv felt the same way.

"I want you. I need you." Honey moaned, and she felt Liv's index and middle fingers flick upwards towards her clit. The gentle but confident motion of Liv's fingers against her, fanned a flame that had been burning steadily for days now.

"You have me."

Honey squeezed her eyes shut, rocking herself back and forth as Liv moved in circles over her. Her breathing increasingly unsteady, she felt her clit twitch as Liv moved in a downward motion, and entered her.

"Fuck, Liv!" she groaned, as the two fingers inside her, curved upwards. She rocked her hips back and forth, slowly at first, allowing herself to adjust to the fullness of Liv's long fingers, before picking up pace to match the release threatening on the horizon.

Honey couldn't remember it ever feeling this good with Andie. She wasn't sure if it was because of the two year stint of only experiencing orgasms she gave herself, or it was because it was Liv, but she couldn't control how fast she felt her orgasm build. She reasoned with herself it was a combination of both. She usually took a while to get to this stage when alone, even with a little assistance, and so she was a little surprised that Liv's touch was coaxing her finicky orgasm out of her with ease.

Honey couldn't speak, but she didn't need to. Liv's fingers slipped out of her, sliding up to circle her clit once more, coating it in her wetness. She nodded her head in confirmation, letting Liv know she was doing exactly the right thing but she knew Liv needed no directions. She was taking from Honey exactly what Honey had to give. Touching her like she had known her before. Playing her like a song she had written every note to and when she felt Liv's tongue flick over her earlobe, sending a jolt of satisfaction through her entire body, Honey let go. A warmth flooded her thighs as she rocked herself hard against Liv's strumming fingers. Murmurs and pleas of Liv's name fell repeatedly from her lips.

"That's it, let go. Come for me." Liv whispered throatily, continuing to flick her tongue over the sensitive shell of her ear. As Honey came loudly, she wrapped her arms around Liv's shoulders, anchoring herself in place as her legs started to shake uncontrollably.

"Where did that come from?" Liv said smugly. Honey could feel her cheeks pinking with a post-orgasmic bliss that flushed over her entire body. A shiver ran down her spine, and she kissed her way along Liv's shoulder, up her neck and licked a line from her jaw to her ear.

"I think we both know that started nights ago, when you first started sending me flirty texts," she teased boldly.

Liv's hands moved to meet at the base of her spine and she stroked at the slick skin there, urging Honey to look at her.

"When *I* first started sending flirty texts? I do believe it was you, Miss Rosenberg, who made the first move."

Honey knew what Liv was playing at. This would be part of another delicious back and forth that they played, and if the results were going to be more of what she just experienced, she absolutely was ready to play along. She dropped her arms and shuffled back to rest on her knees. Liv looked a little confused, until Honey hands found her thighs, pressing them apart and she settled herself between them.

"I think we both know that the person who started all of this was you, Miss Henderson!" she hummed, trailing her fingers over Liv's stomach and watching as her hips lifted into the touch.

She hooked her fingers into the waistband of Liv's boyshorts and began lowering them down her creamy thighs, her breath hitching as Liv's center came into view. Honey licked her lips at the sight of Liv's dark pink folds glistening with her obvious arousal. She felt emboldened now and the heady scent of the woman beneath her boosted Honey's confidence threefold.

"I think you knew you wanted me the moment you kissed me, all those weeks ago. Tell me I'm wrong."

Liv shook her head and closed her eyes as Honey continued to pull the fabric of her underwear down to her ankles. The sight of Liv laid bare just for her, chest heaving with anticipation and biting her bottom lip had Honey's clit twitching and she swore in all her life, she had never seen anyone more beautiful.

"You're wrong. I didn't want you the moment I kissed you," Liv said and Honey paused, her heart thrumming against her chest as she willed Liv to continue speaking. She wasn't disappointed. "I wanted you the moment I met you."

Honey couldn't believe it, Liv had given voice to the feeling she had been wrestling with herself, over the last month. The feeling of instantly wanting someone she had only just met. Wanting to know everything there was to know about that person, but also understanding that none of what she would discover would be new to her, because none of this felt uncertain. Touching Liv for the first time felt like returning to a place she had forgotten, but that deep down she had missed for so long. Having Liv touch her, felt like waking up from a long sleep and being instantly at ease. Being together like this, for Honey at least, felt like coming home.

"You can have me, Liv. Over and over again. But first, I. Want. You," she punctuated each word with a kiss as she glanced up from between Liv's thighs.

On all fours she continued kissing the soft skin of Liv's inner thighs, until her nose bumped against Liv's center. Her tongue darted out of her mouth and parted Liv's folds, gathering her arousal on the tip, she moaned at the taste. Liv's hands tangled in her hair, gently rubbing at her scalp, and her eyes rolled back in her head at the sensation. Not wanting to get distracted she swiped again at Liv, circling her clit and Liv loosened her grip. Honey rewarded Liv's submission by flattening her tongue against her, adding a little pressure and Liv's hips lifted from the bed, urging Honey to taste more of her. She took the opportunity to slip her hands underneath Liv's ass and hold her in place, still licking her with the flat of her tongue. Liv moaned and squirmed, trying to regain some control but Honey refused to give it to her.

Liv could of course have her over and over, all night long. But right now, Honey knew she needed this, and so she allowed herself to do something that felt as inevitable as it was scary. She lost herself in Liv Henderson and she knew she would have no regrets.

Chapter 18

Liv

The smell of peach and cinnamon filled Liv's nostrils, her eyes fluttered open and she noticed the space next to her was empty. The soft blue comforter had been pulled back from the side of the bed where Honey had curled up earlier. The early morning sun was now a burning midday heat, causing a light sheen of perspiration to glitter her skin. She glanced down at her naked body and felt extremely aware of the parts of her that were aching in the best way.

Liv was surprised. Honey had been reserved so far, in all of their sexual exchanges. She had been shy at first in returning texts, but had developed confidence as the days passed by. Last night Honey had asked to listen over the phone, as Liv moaned her release, and it had been wonderful. Surprising but also so sexy, it had spurred her to a second and even third orgasm.

She had considered the possibility that Honey would be nervous the next time they saw one another, and that it would be evident to see when they next spent time together. She had prepared herself for the possibility that Honey hadn't meant to invite her over, and was merely playing along, as she flew down the stairs of the big house, earlier. She had, however, shaken that notion away as she slipped her bare feet into the gumboots she kept by the front door. When Honey had opened the door, all negative thoughts she had conjured flew off in the opposite direction to where she was headed.

The moment their bodies had touched, Liv was certain Honey wanted her, with the same absolute certainty that she wanted Honey. They had both acted on their attraction in small ways, over the last few days and nights. They spent most of the time they weren't sorting the house, talking and making out. Liv had felt sheepish, like she was a teenager experiencing the pangs of first love again. Honey was innocence and excitement and when she touched Liv she lit a spark that threatened to burn brighter than anything she had ever known.

She loved Marcie, and had thought she was in love. She knew what it was to see someone and to be entranced by them. But Liv had never known what it was like to be truly seen. No one had ever looked at her the way Honey did, like she had all the answers to every question.

Like she was the answer.

When Honey had straddled her waist and made love to her a few hours ago, Liv wanted nothing more than to be exactly that.

They had pored over one another's bodies with gentle caresses of hands that have held others, but had never felt home until they touched one another. They had shared secrets, wants and needs in silent movements, and kisses that left invisible declarations of adoration in places they needed each other most.

Liv had leaned into each touch with an ease that told her they were meant for this. Liv was a rational person who believed in what she could see, rather than what she felt, but how she felt for Honey was difficult to ignore.

Lust was different to love, it was unapologetic and strong, but what Liv felt was more than that. The deep feelings she had for Honey hadn't come all at once, like love was known to do. They hadn't rushed in head first and revved her heart into an irrational frenzy. In some ways she felt like her feelings had always been there, burning in the background, long before they had known one another. Their connection was something instantaneous, it was deep and heavy and real. Honey was embedded into the rhythm of her heartbeat, and when she had placed her hand over Liv's heart and gently tapped out each thrum of desire, Liv had known there was no turning back.

She pulled the sheets back and scanned the room for sight of the t-shirt Honey had thrown from her, prior to lavishing her with long sought after attention. She found it folded up neatly on an old rocking chair, in the corner of the room. It made Liv smile, how careful Honey was. The little acts of kindness she often indulged in, were very much one of her most attractive qualities. Knowing she was this careful with her belongings made Liv a little more at ease with how her heart would be cared for.

"So sweet," Liv said, swinging her legs from the bed and crossing the room to retrieve her clothes.

She allowed herself a moment to take a look around the room. Liv had always thought you could tell a lot about a person from their bedroom. Marcie had been insistent that everything be white, chrome and clinical. This was indicative of their relationship too. Honey was the polar opposite. Everything in this room screamed comfort and warmth. From the cottagecore decor, pastel walls and wooden furniture to the crocheted blanket that was folded over the back of the rocking chair. It struck Liv that it was almost identical to the one at her grandparents' place. She wondered if Honey had made them, Liv could imagine her dexterous fingers conjuring something from nothing.

She sucked in a breath as a flash of those dexterous fingers swiping through her folds, entered her mind. Honey absolutely knew what she had been doing. Although her words were playful and teasing, she had been soft and slow as her confidence built. Before Liv knew what was happening she had seen stars form behind her eyelids as orgasm after orgasm had rippled through her. She absolutely wanted to experience that again.

Liv pulled the t-shirt over her head and headed out of the room. Making her way down the stairs she followed the homely scents and sounds of Honey's stand mixer. She stepped into the open space of the cottage and the sight before her took her breath away.

Honey had her back to Liv and her hips were swaying to the Taylor Swift song that was playing quietly through the speaker system. Her messy hair hung around her shoulders, and she wore nothing but an apron and a pair of pink lace, see through, boy shorts. Liv swallowed as Honey continued to dance, unaware she was being watched. She picked up a spatula and used it as a microphone as she sang the words to 'Message in a Bottle', out loud.

A heat made itself known between Liv's thighs as she took in the almost liquid way Honey moved. Her hands itched to reach out and touch, to hold onto those swaying hips and guide them into her own. Before she could stop herself she had stepped up behind Honey and pressed her into the countertop. Honey stilled, spatula in hand and for a brief second Liv worried she had overstepped but then she felt Honey lean back into her chest. Arching her back and pressing her ass into Liv's middle, a groan escaped Liv's mouth.

"I never knew you were a Swiftie!" Liv teased, slipping her hands around Honey's front and fingering the bow that had been tied a hand space below her generous breasts.

"You don't know *everything* about me. Not yet anyway." Honey said.

Her head fell back to Liv's shoulder as she negotiated the tie open and the soft pink cotton billowed around her curvy frame. Liv smoothed her hands back and tucked them under the apron, cupping Honey's breasts in almost a mirror action to how Honey had taken her earlier that morning.

"I know enough to know that you like it when I do this," Liv teased, her forefingers and thumbs rubbing against Honey's stiff peaks.

She could feel Honey's breathing become labored and when she gave a light tug it elicited a mewing noise that Liv had played on repeat in her head since she first heard it.

"Mmmmm…" Honey moaned, dropping the spatula and gripping the countertop as Liv continued her ministrations. "I really *do* like that."

Liv stopped tugging on her nipple and danced one hand down Honey's stomach, pushing past the waistband of her boyshorts and parting her folds with a single digit. She rested her head on Honey's shoulder and smirked as she noted the white knuckled grip Honey had on the counter. She circled Honey's clit with her forefinger and began peppering kisses along her shoulder, up her neck and to her ear. She took her lobe into her mouth and remembering how it had affected her so much last night, flicked at it with her tongue.

"Liv!" Honey said in breathy whispers, "Please, Liv. More."

Not one to disappoint, Liv did as requested. She slipped a second finger between Honey's folds and moved in larger circles over her clit, adding more pressure.

She knew from their text exchanges, what Honey required in order to climax. It made her happy that Honey trusted her enough to vocalize her wants and needs. That she had felt comfortable enough with Liv to express those without fear of being judged. Liv had offered up her own preferences too, and when they finally came together, they felt well versed in how the other liked to be touched.

Liv gulped as Honey once again begged for more and she stopped everything she was doing to spin her around. Hands firmly on

Honey's hips she lowered herself to her knees. The wooden flooring was cold against her bare knees but her entire body warmed with the sight before her. She looked up at the woman above her, Honey's eyes were hooded and filled with wanton desire. She was breathtaking. A perfect picture that Liv knew she would commit to memory.

Lifting the soft cotton of the apron, Liv could already taste Honey's arousal in the air. She leant forward and kissed her center through the damp fabric of her shorts.

"Oh!"

A soft moan reverberated from above her as Liv hooked her fingers into the waistband of Honeys boyshorts. Lowering them slowly, she savored every second. She had watched Honey writhe above her earlier, taking control between the sheets, but right now Liv wanted nothing more than to have her lover submit to her a little. To show her how much she wanted her. To do to her all the things they had teased over the last few nights.

Above her, Honey faltered, her knees buckled as the boyshorts came to pool around her ankles. She widened her stance automatically, making room between her thighs for Liv and she didn't falter. Shuffling forward slightly, hands moving to cup the soft skin where Honey's thighs met her ass, Liv leaned into her, slipped her tongue out of her mouth and swiped upwards.

"F...F....Fuck!" Honey said, rocking her hips into her face and causing Liv to tighten her grip. She flicked Honey's clit with the tip of her tongue, then flattened it against her.

Again, in no time at all, Liv felt Honey squeeze at her shoulders, an indication that she was close. Liv held on a little tighter as she sucked her throbbing clit into her mouth and moaned, the reverberation sending Honey over the edge. A gush of arousal coated her chin and she lapped at Honey with a hunger that surprised even herself.

"Well, Good Afternoon to you, too!" Honey said, pulling the apron back over her, as Liv got to her feet and licked at the remnants of Honey's orgasm that coated her lips. "I didn't expect that when I came down to make breakfast."

"Well, what can I say? I woke up and you weren't there then I came down here and saw you in nothing but those shorts and that apron. I couldn't help myself. I had to have you."

"You have me, entirely."

Liv had suspected this admission was a slip, something Honey hadn't expected to have fallen from her mouth but she took a chance.

"Do I?"

Nerves took over the minute the question hit the air but Liv knew that she wouldn't take it back if she could. She wanted to hear the answer, wanted to know where they stood. She needed the truth, even if she wasn't sure she was ready for it. She wasn't entirely sure anyone was ever really ready for the truth. But as she looked at Honey, standing there glowing from her release, breathing heavily and with a look of adoration on her face, she knew she hadn't needed to ask.

"I think you already know the answer to that."

A silence filled the room. Not an awkward silence that geared a person up for running, no, this one washed over them and comforted them, rather than causing fear and anxiety. Liv marveled at Honey's openness, at her ability to be honest and true, even after everything that had happened to her. She wasn't sure how she had come to be in the presence of someone who had experienced all the loss that Honey had, and yet who still loved as openly and freely as she did. Liv kept a lot of her own life locked away inside her, but Honey made her want to share everything.

Her past, her present, her future.

She wanted to reassure Honey that she wasn't alone in her feelings and ease some of the obvious uncertainties that were written across her beautiful face, but now wasn't the right time to get into anything heavy. Liv still had so much to do here, so many things to pack away, so many decisions to make... a book to find.

Her father had called again last night and she had ignored his call. Not one to be deterred, he had left a voicemail demanding information as to exactly what was taking Liv so long, and why she hadn't found something as simple as a book. A knowing smirk had crossed her face while listening to his rant, he absolutely didn't want to know what she was doing in Verity, that had distracted her from finding the book. Especially as, while she was listening to his stern demanding tone, the humming of another sext from the cute girl across the field, sounded through her phone. Honey was a much welcomed distraction and last night had been exactly what Liv needed, but she couldn't shake the churning in her stomach, at the weight of expectation her father had burdened her with.

"Are you okay?" Honey said.

Liv shook away her thoughts and brought herself back into the moment, her gaze sweeping over the kitchen and the utensils spread out over the countertop.

"What are you making? I could have sworn I smelled cinnamon?" She said, trying to move past getting into anything too deep but also not wanting to ruin the moment and potentially hurt Honey.

That was another weight she was carrying in her emotional baggage, the fact that she could potentially hurt Honey with one of the decisions she had to make. Mentally, she tightened the zipper on that particular notion and hoped it would hold, for now at least.

"You did! Great nose!"

"I happen to think all of my face is great, but it's good to know you like the nose." Liv teased and she felt Honey's curves press into her side as she hip checked her and moved to take the bowl from the standmixer.

The way she stepped around the kitchen was practiced and Liv found herself entranced with each of Honey's movements. As she grabbed a dish cloth and bent to pull a tray from the oven, Liv inhaled deeply, her eyes widening.

"Mmmm, what are those?" she asked, getting off her seat and rounding the counter, any excuse to be closer to Honey.

The tray was filled with soft, fluffy looking, individual golden brown muffins, dotted with small pieces of fleshy fruit.

"I'm thinking of calling them Peach Pastimes Muffins." Honey said, scooping the tray up with the towel and holding it in front of Liv, "Here, smell them. Careful, they're hot."

She tapped away Liv's roaming hands, before Liv had noticed they'd even reached for the tray. Her mouth was salivating at the thought of tasting those delicious little parcels. She inhaled once more and felt something still her, a memory lingered on the precipice of her mind and she narrowed her eyebrows trying to coax it into being.

"I know this smell."

"You should. I used your grandmother's cobbler recipe and altered it a little. If you can hold off for a few minutes until they're cooled, I made vanilla and elderflower frosting to go on top," Honey said as she placed the tray back on the countertop and carefully removed the muffins from the tray before transferring them to a cooling rack. "Liv, is everything okay?"

Liv felt something catch in her throat, she swallowed it down. "You used my grandmother's recipe?"

"Yeah, it's all written down here," Honey crossed the room and picked up a book, its pages were yellowing and loose.

Liv couldn't believe it. Her heart beat rapidly against her chest, the sound of thudding dampened all other sounds. Honey's mouth kept moving, but Liv couldn't hear a word she was saying. In her hands, her wonderfully delicate hands was the book that Liv's father had been asking for. All sorts of questions ran through Liv's mind. How had it come to be in Honey's possession? Had she found this while helping her pack and decided to take it? She couldn't blame her if that was the case, as Liv had told her that anything she wanted to take she could.

"Of course I'll never be able to make a cobbler as good as Bea did, but I thought, well, I can make a mean muffin so why not try. I've been meaning to find time to try out some of her recipes, but with work and things with my sisters and then getting to know you, I've not really managed to find the time. Not that I'm complaining. I've loved getting to know you."

"You've had this all along?" Liv asked, as a horrible feeling crept up on her, manifesting before she could confront it with rationality.

"I'm sorry, am I missing something?"

Confusion covered Honey's face and Liv watched her eyes flicker back and forth, between Liv and the book.

"You've had my grandmother's book this whole time? I've been ransacking that house looking for something that *you* had all along!" Liv's voice became loud and even though Honey took a step back, in obvious confusion, she continued. "You didn't think to mention this to me, oh, I don't know, the countless times you came over and pretended to help me with packing? You know the pressure my father is putting on me to find this!"

Honey shook her head. "You never told me you were looking for a book, Liv. You never gave me any specifics about what you were looking for. I didn't keep this from you purposely."

It was no use, Liv's fight or flight had triggered, and she found her voice becoming louder, laced with something she hadn't ever expected when speaking to Honey, distrust.

"Was this your plan all along? To get close to me so I'd forget that you live here rent free and that I'd feel bad asking you to leave? To keep this a secret and make money from it when *I* eventually leave?" She stepped towards Honey, closing the space the blonde had created between them.

"I'm sorry, w…what?"

"I can't believe this. I could have had my father off my back by now. I could have been packed up and had the property listed. I could have been back at home. But I've wasted so much of my time looking for this damn book! I've wasted so much of my time–"

"…here with me. You don't have to say it. I can hear it in your voice and see it on your face."

Honey's voice was soft and laced with a sadness that Liv almost didn't pick up on, too lost in her own head. When she took a moment to catch her breath, she noticed how small Honey had become. How she was looking down at her feet, gaze fixed on the floor to hide the tears that had begun to roll down her cheeks.

Shame burned inside Liv, she absolutely hadn't meant to make Honey feel bad. She wasn't entirely sure what was happening right now. There were too many emotions fighting for control of her; anger and fear were waging a war against reason and certainty, and the scales were tipped to the negative. She didn't want this. She didn't want the confusion she was feeling to erase the wonderful things she had experienced over the last few weeks. But standing there in Honey's kitchen, with the woman she had earlier been revering, breaking before her eyes, because of *her* words, the peace and comfort she had slipped into like an old cardigan upon arriving here in Verity, began slipping away.

"Honey, I didn't mean to say that," she tried, wanting to right the wrongs she knew had occurred.

She lifted a hand to reach for Honey, but the smaller woman stepped back again.

"I…I think you did. You were never thinking about staying, were you? All those things you said were lies and I fell for them. I fell for you. Gosh, maybe Kyla is right, I do give myself too soon." Honey brushed a hand over the soft, worn cover of the book and thrust it out in front of her. It lingered between them like an ultimatum. "Here, take it…give it to your father."

Liv reached out shakily and when her fingers connected with the book, she felt the weight of it pressed firmly into her palm. Tears rolled freely down Honey's face and Liv knew she had caused them.

"Honey, I–"

"I want you to know that I loved your grandfather very much. When he died I lost more than a neighbor, I lost my best friend. He was a huge part of my life and my heart and I was so lost without him. When you showed up here, I felt like I'd gotten a part of him back. You're so like him in so many ways, but so *not* like him in others. He would never have made me feel like this. He never spoke words he didn't mean, words he couldn't take back. If I had known that *that* was what you were looking for, I would have given it to you immediately. I would never have stolen from you, Liv. I would never have stolen from him."

The heaviness in Honey's words hurt Liv in a way she hadn't expected it to. She felt tears burning at her own eyes as the realization of what was happening, what those words meant, started to make itself known.

"Honey… I…" Liv tried to speak, but the words wouldn't come.

She wanted to explain how she really hadn't meant to say the things she did, the way she did. That this was a stupid, gut reaction to something that was absolutely nothing to do with Honey, not really. This was her mind convincing her that she had been lied to. Lingering weeds of insecurity that had been planted by Marcie, growing in a place they had no right to. She was projecting onto Honey something she had stupidly convinced herself she had left back in the city.

Honey wrapped her arms around herself, covering the parts of her still on show. She looked vulnerable and hurt, and Liv knew how badly she had messed up. The book in her hands felt like a lead weight, pulling under water and she was struggling to breathe. She wanted to fix this. To go back to minutes earlier when Honey's arms were wrapped around Liv instead of herself. She knew though, that it wasn't as simple as that. This wasn't something that could be fixed with apologies and platitudes, the damage was done.

"I think you should leave," Honey said. "This is still my home, at least for now. I want you to leave. Please."

Liv did as she was told. Still clutching the book in her hands she backed out of Honey's personal space, crossing the room to find the gumboots she had removed earlier that morning. Now she struggled as she pushed her bare feet into them, where this morning they had felt too big, they now felt two sizes too small. Everything in this moment felt like it didn't fit. The t-shirt that hung from her lithe frame felt tight around the neck, felt smothering against her skin and she tugged and pulled at the fabric.

Heading for the door she considered looking back, but she knew what would confront her if she did, and she knew that she wasn't able to handle all of this. In a matter of moments her world had crumbled around her. This hurt so much more than the end of her relationship with Marcie, and it was in recognizing that Liv knew what she had lost.

***

She turned the book over in her hands, the purple fabric felt like prickles in her hands. Her stomach ached with knowing that she had hurt someone she cared about deeply, over what was inside the covers. Honey hadn't fought back when Liv had started spewing her accusations. She could have combated Liv's every word with an explanation, but in true to her nature, she had simply done what was right, even though Liv was the one who was wrong.

Before she had crossed the field, Liv had already realized what a mess she had made. When she stepped into the emptiness of the house, she had pushed the door shut with her back and sank to the floor, unable to function. She was still sitting there now, as the cuckoo clock on the wall began to indicate it was six pm. The noise was deafening and she squeezed her eyes shut, willing it to be quiet, to stop shouting at her in its accusatory tone.

Five hours, she had lost five whole hours sitting with this book in her hands, unable to fathom how she had gotten here.

Her phone began to ring. Liv got to her feet and made her way through the hall, up the stairs and into her room where she had left it, before she made the mad rush across the field earlier that morning.

"Hello?" she said.

Not having glanced at the screen when she swiped, she was uncertain as to whose voice she would hear when they chose to reply. A part of her, a large part, hoped it was Honey. It wasn't.

"Elizabeth, you've been avoiding my calls."

Marcie's voice felt like a punch in the gut. Every word she spoke felt like further blows to her already fragile state and Liv wasn't sure how much more she could take today.

"Why are you calling me? Haven't you taken enough from me already?" Liv asked, her entire body shaking with the anger she felt towards the woman on the other end of the phone. The person to whom all of her anger should have been directed.

"I don't think that it's fair to throw something like what we have, away like that. To just run away to another part of the country and pretend we didn't matter."

Liv pinched the bridge of her nose, sitting down on the unmade bed she leaned forward and rested her elbow on her knee. This was all too much. How dare she call her and try to place blame on her.

"Marcie, you were the one who pretended we didn't matter, and you did it right under my nose. You did it in the city we lived in, in the house we shared and you did it for months. I wasn't the one who gave up. I just accepted it when the time came."

"You didn't even fight for me, Elizabeth! For what we had!"

"What *did* we have Marcie?" Liv asked, throwing her body back on the bed and closing her eyes. "A life built on lies. A relationship that neither of us really wanted to be in. You knew we wanted different things and you went and found exactly what it was you *did* want. You found someone who wanted the same life you do. I just wish you had been more honest about it, and I wish I had been strong enough to have let go earlier."

"You don't mean that, Liv. This isn't you speaking. I know you."

"No Marcie, you don't. How can you, when *I* don't even know me? Please don't call me anymore. We don't have anything to say to one another. I don't even know why you would think we would."

"Because I love you, Elizabeth."

There they were, the words Marcie used when she wanted to gloss over things. Words she used to control Liv, only she didn't feel their effects in the same way she used to. They didn't make her feel warm and wanted, they made her feel sick. Marcie wasn't the person she wanted to hear those words from, not anymore.

"Don't! Don't say things that aren't true. Because love isn't a word you should throw around like that. Love isn't simply saying it. It's really meaning it, Marcie. You shouldn't say them to try and control someone. You should say them because they're the only ones you can think of when you're with that person. Love is feeling it. It's feeling it with every part of your being. It's knowing you can't breathe without that person next to you. Knowing you can get through the days without them, but not wanting to. Because without them you're not really living, you're just existing. What we had was an existence and for a while it was enough. But I want to live, Marcie. Really live…and I want to love. I think I deserve that."

"Is there someone else?"

That question stirred feelings in Liv that she couldn't quite place. She didn't feel the need to justify herself, or her relationships, with someone who really didn't have the right to know about them, not anymore. Marcie wasn't entitled to know about Honey, or that she was the first place Liv's mind went to upon hearing the question. She didn't know what it was she would say, even if she did want to share that part of her life. Telling your ex about someone you had potentially fallen in love with wasn't your average conversation.

Someone she had potentially fallen in love with. Liv ran that thought over in her head. Had she fallen already? She considered how and when it had happened, searching for the exact moment she had fallen in love with Honey. Had it been earlier this morning, when Honey's body had moved with hers between the cotton sheets of her bed? Had it been at Ariellas party, when they kissed for the first time, and she felt her entire world tilting on its axis? Maybe it was the night they lay under the stars and for the first time the world didn't feel like it was spinning too fast, it felt still. Maybe it had been that first day she had pulled up in this town and she fell head first into Honey's waiting arms. Liv felt her heart jackhammering truth against her chest, telling her it was absolutely a combination of them all. There was no denying it, she was absolutely, irrevocably in love with Honey and she might have ruined it already.

Marcie's voice filtered through her ears once again. "Have you found someone else, Elizabeth?"

"Yeah, I have." Liv replied,"…Me."

Chapter 19

Honey

Honey was glad she had pulled on a cardigan before she left the house this morning, as the sun hadn't yet made an appearance, and the heating in her Jeep was a little unpredictable. She knew that it was a cop out, heading back to work without an apology from Kyla, but she also really needed to get away from the cottage, at least for a little while.

Everywhere she looked she could see Liv, and it was overwhelming. She had sat in the bathroom for hours after she left, crying until she was pretty sure there was nothing left in her. Exhausted and tired she had crawled into bed, but the smell of Liv clung to the cotton sheets and her stomach churned. Honey hadn't been able to stay there, the memories were too painful and so she had schlepped herself downstairs and slept on the sofa. *Slept* was used loosely of course and her mirror had reminded her of how loosely this morning, as she had tamed her messy curls into two space buns and tried to hide the puffiness under her eyes.

When she pulled up outside the deli, she noticed a line had formed outside. It wasn't out of the realm of possibility that this would occur, but at this time of day it wasn't something that happened often. Confused and a little worried, she got out of her car, walked to the doors and found them locked. She reasoned with herself that everything was okay because the wooden shutters weren't closed and the lights were on inside.

Chatter filled the street, as the patrons stretched in a line that she now saw lead all the way down past the doors of The Nook. She made a note to pass Laura, its owner, a Boston Imposter, a vegan chocolate take on the classic Boston Creme, by way of an apology for the chaos that was unfolding. The line didn't seem to be lessening and she saw Mrs Robbins at the front, her knitted bag devoid of its usual goodies.

"What's going on?" Honey said.

"Oh! Thank goodness you're here. I'm not sure what's going on but when I got here everything was locked and there was a note on the door."

Honey wasn't sure how she had missed it, looking at the note she could make out Sasha's somewhat rushed handwriting declaring she would *Be Back Soon.*

"I've been waiting here over an hour, and they're still not back. A lot of people have already given up waiting and taken themselves over to Irregular Blows. Deserters." Mrs Robbins clucked, shaking her head and Honey snorted a little at the nickname.

"I'm so sorry Mrs Robbins, let me open up and get you all served."

It took a little under twenty minutes for Honey to get the morning madness under control. She hadn't had time to think, and so she was still none the wiser as to why the deli was shut when she arrived. The tables were now filled with customers sipping happily on freshly brewed coffee and munching away on the small selection of her baked goods that thankfully, must have been stocked before her niece and sisters left this morning.

She had fired off a text to Sasha the minute she had a lull at her counter, but didn't expect an instant reply. Afterall she had avoided *her* calls for a little over a week now.

Panic rose in her chest and she slipped her hand under the counter, running her fingers, in an attempt to ground herself, over the scar in the wood where she had engraved her name as a child. Her counter was almost empty and the clock hanging to the right of the doors reminded her that the lunch time rush would be coming soon. Her growing anxiety from not having enough sweet goods made and having to close up early, was lingering, then a voice piped up from the other side of the counter.

"You look like you could use some help," it said, and Honey sighed a breath of relief.

Standing in front of her with the widest smile on her face, was Lara, the cute redhead Honey had babysat for as a child.

"I could use a miracle. My cabinets are a little low on sweet treats and I can't leave the front unattended but if I don't get back there and get baking, I'm going to have to close up shop."

"Well we can't have that, can we now? Do you have one of those for me?" Lara asked, nodding her head at Honey's apron before rounding the counter, smiling widely still.

Honey reached under the counter and grabbed the apron that Lissy usually wore. Handing it over she watched as Lara slipped it over her head and tied it deftly in a bow in a matter of seconds.

"Are you sure you don't mind doing this? It won't get you in trouble with your boss over at Joe's will it?"

Honey knew that Lara had worked at Joe's since it opened, as it was a convenient way for her to make money while at school. She had wanted to hire her at the deli, but Kyla was insistent on keeping it a family run business. Lara's mom hadn't been the most loving or supportive growing up. Honey could recall a few nights she had come home later than expected, smelling of alcohol and looking like she had been hit by a semi. Those nights Honey hadn't gotten paid for her babysitting job, but she hadn't cared. At least she knew Lara was safe.

"Joe's blows!" Lara said, flicking her comment away as if it was common knowledge... and it was. "You need someone to help you. Besides, you were always there for me when I needed you."

Honey looked directly at Lara and those words hung in the space between them. She felt her lip quiver as emotion built in her and she urged herself not to cry. She didn't think Lara really remembered much about their time together. Honey had been sixteen and Lara had been a typical six year old, who ran around the house speaking gibberish to her make-believe horse.

"Thank you, Lara."

Lara shrugged her shoulders as if it was nothing before turning to greet a customer that had just approached the counter. Honey listened to the exchange, it was entirely natural. Almost as if Lara had always been behind the counter here at Rosenberg's. Knowing that the shop floor was in good hands, Honey rushed into the kitchen. Before she started baking she pulled her phone from her apron pocket and tapped the screen, hoping for a reply as to what was going on.

Still nothing.

Anxiety balled itself in her chest. She couldn't wait any longer; she had to know what was happening and so, rather than wait around, Honey called Sasha.

The phone rang out continuously and no one picked up. Honey bit at the skin surrounding her thumbnail, a nervous habit she had engaged in since she was a child. Biting down harder as the call continued to ring out, Honey groaned and ended the call. She tucked her phone away in the pouch on the front of her apron and began to lose herself in her baking. The last few days, especially yesterday, had been hard and nothing seemed to be going right, but one thing that never changed would be the way she felt right here in her kitchen.

She sifted sugar into the softened butter that was already slowly churning in her mixer. The gentle hum soothed some of the restlessness she felt deep inside her. Baking was an art she had perfected over the years, her love for it picked up at her grandmother's side, most of it standing right here, in this very spot. Honey felt like this place was everything that she was. She had given herself to Rosenberg's, to the town of Verity, and she hadn't ever regretted that... until yesterday.

Yesterday, as the door closed behind Liv, Honey had felt like she was stuck in a place entirely too small. Like the safe road she had been walking had turned into a tightrope, and the walls of her once comforting cottage felt like they were closing in on her. She hadn't ever felt like this before. When Andie left to go volunteer in Australia, Honey had felt like the cottage was too big without her. She felt so alone, like she would get lost in the gaping space left by Andie.

When Liv left yesterday Honey had to resist everything in her that told her to go after her. To chase after Liv, across muddy fields and demand to know what was happening. To explain her side of the situation and hope she would be heard. But she was so scared of what would happen if she did. There was too much to risk when you gave someone access to you like that, to your vulnerabilities.

She was angry at Liv, for coming into her life and upending it. She didn't understand why after thirty years of feeling like she wanted for nothing, this woman had made her want...everything.Like a careless baker who doesn't take the time to sift the ingredients in but instead throws them together and hopes for the best, Liv had thrown affection, and adoration at Honey. She had made her believe that not everything had to be done carefully. Convinced her with her lips, to rush into things with her eyes closed.

Each gentle caress of Liv's hand had made her believe that everything would work out fine. She had convinced Honey to freefall, but hadn't told her how much the landing would hurt.

Her phone buzzed in her apron pocket and as she fumbled to retrieve it she almost dropped it into the standmixer.

"Hello, Sasha?"

"Hey Buzzy, sorry I missed your call. We had to close the store early today." Sasha's voice was tired.

"Is everything okay? Are you okay?" Honey said, lifting a hand to rub at the dull ache that had settled between her eyebrows.

"I'm fine Buzzy, It's Kyla. She surprised us all and went into early labor."

"Oh gosh! Is she okay? Are the babies okay?"

"They're all fine, Buzzy. They have to stay at the hospital for a few days but they're all doing great. Naturally, now that they're safe, Kyla is more concerned about the fact that we had to shut up shop and lost business. She spent a lot of time ranting about the cost of diapers, rather than focusing on her breathing. Poor little Sera and Della, they're going to have this held against them forever," Sasha joked and Honey felt a little smile appear on her own face at the ease with which her sister communicated with her.

"She had two little girls?"

Honey was so happy at this news, although she had no preference over the gender of her worker bees. She loved them all unconditionally. Kyla had told them all, that with these being her last, she wanted it to be a surprise. So it made perfect sense that just like their mother, they were impatient enough to ignore their due date and arrive early, on their own schedule.

"She did. Little is the right word too, they're so small Buzzy. The tiniest worker bees there have ever been. You should get yourself over here and see them."

As much as she wanted to see them, discomfort still lingered in Honey. She knew that eventually she would have to talk to Kyla, air things out and if she was lucky she would possibly receive a small apology. But she didn't hold out much hope. She didn't want this negativity to surround what should be a joyous occasion, and so she knew Sasha would understand when she excused herself.

"Maybe in a few days. I'll let them get some rest. Oh, you can tell Kyla that we didn't lose any takings, the tiny worker bees will have their diapers."

"You opened up?"

"I did." Honey said.

She flicked the stand mixer to a slow setting and brought her hand to her mouth to chew at the skin on the side of her thumbnail.

"Cute neighbor chick was willing to give you a hand outside of the bedroom?"

Honey felt sick, her stomach churning as she thought of Liv and how they had ended things. She didn't want to get into it right now, not over the phone, not when she was still trying to work out in her own head how things had gone so horribly wrong. Sasha wouldn't judge her, Honey knew that, she just wasn't ready to hear the words spoken out loud yet. To admit that once again she had failed.

"Erm... no."

"Is everything okay with you two?"

Clearly Sasha could hear the sadness in her voice, no matter how much Honey had tried to disguise it.

"There is no us two, Sasha. She is her, and I am me, and we are definitely not a we," she said, no matter how much Honey *really* wanted them to be. It didn't feel right to say that her and Liv were nothing, because regardless of what was happening there was definitely something there.

"Okay Dr Seuss! Is running the deli alone getting to you, because you sound stressed?"

Honey tucked the phone between her shoulder and ear, flipped the switch and unclipped the metal bowl from the stand. Moving over to where she had already laid out the greased up muffin trays she began to distribute the mixture evenly with her spatula.

"I didn't open up alone." she admitted. " Lara is here helping me, she's outside running the counter."

"Little Lara Lovett? You let Little Lara Lovett run loose in the deli?"

Sasha's surprise was expected, but Honey was still feeling oversensitive about everything that had happened, and was not about to have someone talking poorly about the one person who had stepped in and effectively saved the day without asking for anything in return. Lara was a sweetheart and it had always saddened Honey that not everyone in this town saw that.

"Relax, she's not six years old and riding around her pretend horse anymore, Sasha. She's almost twenty-one, that's practically an adult."

"If it's all the same with you, when we retell this story let's leave her out of it. You know how Ky feels about having people who aren't family working with us."

It was true, Kyla was very much a person with trust issues and that didn't just attach itself to people outside of the family. Honey wished that for once her sister would try and view people how she did, give them a fair shot, rather than write everyone off before they had even been allowed to try.

"I know, I'm surprised she even lets me in here and I am her family. But Lara has been great, more than great, without her we absolutely would have had to close for the day."

"Thank her for me." Sasha said softly, and Honey knew she meant it.

She scooped the spatula around the rim of the metal bowl, getting the last remnants of muffin mix into the trays before popping them in the oven.

"I will. Say hi to everyone."

"Oh I will. Honey, are you sure you're okay?"

"I don't know Sasha. But right now I just sort of have to be."

She wanted to get off the phone as quickly as she could, tears burned her eyes and emotion clogged her throat. If she confessed everything to Sasha it would all feel real and right now there were more important things Honey had to take care of. She couldn't afford to fall apart, not yet, anyway.

"I told you that you were the backbone of this family, Buzzy and I meant it. You're the most important piece in all our lives. You're always there to fix us when we fall apart. But I want you to know I'm here for you, should you ever feel like you're falling." Lissy was right when she said her mom gave great advice, Sasha always knew what to say. She felt the urge to tell Sasha that she had already started to fall. She had fallen too hard and too fast, for the woman across the field. Honey had done everything she knew she shouldn't have done and she didn't regret it, not one little bit.

"I have to go, it's really starting to pick up out there," she lied and hoped that the emotion would dissolve in her throat instead of betraying her.

The deli was busy, sure, but sneaking a glance out of the swing doors, Honey could see that Lara had it all under control. Of course she did. With her magnetic personality she was a veritable rockstar with the customers. She fit in perfectly at Rosenberg's and Honey wondered how much convincing it would take to try and keep her here.

***

Five o'clock rolled around quicker than it ever had before. Honey and Lara had managed to make sure that between them, Rosenberg's lived to open another day.

"I don't know about you, but I am so glad that today is over," Honey admitted, putting the takings into the safe and locking it.

She lifted her apron over her head, folded it over her crooked arm and reached to free her curls from the ponytail holder she had scooped them into when she began baking.

"I had fun," Lara shrugged, pulling the apron over her head and folding it neatly.

"You had fun working here, on your day off?"

"Yeah. It's nothing like being at Joe's. I mean that in the nicest way possible, of course. The customers here are all so friendly and they actually want to talk to you. The last time I had more than a grunted coffee order of an interaction with someone was over a month ago. Although come to think of it she never came back in so maybe I came on a little too strong." Lara trailed off, and Honey giggled a little.

"Was she cute?" she asked, noticing the way a pink blush rushed across Lara's face. Walking out of the back room, Lara followed.

"Oh! I mean, I guess so. She was a little older than I am. Not from around here either, so maybe she just went back home. How did you know…that I like girls too?"

Honey picked up the bag Lara had left under the counter and handed it back to her, "I saw the patch on your bookbag, earlier, and I *know you*, remember. You didn't ride that imaginary horse around your house because you enjoyed brushing its hair. You used to go on rescue missions and I think you spent the best part of a year looking for a damsel in distress."

Lara, still blushing, looked down at her feet and shook her head. "Never did find her. You know when I was younger I used to idolize you. When you would come babysit, I always knew I was safe. You always made me feel safe. It was like having my very own superhero. As I got older, I remember thinking that I couldn't wait to grow up and have it all together, like you do. You were always so comfortable in your own skin. You never had to hide who you were, because this town and everyone in it loves you, for exactly who you are."

"You don't have to hide who you are, Lara."

"You come from a good family, Honey. Not me, though. I'm just little Lara Lovett, daughter of the town drunk. People already look at me in pity and disgust. I could never really be out, not here…not like you are."

"Lara, you can't hide who you are just because you're worried other people won't like it. You have to give people a chance to prove they are here for you, that they care. But, you're more than someone else's opinions of you. You are exactly who you are meant to be right now, and you will become exactly who you are meant to become. You have to allow yourself the space to be that though. Be kind to yourself. I mean, you're plenty kind to others. I wouldn't have gotten through today without you."

Lara looked up at Honey's admission, a smile tugged at the corners of her mouth. Although she put on a brave face often, Honey knew Lara was laden with uncertainty, she could see it in her eyes. As she watched Lara ruminate over her words, Honey felt a little like this is what it must have been like for Marvin, every time he gave her advice. For the first time in weeks that connection to him didn't fill her with sadness, instead a warmth spread through her, a calm of sorts. She still had one thing of his and Liv could never take it away.

"I'm sure you would have. You're a superhero, remember!" Lara said, dropping her bag to the floor. The contents inside caused a thud that traveled through the empty shop. She reached into her book bag and pulled out a sweater to combat the cool breeze that filtered under the now closed doors of the deli.

"You know, Lara. I don't have it as together as you think I do," Honey said, reaching into the cabinet and grabbing two of the leftover muffins. She handed one over to the younger girl, hoisted herself up on the counter and began peeling the casing from her treat. "My girlfriend left me two years ago. She went all the way to Australia and never looked back. Then my best friend died and I fell in love with his granddaughter, who doesn't think the greatest things about me right now. I might very well lose my home, a place I love so very much. I had a huge disagreement with my sisters and haven't talked to them in over a week, that's been rough. Actually, the only thing that's going right for me, is this, here, and that's only because you stepped in and saved the day. You're *my* superhero, Lara. And if you can be that for me, you can be that for yourself. Maybe you never found your damsel in distress because she was never in distress, just a little lost."

"I guess we are all a little lost," Lara conceded before taking a bite out of her muffin and Honey nodded in agreement.

***

The gravel crunched beneath the tires of her Jeep as Honey pulled up in front of the cottage. She had debated not returning home right away and considered taking a stroll through the town, but she was exhausted, both physically and mentally. As she stepped out of the car she noticed Lissy was sitting on the front step, looking as tired as Honey felt.

"Hey you!" Honey said, walking towards where her niece sat.

Lissy got to her feet and wiped the dust off her denim cut offs. For a split second Honey saw in her niece, a glimpse of the small, uncertain, quiet little girl she used to be.

"I didn't know where else to go," Lissy said, her voice small. Honey tilted her head and shook it, uncertain of what was going on. "I've seen new worker bees come into our family regularly over the last fifteen years. I know how babies are born, but I don't think I ever knew just how scary it all is, until I saw Aunt Ky screaming in pain. She looked so scared, Aunt Buzzy."

"Hey, everythings okay," Honey assured her niece, wrapping her arms around her and holding her close. "Ky and the babies are just fine. They're okay."

Lissy shook in Honey's arms, sobs sounded against her chest and Honey tightened her hold, hugging her impossibly close.

"I…I didn't stay. I couldn't. I..r….ran. I let everyone down," Lissy said and Honey pressed a kiss to her niece's head. Even though Lissy was a good few inches taller than Honey, she was still a child. She was still someone who needed protection, who needed comfort and care.

"You did not let anyone down, Lissy," Honey said, pulling back a little. "Have you been sitting here the whole day?"

Lissy nodded and Honey felt her heart break at the fear in her eyes. "You must be tired and I'll bet you're hungry too. Let's get you inside."

Lissy didn't protest when Honey fished the keys out of her pocket and moved to open the front door. She reached for Lissy's hand and guided her inside. Walking over to the sofa, she lowered her niece onto the seat next to the pile of blankets from last night, which had been tossed to one side, in a jumbled heap.

"Take a seat and I'll bring you a cup of cocoa and some food."

Lissy looked as if she was experiencing a little shock and with what had unfolded today, Honey couldn't blame her. The exhaustion she herself had felt lingering in the background dissipated as she slipped instantly into caretaker mode. Glad for the distraction, she rushed around her small space, gathering dishes left out the night before and placing them in the sink. The muffins she had baked with Liv in mind, were still sitting on the cooling rack and had gone hard. Left overnight without proper protection they had spoiled, gone hard before they could be enjoyed. Honey couldn't help but balk as the events of yesterday played over again in her mind.

She still couldn't believe that Liv had said the things she did. How the mouth that had kissed Honey so passionately, that whispered such beautiful promises in her ears, had then accused her of what she had.

That afternoon Honey had woken up after being worn out in the most delicious of ways and had wanted to do something nice for Liv. Wanting to give her a little part of her grandparents back, she had finally plucked up the courage to open the pages of the little recipe book. For the first ten minutes she had allowed herself to get lost in the familiarity of Bea's handwriting and the little drawings she left in the margins. When she reached the page containing the recipe for her cobbler, Honey had known there wasn't anything else she could have made. It had to be that, it was the right choice.

But everything had gone wrong, she had lost the birthday gift Marvin had wanted her to have and more importantly, she had lost Liv, a gift she never saw coming.

Shaking herself back into the present, Honey scooped up the stale muffins and tossed them into the trash. She slipped the cast iron kettle under the faucet and filled it with water before placing it on the stove. Then she headed over to the refrigerator to find something that would fill Lissy's empty stomach.

Even though she was busying herself trying to take care of her niece, Honey had almost forgotten she was there, the house was so quiet. When she looked up from her task and across the room where she had left Lissy, her heart warmed at the sight before her. Lissy was curled up tight, knees tucked underneath her, fast asleep and looking like she didn't have a care in the world. The stress that was so obvious on her face a few moments earlier was fading with each deep pull of breath that ushered her further into sleep.

She walked over to Lissy and pulled a blanket over her. She leant forward and planted a kiss on her niece's forehead like she always had when she was little. You are never too old for a forehead kiss.

Honey knew Sasha would return home, find Lissy not in her bedroom and panic, so she fired off a text to let her know that Lissy would stay over, for tonight at least. Then she set about doing something she never thought she would have to. Soon Liv would begin the process of listing the house, having no reason to stay anymore, and rather than wait for the inevitable to happen, Honey decided to take control. Slowly and with great care she began to remove the instruments from her wall. One by one she brought them down to the floor, holding each one briefly and taking a moment to remember the last time she had played them.

Honey was a gifted musician, something she never told anyone. Although she recalled having almost told Liv that first night here. She had, in her youth, been offered scholarships to many different colleges, but as much as she loved music, it wasn't her passion, baking was, being close to her family was. Her parent's weren't ones to push her into anything, they prefered a more relaxed style of parenting and always championed the notion of 'you'll go where you're meant to and be who you're meant to'. Honey knew exactly who she was, without going anywhere.

She was Verity. Verity was her.

She wasn't sure what would happen now. Although she was someone who liked to give a person the benefit of the doubt, panic had set in the minute Liv had walked out of the door. A part of her had hoped, as she lay on the sofa all night, that Liv would have come to her senses, crossed the field and wearing that wickedly delicious smile Honey had come to adore, knocked on her door with an apology. She had even hoped that she would wake to find Liv standing there this morning, but she hadn't.

Honey had tried to understand Liv's reaction. She knew what it felt like to have a family member pressure you to the point you couldn't see the stars for the clouds. She had wanted to explain herself to Liv, to tell her about how she came to be in possession of the book, but it wasn't the right time for that last night. Liv would have seen it as an attempt at keeping hold of something that rightfully belonged to her family, a guilt trip or excuse of sorts, and no matter how important the recipe book was, Liv's heart was more so.

"No more of that," Honey told herself.

Liv's heart wasn't hers to worry about. She had made that abundantly clear last night. Honey knew she couldn't go through this again, to allow herself to get lost in someone else's mistrust. She couldn't be the girl who gave so much of herself to someone who wasn't willing to at least give a fraction of that back. It wasn't fair. Relationships like that didn't work. But she allowed herself to be sad that what she and Liv had, never got the chance to develop into anything. It was finished long before they had seen through the storm.

It was a shame really, Honey thought. A relationship with Liv was definitely something she had pictured over the last week or two. Something she had dreamt about settling into. But then, she also knew that they had- —in their time together— barely touched the surface of who they each were as people. There was still so much to learn about one another, and realistically they were still strangers. Two people who had come together in their loss, but who absolutely felt found in one another. At least, Honey had.

She sniffled a little at that thought. In her head she made a plan of action. She would take the next few days to pack the things she didn't need to have on hand. First her instruments, which she would take to the Hive for storing until she found a place, then her books and other non-essential items. She knew her parents would try and convince her to move back in. They hadn't wanted her to leave in the first place, but Honey had wanted to carve her own place in her hometown.

When every item was off her walls and packed away neatly into two cardboard boxes she had left over from when she packed up Andies belonging, Honey stood still and took in the emptiness. A wall with no decor, just faded patches around where her memories had been. It made her feel hollow.

"What are you doing?" Lissy croaked as she opened one eye, the other still heavy with sleep.

"Just preparing," Honey said. She didn't have any other words for it. How was she going to explain to her niece what had happened when she wasn't entirely sure of it herself?

"Preparing for what?"

"To move on."

***

After letting Lissy know that she had told her mom she would be staying over, Honey had made them an entire pan of what she called popcorn crack, complete with chocolate chips and skittles. They had contemplated loading up a movie and Lissy as usual had requested they re-watch *The Breakfast Club*, but there was only so many times Honey could get into a debate with her niece over Molly Ringwald vs. Ally Sheedy. Her answer hadn't changed in all the years they had watched it and it would always be, rightfully, Ally Sheedy.

Thankfully, they had become so sidetracked after Honey had asked about Lissy's school life, that time had run away with itself, and before they knew it the clock on Honey's phone read ten-thirty pm.

"Soooo... you and the Henderson hottie?" Lissy teased, clearly not tired despite the redness around her now wide eyes. She held a fistful of popcorn mid-air awaiting Honey's reaction.

"Excuse me?" Honey spat, choking on a rogue kernel and her niece's exclamation. "Henderson Hottie? Who is calling her that?"

Lissy blushed a little and shrugged, before popping a few pieces of popcorn into her mouth. "Everyone one is calling her that. Mr

Jenkins at the convenience store, Alex at the hardware store, even Lols from The Book Nook."

"And you know how exactly?"

"What? It's a small town, Aunt Buzzy. Everyone knows everyone, and that includes all their business."

"The whole town's talking about Liv and I?" Honey balked at the idea.

Sometimes she wished she lived somewhere where nobody knew her business. Some people got *too* involved. "You think they'd have something better to discuss. Kyla's new arrivals for example."

By now the small town would have heard the reason for the late opening of Rosenberg's and gift baskets, well wishes and enough casserole to feed a small army, would be winging its way towards Kyla's family home. That was the kind of town interference Honey could get behind. Anything but a focus on her love life or lack thereof.

Tossing a piece of popcorn into the air and catching it like a pro, Lissy smirked. "Some people live for gossip, others for romance. When the gossip is romantic, who can blame us for being a little jealous?"

Honey didn't attempt to copy her niece's actions, knowing with her current run of luck the popcorn would probably miss her mouth entirely and end up falling down the back of the sofa. Another clean up job she absolutely wanted to avoid.

"Believe me, there is nothing to be jealous about. There is nothing romantic going on with Liv and I. Not anymore, anyways."

"That's a shame, you looked really good together at Ari's party. I haven't seen you that happy in a long time." Lissy said, reaching for another handful of popcorn.

"I was happy."

That had hurt to admit. She had known Kyla had seen Honey's reactions to Liv, but Kyla always seemed to be honed in on her actions. She hadn't realized their attraction had been the focus of everyone else. That her eldest niece had picked up on whatever had been brewing between them that day, the longing... the lust.

Honey knew she could have just blown away Lissy's words, quickly changed the subject and took the focus away from what would be a tough conversation, especially as her heart was aching from all the uncertainty that lingered still. But Honey was never one to lie, and she wanted Lissy to understand that even the hardest topics to talk about could be discussed freely over a bowl of popcorn, while snuggled safe under a blanket.

Lissy moved the bowl of popcorn to the coffee table in front of them and spun herself so they were now face to face. Honey felt her attention like the heat of a thousand suns.

"Do you wanna talk about what happened?" Lissy asked and it hit Honey that it had finally happened. Her niece had grown up before her eyes and was now offering her the sympathetic ear her mom usually did.

Honey didn't know what there was to say, she hadn't entirely worked through her feelings. With everything that had occured in the last twenty-four hours, there hadn't been much time to really think about everything. She leaned back against the armrest of the sofa and blew out a breath.

"Honestly, I'm not sure what happened, so I can't really talk about it. All I can say is, as much as you might feel ready for love, when it's your turn, listen to your head as well as your heart. Think practically before you rush into anything."

Lissy listened intently, nodding her head at Honey as if she was allowing the advice to sink in momentarily but then her demeanor changed and she shook her head.

"Doesn't that take away a little of the magic of falling in love, being practical? I thought your heart was exactly what you were supposed to listen to."

"Yeah well, sometimes your heart is a loudmouth and it can drown out the rational with silly notions of romance, and how it's supposed to be." Honey winced as she heard the bitterness in her tone, she wished she could take it back but honestly it was indicative of how she felt right now.

Lissy sat back a little, looking confused. "Okay, did you and Aunt Kyla have some sort of Freaky Friday experience and switch bodies, because that sounded eerily like something she would say."

"Oh gosh, I absolutely don't want to sound like that! I don't mean to trample all over something that should be so exciting for *you,* because it's not gone right for me. But, be careful with your heart Lissy. You're so incredibly special and I don't want you ending up like me; a lonely thirty-year-old who keeps waiting for love to walk through the door and sweep her off her feet, but keeps getting her feet swiped from underneath her instead."

Honey brushed her hands over the blanket covering her legs and chewed on the inside of her cheek, trying to staunch the tears that were threatening to spill over. She had allowed Liv to get close to her, to become someone to her and yet Liv had always kept her at a distance. She hadn't opened up, not really. She kept everything close to her chest and Honey had played all her cards for everyone to see. She went all in.

"I'm sorry she hurt you, Aunt Buzzy. Really, I am, but you know that's not a reason to give up on love, right?" Lissy asked, reaching for her hand and smiling softly, "The smartest woman I know would tell me that when people crash through your doors, it doesn't mean you should lock them. Give love space to show up unannounced. Keep your door open. All messes can be cleaned up and sometimes fixing them is half the fun. If it means anything, I know love is out there for you. I think it's out there for us all...at least I hope she is."

"Lissy... did you just?" Honey asked, unsure if she had heard her niece right. Had she just admitted that she was into girls?

Lissy blew out a breath, "I don't want this to be a big deal. I haven't talked about it with mom or dad yet, and I was going to wait until after my Europe trip, but I don't know if I can wait that long. I have to be honest with myself. My friends keep gushing about all of the European boys they're going to see, and how we will be visiting the most romantic places in the world. You know, typical dreamy teenage girl stuff, and honestly, I'm excited. I can't wait to see everything. I can't wait to fall in love. But I'm not like most teenage girls. I think, no, I know that when I fall in love...it will be with a girl."

Honey knew she could handle this in one of two ways, and while the super proud gay aunty in her wanted to geek out and gush over the fact that her niece had come out, she also knew Lissy would appreciate the low key approach. So she tampered her excitement and made sure she spoke from the heart.

"Thank you for trusting me, Lissy."

Lissy smiled and reached for another handful of popcorn, she popped it in her mouth and Honey mirrored her actions. She was so happy that her niece had felt safe enough to open up to her, and there was no doubt in her mind that when she did finally tell Sasha and her husband, they would handle it perfectly. She snuggled into her niece's side and rested her head on her shoulder.

Maybe her words earlier had been too harsh, too cynical. She didn't want Lissy to give up on love before she had ever experienced it. She wanted it all for her. The excitement of first glances, the heart rush that came with the first time you held someone else's hand. She willed romance to find her niece's life, to fill it in ways Honey herself longed for. At least one of them deserved that.

Chapter 20

Liv

Her head hurt.

Her head hurt and her eyes stung, but it was nothing compared to the pain Liv felt in her chest. It had been three days since the fallout with Honey and Liv hadn't managed to do much of, well, anything.

At various times during the day, regardless of what she was doing her chest would fill with sadness. She would stop what she was doing, sit and think about Honey. About how something that had started out so wonderfully had come crashing down so fast and had left her doing the walk of shame across the field in nothing but her boyshorts and t-shirt. Everything had happened so fast, her words had snowballed until her reactiveness chased her out of Honey's home, and out of her life. Liv didn't know how to come back from that. If it was even possible.

She sat on the porch swing, from the moment she woke up, or rather from a socially acceptable time to be seen sitting outside, not that anyone was around to watch her. She had hoped to catch glimpses of Honey, either coming outside to water her flowers, or taking some of her delicious muffins to the deli, but she hadn't seen her yet. A few times she had looked over at the cottage and noticed the bright yellow Jeep missing, or parked up, but she had never seen Honey getting in or out. It was for the best though, Liv reasoned, she wasn't sure what she would say to her. She didn't know if her neighbor would listen to her right now, or even if she deserved to be listened to.

For three days Liv had been lost in her own thoughts. Although the birds still sang the morning into existence and the sun still rose on the horizon, warming the wooden deck the way it always did; nothing felt right. Liv didn't feel the comfort she had felt since arriving in Verity, in fact she felt very unwelcome. Something about how the birds sang felt accusatory. When the sun crept over the decking it moved around her, instead of over her. It was as if the universe knew, the town knew that she had hurt one of its residents, that she had broken the heart of someone so precious.

Liv had seen it in Honey's eyes that morning when she walked down the stairs of the small cottage and found her singing. She could have sworn she tasted the word 'love' on Honey's tongue as it swirled with her own. She was so very desperate to taste it again.

She glanced at the book in her hand, with its frayed cover and loosely bound pages. This was what she had been looking for. This was the only reason her father had called her in months. This was the only thing he spoke about, the only thing he cared about. It felt like a brick in her palm, capable of destroying everything and all she had to do was let it go. What was so special about it, she didn't know. She had asked herself this question countless times over the last few days. The recipes inside were years old, and the company that once wanted to buy them, would now have had millions of other recipes for similar products. It was worthless, to everyone but Honey.

Honey, who had handed it over without a fight. Who even though she had been hurt, was sweet and accommodating, and everything Liv never knew she needed.

A high-pitched beeping broke her thoughts. Her phone rang from the pocket of the cotton robe she had wrapped around to stave off the early morning chill. Her fathers name filled the screen and Liv didn't know if she was ready to do this, to have this conversation with him, not after everything that had happened.

"Elizabeth."

His tone was curt, clipped and tense. She didn't know what she had expected but it didn't help her own feelings. She was so angry with him and with herself. Rather than wait, she decided to come straight out with it and leave him no room for pretense. He was never good at that anyway.

"I found the book you wanted."

"That's good. Now you can concentrate on packing up and leaving that place."

His reply was exactly as she suspected Her father had a way of controlling with fear, his entire tone exuded it and yet, she didn't feel the urge to comply with his request.

"No dad, I can't. You can't have the book, it belongs to someone else now."

"I'm not sure what you're saying Elizabeth, either you have the book or you don't. Which one is it?"

His patience was wearing thin and normally that would have prompted Liv to go into preservation mode and comply with his requests in order to maintain the peace. She was tired of living her life via a guideline of trauma responses. She cleared her throat.

"The book belongs to Honey Rosenberg, now. The girl who lives–"

"In the cottage at the bottom of the field," her father said, "I know who she is, Elizabeth! Her family has been stuck in that place longer than mine were. No desire to get out, no drive! So, she has the book and what, she's refusing to give it back? You'd think she would have been satisfied with the fact that my father willed the cottage to her! Typical! Figure this out Elizabeth!"

She wasn't sure she had heard her father right. Honey owned the cottage at the bottom of the hill? How had she not known this? How did Honey not know this?

Sweet, beautiful, gentle Honey who had slipped from between the sheets they shared and made something from nothing. The woman who had conjured up a taste of Liv's past in order to help her feel safe, comforted and happy, despite not knowing if she was safe herself. The sweet woman who had stood there while Liv said some spiteful and nasty things and handed over the book, without so much as trying to reason why she shouldn't.

"Did you hear what I said, Elizabeth? Figure it out and get home!" He abruptly ended the call, not waiting for an answer.

She sat for a moment, frozen in disbelief, the phone in her lap. Her mind raced with the things she now knew. Her body itched to spring from its stationary position and race across the field to let Honey know that she didn't have to worry. She didn't have to leave the cottage, it was hers. The book was hers.

She was hers… if she wanted her.

But the reality was, Liv would be lucky if Honey opened the door, let alone gave her a chance to speak. She had *really* messed up.

"What have I done?" Liv asked herself, closing her eyes and lifting her face towards the light that crept across the wooden decking. Despite not knowing the answer to her own question, she knew what she had to do.

***

"Just knock on the door. If she opens it, then you can panic." Liv told herself as she hooked her leg over the stile and jumped to the ground with a flourish. The grass had grown exponentially over the last few weeks and now reached her waist. She brushed her hand to remove the dried seeds that clung to her jeans and tucked in white t-shirt.

Honey's Jeep had pulled up ten minutes ago and Liv had caught a glimpse of blonde hair over the top of the tall grasses. She had almost decided against coming over, but the news of the cottage's ownership wasn't something she felt she could sit on any longer.

She walked up the gravel footpath, under the flowering arch and towards her front door. Liv loved Honey's little home, the pops of color from the window boxes, the vegetable patch where the zucchini were now sprouting yellow flowers and the blue bench where Honey would sit reading, during her days off. She knew how much Honey loved being here, it was only right she gave her some semblance of safety back. Especially after everything she had taken from her these last few weeks.

She raised her hand and knocked on the door, her whole body shook with nerves. When the door opened, and Honey stood in front of her with her blonde hair loose around her bare shoulders and wearing dungarees with one strap fastened, it took her breath away.

"H...Hi," Liv said. The door didn't slam in her face instantly and so she took it as a sign to continue, "I um, I came to return this."

She held out the book filled with her grandmother's recipes. She hadn't planned to do it this way. She hadn't planned how this interaction would go after Honey opened the door, if she was honest. Everything in Liv had told her to prepare to be shut down instantly, and so when Honey tilted her head to the side and reached out to take the book from her hands, she unraveled.

"I want you to know that I'm sorry for what I said. What I did. I don't know what came over me. I'm not like him, my dad. I'm not. I should never have said the things I did. I know who you are and I am so sorry. This belongs to you."

Honey looked at the book with reverence, Liv watched as she furrowed her eyebrows and then brought the book to rest over her heart.

"I...I don't understand. What changed?"

"Everything," Liv admitted. Since Honey had appeared in her life, everything had changed for the better. She hoped one day she would get to tell her that properly. "I'm not here to ask you for forgiveness. I know I messed up. You don't owe me anything. I just wanted to return that to you. It's yours, my grandmother gave it to you for a reason."

When Honey leant against the doorframe, Liv felt her nerves lessen. She watched as Honey's rigid posture seemed to resolve a little. She wished her own would.

"Actually this was a gift from Marvin. It was the last thing he gave me before he... left. I know you probably don't want to know the details but I want you to know. He gave this to me on my birthday, we sat down to drink cider and play some chess and I asked him if he was sure he wanted to give this to me, rather than you or your brother. He said that you had stopped calling after Bea passed. He was pretty sure you had forgotten all about him."

"He was right. Not only did you love my grandfather when the rest of us forgot about him, you lost him on your birthday. I can't believe this. You've spent these last few weeks telling me how sorry you are for my loss, and yet you're the one who actually lost him. I'm so sorry, Honey."

"I miss him so very much. Sometimes I forget he's gone, you know. I'll come over the field and see the light on and now I know it's just you, but for a second... just a split second, I swear I can see him shuffling across the deck to the porch swing, clutching a Jamesons and one of his battered classics. I can still hear his warm laugh and his soothing voice calling me across the field to join him." Honey's voice trailed off and Liv noticed tears rolling down her neighbors cheeks.

She wanted to step towards her and wipe them away, hold her tight and promise her that everything would be okay. But Liv wasn't sure that this would be okay, no matter how much she wished it could be.

"You make him sound *so* real,"

The way Honey looked up from the floor and right into her eyes, startled Liv. Her gaze was firm and certain, even in her heartache.

"He was. To me he was *very* real. He was my best friend when I sorely needed one, and he never once judged me for falling for Andie's stupid antics. When I was with him I always felt like I mattered. He had a way of making you feel like, even with all your flaws, you were perfect, exactly as you were."

"He wasn't wrong, Honey. You are perfect, exactly as you are. You've been nothing but nice to me since I got here and I've taken so much from you. Your food, your time, your kindness… I even took your sadness. You've comforted me through a loss that has been eating *you* up inside. You're amazing Honey and I'm so sorry, because you asked for nothing and I gave nothing in return."

Liv wished she had known him, the man Honey was describing. She thought about how her life would have been different if she had that kind of influence growing up. Maybe she wouldn't have flown off the handle like she did the other day. She had spent her whole life carrying around her fathers shame about being born here, raised here and yet with each day that had passed since her arrival Liv had come to understand that it was all for nothing. It wasn't hers to carry, sure she had her own but none of it was linked to this place.

She offered Honey a sincere smile, one that she hoped would show how genuine her words were. Honey's eye contact was unwavering as she sniffled and wiped at her cheeks.

"You're wrong, Liv. Spending time with you over at the house, sitting on the deck, laying under the stars. You gave me a little of him back."

Liv blew out a breath at Honey's admission. This wonderful woman was still trying to make her feel good, still thanking her despite the hurt she had caused. She couldn't keep it from her any longer, she had to tell her about the cottage.

"I actually have something else for you," she said, daring to step a little closer. "But it's not from me. I can't take credit for this, I'm just the messenger."

"Okay," Honey said, confusion written all over her face.

"It turns out, the book wasn't the last thing my grandfather gave you. I spoke to my father earlier and it turns out, you never had to worry about leaving here. It's been yours all along."

As she waited for Honey's response it hit Liv exactly how deeply she cared for the woman in front of her.

"I'm sorry, what?" Honey said, standing up straight and taking a step towards her. Liv raised her arms in the air and gestured around her, smiling.

"The cottage is yours, Honey. He left it to you." Liv noticed the look of disbelief on Honey's face and she was determined to watch it evolve into joy.

"It's mine? I don't have to leave? I don't understand, how do you know this?"

"My father let it slip this morning, after I told him I wouldn't be giving him the book. That it belongs to you now."

"Wow, I know that must have been hard for you."

Liv shook her head, "Not as hard as you might think. Doing something scary can be incredibly easy when you know it's the right thing to do."

Honey's shoulders dropped and Liv watched all the tension fall from her body. A few days ago she would have held Honey in her arms and hugged her while they celebrated this news. If she hadn't messed things up.

"Are you sure that I really get to stay?" Honey asked, her voice showing small hints of excitement amongst the disbelief.

"For as long as you want. For forever, or until you decide that this place is too small for you."

"I can't believe it. Thank you for telling me," Honey said, still clutching the book tight to her chest. Liv smiled softly, feeling some of the weight she had been carrying, fall from her own shoulders.

"Please don't thank me. I'm sorry nobody told you before and that my father kept that to himself, as if no one else is affected by this. I always knew he had a selfish streak, but I want you to know it's not a family trait. I came over to tell you as soon as I knew. Well, as soon as I could muster up the courage to come, that is. I never wanted you to have to be scared of losing your home. I'm sorry, Honey."

She had said what she came to say. It was a great time to end the conversation and head back across the field to the big house. As she turned to leave, her dirt-trodden Vans kicking up small dust clouds from the dried up pathway, Liv's heart felt ten times lighter. Seeing the smile she had been able to put on Honey's face, giving her selfless neighbor the peace she so desperately deserved, was the confirmation she needed to move forward.

"Liv!" Honey's voice floated through the air, causing her to spin on her heels, "I don't think you're selfish. I never did, not for one second. Thank you for coming to let me know."

"Thank you for keeping your door open," Liv said, giving a gentle nod before continuing to move towards the stile. She stepped up and hooked her leg over the wooden fence, she chanced a glance over at the doorway and saw that Honey was still standing there, watching her leave. Liv thought she saw some sadness there in Honey's warm eyes.

"Do you think maybe there's a way we could get back to being whatever this was becoming?" Liv shouted, trying to keep her voice from cracking with the emotion that filled her. Hope blossomed in her chest as she took a chance. She knew it was potentially the wrong thing to ask, at the wrong time. But if she didn't try, she wouldn't be able to live with herself.

Honey shook her head.

"Honestly...I don't know, Liv. I think you're still a little lost, and it's okay for you to take time to find your way. I think we just happened to come across one another at the wrong time. I do hope everything works out for you and I really do appreciate you coming over here to apologize and tell me about the cottage. I'm just not sure if I'm there yet. I don't know if I can do this again. Do us again."

Her heart plummeted into her stomach, and her whole body went cold as if immersed in open waters. Liv didn't want to press her any further. Honey had already given her more than she deserved after her reaction the other day. She nodded softly.

"I understand. I appreciate the time you've given me and the chance to talk about things."

She glanced over Honey, how she held onto the book with careful hands that Liv knew would treat each page with care. Honey's hands were wonderful, Liv knew what it felt like to be touched by Honey, to be revered by her even if it was only for a short while. It was something she would hold onto forever even though she had to let go.

"Happy Belated Birthday, Honey!"

Liv swung her other leg over the stile and jumped down into the tall grass, allowing it to cover her clothes with seeds this time. Heading back across the field slowly, she took deep steady breaths and blinked away the midday sun.

Halfway across the field she stopped, lifted her arms out to either side of her, and let her fingers tickle the tops of the grass. She was done fighting. She was done seeing this place through someone else's eyes. She was ready to experience Verity for herself, the way she should have as a child. Her stolen memories could be replaced, all she had to do was try and Liv was so ready to try.

***

The sound of a car engine revved angrily as it made its way up the driveway. Liv stood from the porch swing and it creaked in relief. She made a note to oil the chains, or consider replacing them, and then squinted in the direction of the sound. A sleek black Mercedes crept up the dusty driveway in a series of fits and starts, punctuated by the growling engine. She winced at the way the dirt clung to the car, a car she recognized instantly.

Long legs swung out of the driver side door as the car came to a stop. High heels that cost a month's pay sank into the dirt and a scoff of disgust filtered through the air. When the woman stood upright and closed the door behind her with a loud bang, Liv felt her heart fall into the pit of her stomach. What the hell was Marcie doing here?

"Well, aren't you going to say hello? Haven't you missed me, Elizabeth?"

Liv wasn't sure what her mouth was doing, but her head was screaming at her to walk inside the house and lock the door. This was a situation she absolutely didn't want to have to deal with. Why was Marcie here in Verity? The last time they had spoken she thought she had made it abundantly clear that there was nothing more to be said. Yet, here she was. Standing in the middle of Liv's driveway looking, nothing less than her perfectly put together self.

"What are you doing here?" Liv asked, her tone laced with confusion and disdain she hoped Marcie could hear.

She obviously did because a frown appeared on her face and she stepped cautiously towards Liv, taking in her surroundings with a wrinkled nose.

"Not the greeting I was hoping for. You've been here for almost six weeks now and honestly, I think it's time you stop hiding out here, and think about coming home."

"We already discussed this, Marcie. More than we probably should have. I thought I made it clear last time you called, that there was nothing more to say."

Marcie wasn't deterred by Liv's words, she continued walking up the wooden steps until they stood face to face.

"You said that there wasn't anyone else and so I had to try. I have to get you back," she leaned in and caught the corner of Liv's mouth with a kiss.

"Marcie!"

"Elizabeth, please. I'm here, doesn't that count for something? You've been hiding out here all this time and it looks like there's still so much work to be done before you could even consider selling it. Especially if you want a half decent price for it. Let me help."

This woman was unreal. Typical Marcie, she had only heard what she wanted to but this was a conversation that Liv didn't want to continue on the front porch, where anyone could see and hear them. Marcie did make a good point, the house did still have a lot of work to be done to it, even if Liv had no intentions on selling it. It could be good to get an eye for ways to improve the space and Marcie's opinion would be well informed. She had drove hours to get here and Liv couldn't turn her away, that would be rude.

"Come inside," she said, reluctantly.

Liv headed towards the door, stepped inside the hallway and turned to watch as Marcie tentatively crossed the wooden decking, being careful not to touch anything on the way.

"So have you missed me?"

Liv blew out a breath, stepping aside she ushered her ex through the door and closed it behind her. Marcie was like a dog with a bone when she latched onto something. She was relentless, and once upon a time that was a quality Liv would have said she admired. Now, she realized how much it actually annoyed her.

"We aren't doing this, Marcie. You can stay overnight, I know how long the drive is. We can talk about the house and about how we move forward from this, but we aren't talking about us. There is no us. Not anymore."

She expected a fight, more attempts at trying to win her back, reminders of what they were and pleas to not forget. But Marcie simply brushed her hands over her navy a-line skirt, nodded her head and followed Liv inside. She wondered if maybe acceptance was something Marcie was capable of working on too.

Chapter 21

Honey

The cottage was hers. She didn't have to leave.

Honey took in her surroundings and for the first time in a long time, it was like she could really see. Everything was in technicolor, rather than the dulled tones of self-pity she had been walking around in these last few days. She glanced at the boxes that would need unpacking, the half filled bookshelf that she had started emptying last night, but couldn't finish. Now she didn't have to. She couldn't quite believe that this was happening, that this was real. She could stay. But why did everything still feel too small?

It had been both wonderful and heart wrenching, seeing Liv. Honey knew she missed her, but hadn't known exactly how much until she stood in front of her. Liv looked amazing. Verity had grown on Liv. She no longer looked like the city chick, who almost face-planted into her arms all those weeks ago. With her soft denim jeans, slip-on Vans covered in dry dirt and her t-shirt covered in grass seeds, Liv looked every inch the small town girl she could have been. Behind her blue eyes though, Honey saw a sadness, a tiredness that made her wonder if Liv had been losing sleep also. She wished there was more to say, some way of taking back the events of the last few days and falling back into the comfort that had come so easy to them. But moving backwards would never get them anywhere. So, Honey decided to move forward in the only way she knew how.

She crossed the messy living space, rounding the boxes on her way to the kitchen and scooped her blonde hair into the ponytail holder she kept on her wrist. Once her curls were secured, she bent low and opened up the cupboard under her sink, where she kept her mixing bowls. For the first time in days, Honey moved around her kitchen with a fluidity that she had missed. The fear of losing this place, the memories that lingered between these walls, the possibility of losing another connection to Marvin, all dissipated with each utensil she reached for, with each ingredient she procured.

"I can't believe this is mine," she whispered into the air and a shiver traveled down her spine, triggering the hairs on her forearms to stand on end.

As she whipped up a thank you in scents of cinnamon and fresh peaches, she continued to turn this thought over in her head. How surreal it all felt, but how grateful she was.

A short while later when the timer signaled that her dish was done, Honey bent low and with her bright pink oven mitts, dotted with cacti, retrieved the large glass dish from the oven. The smell of nostalgia hit her first, summer days she could taste at the back of her throat. Warm spices and ghosts of vanilla followed, swarming her taste-buds and leaving her salivating.

She placed the dish on the countertop to cool, and leaned over the glass dish to inspect it. It was beautiful, a light brown crumble oozing with clear juices from where the peaches had burst through the top layer. She wanted to grab a spoon and dig into it just to be sure that she had gotten it right, but this wasn't for her.

She wanted Liv to be the first to taste it.

Honey remembered how special that first bite had been as a child. That feeling of exhaustion from running the dirt path while the shouts and giggles of her siblings and friends surrounded her. The deep breaths that were taken while a warm bowl was placed into one hand and a cold spoon into the other. That first scoop and the sweetness of the peaches as they hit her tongue, making her feel like all was right with the world. She figured Liv could use a little of that right now.

Honey had been trying to replicate that feeling as closely as she could, the afternoon when she made those muffins for Liv. When she had woken in Liv's arms feeling more complete than she had in the longest time something had urged her to try. To give the beautiful woman who had spent hours poring herself over Honey's body, something that would make her feel equally as wonderful. She hadn't been brave enough to tackle the cobbler itself that day. She knew it would have been like trying to step into shoes too big. Kind of like those ridiculous gumboots Liv insisted on wearing.

After Liv had given her back the book, something inside her had yelled loudly again, telling her to make it, just in case Liv changed her mind, or she never got the chance. The universe screamed at her that now was the time. A feeling of pride washed over her as she continued to look over her creation. From inspection alone it looked to Honey like she had done it.

It was perfect.

She had made Bea's cobbler and it smelled like home.

***

"Hey Liv, I thought you might want this," Honey mumbled to herself, gripping the dish with both hands, as she moved through the grass towards the big house. "No, that sounds weird. Gosh, why is this so hard? Why can't it be as simple as *'Hey I know things are weird between us right now and I know I said I wasn't sure about being friends, but I want you to have this.'* Why does it always have to be so complicated?"

The sun beat down on her, a trickle of sweat slipped from the nape of her neck and rolled down her spine. She hadn't noticed the weather when she was doing her morning delivery to the deli. If she was honest, she hadn't noticed much of anything the last few days. Heartbreak was really good at muting everything but the sick feeling in your stomach and the loneliness in your head.

She had waited a while for the cobbler to cool and during that time she had called Sasha at the deli to let her know she would be a little late getting back. When she had given her the news about the cottage, her sister's squeals of delight had reminded Honey exactly how important all of this was. The relief that should have washed over her the moment Liv told her the news, hadn't truly settled in yet. It wasn't that she didn't believe it, she knew Liv wouldn't have told her if she wasn't sure. It just felt like there was something missing, a piece of this puzzle that wasn't fitting into place, something stopping her from feeling complete.

A strand of blonde hair escaped its ponytail confines and settled in front of her face. She blew a breath from the corner of her mouth to move the hair out of her vision. She had almost reached the otherside of the field when the sound of Liv's voice —and another unfamiliar one— stopped her in her tracks. Tightening her grip on the dish, she strained to hear what they were saying. She wasn't trying to eavesdrop, she just didn't want to interrupt anything. The other voice was smooth, syrup like in its delivery and made Honey feel uneasy as she pieced together words.

"You've been hiding out here all this time—"

It was an accusatory tone that confused Honey. Hiding out? Why was she hiding and who was she hiding from? Then it hit her in the chest, Liv had someone to hide from. She shuffled a little closer, being careful not to make too much noise but also not trying to be sneaky. She just wanted, no, needed, to put a face to the voice. A tall woman came into view, blonde hair pulled back into a severe bun, A-line skirt that brushed just above the knees, paired with a white blouse that almost blinded Honey. She couldn't make out her shoes, but Honey would wager that some form of expensive heels were holding up this incredibly attractive woman. Standing in front of Liv's home like some modern rendition of a Greek goddess, this woman was stunning. Not in the same way Liv was, with her angular jawline and beautiful blue eyes, but in a way that had Honey's warm brown eyes turning green.

"Come inside," she heard Liv say and the goddess complied, taking each step like she was on some sort of runway. Honey inched forward, battling with the dilemma of either making herself known and inserting herself into this situation, or lingering and watching as it unfolded.

As the goddess reached the door and her syrupy voice asked "So, have you missed me?" Honey was glad she had chosen to stay quiet. It was obvious that she had walked into something she absolutely shouldn't have inserted herself into. This mystery woman clearly knew Liv, in what capacity Honey wasn't sure and as much as she wanted to know, she also didn't.

She glanced down at the dish in her hands feeling a little foolish for having put herself in this situation. Her stomach turned somersaults and she began to feel a little lightheaded at the endless scenarios that now ran through her head. This could be a friend of Liv's, a work colleague, a girlfriend... *a girlfriend*. Nausea washed over her and the heat of the sun became noticeably uncomfortable. Honey moved towards the stile and placed the dish on the top step, not wanting to take it back over to the house. She wouldn't eat it. She knew that if she dug her spoon into it now she wouldn't be able to taste the love and thought she had baked into each piece, it would taste bitter and bland.

She left the dish where it could be seen then began to walk away from it, from the goddess, from whatever was going on inside that house, and from Liv.

***

"What did she look like?" Lissy asked, swiping her finger around the glass bowl and sucking it into her mouth.

"Like a literal goddess," Honey lamented, and pushed another tray into the oven before pushing the buttons on the digital display, to set the timer.

"So tall, curvy and make-believe?" Lissy snorted back a laugh and Honey narrowed her eyebrows at her niece, before throwing a dish cloth at her.

"Sometimes you're a real smart ass, you know that?"

Lissy dabbed at her hands with the cloth before throwing it back at Honey.

"It's one of the things you love most about me. It's also why I'm your favorite niece, don't worry I won't tell the other worker bees. I just happened to have met you first."

After the whole eavesdropping incident, Honey had scolded herself for listening in and returned back to work. Throwing herself into making sure her cabinets were full was a great distraction and required a lot of her attention, because today her muffins were flying off the shelves.

Lissy had noticed her low mood and had, during the mid-afternoon lull, slipped into the kitchen to press her for information. When Honey couldn't take her niece's doe eyes and eyelash batting any longer she told her all about Liv's visitor. As much as a problem shared is often said to be a problem solved, Honey wasn't sure she had enough information to solve this one.

"So you just left the cobbler and ran? Smooth moves, Aunty Buzzy," Lissy teased and Honey was thankful for her niece trying to lighten the mood.

"What was I going to do? It wasn't like I was going to take it back home with me, sit in my sadness with a spoon and eat the whole thing like they do in those rom-coms you make us watch."

Lissy reached for a cookie from the cooling rack and paused mid-swipe.

"Firstly, you love rom-coms, don't act like you don't. Mrs Robbins keeps telling me about those books she gets in for you at the library. Erica Lee, Sabrina Kane…sapphic romance is clearly your thing. Secondly, yes you take it home, you throw on *You've Got Mail*, you grab a spoon, a pint of vanilla ice cream and you call me so I can come wallow with you."

"No. There's not going to be any wallowing. I told Liv we couldn't be more. I told her that I wasn't sure I was ready for anything again. I don't get to wallow, my pity pass is denied." Honey said, taking a tray of cooled down cookies and transferring them into a Tupperware container.

"But you two were… something," Lissy said, still eyeing up which cookie she was intending on swiping.

"And now we are something else, nothing else. I don't know what we are. I also don't know what Liv and the goddess are and I'm not sure I want to know. Because all avenues don't look great for either of us."

"What do you mean?" Lissy asked, as she picked up one of the still warm cookies and broke off a piece.

"Well, if she's an ex, that means Liv didn't tell me about her. Not that she should have to, but she had a chance to. I mean, I shared about Andie. Which then prompts me to wonder if I didn't give her room to talk, or if I overshared, or if she just simply felt like she couldn't open up to me, or trust me and aren't relationships supposed to be built on trust?" Honey sighed, "Then there's the possibility that she's not an ex, and that thought alone means that Liv lied to me. Which brings about a whole other set of feelings I'm not sure I'm ready to deal with."

"Wow, you really overthink things. I get it, this all sucks. I'm sorry Aunt Buzzy, but wouldn't you rather know for sure?"

"What was I supposed to do? Just go up there, knock on the door and say *'Hey I was just watching you both from the grass over there like some peeping Tom. Wanna tell me who this is?'*. You and I both know that confrontation is not my forte. I prefer the 'stay quiet and pretend it didn't happen' approach."

"But, Aunt Buzzy, it did happen and now you're in here trying to overbake your problems away."

"I am not overbaking," Honey balked. As her niece lifted her hand indicating the space around them, every surface of the kitchen covered in trays of muffins and cookies in every flavor imaginable, Honey sucked in a breath. She was such a smart ass. "Okay, maybe I am baking my feelings away."

"They're not leaving though are they?" Lissy asked and Honey wondered when this shift had happened. When she had gone from being the one giving advice to the one needing it, "Look, why don't you just head over there after closing and ask her what is going on?"

"Because I can't. She doesn't owe me an explanation, Lissy."

"No, she doesn't. But, maybe she will give you one regardless. Take a chance, Aunty Buzzy, just this once. Don't run and hide from things. Be the superhero we all see you as."

Honey couldn't stop the truth from tumbling out, "What if I hear something I don't want to hear?"

Lissy jumped off the countertop where she had sat swinging her legs and placed a hand on Honey's shoulder. "Then you call me. Quicker than you can say Lissy is my favorite person in the whole world, I'll come over with a pint of cookie dough ice cream and a hug you know you're gonna need."

She turned to her niece and took her in, with her wide eyes and soft smile she was her mother's daughter.

"You really are the best niece, Lissy."

"Remember that when I'm gone next month," Lissy smirked and popped another bite of cookie into her mouth.

Honey laughed gently. As if she was ever going to forget.

***

After locking up the deli and saying goodnight to both Sasha and Lissy, Honey drove home slowly. The town square was full of people carrying foldaway chairs and picnic baskets, ready for the monthly movie screening that was being hosted by Lol's from McCormacks Book Nook. It had been something she would have loved to have taken Liv to, snuggled up under the night sky and eating their fill of whatever goodies Honey would have packed for them both. Another experience that their short-lived relationship wouldn't afford them.

Honey hated the idea of calling it a fling, it made it sound so far from what it had felt like. But since the arrival of the goddess, Honey was almost certain that she had participated in some form of sordid affair. That made her feel uneasy, so she determined she would do what Lissy said and find the time to talk to Liv about it.

She had almost reached home when she noticed something at the bottom of the driveway that led to the big house. A pile of broken wood that looked uncannily like Liv's porch swing.

It couldn't be though. Honey reasoned that there was no way Liv would have taken that down, she loved sitting on that swing to drink her morning chai and work on her book. Honey loved watching her, even in the days that passed after their argument she had watched Liv sitting in the swing. Her heart ached each time she saw her and more than once she had stopped herself from going to join her.

Driving a few yards further until she reached her own small driveway, Honey parked up and got out of the Jeep with a jump. She retraced her steps and ran her hands over the broken swing. Anger rose up in her as her suspicions were confirmed. Without a second thought she began to scoop up the remains of the swing, using all the strength she could muster to carry it the short distance back to the cottage. Placing it down with care, so as not to cause any more damage, she noticed one of the arms had broken in half, its pieces jagged and unwelcoming. The bottom of the seat was scuffed too, Honey imagined this had been the result of being dragged carelessly down the gravel driveway.

She couldn't believe Liv would just throw the swing away like that. Sure she didn't know the sentimental value of it, and that her grandfather had built it with his own two hands, as a wedding gift. But none of that mattered.

Honey wasn't able to control how her hands shook and her breathing became labored. She turned to look across the field and before she could ask herself what she was doing, she was standing in front of Liv's home ready to demand answers. What she hadn't expected was to see the goddess sitting on the top step of the porch, clutching a bowl of Honey's cobbler and wearing the oversized t-shirt Liv had worn that morning when they –

"Where's Liv?" she demanded, her voice shaky and a little uncertain.

The goddess looked up at her confused and dropped the spoon she was holding into the bowl with a clatter. "Excuse me?"

"Where is Liv?" Honey tried again.

"She's inside sleeping. She's had a rough few weeks and now that I'm here she's able to finally get some rest," the goddess stood up and walked down the steps towards Honey. She extended her hand and Honey stepped back, "I'm Marcella Jacobs, Elizabeth's girlfriend and you are?"

There it was. The words she hadn't wanted to hear. The goddess had a name... Marcella.

No wonder Liv had been reluctant to talk about her life back in the city. She had a girlfriend, a very tall, very beautiful girlfriend, one she had cheated on with Honey. That notion made her feel sick.

"I'm nobody. When she wakes up, tell her... actually don't tell her anything. I wasn't here." Honey turned and walked away.

"Strange people around here..." she heard Marcella say and again her body reacted before her mind could control it. Honey spun on her heels and blew out an exasperated breath.

"Did you take the porch swing down?"

"God, yes! That thing was an eyesore and will absolutely not help with the sale of the house. Better no swing than one practically falling apart."

Honey's fists clenched at her sides and she bit hard on the inside of her cheek. She had to steady herself because by now she could feel herself spiraling.

Marcella the goddess lifted her pointy nose in the direction of the driveway, "If you want it for firewood, or whatever you use to heat your little shack, it's down there."

That was all she needed to hear. She shook her head and bit back any more words that threatened to make themselves known. Marching away from the house and back towards her own, Honey wondered how someone she had felt so deeply within her heart could now feel so far away. How had Liv, who Honey had thought was so sweet and caring, ever be with someone so...cold. Liv and her girlfriend were the least of her worries. Sitting on the floor outside of her home was a memory Honey wasn't ready to let go of, something she had the power to fix and she was determined to do so.

Chapter 22

Liv

"Ugh!" Liv's entire body felt like she had just ran a marathon.

Sleep had come easy after Hurricane Marcie had arrived in Verity. The minute she crossed the threshold of the house and started rambling off a list of things that needed to be fixed, punctuated by affirmations of affection and love, Liv had been exhausted. She had shown Marcie to the spare room at the bottom of the hall, told her where the bathroom was and excused herself for a lie down. Sometimes she wondered how she had managed so many years living with her, when those initial five minutes had felt like a lifetime.

She stretched her arms into the air and rolled her head back on her neck until it gave that familiar pop that released some of the tension. Some, not all, would remain until the woman down the hall left. Marcie was relentless, Liv would give her that, but she herself had changed since she came to Verity. Now she felt so much stronger in who she was and what she was capable of.

Glancing at the clock she noticed late afternoon had arrived. That meant she had napped for three hours and missed lunch. When her stomach gave a warning rumble she knew it wouldn't be long before the hangry kicked in.

"Better go fix up some food for my guest too," Liv groaned as she moved off the bed and headed downstairs. What she found was Marcie walking back inside the house clutching a bowl of something and wearing her favorite t-shirt. She looked...entirely too comfortable.

"Elizabeth, darling! How was your rest? You look like you need it."

Marcie had always been queen of the back-handed compliments.

"I slept well, thank you. You've eaten already?" she lifted her chin at the empty bowl in Marcie's hand.

"I did. Someone had left a rather delicious peach concoction on your wooden gateway over there. So I took the liberty of bringing it inside and helping myself. Normally I would be wary of gifts left out in the open like that, but I figured this is a small town and isn't that what neighbors in backwater towns like this are known for? Besides, it smelled divine and I couldn't resist."

Liv furrowed her brows as she tried to allow her still waking brain to catch up to Marcie's mile-a-minute way of telling her something. Marcie shuffled past her, heading for the kitchen, clearly she was already familiar with the layout of the house. Liv followed.

"There's some left over for you. don't worry I didn't eat it all. The dish was rather large, especially for one person. I guess they're not really interested in portion control here. Or she hadn't intended on letting you eat it alone."

An audible sigh escaped Liv's mouth and she felt herself becoming extremely tired once more. This was draining. She hadn't been here long and yet Marcie was already pushing Liv to the limit of what she could take. Her stomach ached and she felt like she had to internalize her thoughts in order to keep the peace. In all the time she had been here, this was one thing Liv hadn't missed. Not sure how long she could pretend she was okay with her ex being here, she decided to give her the night to rest and then tomorrow she would talk to her about leaving.

"Wait, did you say this was left outside?" Liv asked, as she gently ran her fingertips over the rim of the glass dish.

"Yes. I think it was from the cute blonde who lives in that little shack over there. She was over here not long ago asking where you were and I—"

Anxiety hit Liv full force. Honey had met Marcie, they had been in each other's space. They had talked. She hadn't purposely not told Honey about her ex; she just hadn't felt like it was something she needed to talk about. Marcie and their issues had been left behind in the city. Never in her wildest imagination could she have predicted that Marcie, having done what she did, would have followed her here. They were over, there was nothing to tell. And yet knowing they had been in the same space made Liv feel guilty for having not told Honey about her.

"What did you say to her?"

"I told her you were in bed. That this has all been a lot for you but now that I'm here–"

She felt frenetic, Marcie's words were silenced by the sound of blood rushing in her ears and her heart pounding in her chest. She shook her hands and moved to leave.

"I have to go."

"Elizabeth! What is happening?"

She couldn't hear anything else as she ran out of the front door without stopping to put her shoes on. Taking the wooden steps with a jump, she headed towards the field, climbing the stile steadily, rather than with the uncertainty she had a few weeks ago. The tall grass tickled at her bare arms, leaving light pink marks as she raced her way past them. She could probably do this with her eyes closed now, but she needed to keep them open. She'd had enough of pretending not to see what was right in front of her. But, even with her eyes closed, Honey was someone Liv couldn't unsee.

When the bright yellow siding of the cottage and the wooden arch trellis, woven with green climbing plants that had blossomed overnight came into view, Liv stopped. What was she going to say? How did she explain everything without losing someone who had become the most important person she had ever known? She didn't have time to ruminate on that thought, because when she glanced down she saw Honey hunched over on the floor, a hammer in one hand and a pile of wood at her feet.

"Can we talk?"

Honey looked over her shoulder and Liv felt cold. The hairs on her arms stood on end. Honey's normally warm brown eyes were hardened, red and puffy from tears she had been crying.

"We have absolutely nothing to say to one another," she said, turning back to the pile of wood on the floor and shaking her head.

"Honey, please!" Liv moved slowly towards her until she stood by her side.

"Did you tell her to do this?"

Liv took in the pile of wood on the floor and narrowed her eyebrows, "Is that my porch swing? Marcie must have–"

"Marcella?" Honey spat, moving a piece of wood into place before reaching into the pocket of her dungarees and pulling out a nail. "The woman over at your place eating the cobbler I made for you? The girlfriend you forgot to tell me about?"

"Honey, I… she's not my–"

Liv wanted to reach out for her. As if by making a connection, she could convey with her touch everything she was struggling to say with words. It had been days since she had known the warmth of Honey's body against her own, it felt like far too long. But she also knew contact wouldn't be appreciated right now. She needed to set her straight, let her know that she had gotten the wrong idea about Marcie. A wrong idea that had been entirely Liv's fault for not telling her the truth in the first place.

"Marvin built this swing with his bare hands, and I know you didn't have any feelings towards your grandparents at all, but I did. I loved him and he built that for your grandmother, as a wedding gift. It was all he had to show her how much he loved her and you let that woman tear it apart."

Liv shook her head. Honey was clearly not interested in entertaining any further talk about Marcie. Instead she was fixated on the swing that lay on the ground in front of her. Liv watched as she carefully hammered a nail into place, securing the broken slat where the arm had been damaged.

"I didn't know she had taken it down, Honey. I didn't know he had built it."

" Just…go away, go home,"

Her hands moved of their own accord, reaching to touch the sun-kissed, freckled skin that lay bare under the straps of Honeys dungarees and off the shoulder top, "Honey please let me explain. You know how much I care for you."

Before she could make contact, Honey had gotten to her feet and was staring her down. "Stop! Don't lie to me Elizabeth. I thought I knew you, I don't think you know yourself. All those things we spoke about, when you talked about the life you wanted. You already had it, you already had someone."

"No. It's not what you think Honey." Liv held her hands out in front of her and moved to take a step, but when Honey stepped back once more she dropped her hands in defeat.

"You don't owe me an explanation but I am not a cheater, Elizabeth. You know how things with Andie ended and I don't do that. I won't be that other person. I deserve to be more than a back-up."

"It's not like that, Honey. I need you to understand. You were never a back-up, Honey. Ever. I'm not with Marcie, not anymore. We were over before I got here and she knows that. We wanted different things."

"What do you want, Elizabeth?"

That was the question. Six weeks ago Liv wasn't sure what she wanted. She had spent so long unable to voice her desires, hiding her wants and needs under the pretense of a happy life and a seventh floor view of the city. She hadn't even known the possibilities of what she was missing, but now she knew everything she could ever need was here. Not in Verity, not in that big house she had come to adore, but here, in the arms of this woman. This beautiful, breathtaking woman who baked cakes that tasted like heaven, who kissed like she was made of magic and whose eyes felt more like home than Liv had ever known.

"Please don't call me that. My name is Liv."

It was like a punch to the gut hearing Honey use her full name, too reminiscent of the way Marcie held it in her mouth, she wondered if it tasted bitter on Honey's tongue too. She considered that it might be too late to plead her case, but she had to try, she deserved the truth.

Glancing around at the place she had come to love, at the woman she had come to love, Liv sucked in a deep breath and let it all fall out.

"I want this. I want to be here. Everything I have here, the house, the stolen kisses at family birthday parties, the late nights watching the stars and early mornings cuddled up in bed with you. I want that. I want a family and I want it all with *you*. I never knew I could need someone as much as I need you, Honey. What I want is you. I lo–"

"Don't. Don't you dare say it, because once you do you can't take it back and the first time you say it can't be something you say on a whim, in an attempt to sway me. Not when we are standing in the middle of my driveway shouting at one another because every word you spoke was a lie."

Liv shook her head and stepped towards her, Honey didn't move. She reached out tentatively and cupped Honey's face, her thumb interrupting the flow of tears that had started rolling down Honey's cheeks.

"It was never a lie, Honey. I've spent years of my life keeping everything I knew I wanted to myself. I had resigned myself to believing I would never have the things I dreamed of. Then I came here and I didn't have to dream anymore. The moment I met you, everything I ever wanted felt possible. It felt real. I never lied to you, not once. I meant every single word."

Honey closed her eyes and leaned into Liv's palm, sniffling lightly as she bit back the sobs that were wracking her now shuddering chest. Liv brought her other hand up to cup Honey's face, she looked so sad that Liv could actually feel her heart breaking. They stayed in that moment for a while, Liv holding her heart in the palm of her hands, before Honey broke the silence with a whisper.

"You should go, before you break my heart entirely."

Liv didn't want to leave. Now that she had Honey this close she wanted to beg her to listen to her, hear her out but loves funny like that. You find yourself torn between wanting to hold on, because you can't let go and letting go because it hurts to hold on. Liv wanted to keep Honey close, but being close was hurting her. That was the last thing she wanted. Honey deserved the world and Liv knew that if she didn't get to be the one to give that to her, at least they'd always have the stars.

"You know how I feel Honey. I don't want to lose you and this feels like the beginning of an end and so I need you to know that none of what we shared was a lie. I'll leave you alone now. I am so, so sorry."

Liv dropped her hands to her sides and stepped backwards still focused on the beautiful blonde who was crumbling before her eyes. Her breath caught in her throat, eyes blurring with the hurt she was feeling right now, she turned away and headed back across the field. The tall grass scratching at her skin didn't register now, her whole body was numb. She didn't notice the way the sun dipped behind the clouds and sent a cold gust whipping through the air, or the birds chattering amongst themselves. Her heart hammered loudly in her chest and soon her pace began to match its beat.

"You can stay tonight but you leave tomorrow," she said, stomping up the steps and walking right past Marcie, who was standing in the exact same place she had left her, moments before.

"I'm sorry, what?"

Liv spun around and marched towards her ex-girlfriend, her whole body was shaking. She breathed deeply through her nose and clenched her jaw. "You heard me. Don't unpack. Don't get comfortable. You can stay tonight and get some rest but tomorrow I want you to leave."

"You've been acting incredibly strange since you got here, Elizabeth. This is not like you," Macie said, leaning back a little and running her gaze over Liv.

Liv snorted. "That's the thing Marcie. This *is* me. I am more me here than I have felt in years. Since before I met you, even. I'm staying here, Marcie. I'm not selling the place. This was my grandparents' home and I want to keep it. I feel connected to them here."

"Please," Marcie snorted, stepping closer to Liv, "You saw them a handful of times in the thirty-two years you've been alive, Elizabeth."

"I was lost, Marcie! I've been lost for so, so long."

"Oh and six weeks here frolicking in the mud with Backwoods Barbie over there has suddenly made you find yourself?" Marcie snarled, and Liv's eyes widened with disbelief, "Don't look so shocked, I know there's something between you both. It was written all over her face when she came here earlier. She looked like I'd kicked her puppy."

"You're unbelievable."

"So, a younger woman takes a shine to you, shows you a little attention, makes you feel special and now you're uprooting your life? She must be adventurous between the sheets because we both know it wasn't her aesthetic that drew you in. What self-respecting grown woman wears dungarees and Doc Martens?"

Liv had heard enough, she wasn't about to allow Marcie to continue degrading Honey like that, "You don't get to talk about her like that! You don't know her. You don't get to have any sort of opinion on who I choose to spend my time with, or how I choose to spend it. I suggest you think carefully about what you say next or you can get back in your car and leave now."

Marcie ran her fingertips along the weathered wood of the porch and blew out a breath as she moved out of Liv's firing line, "Look, Elizabeth, you've had your fun. Let's not pretend that this... here, with her, was ever going to be anything serious. You aren't made for life here, Liv. You're meant for more than this."

Meant for more than this.

Liv had heard utterances of that phrase her entire life. It sounded like a mantra lifted directly from her father's vernacular. She wondered exactly how many times Marcie and her father had spoken during her time here in Verity.

Marcie paused in her tracks, "You know she won't ever be able to give you the life you want."

Liv felt every emotion she had ever kept inside tumble out of her, she unclenched her fists and her shoulders settled on an exhale that released all of the stress and uncertainty she had carried for too long.

"She's already given me more than I ever knew I could have. The reality is, you cheated on me, Marcie! You had been cheating for a year! You don't want me and I don't want you. You and I are a two woman demolition squad. We shouldn't have been together for a long time. We both know it." Marcie's eyes were wide, her mouth agape as if she couldn't believe what she was hearing. Liv watched her face move from disbelief to some sort of sadness, as her ex blinked back tears. Maybe she wasn't as unfeeling as she came across, "Can you honestly tell me you were happy? Happy people don't cheat Marcie."

Marcie shook her head and moved to sit on the top step, looking down at her feet, her voice gravelly and small. "I know I messed up, but… what happened to us?"

Past Liv would have comforted Marcie by now, and would have pretended everything was okay. She would have slipped into survival mode rather than deal with the difficult feelings that arose from seeing Marcie upset. It still made her feel sad, despite their differences. She never wanted to hurt Marcie, despite having been hurt herself. But she couldn't go back, she needed Marcie to understand, to hear her. Really hear her.

"We grew up… grew apart. You should be with someone who will grow with you, alongside you. You should be with someone who flowers in the spaces you leave, and will encourage you to blossom too," Liv smiled softly and sat down in the space next to her ex.

Their shoulders brushed and the contact didn't light Liv up like it used to. She no longer came alive under Marcie's gaze, and that was okay. Liv needed her to know that she wasn't mad, she didn't hold any grudge against her. Acceptance means finding peace in knowing that sometimes the people who once meant everything to you could become a stranger who knew all your secrets.

"She does that for you? Encourages you to blossom?" Marcie turned to look at Liv and she could see remorse there, hiding within her steely gray eyes.

She thought of Honey, lying next to her under the stars, kissing her behind the foliage at her parents home, dancing around the kitchen in her underwear, sitting on the floor outside her home fixing another thing Marcie had broken. Just like she had fixed Liv, one delicate but meaningful touch at a time.

"She does." Liv admitted on an exhale. Not willing to give any more than that. Even though her whole body was screaming with the things Honey did for her and to her, Marcie wasn't the person who got to have that information.

Nodding her acceptance, Marcie turned her gaze back to her feet. Liv felt a weight settling into her side, as Marcie leant on her for support for the last time.

"I remember you used to look at me like that. That dreamy look you get in your eyes when you think about her. You really do like her, don't you?" Liv's breath halted and Marcie's shoulders dropped, "Oh, you love her?"

Liv wasn't sure how to respond. It wasn't something she wanted to talk about with Marcie, not when she hadn't even told Honey yet. But staying quiet would say more than words ever could. The problem, Liv mused, was that simply saying yes to liking Honey didn't feel right. It didn't feel sufficient enough or accurate enough to convey exactly how she felt about her.

The truth was, Liv didn't *like* Honey. She wasn't sure that what she felt for her had ever been… *like*. Liv was absolutely certain that from the moment she had fallen into Honey's arms, she had loved her. First in that tender way someone loves another person who slips into their life unnoticed and with such an ease it's as if they've always been there. Then in the way love blossoms with each new piece of information you discover, each connection you make, until you're not sure how you ever grew without her. The kind of love that brings out the beauty in each person. Liv loved Honey through every stage of their development, more and more with each passing day. She wasn't sure if she would ever be capable of *not* loving her.

But Honey was right, saying it earlier would have been wrong. Its meaning would have been muddied by the moment. There were so many things that needed to be fixed, worked on, before Liv could say those words. But being here in Verity had taught Liv that nothing was irreparable. Like the porch swing Honey was nursing back to life, everything could be mended with time, patience and a little love.

She looked up at the sky, night was drifting in as the sun set on the horizon. The warmth of Marcie's weight against her side no longer felt like an anchor dragging her down, it felt almost comforting.

A few months ago Liv would have done all she could to placate Marcie. Given her all the information she needed to dampen what was destined to become an explosive situation. It felt oddly satisfying to know that she no longer owed her that. She wasn't laden with obligation anymore and it felt... freeing. So, rather than answer her questions, Liv simply exhaled the breath she had been holding, stayed silent and allowed Marcie room to grow.

***

In the two weeks since Marcie had left, Liv had thrown herself into repairing the things she could. The paintwork on the outside of the house had been an arduous task, but Liv had made friends with Alex from the hardware store, who had come over occasionally to drop off supplies, but ended up staying and lending a hand... and an ear. She had come to appreciate the close knit community of Verity, outside of the four walls she now called home. Her life these days was very different. Although she had never felt out of place in the city, she hadn't felt settled, not the way she did each day she woke up here, to the sun streaming through her open window.

She rinsed her cup in the sink and placed it on the side, with her morning cup of tea out of the way, Liv was ready to start her day. Looking out of the kitchen window and seeing rain droplets rolling down the pane, she sighed. "I guess painting the step and decking can wait a while longer."

Still, she stepped outside and checked to see how heavy it was coming down. The now neatened gravel driveway was turning to mud. Dashes of rain slipped under the porch and onto the decking, splashing her socked feet. In the distance, the familiar grumble of Honey's car signaled to Liv that her neighbor was headed to work.

They hadn't spoken at all over the last two weeks. Honey had made it clear where she stood and although Liv missed her terribly, she respected her enough not to press it. Still, she saw no harm in finding comfort each time she heard her engine, or saw the cottage lights flicker on at night. Honey was only a short distance away, even if sometimes it felt like a lifetime.

"Morning, Liv!" came a voice from the bottom of the steps. Alex stood at the bed of his truck, clutching two buckets of wood stain Liv had ordered a few days ago. Liv mused that he must have crept up the pathway while she was lost in another Honey induced daydream.

"Alex, hey!" she greeted him, walking further out onto the porch.

He held up the buckets and jostled them about as he climbed the steps, two at a time. "I figured you'd want these as soon as possible!"

He bent to place the buckets next to the potted fern that sat at the side of her front door. Liv slipped her hands into the back pockets of her now well worn jeans and smiled.

"You didn't have to come all the way over here, I could have come and picked them up."

"It's no bother, Liv. Besides, I wanted to take a little look at how it's all coming together here." Alex looked around and Liv hoped he would be impressed with what he saw.

When she had purchased an orbital sander from him a week ago, explaining her intentions for the house, his eyes had lit up as he told her what a mammoth job it was going to be. He had offered her some help –like she suspected he would– but she had been determined that it was something she wanted to try herself. It was great knowing that if she needed him he would be there, but she had relished the opportunity to learn something new and lose herself in the process while she did.

"What's the verdict?" she asked, wrinkling her nose in preparation for his professional answer.

"You did a great job, Liv! Marvin would have loved to see this restored like this. I know it used to upset him that he couldn't fix things the way he wanted to. He was too proud to let the rest of us help him, no matter how much we assured him we would love to."

That meant the world to her. She blew out a breath and rocked back and forth on her heels. "Well, I am not too proud to accept help and yours has been invaluable. Honestly, Alex. I don't think I would have had half this stuff done without you and your expert eye. So, thank you, really."

Alex smiled that full smile of his, the one that reached his kind eyes and made Liv feel instantly safe in his company.

"My pleasure. We help our own here. Anyway, I'd better get back to the store before this rain really picks up." He hitched his thumb over his shoulder and began to head back down the steps and towards his truck.

"It's going to get worse?"

"Things always get worse before they get better," he said, and for a moment Liv wondered if he was talking about something else. She was sure by now the whole town had heard of her falling out with Honey. "If you're heading into town for Lissy's send off party, you might wanna consider some shoes."

That was right. Lissy was leaving for Europe. Liv hadn't realized exactly how much time had passed since the party at Honey's parents home. She hadn't truly allowed it to sink in, how long she had been here for. The only concept of time her brain recognized was time spent without Honey.

"I think I'm just going to stay at home, give this one a miss. I'm not sure how welcome I am at the deli these days," she said, glancing off into the distance to try and avoid openly displaying the level of sadness she was feeling.

She had avoided going into the deli during her visits into the center of town. Naturally she had to get her groceries, pick up supplies from Alex's Hardware Store, and some new reads from The Book Nook. But when she had felt the need for a cup of tea and a sweet treat she came home. Even though she and Honey were still not speaking, she wouldn't step foot in Irregular Joe's and be accused of adding fuel to the fire. Of course, she knew that Honey wouldn't ever see it that way, despite everything, but Liv's conscience just wouldn't allow it.

"I still don't know how you've gone so long without one of her treats. My wife keeps telling me I need to consider investing in the deli, the amount of times I visit. It's those Peach Passion Promises they're –"

"Divine!" Liv's stomach groaned, her mind swirling with the first time she had tasted Honey's muffins, she could feel her taste buds tingling at the memory.

Alex cleared his throat and chuckled, "Although her newest addition is a close second. Bea's Peach Pastimes. Now that's a fitting memory the town needed."

Honey had put her creation on her menu, of course she had. It probably tasted amazing. Liv had tried a bowl of the cobbler she had left the day Marcie arrived, and it had been delectable. She couldn't imagine Honey making anything less than spectacular.

"Anyways, I better go. Don't go staining that deck in the rain. Give it a few dry days for the wood to settle before you go about doing anything." Alex nodded and Liv nodded back her compliance.

"Yes, sir!"

As she watched him reverse down the driveway –a skill she hadn't yet mastered for fear of hitting the overgrown bushes that were next on her to-do list– Liv sighed. Lissy leaving was probably hitting Honey hard, she knew how close they were. She wondered if the secret Lissy was keeping had ever come to light, if she had trusted Honey enough to share it with her, she hoped it wouldn't be sitting on Lissy's shoulders the entire time she was traveling.

Europe would be an experience the young girl would never forget. Liv couldn't, even after all these years. There were things she would like to tell Lissy to see, things tourists never really knew about because they would stick to the main sights, too afraid to go off the beaten path.

She wanted to tell her to take her camera, but rather than focus it on Big Ben or Buckingham Palace, to take a walk around Camden and snap as much street art as she could. To grab lunch from a street vendor and go sit by the lock. To take time for herself and just be still, in such a busy part of the world. Liv wanted to tell her to take a train into Wales, or rent a car and drive to Llanfairfechan, a place whose name she'll never pronounce properly no matter how many times she tries. American tongues weren't meant to wrap around a language that beautiful and historic. To head into a village called Abergwyngregyn, find the steep stone pathway, wide enough for one car, and take it all the way until you reach a car park surrounded by trees. To get out and listen… just listen. She wanted to tell her to follow the sound of running water, until it became so clear it felt like it was a part of her. To take a moment to fall in love with Aber Falls and its surroundings. To give herself something to hold onto for when she returned, so she could remember that beauty exists outside of our comfort zones.

As much as she wanted to share this with Lissy, she was fearful of seeing Honey. A huge part of her ached, still, at how things between them had ended. How she had been on the precipice of something wonderful and it had slipped away in a moment she wished she could take back. Ever since, Liv had been taking stock of her actions, of her reactions and behaviors that she knew needed work. Every time she had contemplated walking into the deli, her stomach had reacted with a dull ache. Still, something was pulling at her, telling her to take a chance. If Liv wanted to tell Lissy to find beauty outside of her comfort zone, then she had to challenge that notion too.

The oversized gumboots called to her from their resting place just inside the doorway. She slipped her feet into them, her hands shaking with anticipation of what she was about to do. She ran the gamut in her head. She could show up to Lissy's party and try to say goodbye without bumping into Honey, or she could run headfirst into the woman who had stolen her heart.

"Suck it up Buttercup!" she said to herself, reaching for the keys she kept on the table near the door and tucking them into her back pocket.

She stepped outside and although the weather was less than desirable, she made the decision to walk into town rather than drive. Her shaking hands made for uncertain driving conditions and the last thing she wanted was to get herself or anyone else in trouble. Besides, a little rain never hurt anyone.

***

The noise from the deli filtered through the air. Liv was two blocks away but could hear the cheers, chatter and music as if she was standing right in the middle of it all. Oh, how she longed to be in the middle of it all. Liv yearned for the feeling of comfort and welcome she had felt all those weeks ago surrounded by Honey and her family at the birthday party. Back when things were good, when they were right.

She came to a halt and took a deep, steadying inhale, filling her chest as much as she could in an attempt to staunch her nerves. People were moving in and out of the deli in a steady stream. Balloons in red, white and blue dotted the exterior of the store, the rain bounced off them in a welcoming melody and banners wishing a *'Bon Voyage'* flapped in the light breeze.

She walked slowly towards the store and peered through the window, each table and all the space between was occupied. Liv could absolutely hide amongst the throngs of people and so she began to formulate a plan in her head.

Go in undetected, slip past crowds, find Lissy, wish her luck and leave. Simple really.

Except Liv knew it wouldn't be *that* simple. That had been evident the minute she opened the door. Alex had caught her eye from across the room and lifted a muffin in Liv's direction, a welcome Liv wasn't sure she was.

Children ran around, weaving through the crowds, blowing noise-makers and laughing as they unfurled dangerously close to each other's faces. Before she could find Lissy she felt her gaze being pulled to Honey's counter.

There she was.

Liv's breaths became heavy as for the first time in weeks, she allowed herself to look at Honey. She was sitting on her countertop, looking breathtaking. Her curls were scraped into messy space buns and she was wearing a soft pastel yellow t-shirt with the sleeves cuffed to her shoulders. The rest of the outfit had been paired with washed out gray short dungarees, covered in white daisies and her legs were swinging back and forth playfully. The heels of her white patent leather Docs hit the counter with each motion and Liv felt each thud like a beat of her heart. Honey was perpetual sunshine on the rainiest of days.

Liv's throat dried out instantly, she needed a drink of water but instead tried to cough away the dryness. Of course in doing so she managed to alert Honey to her presence, and the minute those warm brown eyes fixed on Liv she knew she couldn't just leave. She wove her way through the crowd –crossing the floor in what felt like a slow-motion scene from a movie– until she stood in front of Honey.

No barriers, no pretense, no more secrets, just her in her most raw and vulnerable form.

"You're here." Honey's legs stopped swinging and she ran her eyes over Liv's body.

Not expecting to have left the house today, she was sure Honey would be cringing internally at Liv's denim jeans, paint-stained t-shirt and her grandfather's gumboots. Liv felt underdressed and really small all of a sudden. She looked over her shoulder, trying to find Honey's niece to no avail before turning back and speaking quietly enough that she wouldn't bring more attention to herself.

"I just wanted to say goodbye to Lissy. I hope that's okay."

"Of course. She will be happy to see you. We haven't seen you around for a while." Honey ducked her head and started fidgeting with her hands in her lap. Liv wondered if she too was nervous, "Everything was sort of quiet for a while and I thought maybe you'd gone back to the city but then I noticed noises coming from the house."

"Yeah, It's turning out to be a bigger project than I thought. But it will be worth it in the end," Liv said, no longer examining the floor and instead taking a chance to look at Honey directly, "You were looking for me?"

Honey lifted a hand and motioned towards the entrance where people still filtered in and out. "Do you think we can go outside and talk for a minute? I don't really want to do this here and I can barely hear myself think."

"Sure."

Liv watched as Honey jumped down from the counter with ease. Still, her hands automatically reached out to steady the smaller woman, wanting to keep her safe. She berated herself internally for not having control over those compulsions, and yet she wasn't sure that was something she was capable of controlling. Her need to protect and take care of Honey was something intrinsic.

Honey moved towards the door and Liv followed at her heels, careful to stay a respectable distance. Outside, the rain was still coming down, splashes bounced off the pavement and snuck under the shelter of the canopy seeking solace in their clothes. A cold shiver ran the length of Liv's spine, she wrapped her arms around herself for comfort and wished they were Honey's. Although she had set this in motion by approaching Honey inside, and her tone wasn't unwelcoming, the way Liv's stomach churned told her to prepare for the worst.

A warmth moved its way up her arm, Liv looked down and realized Honey was touching her. Her gentle fingers were rubbing soothingly at Liv's skin, a touch that felt both familiar and almost forgotten.

"I owe you an apology," Honey stated, her voice low and uncertain, but then it was if she had been a bottle uncorked as the words started to spill out of her, "I have been so mad at you these last few weeks, and I had to work through some things that I never saw coming. It wasn't fair of me to tell you that we couldn't be anything, and the moment someone else came into the picture, act like you belonged to me. When you came here, I wasn't looking for a relationship. I wasn't even looking for a friendship. But I found you, and I knew the moment I met you that you would become someone to me, someone special. We had this connection that I couldn't explain but I haven't been able to stop thinking about it. How easy it was to be around you, to just exist with you. Liv, you changed my life the day we met. It would be a lie if I told you that I was ready for you then. I wasn't, but I *so* wanted to be. I've watched and waited for years as my sisters met the love of their lives and got the families they always wanted. I watched them fall in love and saw that love grow exponentially, while I went home alone. I wanted just a fraction of that kind of love. But even when Andie and I were together, we weren't. She was never really here…she was never really mine. I think I placed too much of my dreams on her. She wasn't like me though, her dreams weren't the same as mine. She wanted sunny beaches and bikinis, and I wanted picnics in open fields, visits to the ocean and sandcastles built by hands that fit inside my own, just right. She wanted to see the world and I thought I'd see the world in its entirety the moment I looked into my person's eyes. I didn't see the world in her eyes, then I met you."

Honey took a deep breath, lifted a hand and pressed her palm flat against her clavicle as she tried to catch her breath. Liv couldn't believe what she was hearing right now. Honey wasn't nervously ranting, every word she spoke was laced with love and deep meaning. She was speaking from her heart. This incredible woman, who was so adorable, standing there with her wide eyes and sheepish expression and chewing on her bottom lip, while looking like a love Liv wanted to drown in.

"Me?" Liv asked, unsure if she had heard correctly due to her heart pounding rapidly in her chest. Honey was looking at her like she saw right through her, and her voice was like the warmest hug. Liv wanted to lean into that warmth, collapse into Honey's arms.

"Yeah, you. You walked into my life in those ridiculous gumboots and the moment I looked at you I saw it all. You look at me and I see entire galaxies in your eyes. Everything is right there in shades of always and forever, and I got scared. I was so scared of trying to keep you when you weren't mine to keep. Of both holding onto you too tight, and pushing you away, when I had given myself over to you entirely. I didn't know what to do, I just knew I didn't want to lose such a deep connection, not again. I couldn't put myself through that, not with you. There are people who come into our lives so unexpectedly, but when they do it's like they've always been there. Something in me recognized something in you…instantly. I don't know what this means for us Liv, all I do know is… I miss you, so very much."

"I miss you too," Liv swallowed her disbelief and allowed Honey's words to wash over her.

She pulled her arm away from Honey's touch, gently, until their fingers found one anothers and tangled together. She had to forge a connection between them, she had to hold on tight. She needed to let Honey know that she felt all of this too, and as unexpected as it was, it was real. But her words kept getting stuck in her throat, so all she could do was keep their gaze locked and hope those galaxies were visible… and enough.

The deli doors opened behind them, as they both turned towards the sound, Lissy peeked her head out. Liv saw a sparkle of something in her eyes, at the sight of them, something close to happiness, maybe.

"Hey Aunt Buzzy, are you coming back in?" she said.

Liv watched Honey's gaze move from where their hands were connected still and then flick cautiously back at the door. A pink blush rose on her cheeks and Liv guessed it was from being caught in such an intimate moment. Honey looked back and forth between Lissy and Liv, her eyes wide and telling. She dropped Liv's hand and took a step back. Liv felt the loss immediately. She tucked her hands into her back pockets to stop the shaking and pressed her lips together, smiling at Lissy, who smiled widely back.

"Yeah Lissy, I'm coming," Honey said almost apologetically, her eyes now fixed firmly on Liv's.

Lissy stepped back inside and the door closed slowly. Liv was confused, Honey had just all but told her those three words and yet the minute they had been seen together she had pulled away. It felt like the conversation was over, Honey was ready to go back inside. Liv wondered if maybe Honey just said what she did to get it off her chest, to release some of the weight she was carrying.

Not wanting to create any more awkwardness she decided to forgo speaking with Lissy. She would walk away once more, only this time, she would do it differently. She would make sure to leave the door open and be transparent with Honey. If there was to be any hope of them being together and from Honey's words, Liv was almost certain there was, she had to exhibit a little patience. She had time, Honey wasn't going anywhere and neither was Liv.

"I'm here, anytime you need me. Remember, I'm just a field away," she said and turned to begin her walk back home.

With each small step she took she felt a little lighter despite the heaviness of the rain that pelted her entire being. Within seconds of stepping out from beneath the dark green shelter her t-shirt had become so wet it now clung to her lithe frame. Her hair, which she had left loose, was stuck to her forehead and shoulders and her teeth chattered despite the absence of cold. Her ears pounded with the sounds of cars passing through the puddles on the wet road and her mind played Honey's words on repeat as she tried to figure out how to move forward from this.

"What about now?" Honey shouted and Liv thought for a moment maybe she had made it up, but she stopped nevertheless and turned around in confusion. Honey took a step out from under the canopy, "What if I need you now?"

Honey continued to close the space between them, until she too, was soaked from the rain that showed no sign of letting up. When they stood face to face, both breathing heavily and focused only on one another, Liv remembered she had been asked a question.

"Do you? Need me now?"

Hope.

It filled Liv's chest, pushing past her uncertainties and taking possibility by the hand. She looked into Honey's eyes, those warm eyes that had always felt so familiar to her. When Honey nodded, Liv wanted nothing more than to take her into her arms and kiss her senseless. She took another step closer and looked down at the smaller woman. Neither reached out just yet, but they didn't need to. Honey's touch was one Liv could feel with her eyes closed, from the furthest distance. Her chest rising and falling rapidly she allowed the feeling of being within such close proximity to Honey to finally register. Her head spun and she closed her eyes to steady herself, as her nose bumped against Honey's forehead.

That was all it took.

As if she didn't care that Liv was soaked through, Honey's arms wound around her neck, anchoring her in place. Liv felt soft kisses on the skin just behind her ear, as Honey buried her face in the crook of her neck. She slipped her own arms around Honey's waist, clinging onto her for dear life, tired of swimming stormy waters and ready for reprieve. Their bodies flush, Liv moved one hand to the nape of Honey's neck, pressing lightly with the pads of her fingers, hoping her touch conveyed the words she couldn't say right now. She never wanted to let go.

Honey's hot breath tickled the shell of her ear when she whispered words that set Liv aflame. Words that Liv knew she would never forget for the rest of her life, "You were never a stranger to me, not really. I've been thinking about this so much and I keep coming back to the notion that I think I've loved you before. No, I know I've loved you before… in another lifetime maybe. And if you'll let me, I want to love you in this lifetime, too. So yeah, I need you, Liv. I need you…always."

Epilogue

(Six Months Later)

"Are you sure you don't need my help locking up?" Honey asked, lifting the apron over her head and folding it neatly.

She looked up at her eldest sister who was busy cleaning the tables after what had been another long and busy day. Sasha shook her head and nodded across the room where the chairs were being stacked away by a petite redhead.

"We've got this covered, right Lara?"

"Absolutely!" the girl replied, walking over to Honey and holding out her hand, nodding at the apron Honey still held onto. She smirked over at Sasha, waggling her eyebrows like they shared a secret Honey wasn't privy to, "Go on, you get out of here. You don't want to be late for your date night."

Pressing the apron into Lara's palm, Honey narrowed her eyes at her and then smiled. Lara had been such an incredible help in the months after Kyla had given birth. So much so, that she had called an emergency family meeting and pressed for them to keep her on at Rosenberg's. It was a no-brainer they had decided. Kyla had her hands full, settling into her stride as a mother of six, and they needed to accept all the help they could get. Lara had jumped at the chance to work with them and had immediately handed in her notice at Irregular Joes.

"Do you both wanna tell me what it is you seem to know that I don't, or –" Honey asked.

Sasha raised her eyebrows and gave her the older sister look she had perfected over the years, "I'm gonna go with 'or', how about you Lara?"

"Yeah I'm gonna go with 'or' too," the redhead said, still smirking widely as she tucked Honey's apron under the counter and reached for the cloth and spray that sat on the top.

"Fine," Honey huffed in mock annoyance, the two of them were like a brick wall. A solid alliance Honey loved to see, even if they were teamed up against her, "Thank you both for letting me slip out early. I'll see you tomorrow."

She could have sworn she heard whispers and muffled laughter as she excited the deli and stepped out into the night. Cars slipped past and families clutching blankets and chairs headed for the open green space opposite the deli where The Book Nook was hosting its usual movie night. Honey and Liv had attended two of them on their scheduled date nights. They had taken in Dirty Dancing and While You Were Sleeping, both movies that Honey was amazed to find Liv had never seen before. Tonight however, they had agreed to keep it low key. Liv had agreed to cook dinner for them both at the cottage, where they had both been cohabitating the last three months after a patch of bad weather had caused problems with the roof of the big house. A home cooked meal was exactly what Honey needed after a day as busy as today had been, that and a hug from her girlfriend.

Slipping into her car she pushed the aux cable into her phone and Taylor Swift began to play through the speakers. Liv had offered to have the Jeep fitted with the same touchscreen technology she had in her car, but Honey only used it for short trips, so she didn't see the point. Singing along to 'Stay' as she drove through her tiny hometown she felt her body relax. Only a few more minutes and she would be settled down for the night, happy and right where she needed to be.

Pulling up the gravel driveway she noticed the cottage was in darkness and her eyebrows furrowed.

"Liv did say she was going to cook dinner tonight, didn't she?" Honey said to herself, coming to a stop and taking the keys from the ignition. Crossing the distance to her front door she slipped the keys into the lock, pushed the door open and was met with silence.

"Okay, that's odd," Honey said, reaching out to her side and flicking the lights on.

The cottage was unmistakably empty, actually too empty. She glanced around the room and saw that the boxes of her things that they had piled up in the space under the stairs, were nowhere to be seen.

Two months ago, after only a month of living together, Liv had asked Honey to move in with her when the big house was ready. Not wanting to be apart from Liv any longer, she had agreed.

"Liv?" she shouted into the open space. No reply came.

Turning back on herself, Honey headed for the front door and noticed in the distance, lights coming from the big house. She shut the door behind herself and headed for the field. With the grass back to ankle height, renewed after the winter, she crossed the land in no time.

"Liv?" she shouted again, as she walked up the stairs and pushed at the front door which again was locked.

She made a fist and banged on the door, lightly but loudly enough to be heard. Still no answer. She leant back and scanned the surrounding area, the deck was empty and there was no sign of anyone. The only movement was the porch swing, exactly where it should have been, restored to its former glory, swaying back and forth on the gentle February breeze.

About a month after Liv and Honey had made up they had agreed to move the porch swing back. Honey had been reluctant at first, scared to let go of something that precious. Especially after how it had come to be in her possession in the first place, but Liv had told her that she understood.

Their relationship had developed so much over the last six months, they found that they both really enjoyed getting to know one another but that in some ways they felt like they already knew one another, incredibly so. Liv would always repeat the words Honey had said to her back when they made up. How she believed they had known and loved one another before. How something inside them had recognized the other the moment they met. Honey still believed that to be true.

Liv had settled into life in Verity with such ease Honey felt like she had always been there. After publishing her book, Liv had submitted her resignation at the university outside of the city where she used to live and landed a job at Verity Community College. Everything was going well, except for the fact that now Liv seemed to have gone missing.

Honey took the steps with a leap and headed around the back of the house, although she wasn't sure why Liv would be there, unless she was helping Alex with the roofing, as she sometimes did.

Noises started to filter through the air. A low hum, the gentle twinkle of music and then…laughter. When Honey rounded the corner what she saw caused her to step back in amazement.

String lights hung from the branches of the trees to the left of the house, tables were laid out containing food and drinks in abundance, and soft music was coming from the speaker system Liv must have unhooked from the cottage and hauled across the field while Honey was at work. The entire space was filled with people. Everywhere Honey looked, family and friends were mingling and chatting, raising their plastic cups in cheers and the children were sitting on the floor in a circle passing a ball back and forth.

Alex from the hardware store, who had been so integral in getting the repairs done on the big house, stood chatting with Lols from The Book Nook, who must have snuck away from her own event to be here. Chatting away with them was Mrs Robbins, who clutched a flute of champagne in one hand and her chunky orange tabby, Keats, in the other hand. Keats looked less than impressed by the company, or maybe, Honey mused, it was the tweed bow tie Mrs Robbins had added to his collar.

Honey walked towards everyone. Over at one of the tables, she recognized Jen and Taylor, Liv's friends from the city, who she had only spoken to via Zoom. Her mom and dad were moving from the drinks table to the circle of children, handing out drinks to the drones as they enjoyed each other's company. Even Kyla, who was pushing a double stroller back and forth in the grass, looked happy, tired but happy.

There, standing front and center, in the fading light of day was the most beautiful woman Honey had ever seen. Liv, with her long dark hair curled around her shoulders, smiled back at her like Honey was the most beautiful thing *she* had ever seen.

"What is all of this? What's going on?" Honey asked, when she finally reached her girlfriend.

Liv pulled her in for a hug and the minute their bodies met Honey melted into her. She lifted a hand and waved it about nonchalantly, scanning the faces whose gaze were now focused entirely on them.

"Well, this is a housewarming party. It's customary to throw one when you move into a new home. I know I've lived here before but you haven't. We haven't, so."

Honey kept her arms tight around Liv's waist but leaned back a little, tilting her head questioningly. "Wait, do you mean? It's ready? How long have you known about this?"

"It's been ready for about two weeks now, but I wanted to make sure that everyone could be here with us." Liv's smile was the perfect mixture of mischievous, entrancing and downright adorable that all Honey wanted to do was kiss her until they both needed air.

She lifted herself on her tiptoes and placed a gentle kiss on Liv's full lips. "This is… Liv this is everything."

Liv wrinkled her nose and Honey mirrored the action. It was something they both did when they wanted to convey something words couldn't. This was all so much, not too much though, Honey thought, just right. Perfect even.

"There are a few people who want to meet you in person, are you ready to come say hi?" Liv asked. Glancing around she noticed that everyone had gone back to their conversations and were no longer looking at them. Honey was thankful in the moment for all the background noise as she felt nerves start to bubble in her stomach.

"Absolutely," she nodded, hoping her nerves didn't show but as she knew she would, Liv saw right through her.

Dropping her arms from Honey's waist and reaching behind her for Honey's hands, Liv squeezed comfortingly. "You're not scared are you?"

"When I'm with you, there's no reason to be, right?"

Honey knew the answer before Liv had uttered it. The softening of the waves in her ocean eyes spoke before her words could find Honey's ears. The warmth of her touch filled Honey with all the courage and strength she knew she would ever need, it both grounded her and lifted her in equal measure. Liv was everything she needed and more.

"Never."

Honey took a deep inhale and held a little tighter to Liv's hand as they began to head across the land towards an older couple, one Honey didn't really know by face but by reputation however the minute the man spun around and took them in with his familiar eyes she needed no clarification as to who he was.

He cleared his throat as Liv nodded at him before momentarily let go of Honey's hand to hug the woman accompanying him.

"Mother, father… this is Honey," she said, moving back a step and reaching for Honey's hand once more.

"It's lovely to finally meet you, dear," the woman said, smiling so wide Honey could see nearly everyone of her perfectly white and straightened teeth. She smiled back and went to say something similar, but was taken by surprise when Liv's mom stepped to her and pulled her in for a hug. She wrapped one arm around Liv's mom's back, tentatively, and rested it there gently.

Her father, thankfully made no move to do as his wife had done, and for that Honey was thankful. She knew far too much about this man and how he had not only made Liv feel but how he had made Marvin feel. She wasn't sure she would be able to maintain the same decor with which she had interacted with Liv's mom.

He looked Honey up and down, then Liv, settling his gaze on where their hands remained joined, he sighed. "You're different here."

Honey felt Liv stiffen beside her, she knew how much power this man's words had over her girlfriend, despite the distance and time that now played a factor in their relationship, and how far Liv had come.

Liv and her parents had spoken a few times over the last few months, once they realized Liv was serious about staying in Verity. The reality of having a child live so far away had prompted a change within their relationship. A small change, but a change nevertheless.

He reached out a hand, settling it on Liv's shoulder and Honey watched her girlfriend flinch and clench her jaw.

"I mean that in the nicest possible way. This place looks good on you. You fit here, in a way I never felt I did. I owe you an apology. I was wrong to keep you from them, from knowing them and this place. It wasn't all bad, it just wasn't what *I* wanted. A parent shouldn't ever assume that what they want is what their child would want. You've always been so strong-minded. You've always known what *you* wanted. I'm sorry for stealing those experiences from you. For not listening to you and for making you feel like you had to stay in a relationship that you weren't happy in, all because I had put in effort to accept her into our lives. I shouldn't ever have made it feel like it's a chore to accept any part of you, Elizabeth. It's not and never has been. I'm not the perfect parent, far from it but I'm willing to try and be a better father. The father you deserve. All I want, *we want*… is for you to be happy."

Honey felt Liv soften next to her, she turned to give her a warm smile and what she saw reflected back was breathtaking. Liv always looked stunning to Honey, but in that moment, with that little bit of peace, of closure Liv looked radiant.

"I am so incredibly happy here," Liv admitted with a smile and both of her parents smiled back.

"I see that. I know it has so much to do with this beautiful person right here. It's good to finally meet you in person." He reached out a hand for Honey to shake and she did, the moment her hand touched his she felt a pang of sadness deep inside of her. His touch felt like one she had almost forgotten.

"You too," she whispered softly, her voice cracking a little.

"Liv!" Jen's voice interrupted them, and Honey's gaze instantly sought out Liv's friend in the crowd. She had the arm that wasn't holding Theo against her chest, raised up in the air waving frantically.

"Sorry, we will talk again but there's someone desperate to meet Honey." Liv apologized.

"Go, enjoy your friends," Liv's father said, waving them off, "but before you go...I want you to know, I'm proud of you, Liv."

Honey watched Liv's eyes well up, felt her hands shaking and so she did exactly what she knew she had to do in that moment. She stayed quiet and allowed Liv to lean on her, the way she knew she always would.

"Thanks Dad."

To say Jen and Taylor were excited was an understatement. Of all the people at the party, Honey was the most nervous to meet them. Of course they had already met over Zoom, countless times in the last few months, but meeting someone in person was so different. Honey was scared they wouldn't like her in person. She was aesthetically very different from Marcie, aka the goddess, after all.

"Hey you!" Liv sidled up to Jen and tickled underneath Theo's chin. He giggled and wriggled, arms out-stretched, clearly wanting Liv to hold him. Jen shifted him on her hip and nodded towards the direction they had just come from.

"I figured you might need an out. Was that as awkward as it looked?" she asked, still struggling with a jostling Theo who was nothing if not determined to land himself in Liv's arms. Liv reached out for him and signaled to her friend to hand him over, transferring him to her own hip, and bouncing him softly.

"Actually it was... perfectly normal." Liv said, not taking her eyes off her little playfriend who was now tangling his chubby little fingers in her curls and tugging gently.

Honey felt Jen's attention switch to her, "Wow! You're even cuter in person."

Her cheeks burned and she looked to Liv for help with a response. Not one to disappoint, Liv slipped her other arm around Honey's waist and pulled her closer to her side. Honey let her head fall to Liv's shoulder.

"Steady now. She's spoken for."

"It's so good to finally meet you both," Honey said, reaching out a hand to meet Theo's who had moved on from Liv's curls and was now staring at Honey with laser focus, "and this little watermelon."

They all laughed at the nickname and Jen shook her head. "He'll never outgrow that name and I'll make sure he knows who is to blame."

"What can I say, he's the cutest watermelon," Liv smirked and Honey felt the sound warm her from the inside out.

"Yeah well, one day you two will have a baby of your own and I will get to pick the fruity nickname." Jens finger moved back and forth between Liv and Honey and she pursed her lips together in mock indignation.

Honey laughed, "I think that's only fair."

Watching Liv with Theo on her hip, bouncing him and swaying with such natural movement, was such a turn on for Honey. She was so ready for this to be part of their narrative, for this chapter of their life to begin and she knew Liv was ready too. Theo began to fuss and reached out for Taylor who took him in her arms and glanced over at the house.

"Liv, do you mind if I take him inside and try to get him to sleep. He didn't nap on the drive here. I guess he was as excited to see you as we were."

"Of course. Go right ahead." Liv nodded towards the door at the back of the house that led to the kitchen.

"I'll come with you. I could use the bathroom," Jen said, looking at her wife and then back at Liv and Honey, "It's so lovely meeting you. We have all weekend to get to know one another better, why don't you two go see the rest of your guests.

Honey listened as Liv explained that Jen and Taylor had decided to make a real trip of it. They were staying in Verity for the next three days, at the new BnB that had opened up just down the road from the deli. Honey was so happy that Liv would have the chance to spend some time with her friends, she knew how much she missed them.

From over in the distance Honey saw Sasha appear, Lara following beside her looking a little nervous. It didn't matter how many times Honey had invited her around for dinner or assured her she was welcome to come to their family get togethers, Lara always retreated into herself a little when surrounded by so many people. Honey knew it wasn't the people, it was the kindness Lara struggled with. The feeling of belonging in a world where she had always only ever really experienced being told what an inconvenience she was, or the pitying stares from those who knew her background.

Honey waved to them both and they approached, carrying the leftover baked goods from today's stock.

"You two knew all about this, didn't you?" she accused, narrowing her eyes and shaking her head jovially.

Sasha and Lara looked at one another conspiratorially and after a moment of silence both just shrugged their shoulders and laughed.

"You better go put those on the table before you lose a limb," Honey said to Lara, who looked confused, until a swarm of small humans began to form around her.

The worker bees had never been able to resist Honey's Blueberry Banana Bonanza muffins and they could smell them a mile off. Lara held the bag aloft and began to head over to the table, the children still following at her heels.

"How did you get her to come?" Honey asked Sasha, who just shrugged and acted like it was nothing.

"That girl worships the ground you walk on. All I had to do was tell her that you'd be sad if she wasn't here and she was putty in my hands. How does it feel, to finally have a little sister?" Sasha said, looking smug.

"I sort of already felt like I had one in Lissy, but I'm good having another. Lara's really sweet. I'm glad she's here. She needs people around her and I like having her close by." Honey looked over at the table where Lara was chatting away comfortably with Lissy, both handing out muffins to the smaller children. Lissy played nervously with the ends of her waist length hair, twirling it around her fingers as Lara handed her what looked like the last muffin. Lissy reached out for it, her gaze not wavering from the cute redheads, broke it half and handed some to Lara.

"I'm glad you like her being close by because I was thinking. What do you think about letting her move into the cottage?" Liv said, hip checking Honey and waggling her eyebrows at Sasha.

That sounded perfect. Lara would be able to have a space of her own, some security finally after everything she had been through. Liv really had thought of absolutely everything. Honey almost jumped into her girlfriend's arms upon hearing her proposal. Instead she reeled back her emotions, although her voice still cracked as she spoke.

"I think that sounds absolutely perfect."

She would have plenty of time to thank Liv properly tonight, once everyone had left and they were alone, in their new home.

***

Night came fast, settling around the garden and guests until it was hard to make out their faces, even by the string lights and the glow of the small fire Honey's father had lit for the remaining adults. Honey and Liv were sitting by the fire, side by side, on a log from one of the few trees they had cut down during the winter cull, in an attempt to make room for new life. Lower registers told stories of love, life and local happenings and Honey knew she should be feeling at peace, but something wasn't sitting right with her. Something felt missing.

"Come with me," Liv whispered in her ear, standing up and reaching out a hand to help Honey to her feet.

They made their way across the garden towards the front of the house where it was completely dark with the exception of the night sky. Coming around to the front porch they stopped at the steps and Liv sat down first, patting the space next to her for Honey to join.

She lowered herself into place and sighed, "I'm sorry."

"What for?" Liv asked, shuffling closer and wrapping her arm around Honey's waist.

"You've done all of this for me, for us and I don't want to ruin it by being sad," she admitted.

"It's okay to feel sad, Honey. Changes can be sad as much as they can be happy. They can be a whole array of feelings and emotions that don't necessarily normally co-exist. It's okay to feel exactly how you feel, right when you feel it."

"I don't want you to think I'm not happy, because I am. I am so incredibly happy, Liv. This is the start of something wonderful for us. It just feels like something is missing."

"My Grandfather?" Liv asked and all Honey could do was nod.

They sat in silence and allowed the moment to take hold, allowing everything that had happened tonight, all the interactions, all the surprises, everything…to just settle.

"I really wish he could have been here to see this. To see the house like this, so full of life and love. He would have been the life of this party and everyone here would have adored him. It's been almost a year and I still miss him incredibly," Honey sniffled and wiped at the tears that were spilling down her cheeks, "When it gets like this, when I feel this heaviness inside and I get scared that I'm forgetting him, something always pulls me back to him. Something reminds me that he isn't really gone. When I speak to Lissy or Lara and offer advice, I hear him in the words I speak. When people come into the deli and set up at the chess table I can see his face. Everytime you walk into a room barefoot, clutching a book so close to your face I'm worried you're going to trip, I see him. I wish you could have had the chance to talk to him, because you both would have been inseparable. I might even have had competition for best friend bragging rights. I am so thankful that you're here and that I get to love you, Liv. I just miss him."

Liv hands cupped Honey's face, her thumbs brushing away the tears as she leaned in and kissed her softly. "I know I tell you this so many times a day you're probably bored of hearing it, but I love you, Honey. So very much."

"I could never get bored of hearing that, Liv. I love you too, more than you'll ever know. Thank you for all of this. I can't believe you did this on such short notice. Actually, I can. You're incredible. All of this is just perfect."

Honey leaned in, the magnetic force that always seemed to linger between them, pulled them together until they collided messily in a kiss that made the rest of the world seem to disappear.

Liv's tongue swiped a path along Honey's bottom lip and she opened her mouth, deepening their kiss. She could taste the salt on her lips from where her tears had fallen, and she knew Liv must have been able to taste them too. They lost themselves in one another, while their guests continued to celebrate out back. When they finally broke apart they agreed to sit a little while longer, just enjoying the quiet and each other.

"I'll never get over just how bright they shine here," Liv said, looking up at the stars in the night sky.

Honey nodded, remembering the first time Liv had noticed the stars here. So much had changed since then. "Everything shines a little brighter here."

There was a hidden meaning in that statement. Honey wasn't just talking about the stars, Liv was brighter since her arrival. Her father was right, Verity looked good on Liv.

"It's him, isn't it," Liv asked, still focused on the constellations that dotted the darkness, "Somewhere, somehow… this is partly to do with him."

Honey knew exactly what she meant by this. She had always been a believer in fate, destiny, providence, kismet and all the other words used to describe that underlying feeling that the universe has a map that we all blindly follow, until we reach the place we were meant to be, or person we were meant for. She was sure that Marvin had felt the same when he had met Bea and they had decided to stay in Verity Vale. She was certain that her parents and sisters had all experienced this too when they met their partners. For the longest time, Honey had wondered if the universe had forgotten about her. Everything she held dear seemed to disappear. Now she knew the universe hadn't forgotten about her, her path to love had just been a little longer than others.

Marvin's last piece of advice ran through her mind, *"You'll get the reward you deserve in the end regardless."*

A shooting star zipped across the sky, racing to reach its destination. She blinked back tears that burned at the corners of her eyes and shook her head at the sky, knowing that if he was out there, he was absolutely with them at that moment. In life he always shone brighter than any star in the sky, there was no way he wasn't part of something bigger now.

"I know you said once that the cottage was the last gift he left me, but I don't think that's true. I think the last gift he gave me is by far the best one I could have ever asked for, and one I didn't know I needed. "

"Do you mean–?"

"I'm so lucky to have you Liv," Honey smiled, reaching for Liv's hand and giving it a reassuring squeeze. Liv squeezed back but neither looked down.

"I didn't know I was going to meet you and yet the moment I did. It was like I'd always known you. We now know how true that is. It's funny how the universe works. I had no idea that coming here would change my life."

Finally looking across at her girlfriend, Honey saw everything reflected in the watery depths of Liv'e eyes as she too had tears rolling in rivulets down her face, "Coming *home*, Liv. This is home now."

Liv nodded, "I think you've always been my home, Honey. I just went away for a little while."

They sat together a little while longer on the wooden steps of the house they had planned to fill with the love and life it deserved. When the cold eventually slipped beneath their layers, they stood up and moved inside. Liv unlocked the front door and they crossed the threshold together, holding hands tightly.

Warmth welcomed Honey as Liv flipped a light switch on in the hallway. She glanced around and noticed that everything looked new, but still felt so familiar. The once yellowing walls were brilliant white, but not clinical. They provided the perfect background for the frames that hung in place, holding smiles of faces they had come to love and lose.

Marvin and Bea smiled at them from pride of place in the center of the wall, all other pictures of their family surrounding them. To the right, Honey's entire family at Lissy's welcome home party, after her return from Europe. Liv stood next to her girlfriend looking like she had always been there. To the left, a picture of Liv's side of the family that her parents had sent them at Christmas. Honey held out hope, after tonight's interaction, that one day, Liv and herself would be standing next to them having celebrated a holiday together.

And just below the photograph of Marvin and Bea, sat a framed image that they had discovered a few weeks ago whilst sorting into albums, all of the photographs Marvin had kept. Staring back at them were two little girls, about four and six years old. One with her blonde hair scraped back into messy pigtails, the other with long black hair pulled neatly into braids, with their arms wrapped around one another, smiling widely from the safety of a porch swing.

THE END

About The Author

S-Jay Hart can be found sipping tea and reading, most of the time. When she's not doing these things she can be found camping, hiking or shamelessly pretending she's a dinosaur, astronaut, or butterfly, with 30 small children. She started writing when she was a teenager, creating a fictional world with friends, and has over sixty notebooks filled with stories and ideas. She lives with her two teen humans, her two doggos and her furry beta-buddy Brenda.

Printed in Great Britain
by Amazon

84479334R00159